Praise for *The Divine Flesh*

"Timely, vicious and, at times, gleefully wicked, Huff's *The Divine Flesh* is a mashup of David Cronenberg via Clive Barker via Poppy Z. Brite. Readers better buckle up and submit to what's about to happen to them. It's for the best."

—Steve Stred, author of *Mastodon* and *Churn the Soil*

"Take Clive Barker's lurid worldbuilding, mix in Chuck Palahniuk's audacious nerve, and top it off with Rachel Harrison's storytelling, and you have something approaching *The Divine Flesh*. With her sophomore novel, Drew Huff presents a book that roars, equal parts rage and redemption, terror and transformation. This is what modern horror should be doing."

—Brennan LaFaro, author of *Noose*

"From the first page, this book grabs hold and takes readers on a full-speed acid trip that doesn't slow down until the very end. A superb blend of heartbreak and humor, body and cosmic horror, human suffering and love, Huff takes readers somewhere truly unique and strangely beautiful."

—Emma E. Murray, author of *Crushing Snails*

"Comfort zone be damned. This is some no holds barred, indie horror right here. Huff puts pedal to metal before you can even strap on a seat belt. Still have whiplash from how she takes the turns."

—Scott J. Moses, author of *Our Own Unique Affliction*

Books by Drew Huff

Free Burn

Landlocked in Foreign Skin

The Divine Flesh

THE DIVINE FLESH

Content Warnings

Violence, death, murder, profanity, body horror, drug abuse, drugs, suicide, self-injury, body dysphoria, emotional abuse, homophobia (f-slur at a few points), transphobia (implied/off-page), racism, sexual assault/rape, infidelity, animal death (mentioned/off-page), death of a child/infant, child abuse (brief mentions of physical and verbal abuse. Someone mentions a past sexual abuse from a foster family), eating disorder (off-page/mentioned).

This book is intended for adult audiences only. Reader discretion is strongly advised.

Edited by Maddy Leary
Book Design and Layout by Rob Carroll
Cover Art by Evangeline Gallagher
Cover Design by Rob Carroll

Library of Congress Control Number: 2025932492

ISBN 978-1-958598-59-7 (paperback)
ISBN 978-1-958598-83-2 (eBook)

darkmatter-ink.com

THE DIVINE FLESH

DREW HUFF

For everyone that's woken up in a bad place.
And then gotten into a worse place right after,

falling,

falling

into a series of increasingly-shitty places, drug-addled people, and traumatic
flashbacks so bad, you shiver and puke (you say it's because of the booze
you can't stop drinking but you know you're lying to yourself)

falling,

Puking, shivering, feeling the lub-dub of your heart as the people who abused
you end up getting exactly what they wanted.
The fruits of life.
You ferment the fruits of life and drink it down, because it keeps the
flashbacks from getting bad.

And you just keep on

falling,

then you hit rock-bottom with your head spinning,
wondering how the fuck you turned thirty.
Because you were eighteen just yesterday.

Right?

For everyone at rock bottom:
You can only go up from here.

"The darkness drops again; but now I know
That twenty centuries of stony sleep
Were vexed to nightmare by a rocking cradle,
And what rough beast, its hour come round at last,
Slouches towards Bethlehem to be born?"

—William Butler Yeats
"The Second Coming"

"You can turn your back on a person, but never turn your back on a drug, especially when it's waving a razor sharp hunting knife in your eye."

—Hunter S. Thompson

Part One

Can't Get There from Here

1

"All I wanted were those bodies, Jennifer-baby," the Divine Flesh said. "Just those silly little cadavers. Or even just *one* cadaver. Why do you keep hurting Me?"

I woke up in a ditch, which wasn't so bad. The Divine Flesh didn't stop talking. She never stopped talking.

"Jennifer-baby, I want to create," She said.

The ditch rutted either side of some county road. Cracks marred asphalt, webbing the road's lines. Tumbleweeds filled the ditch, forming a river of dead and desiccated plants. All the midsummer grasses were here: cheatgrass, sagebrush, goathead. Bits of cheatgrass itched inside my jeans. Farther back from the road, cherry orchards rowed the land. They smelled green, like weeds and grass and dirt. White-hot noon blazed over cherry orchards and washed out the gold hills on the horizon.

Ash coated my hands—

—he's in the beige bathtub when She finds him, all alone in his mobile home except for the yipping worried Chihuahua, he's lying in the red, red water, so very pale, the slit on his thigh hanging open, exposing treasures, the white sliver of his femur; he tastes like sweat and ethyl alcohol and tears. She bundles his flesh to Herself, She's crying, She repairs the wound and he lives again, She licks the suicide-blood off him and bathes him instead in love, asks him gently, Would you be Mine? But it's a silly question, the answer's always yes, yes, and so She sanctifies his flesh as his little dog chatters—

The Divine Flesh had taken control of our shared body and revived some random dude. Great. Fantastic.

I staggered to my feet. I picked under a nail.

The Divine Flesh cooed, "And then he was SO happy!"

"He's dead."

"He *was* dead, silly. Until I recreated him. God, you're depressed. I didn't hurt anyone."

I sucked gore out from under my nails. Salty-sweet. Blood.

"Be quiet and think. What time is it? We're supposed to be at Daryl's tonight," I said.

Even saying that made my heart beat faster.

"I'll tell you if you let Me out."

"You had Your fun last night."

"Fine, then. I'll tell you if you let Me *show you* some of what I made. Take a look," She said.

I did not take a look. I did not ask to be shown whatever fresh horror She'd molded out of a casualty list, and for once, the Divine Flesh didn't play show-and-tell. I dug into my pockets. C'mon, God. I need cash. *Jesus loves me, this I know, so can I find a twenty or even a C-note, here? A gift card to Denny's?*

My pockets were empty.

Current inventory: one dirty Metallica tank top. One pair of stained—*bloodstained, Jennifer, let's not kid ourselves*—skinny jeans. No socks. No shoes. No purse, phone, wallet, or money, but also no corpses…within sight. The road gaped. I stuck my thumb out for luck.

Let Me make you something, She thought.

Suddenly, the smell of bacon. Heat shot through my jaw. A rush of saliva filled my mouth.

That wasn't good. It meant She currently had enough power to control my senses. She could make me see things, hear things, smell things…and, if She felt like it, She could make me see a stable patch of ground instead of a cliff, a green traffic signal instead of a red. Whatever creative way She could think of to kill me. Then She'd take control of our body. Again.

I had to distract the Divine Flesh.

"You wanna help? Tell me where we are, and how we got here," I said.

"Don't remember. You've got the part that thinks about all those silly things like spatial distance and time. When you're not burying our brain in…chemicals?" She fished for the word. "…drugs."

"It's Thursday. We're supposed to be at Daryl's at six."

Yes, think about Daryl. You love Daryl. We're going to see Daryl.

"Let Me out. I can get us anywhere in five minutes, babygirl. I see where the skin's thin," the Divine Flesh said.

"Absolutely not."

She giggled. "Have it your way. You're the one who's in trouble with Daryl, not Me. He loves Me."

I waited by the side of the road for a few minutes before a fruit truck, laden with splintered crates of Rainier cherries, slowed. The wrinkled driver smiled at me. An easy, howdy-missy smile.

"Need a ride, ma'am?"

I smiled back, hands on hips. "Appreciate it, thanks."

So far, so good. If Mr. American Farmer wanted sex as payment, I'd have expected nothing less. I would have done a good job of it. I didn't put my thumb out if I wasn't prepared to suck someone off for the car ride. Believe me—I'd done worse.

"Hop in," he said. "Name's Clay."

I used my standard fake name. "I'm Molly."

I entered. It smelled like dust and soured fermented fruit.

Don't worry, the Divine Flesh thought. *If he tries to hurt you, I'll protect you.*

I'm not worried for me. I'm worried for him, I thought.

She laughed. *You're so silly.*

The fruit truck jolted over a bump.

"You okay?" Clay asked, cigarette between his lips.

No, random American farmer, I wasn't.

Sometimes it would almost burst out of me, in moments like these. Freakazoid Jennifer, freakazoid me, so self-destructive that any semi-kind statement made her chest ache. Sometimes I liked to pretend someone was listening. I'd snap, make some sappy, tear-ridden emotional monologue about my life and my problems, and they'd listen. They'd care.

They'd ask, *Jennifer, what's wrong?*

I'd tell them: I've got a flesh-bending cosmic goddess trapped in my skin, and both of us hate each other.

Holy shit! Jennifer, how long's that been going on?

In my earliest memory, I'm three years old, sitting on cold, kitchen linoleum. Sitting in a pool of blood. Two dead bodies lie on the water-stained floor nearby. Bio Mom and Dad. It smells like speed. Speed's crackling in an old used two-liter bottle in the trailer sink, because they're using the Shake 'N Bake of cooking speed, no lab needed. Chemicals fizz in the bottle. It's bulging from gas buildup. Nobody's loosening the cap every five minutes to let the gases out. Soon, it'll explode, splattering the trailer and three-year-old me with caustic, dangerous liquid—basically Drano. Products line the kitchen counter: Sudafed, instant cold packs, camp-stove propane, fertilizer, Drano…other stuff, too. Spice bottles roll across the floor: McCormick Salad Magic and Poultry Seasoning, desiccated bay leaves in their jar, pretty spices I want to touch and smell because the chemicals stink. My nose burns. My cheeks burn, raw from crying. And the Divine Flesh is there, shushing me like an older sister. She soothes, *They wanted to hurt you. It's okay, babygirl. I'll always, always be here. FOREVER. I LOVE YOU!*

My listener would ask, *Jennifer, have you tried therapy? Antidepressants? Prescribed drugs instead of self-medicating?*

Jennifer, are you insane?

I'd laugh. I'd tell them about all the times I've died. I'd tell them that a shotgun blast to the head hurts less than a bullet. I'd march them over to Daryl Plummer's storage unit in Coeur d'Alene, pull out the black plastic storage bin marked *Jennifer's Body*, and show them the wet-preserved fragments that the Divine Flesh bequeathed to him when he was in that creepy taxidermy phase. I'd dust off the jars and juxtapose them against my body.

The Divine Flesh crawled in my skin, but She was kind enough to repair the damage.

Jennifer, you wouldn't, like, kill yourself or anything, right? You're not gonna pull a Jesus-Savior thing?

Jennifer, you're self-destructive.

This is where we'd start fighting, and then it'd get too heated.

The Divine Flesh would possess me, rip out their throat or heart, and transmute them into, like, an eldritch horse or something. No matter how much I begged Her not to.

"You look like you just took a shit and saw your liver floatin' in the toilet," Clay said.

"If someone gave you one last chance to redeem yourself, and you might've blown it because you got drunk and then woke up on the side of a road in the middle of nowhere, how would you feel?"

"You need some of those AA meetings?"

"Where am I? What time is it?"

He jerked his thumb at the dashboard. Duct tape held a cheap wrist-watch to the left of the radio. The clock hands said 12:30.

"Can I have a smoke?" I asked.

"Ain't good for your body."

"Do I look healthy?"

His muddy eyes scanned along my arms. Dash-shaped scars meshed every inch of skin, rowing from armpits to wrists, each one about a quarter-inch long. The colors ranged from silvery to cherry-red.

"Can I have a smoke, pretty please? I'm legal," I said.

"Center compartment."

I fished around a pile of dusty receipts and glass vials. A molar rotted in a corner of the compartment, dotted in dried blood. Cigs spilled out of a crushed Marlboro pack. I selected one, rescued a BIC lighter, and lit it. Drew in smoke.

"Lotta orchards. We in Washington?" I asked.

"Yakima. You got a home?"

I kept expecting him to reach over. Waited for the hand on my thigh.

"Y'know, I gotta say, I ain't all that impressed with you," he said, rubbing his age-spotted jaw. "It's cherry season."

I blinked.

Cherry season.

Something tickled the back of my brain. Why...did last night seem so important? I mean, beyond the need to get high—that was a given. Teeth. Teeth in glass vials. Exonumia, slicked in blood. Dixie cups half-filled with pinkish slime, spit, water. Pliers on a table, pliers grasped in non-hand appendages. A forked tongue, working between my thighs. Pleasure. Rough, slick texture. A rowdy butch's voice, telling me about Spine and good hard whiskey. How if we went to another place, there'd be better stuff. She wasn't a Mirror Person; I let her fuck me. Her forked tongue worked and worked, *so good, keep going*, and her hair was banana-candy yellow, cropped close to her skull.

I probed an empty space in my gums that hadn't been there yesterday.

Another fragment of last night flickered by. *Cherries.* Maraschino cherries, bobbing in last night's pineapple upside-down cake cocktail like bloated corpses. I'd been talking about a job, a shipment of something. Cute forked-tongue butch said, *Listen for cherries, Jennifer. You're holding the shipment for a few days, then taking them to—*

"These cherries are goin' to Mesa, Arizona," Clay said, and his grip tightened on the steering wheel.

So this was why I'd ended up here. I'd gotten blitzed, gotten bored, taken a job, trekked off into the night, accidentally let the Divine Flesh loose, and then collapsed at the pickup rendezvous.

"Kinda funny," I said.

"Hm?"

"If this is a shipping route for the orchards, where are the other fruit trucks? Road should be full of 'em, Clay."

"You figure it out, *Jennifer*?"

I nodded. "Want me to drop you off in a better location before I take over—"

"No." He swallowed. Hard. The flesh on his neck jiggled.

"Doesn't have to be your house. Or anywhere associated with you, your family, or your friends. It can be the next gas station we drive past," I said.

"You don't gotta."

I exhaled smoke. "I don't like leaving people in the middle of nowhere. It's bad for morale. Shitty business practice."

"You care?"

"More than I should," I said.

"You're the Flesh Failure. I don't want you caring 'bout me, understand?" he said.

Cornfields rippled on both sides of the freeway, crowned with green silk. I cranked the window down. July air, humid. Thick with the gamy smell of growing things and pesticide. Rainier cherry season. Too early for Bings.

"I won't even remember your face or name, trust me," I said.

None of it mattered. Mr. American Farmer's name wasn't actually Clay. He wasn't human, and I wasn't moving a shipment of cherries.

Most likely, I'd be safeguarding a clutch of parasitic babies from vigilante exterminators. Or bits of dried Mirror Person, called Spine. Or plain vanilla fentanyl. They moved a lot of fentanyl in rural areas.

I never said I was a good person.

I crushed out my cig. "Spine or babies?"

"Both," he said. "Eggs. Not larvae."

Jennifer, I wanna DO THINGS, the Divine Flesh whined.

I thought, *Okay, what brand of non-human is this guy?*

She thought, *He tastes like one of the Mirror People. He has skin cells. He's shedding them off and I can TASTE the dust. I like it. I wanna clothe him in something slippery. He'd look better—*

Mirror People.

My guts clenched.

I should have felt sorry for 'em. But I didn't. Mirror People were genderless, supercoiled, silvery wasp-like beings with the "empathy" of a billion saccharine therapists hopped up on pure oxytocin. They reflected the environment around them, changing their appearance and bodies at will. Mirror People were great. Super nice. Until they went into heat, lost their hyper-empathy, and went into sociopath mode, looking for some poor victim to impregnate with their larvae. They didn't like to talk about where they were from. The most I ever got out of one was: *God decided to end reality. We had to leave. Now we're here.*

I ignored the Divine Flesh, as usual. I checked a mental padlock, tugged at it. Saw Her contained and docile. For now. She kept trying to get my attention. She kept saying that Clay didn't taste quite right, but I tuned Her out.

Crates rattled as the truck jostled over pitted road.

"Where is it?" I asked.

"Glovebox."

I opened it. Two prescription pill bottles lurked inside. Flyspecks of dried blood covered the labels. A potpourri bag of something called *Lavender Summer* rested under the insurance papers. Not a clever repack, but standard for Mirror People. Spine looked almost identical to dried lavender. Think potpourri at Grandma's crack house.

I lifted a pill bottle.

Mirror-Person eggs shone near to the brim. They gleamed like pellets of chrome, small as aspirin.

"How many in each bottle?" I asked.

"Sixty. A hundred-twenty total."

He pulled off the road, let the truck idle. We switched drivers.

The fruit stand came up as we continued. *Cherries! Rainiers! Antiques!* proclaimed painted plywood signs.

I drove into the fruit stand's parking area.

"Crates are for show. You can hock 'em or burn 'em or what have you."

"All right."

Five hour drive from here to Daryl's.

Something fluttered in my chest.

I could still meet up with Daryl. I could still save this. As long as I drove continuously and nothing went wrong. It'd been a whole year since we'd talked. Since he'd kicked me out. Would he look different? Would his new friends think I was okay? What did Daryl say when he talked about me?

Jennifer, yeah, my ex, she's a junkie.

Jennifer's a mess.

Oh, we knew each other back from the foster care system. Way back. She's been the same self-destructive, scar-covered piece of shit that she was when I met her at fourteen.

I needed a different life motto. "No drug left undone" was really starting to fry my brain.

Clay opened the truck door. Then he hesitated, dug in his shirt pocket, and thrust a twenty at me. It smelled like cinnamon Altoids.

"Here. Git somethin' to eat," he said.

"Aw, shit. You don't have to—"

"The hell I don't. You're skin and bones."

Is he implying that I STARVE YOU? the Divine Flesh snapped. *Because it's not My fault I forget to feed our body when I go create My children.*

"Thanks," I said.

Clay grunted approval. Then he practically sprinted out of the truck, gnawing his lip. The Divine Flesh tapped on the door of Her mental prison, saying, *You didn't even see the things I created in Tieton, babygirl.*

Clay became engulfed in the standard fruit-stand crowd: tourists clad in bland designer clothing and cooing over half-rotten past-season strawberries, sour-faced grandmothers yanking grandkids over to the pickling cucumbers, and fecund young fundamentalist families with smartphones and their broods, wearing nervous expressions—*Is this where you go to get produce for Instagram posts on slow living?* Around piles of rusted iron antiques, men long past their prime smoked Camels and wheezed, cancer gestating in their lungs.

I drove on. Why watch "Clay" homogenize?

Can you redeem *the sins of the flesh?*

I cranked up the religious radio stations, for variety. I had a five-hour drive. I spent a lot of it thinking and drinking peach-flavored Monsters.

You had that fight.

You were high! It was over a year ago! Anyway, it was all Her fault.

If someone lived in a trailer in the forest by their ex's cabin, because he kicked them out a year ago, because apparently throwing plates was "inexcusable" now, but it was partly driven by the emotions of the meat-bending horror inside their body…would they still be redeemable?

Cloudless sky loomed over me. Sweat slimed my thighs.

Daryl must've thought so.

It'd been a quick phone call from him, a week ago. He'd said, "Hey. Emily and Javier are coming over on Thursday. You wanna meet them?"

Then me, taking a solid thirty seconds to respond. "What?"

"Not as lovers…Jennifer, I miss you."

Neither of us brought up the Divine Flesh. It was better that way.

I'd said, "Yeah, me too. It's just—Hey, you get custody of the kids?"

"I'm not going to be involved in your lifestyle anymore," he said, in that blunt Daryl-way of his. "No more drugs, none of that. I miss you. Emily and Javier want to meet you, bring you into the fold. You know how it is out here in the boonies."

"My *lifestyle*? Oh my god, Daryl. You bought my supplies and Sudafed when I needed to cook a batch of speed and I was too fucked up to go out in public. You're not the Jesse to my Walter White, asshole. You handed ten high-schoolers thirty bucks to buy a pack of Sudafed for you and told them to keep the change, and then you went to Lowe's for the fertilizer and plastic tubing. For fuck's sake—"

Daryl's voice chilled. "That was enough to keep me from getting custody of Marcia and Isaac when the cops came."

"Hey, I'm sorry. So sorry. So, so very sorry. I'm just Evil Fucking Jennifer, right? I magically possessed you like a demon and made you cook speed with me all these years. Me. I guess I'm fucking magical now—"

"Forget I called," he said.

"—because you had *no control* of your body, right, Daryl?"

My face had burned, and my heart kept pounding in my ears. I tasted metal.

"You had—" My voice broke. "No control. Right? Just couldn't control yourself."

"I'm sorry you're dealing with the Divine Flesh."

"What the fuck did you think was gonna happen when you called me, Daryl? I'd tell you I still love you?"

He sighed. "I shouldn't have cheated on you."

"You finally called it what it is. Cheating."

"Can we—look, Jennifer. You're my oldest buddy. I wouldn't be alive if it wasn't for you. You know I don't got family I talk to anymore. You're it. The closest thing I got to family."

"Same," I whispered.

"Do you wanna come over and meet Emily and Javier?"

"Okay. Okay."

"Can you try to be sober?"

"Yeah," I'd said, because sober meant hope. I could do that.

I missed Daryl. So much. So I drove, and I thought about that little snippet of hope I had left. There was a chance. All I had to do was get to Daryl's cabin at six. I had time. I had hope.

I really did.

Until I hit Moscow, Idaho, and the fruit truck's rear tire blew out at 5:01 p.m., exactly an hour and a half away from Daryl's cabin.

Shit.

2

It happened on the interstate, barely a mile out of Moscow. Worse things have happened. Nobody was shooting at me. Cars whizzed by, none of them slowing. Good. If they slowed, it'd either be because someone was about to pull a drive-by to steal the shipment, or because a predator saw an emaciated twenty-two-year-old alone on the side of the road.

Granted, neither of those could have hurt me.

I'd gotten the truck onto the shoulder. I slithered over, exited on the passenger side. One tire had shredded apart. The others were bald and cracked. No bullet holes. No nails. Probably not deliberate.

One last shot to fix things with Daryl, and you fuck it up. Great going, Jennifer.

I took inventory.

No spare tires. No jack. Thirty wood crates. Twenty-nine empties. There was a .44 revolver in the last crate.

I wrapped my tank top around my hand, wiped the gun, and checked it. Loaded. Okay, good. I stowed it back. Not my gun, not my problem.

Two-hundred dollars lay in an unmarked envelope in the glovebox.

A burner phone—a bona fide Jitterbug—rested in the center compartment.

I flipped it open. The screen glowed to life.

Thanks, God. I knew you'd come through for me.

I could call Daryl and tell him what was going on. Then it wouldn't matter. He'd forgive me. Hell, we'd've laughed it off a few years ago.

I punched in his number. Pressed call.

Ringing.

Ringing.

The number would be unknown. He never answered his phone when he was in the middle of something, and if it was an hour before he was having people over, he'd be cleaning his baseboards with a toothbrush or some shit like that. So. It was fine.

Ringing.

Went to voicemail.

I left one, stating the facts. Shipment came up. Flat tire. Sorry, Daryl, I'm gonna be late, but things are going great. I made it to a week sober. I started eating three meals a day, not just breakfast. The Divine Flesh says that She loves you.

I checked the time. *Friday, 5:10 p.m.*

The Divine Flesh said, "If you let Me out, I could give us wings and fly there."

"Not helpful."

Couldn't google tow truck companies. Didn't know any numbers. I dug around in my bag of gas station snacks and found teriyaki beef jerky. I tore the bag open and chewed a square of jerky, thinking.

Then it hit me.

Flesh.

"We're going to do something even more fun, D. F.," I said, padding over to the tire, bag of jerky in hand. "Let's fix the tire."

She plunged into our body, greedy as a demon on Judgment Day. Our hands stroked tattered rubber. I swallowed every scrap of jerky. *Use the jerky, the dried flesh. Use what's inside me. Slough off my appendix if you gotta, Divine Flesh.*

Like spider silk, filaments of protein unspooled from our fingers.

We worked.

We had a soothing, weaving rhythm as our hands danced over the tire. Filaments threaded through it, pulling, melding. A thick mesh of flesh formed over the breach.

Now, I thought. *Breathe.*

Millions of microscopic primordial mouths formed on the mesh—featureless stomata. They all inhaled. Air bloated the tire, inflating it. The fruit truck shuddered up, up, back to position.

Close, I thought.

The stomata shut and fused together.

I nudged our handiwork with my foot. It felt rock-hard.

"Nice."

She said, "I can't wait to see Daryl!"

"Cry me a river. You see him all the time."

The phone said, *Friday, 5:20 p.m.*

I reentered the truck, fired the engine. If I gunned it down the interstate, I could make Daryl's by 7:00 p.m. A little late for Daryl on a Thursday night, but I had to get there. At least to apologize. Then I could finally be a Good Person, or somewhat closer to that.

I gunned it.

I hit Rosetown, Idaho at 6:50 p.m., and drove the last half mile out to Daryl's.

The only vehicle in Daryl's driveway was his. A black Dodge Ram, streaked with dust.

It should've been a sign.

His cabin jutted from a grassy clearing at the end of a gravel road. It was a one-room shack that was built in 1906. Didn't have electricity until Daryl wired the place as a favor to the owner. The rent was something like $600 a month. Pine shingles littered the yard and driveway like decaying leaves. A lone cedar sheltered the front. Metal glimmered by the east side of the cabin—a tin-can trailer, straight outta the '50s.

No other cars were here.

He could've picked up Emily and Javier, especially if they'd be drinking.

I eased the fruit truck into the drive. Got out.

Only an hour late. Hardly a sin.

I licked my cracked lips, strode up to Daryl's front door, and knocked.

July evening swirled around me, oven-hot. The sunlight had thickened into almost-tangible gold. It gilded the cabin. Shadows stretched. Blue woodsmoke streamed from the chimney.

A creak came from within. Someone getting up, walking over.

How to begin? *Hey, Daryl, nice to see you. Remember when you had to haul me over to Bridgeton Recovery Center, with my wrist still spurting blood? Gosh, remember the time I caught you cheating on me?*

My stomach churned.

The door opened.

Daryl blinked at me. "Jennifer."

The Divine Flesh pulsed, pulsed, going, *Daryl! Jennifer, let Me out. Let Me talk to him! Daryl I love you!*

Daryl looked the same as he had the day he'd kicked me out. Trimmed dark beard, stocky, a bit shorter than me. Whiskey-brown eyes. He had a crooked nose and the slow, methodical gaze of a medical examiner performing an autopsy.

He clutched a Space Dust IPA in one hand, *Preservation of Wet Specimens* in the other, and he wasn't wearing a shirt. He had a dad bod, which made sense, given that he was the dad for his younger siblings. Chest hair carpeted his torso.

Which meant nobody else was here. No way would Daryl casually walk around without a shirt if there were others around, and like hell would he drink on a Thursday night. Maybe more had changed than I'd realized.

Or maybe this whole thing was a setup.

"Where'd everyone go?" I asked, heart hammering in my throat.

He just stared at me, in that expressionless Daryl-way of his.

"Don't—don't stand there and look at me. Where'd everyone go?" I said. "C'mon. I left you a voicemail, I said I'd be late."

He sighed. "Jennifer—"

"I'm not here to fuck this up—"

"Jennifer—"

"I'm sorry I was late. What is this, a setup? You wanted to—to drag me here and pretend that people actually wanted to be around me and that everything was okay, just to fuck with my head? Is that it? Is that what you wanted? The Divine Flesh took over my body, I lost a few hours and I had a shipment I didn't know about, but I still tried to make it. Fuck, I'm sorry. It's Thursday night, maybe we can still do something—"

"It's Friday," Daryl said.

"What?"

He rubbed his temple. "We waited for you last night, but you never showed up."

"Oh, fuck."

I wasn't an hour late. I was *twenty-five* hours late. I'd lost an entire day without knowing.

"Same as usual, Jennifer? You got high?"

"I'm sorry."

"I don't want to talk about this right now."

"You want me to leave?"

"I want Jennifer to leave. Not my sweetheart—"

Then Daryl did that thing where he looked through me. Looked at Her.

His voice got that soft rumble. "You wanna c'mon in, sweetheart?"

The Divine Flesh said, *I LOVE YOU!*

I staggered. Red blotted out my right eye. Feverish blood dribbled down my cheek.

"Oh god, stop it. Please," I said, but of course, they didn't.

He touched my arm, caressing the flesh…touching Her. Not me.

She flooded our body, an ocean, obliterating me in a black rush. My vision was the first to go, as always. *We need our privacy, Jennifer-baby. You aren't in a relationship with Daryl anymore. He's MINE now. MINE. Tee-hee!*

His warm hand rested on our cheek.

Creak.

The door was opening, and I was supposed to leave. Bye-bye, Jennifer. It's time for Daryl and the Divine Flesh to go on a dinner date. Then they'll fuck. Using the body. My body. Her body. Our body. She'll love him the way I used to.

"C'mon in, baby."

Oh god, do you two have to do this now? Right now?

The Divine Flesh tsk-tsked. "Nobody wants you around, Jennifer. Go to sleep and let Me love Daryl a little bit."

Nobody wants a worthless addict, Jennifer. Everyone knows you're snorting coke in the bathroom. You're chugging the Listerine. If I kept myself in a constant state of low-grade oblivion, sometimes I could forget my life.

My sense of touch went next. Everything numbed. I floated in a void, I felt Her stuffing me down. Jennifer-baby, the unwanted parasite.

"Daryl," She murmured, using our mouth. "I missed you."

"Did You learn something new?"

"I learned about cherry season."

"I know a cherry I'd like to taste."

She giggled. "Silly. You taste like sweat today. I like it."

Then my hearing went.

Then I went.

Going, going, gone.

"We told these folks to leave. We've told 'em multiple times," Trojan said to the gathered people. "What do you do when someone's trespassing on your property? You come out with a shotgun and tell 'em to kindly get the hell off your land. And if they don't, you shoot."

They shivered in the woods. It was one in the morning. Before them lay the burned-down shell of a trailer, its blackened metal thin as a wasp's nest. Trojan aimed his flashlight at it.

"Who's been supplying you, Wade?" Trojan asked.

"Oh god, oh god, I don't know," Wade blubbered.

There they were, all gathered: the pastor-man, the junkie, the Trojan, the woman, the twins, and the others driven to protect Rosetown, Idaho. Couldn't have the wrong folks settling in Rosetown. That would have been like putting drops of crude oil into a well and expecting the water to still be sweet. So Trojan had called, and they had come.

More voices. The pastor-man said, "Rutted with a blackbird, didn't ya, Wade? Now you're surprised the kid you bred's hanging out with these folks? What'd you expect? All they do is drugs."

"I left the warning. Did it quick," said the woman.

The woman. Singular. Only one. Her voice was reedy as a nun's.

"I still think the guy's a Jew or somethin'. He's not acting like a white man," the pastor-man said, and straightened up. His tone became robotic. "It's vital that we preserve the integrity of the white race—"

"Fuck, save it for your KKK meetings. I don't wanna hear any of that white pride bullshit. Trojan's right. These kids ain't locals, and they're bringing in drugs. Not good people. I still don't see why we gotta do a repeat of ten years ago."

Trojan walked a few steps closer to the burned-down trailer.

"I'm here to show ya why," he said.

He aimed his flashlight at the ground.

On the dirt rested a corpse. The mostly naked body of a young female. Barely dead. Dead maybe a day or three. A faint smell of rot came from it. Sores covered most of its skin. Purple-black track marks decayed on its left forearm. Its torso had been sliced open. Fishing-line stitches gleamed from sternum to pubis. The top two inches of the slice bulged open, exposing plastic.

Plastic bags of drugs stuffed the cadaver.

"Should I rip the rest of it open for you to see?"

Voices rose.

"Oh god, oh god—"

"Jesus Christ, cadaver drug bags? Here? This ain't the border. We're in fuckin' Idaho."

"Poor girl. Look what they did to her body."

"Dad, we gotta come out here or move the corpse…I mean, we gotta make an official police report on this, right?"

"Hush, son."

Trojan cleared his throat. "See that burned-down trailer? Used to be a meth lab. Inhale, folks. You smell somethin' a little like Vicks VapoRub and smoke? That's meth. Speed. Crank. This trailer used to belong to a certain lil' junkie gal who's living in our town. The junkie's gotta be under the thumb of that fuckin' creep with the beard. One of 'em's been cooking speed."

"His name's Daryl."

"Thank you. Daryl ever go to church? Even once?"

"Naw, not even that Catholic place or the faggy Unitarian joint."

"Folks," Trojan said, "I could tolerate a certain amount of cooking speed. America's a free country. But when we got a man in our town murdering women to use as drug bags…Look at her. She's probably been dead less than a week."

Greedily, the pastor-man hissed, "And we can get rid of that little Mexican faggot, too—"

"Ah, let the Rodriguez family alone. They're hardworking citizens."

"We had a threat like this ten years ago. We took care of it. We take care of our town," Trojan said. "Come real close. I'll show you the plan."

The body isn't real. *The body isn't mine. I am not burning.*

I'm not.

Deep night.

The lurid blue glow of his alarm clock. Heavy air. Flannel sheets strangled me, damp with sweat and hormones.

The taste of him lingered in my mouth. I know that taste. His spit. His skin cells. They coated my tongue and the insides of my cheeks.

I could taste his dick. His semen.

They'd fucked.

I untangled myself. Daryl made a soft sound, rubbed the empty space where She had been, and went back to sleep. I ghosted through the cabin and slipped outside. Gravel hurt my feet. I didn't go back for my shoes. I slipped into the truck. Chugged a half-drunk bottle of water from the cup holder. It was 4:12 a.m. The Gas N' Go would be open. It was only a two-mile drive from there to my trailer, which was great, because I'd probably start drinking on the way back. Cry or drink. One of the two. Probably both.

I drove.

A fingernail moon hung low in the sky.

I wanted to fly up to it. Fly out of my body. Leave it behind forever. Get the taste of Daryl out of my mouth, the taste of them screwing and loving each other. No more drug-fried, scar-covered body to cage me. Just freedom.

The body isn't real. The body isn't mine. I am not burning.

At some point, Clay would call me on the burner phone and tell me to start driving the shipment to Mesa. Until then, I was free enough.

"Jennifer-baby, go back. I don't want to get drunk. I want to sleep with him," the Divine Flesh said.

Gas N' Go shone like a lighthouse in the dark. Fireball. Thunderbird. Jack Daniel's. Smirnoff, strawberry-cream flavored.

"I was so beautiful, you know," She said, voice suddenly flat.

I ignored her. The Divine Flesh didn't have real feelings. Well, that wasn't true. She had three modes. Bored, psychotically happy, and oh-look-I-found-*flesh*.

"So beautiful, Jennifer."

"You're very pretty, Divine Flesh," I said.

I entered Gas N' Go. Warm browns failed to add charm to the industrial space. The windows only looked out on freeway. A smell— kitchen grease and Polyquat. Bright-pink SnoBalls overflowed from every Hostess display.

The booze section took up three aisles.

I selected.

A bottle of Red, White, & Berry Smirnoff, because why not be festive?

The moonshines: a bottle of Kentucky Mist, a bottle of Black Mountain, and a jar of Ole Smoky peaches. See, I was healthy. I ate fruit.

Some warm-ups. A couple mini Fireball bottles and a six-pack of Truck Stop Honey.

As he rang me up, Ol' Monty said, "You're bleeding."

"Oh?"

I studied my left wrist. Some of the scabs had fallen off. Blood beaded.

"You like the company you keep?" Monty asked.

"Huh?"

"You already drunk?"

My hick accent—a relic from my origins—crept in. "Naw, gonna git there. Have a good one."

"You seem like a decent enough kid. Not like the…guy you showed up with. Does he hurt you?"

Just three more seconds, and then I could drink.

"Yeah, yeah. Have a good one."

"You oughta keep better company, is all I'm sayin'. Get some therapy. They got therapy for it, y'know. Could find a nice man."

I reached for my bag. "Sure, thanks."

"They really oughta move."

"We won't."

He slid the booze over. "So it's 'we.' So you're with 'em?"

I didn't respond. I headed for the door.

"I warned you," he said. "Remember that."

I cracked open a beer as I drove. I'd finished it by the time I drove past Daryl's, through the forest, and unlatched the door to my trailer.

I drank.

"Jennifer-baby, are you trying to kill yourself?"

"That's physically impossible," I slurred.

I plowed through an entire bottle of moonshine, then threw up in the sink. It tasted like jerky and acid and synthetic peach. Bits of steak came up. Daryl would've cooked for Her. She and Daryl must've eaten before they—

I drank before I finished that thought.

My hands numbed. My body numbed. I retrieved both pill bottles of Mirror People eggs, little sad unborn things wanting meat. Wanting love. I considered swallowing them. The larvae would secrete feel-good chemicals, synthetic love, as they hatched and consumed me from the inside out. Clay wouldn't mind. Hell, he'd probably throw ten grand into my cut.

Full of little babies, the Divine Flesh thought.

Blearily, half-staggering, I got the Christmas lights out from under my couch. Snow-white twinkle lights. I plugged 'em in. I set the pill bottles on the gray carpet. Warmth radiated off the lights. The plastic cord felt smooth as skin. Alive. I cried. With clumsy motions, I wrapped the lights around my body. My arms. My legs. I wreathed myself in light.

I passed the rest of Saturday in a drunken doze, in the glow of the Christmas lights.

Clay called. I couldn't answer.

He left a voicemail. "Move the shipment. The distribution gal will be expectin' you in two days." A cough. "I might've found something. I reckon you might know what it is."

I think I got up at some point. The next thing I remembered was eating a peanut butter, ham, and pickle sandwich. With raw bacon.

"What the hell is this?" I asked.

I like it raw, the Divine Flesh said.

"Oh, I know. We all know."

Daryl called around 3 p.m.

I answered, slurring out some greeting.

"We're going out to Silver Lake tonight. The gang wants you to come," Daryl said.

"I notice you aren't included in that statement."

"What do you want from me? I loved you. We tried. You're still on my damn health insurance."

"Can't make it. Got a shipment."

"Well. If you decide to, we're meeting at my place."

"Aye aye, cap'n."

Click.

I sobered up around dusk. I packed the fruit truck with food, water, and supplies for a desert drive. It'd be best to drive during nighttime. Less wear on the engine. Less traffic. Less Mojave heat. Underestimating the desert tended to be deadly.

I was heading out of Rosetown when Daryl called again.

I picked up.

"Get over here. Now," he said.

Police sirens bayed in the background.

"Daryl?"

"Get over here."

"I'm running a shipment. I can't—"

"They're dead, Jennifer."

Click.

3

The Divine Flesh slithered into my nerves and nose, taking control of our body, and this time, I let Her.

Daryl.

She knew how he tasted, knew the texture of his skin, his sequence of nucleotides, strung like glass beads on a helix, the array of skin cells, all the silly human bits he'd sloughed off over the course of his life, every hair follicle, every skin cell floating in the dust, dusting cabinets, dusting across his apartment in Coeur d'Alene even though he'd last been there eighteen months ago; they tasted so very old, lifeless.

Almost lifeless. Ah, that was the key.

Trillions of invisible tendrils exploded out from our body, each one thin enough to brush against electrons, worm around, and continue onward. *Find Daryl.*

As one, we searched.

Daryl Plummer, darling loverboy, where are you?

He hates me.

The Divine Flesh spoke through my mouth. "Well, he doesn't hate *Me*, Jennifer-baby."

Daryl's dried blood rusted on a pocketknife in a Goodwill bargain bin in Portland, Oregon. Methodist churches were rife with his skin cells, the dust of him scattered over Bibles and varnished pews, along windowsills. One of his pubes lay in the backseat of an Econoline van, dried splotches of cum on the velvet seats, more skin cells. A Coeur d'Alene storage unit, more hairs. Dust. Skin. Pubes. Hairs in a public rest stop in Montana. Skin cells on a bottle of Perrier on a plane, a dried-up Mormon housewife stroking the side of the bottle, tasting her, *so silly and sad, so covered in decaying aging skin*, Jennifer-baby, *she needs new skin, can I give her something silky? Can I give her gills or fresh eyes, can I, can I—*

"Focus," I said.

I added human logic. *We're in Idaho, so start there.*

If he's in trouble, he could be halfway across the USA.

I bit my wrist. Hard. Pain burned, clearing my brain.

Focus. Don't let Her out.

Skin cells on a cigarette butt littering Highway 395, bloody bits of toilet paper in a landfill, coated with his beard hairs, his old blood on discarded Band-Aids, black from age and moldering, blood—*fresh*—on asphalt—

Blood!

Fresh skin, shredded into asphalt. Skin cells blanketed a nearby truck's interior. Blood. Wet blood. Someone else's blood was smeared across his skin—

pulse-pulse-pulse.

His heartbeat, a low-pitched song.

Daryl!

He was sitting off the side of Highway 93, a couple miles up the road. *Blood on the road. Police sirens. Daryl, what the hell did you get into?*

I drove us along Highway 93. It took us twenty minutes to find the accident.

Blood. Smelled it when I opened the truck door. Blood, glistening on asphalt. A semi-truck lurked on Highway 93's shoulder, its front dented. State troopers in khaki clustered around it, stances casual, motions easy and relaxed. Nearby lay Daryl's Dodge Ram, twisted like taffy. Broken safety glass glittered. Two plastic tarps covered bodies. Red and blue police flashers painted over everything.

Daryl sat by a tarp, shivering. A Mylar blanket cocooned him in silver. A trooper loomed over him. Daryl's lips moved, but no sound came out.

I approached.

The trooper was a blond shitkicker with a double chin and acne.

His mouth twitched as he stared at Daryl. "Sir, the paramedics are on their way. We're goin' to do the Breathalyzer again."

Daryl grunted.

"I can recommend an auto shop, sir. Outta town," the trooper said.

"You saw the brake line," Daryl said.

"You sure you knew what to look for?"

"Oh," he said softly, "believe me, Officer. I know."

Then Daryl Plummer saw me.

"Jennifer. Give him the insurance information," he said.

Daryl didn't have so much as a paper cut. No bruises. No broken bones. No obvious signs of pain. His clothes were ruined, soaked in blood. Tatters of his black cotton shirt latticed over his gut, showing bits of fish-white flesh. An arm-length hole arced up his right jean leg.

"Daryl, when did the accident happen?" I asked.

"Wasn't an accident."

"The hell you saying, *sir*?" Blonde Trooper snapped.

I pasted on a smile. "I'm going to take Mr. Plummer to the hospital. Can we leave?"

"We told you to leave. We told you a million times to leave."

An ambulance rolled up to us, red lights flashing.

"Jennifer has the insurance information," Daryl said.

He let the paramedics bustle him onto a stretcher. I went to get in the ambulance, but they stopped me.

Someone asked, "Are you the girlfriend?"

"What?"

"He said he was driving with his girlfriend and another individual when the accident happened. Are you involved in this?"

"No."

"Then you can't ride in the ambulance with him. Family and spouses only."

"I want her to ride with me," Daryl said.

"Sorry, sir."

Heat bloomed through my face. I yanked out a laminated copy of my driver's license and a copy of our insurance cards.

A paramedic shrugged, hand resting on the ambulance door. "Miss, we really can't let any random girlfriend ride along in the ambulance—"

"I'm not his girlfriend," I said.

I gritted my teeth and held the IDs out.

Say it. Spit it out, Jennifer. Why don't you spit it out, Mrs. Jennifer Plummer?

"I'm his wife."

They let me ride in the ambulance.

I'd seen WinCos larger than that hospital. It'd been built in the 1970s, and still reeked of cigarettes and rubbing alcohol. White vinyl wallcovering browned around the ceiling and light switches, crusted in decades of grime, sweat, and nicotine. Puke-yellow linoleum shone. The ceilings hung too low.

A sour-faced female doctor examined Daryl, lips pursed.

"Take off your shirt," she said.

Daryl did. The doctor palpated, pressing at random intervals, listening for pain or distress. I watched her. She didn't try any bullshit. I felt two bone spurs pulsing, waiting to sprout out from the radii at the base of both my wrists, *grab, kill the meat-doctor, absorb her flesh and stab the threats, Jennifer-baby, because I will protect Daryl—*

Jesus fucking Christ. *Calm down. Daryl's fine.*

I LOVE HIM, JENNIFER! LET ME OUT!

Not now, Divine Flesh. Later.

"You're a very lucky man, from what I can see," the doctor said as she shone a light into Daryl's eyes. "No concussion. No serious damage. You'll probably be sore in a few days."

That was when I remembered. I'd left the truck full of drugs parked on the side of Highway 93.

Well, shit. Was this entire thing a setup? A ruse to steal the egg shipment? Was this guy even Daryl, or was he a Mirror Person pretending to be Daryl? It seemed awfully convenient that Daryl was the only survivor of that car accident.

An invisible icepick stabbed my skull, and a cold feeling crept up my spine. Hangover incoming. I winced.

The doctor hesitated for a minute. "Do you have good health insurance, Mr. Plummer?"

"Yeah, it's from the union."

"It might not be a bad idea to stay overnight. For observation."

"Is there a reason I shouldn't be home tonight?" Daryl asked.

The doctor didn't stare at Daryl. She stared just below him, at the hospital bed rail, and her throat worked.

"Well," he said, "is there?"

"Maybe."

"I'll take your suggestion. Thank you, Dr. Landes," he said.

The doctor nodded, then left.

Hey, Divine Flesh, I thought, *does this one taste like Daryl? Is he really Daryl? Or is this a Mirror Person pretending to be Daryl?*

She responded, *It's Daryl!*

Something burst at my left wrist. Wet warmth trickled down. An inch-long spar of bone jutted out, coated in blood.

LET ME OUT!

"I gotta get my truck and shipment. I'll be back in an hour. That okay?"

"We need to talk."

"No shit, Sherlock," I said.

"Can I see the Divine Flesh? I miss Her."

I forced a laugh. "Depends on if you want Her to massacre every single person in this hospital. She's unsettled right now."

Then he did that thing where he looked through me. Looked at Her.

"I love You, baby," he said, voice breaking.

I LOVE YOU!

My hick accent crept in. "Want me to git your truck?"

He shook his head. "Jennifer, that wasn't an accident. It was sabotage… My brake line was cut almost all the way through…I checked. After I… after it happened. They tried to kill me, Emily, and Javier."

I warned you. Remember that.

"Okay. Okay," I said.

Now Daryl's hick accent started slipping out, too. "You live outside a' Rosetown, you wouldn't have seen how bad it was gettin'. I never wanted to talk 'bout it. It's part of the reason I never let you git close this last year, not just for selfish reasons. I left all of it behind years before that—"

"Oh, please. You were never involved in this shit like I was, Daryl. Not an insult, by the way. That's a compliment. I never wanted you to—"

"I know."

I sighed. "I stopped cooking speed, 'bout six months ago. I mostly move larvae and eggs now, and I don't deal."

"You want a gold star, Jennifer?"

"Look, I'm trying."

His upper lip snapped up. "Maybe if you'd've been with us, the Divine Flesh would've stopped us from dying."

"Blame me for everything. Ain't that some shit?" I said.

"This wasn't an accident. It was murder. Emily and Javier ain't gonna rot under the ground while their killers go free. I'm gonna find out who did this, and I'm getting justice."

"You want my help?"

"I need your help. Know the difference," he said.

The shipment and truck were fine.

Should've been a dead giveaway that something was off. But I didn't think about it, because I was too busy worrying about Daryl and whatever else Rosetown, Idaho had planned for him tonight.

The Divine Flesh sang, *Let Me. Let Me devour them, Jennifer-baby, they won't even suffer. Well. I suppose that might not make Daryl very happy, but love needs to be given to EVERYONE! Tee-hee!*

She whispered, *Is there a morgue in town? I think there is.*

I was driving back to the hospital, white-knuckling the steering wheel.

I want the bodies, babygirl.

About halfway there, buzzing filled my left ear. I wiped dried blood off my face, listening.

(Baby, I love You.)

I sighed. I knew that sound. Daryl Plummer was praying to the Divine Flesh. His voice twined 'round my brain, softer than kidskin.

(Divine Flesh, please help me.)

She crooned something back.

(I can't live in a world where this shit gets to happen and nothing good ever happens, I can't. I fucking can't, so if You ever loved me at all, help me. Fuck, that sounds bad.)

(I know this sounds bad but—)

(I tried to love Emily.)

She said it was okay. How could you expect to contain love to just one person or one god? He would always love Her, and that was enough, silly. She wasn't possessive.

(But I couldn't.)

(Emily wanted to make it work but I couldn't love her no matter how hard I tried.)

(Because I love You and—)

(Fuck.)

(Now Emily's dead. Javier's dead. Here I am.)

(Please help me.)

(Amen.)

Daryl's eyes were bloodshot when I walked into his hospital room.

"We have to get you out of this town," I said.

"You heard?"

"I always hear your prayers."

"I'm sorry. For what I said earlier," he said hoarsely.

"It's okay—"

"No. It wasn't. It wasn't your fault they died. I don't know—I don't what's happening to me, but I feel off. Angry. Impulsive."

"You're angry for a good reason. Okay. Let's do this. I'll get you whatever the hell you want or need, no questions asked. Blank check. You want firepower that'll liquefy an elephant? Grenades? I can give these assholes some drugs that'll melt 'em from the inside out and make 'em scream the entire fucking time they're melting. I'd've helped you no matter what," I said.

He scowled. "But?"

"I can't do it right now. We need to get you outta town, make a plan, and then—"

"Why not now?"

"Shipment. Other reasons."

He snorted. "You always got a shipment."

"Daryl. I know you want me to let the Divine Flesh out so you and Her can go hunting for the people who sabotaged your truck, but that cannot happen. I don't care what fucked-up, quasi-relationship you two have, it ain't gonna happen. You've never seen what She does to people."

"I have—"

"You've seen Her make human hearts out of ground beef and resculpt some rats. Not what She actually does."

"If you treated the Divine Flesh like a human being, She'd act like one. She's full of love, Jennifer. She's beautiful."

YES, JENNIFER! I AM BEAUTIFUL!

I gripped the bed rail. A splitting headache arced through my forehead.

"C'mon out, baby," Daryl said, looking at Her.

DARYL!

"Stop it," I said.

Something warm trickled from my right ear. Blood. She was coming out, taking control.

Sometimes all I wanted to do was reach up to my shoulders, claw into the flesh, and *tear* down until everything slipped off, all the skin and fat and flesh, let it fall off me like some shitty thrift-store coat, slither out, and be free. No more Divine Flesh. No more drug-fried body. Just clean spirit.

I stroked the dash-shaped scars along my arms. Purple-black track marks festered along the insides of my elbows.

Not to mention my thighs.

I couldn't think about what I looked like, really, and the body wasn't mine half the time. I called it *the* body, not *my* body. Why lie to myself? The Divine Flesh manipulated it when She was in control.

A little mirror hung over a sink in the corner of the yellow hospital room. I needed some water, but if I got any from the sink, I'd catch a peek at myself in the mirror. I couldn't handle that right now.

"Tell me about Emily and Javier," I said.

Daryl told the short version. Emily was born and raised here in Rosetown. Her daddy was white and her momma was Black, and Rosetown never let Emily forget it. Daryl and Emily bonded. They started having sex. Emily loved Daryl. Daryl never talked about his piece-of-shit ex-wife Jennifer, and Emily liked that fine. Presumably, Daryl hadn't told Emily that he was fucking a cosmic goddess on the side. Javier was Emily's childhood friend. Javier and Emily had the tight kind of decade-old friendship that only happens when two misfit kids stumble across each other in elementary school.

The kind of friendship that Daryl and I had. Or used to.

As Daryl spoke, I could intuit the dynamic.

Before Daryl Plummer had moved here, there'd been two oddballs. Emily and Javier. The biracial girl and the gay Mexican kid. But there were only two. Emily and Javie. To Rosetown, Idaho, two oddballs was a tolerable number. Two lonely little misfits, tucked out of sight, under the radar. Maybe someone would've tried something down the line, maybe not. But two was the limit, and those two were born natives of Rosetown, Idaho, at that.

Then Daryl came and I came, and Daryl rented a cabin, and then all of a sudden, the misfits gathered right behind him. An infestation. *Stamp it out.*

"So they cut your brake line?" I asked.

Daryl nodded, expressionless. "We went to Silver Lake on Saturday nights, after Javier got off work. Everyone would pile into my truck, we'd pack a cooler, and we'd drive. There's a steep hill on the route. We took the same roads every time, not thinking..." His jaw worked. "Because I got fucking complacent."

"Daryl."

"You and I learned pretty good, going through the foster care system, didn't we? It taught us well. Kept us hardened. You remembered those lessons. I forgot," he said.

"You went to trade school, became an electrician, and didn't become a self-destructive, alcoholic drug mule. What a terrible path to choose."

"Maybe they wouldn't be dead."

I looked him square in the eye.

"They're dead now," I said, "and you can't avenge them if you can't keep your head in the game. I'd know."

"…All right. So. They cut it most of the way, knowing that it'd snap after we took that downhill curve. There was a semi waiting at the base, where the freeway kicks up. Couldn't stop. Rammed into it."

I sat on his hospital bed by him, close enough to smell him. Old Spice, sweat, woodsmoke. I put an arm around his shoulder—

Daryl, Daryl, let Me touch him, the Divine Flesh said.

He relaxed into me, warmth baking off him.

Daryl whispered, "Javier flew through the windshield. His body broke apart when it hit the road, like a doll or a mannequin. I should've made him wear his seatbelt. He was in the backseat."

People ramble, when they describe death, but they gotta. It's how they cope.

"Emily?"

"…She was sitting up front with me, and her head just slammed into the dash and front when it crumpled up and it burst, it broke so fast, one second she was there and then there's this…this shattered body with red pulp on top of its shoulders instead of a head or face. I screamed."

I said the next part very gently: "What killed you?"

"I didn't die."

"Your clothes, Daryl. They were soaked in blood and shredded. I noticed earlier."

"I don't know what happened."

"You don't have a scratch on you. Was it the Divine Flesh? Did She help you?"

"I don't know."

I asked, "What'd they do before this?"

There would've been other incidents before they cut Daryl's brake line. Warnings. They didn't start with cutting brake lines and burning crosses. They built up to it.

"Someone killed my two cats. Slit their throats, left 'em on my doorstep with a note," Daryl said.

"Jesus Christ."

"Note said that huntin' season was coming. Said it was a friendly reminder. Had some coupons for U-Haul stapled to it."

"You go to the cops?"

"Any other place, I might've. Emily said it'd be a waste of time at best."

I embraced him. He startled for a half-second, then hugged back.

"Stay here tonight," I said. "I'll watch over your cabin, make sure nobody burns it down or nothin'. Let's figure out stuff in the morning. If someone tries something, pray to the Divine Flesh. We'll come in, guns a-blazing."

He gave me his house key.

I went to sit vigil for the dead.

4

There!

Susan hissed. Startled.

She'd gotten lucky. She'd been parked outside of the free psych hospital for a few hours, watching staff members enter and exit and working her filaments through walls. She closed her eyes, trailed out, out, and each human life gave a faint *ping* as she detected it. A bell's tone.

Ah. Her own kind felt different. Akin to tapping a guitar string.

There!

She'd just found the bastard who'd stolen her last clutch of eggs.

There you are. I bet they love you. I bet you're the best worker they have. I bet they talk about how good you are with nonverbal patients.

Her skinsuit's legs ached to sprint in and grab them, but she gritted her teeth instead. Best to wait. It wouldn't do to fight here. Too much attention. Too many humans to sedate and soothe and cosset.

July twilight painted everything bruise-purple: the white cinder block hospital and its red roof, the grass around it, the oak tree and its untrimmed saplings. In the parking lot, streetlights flickered to life, lurid purple instead of white from the old LED substrate decaying. Decayed thing. Old thing. She could've laughed. Over in the industrial district, delivery vans thrummed around an Amazon warehouse, their engines droning like bees. Besides that, all lay quiet. Humans entered and left the psychiatric hospital, *pinging*. Susan waited for the thief to emerge.

She had time. She tasted the emotions quivering up and down her filaments:

Lots of *(resentment)*, bitter as a mouthful of pennies.

Two schizophrenics having *(happy) (pretty)* visions, sweet tasting but chemical: bad candy, soft circus peanuts, too squishy, too labile—

(do you want)

(do you wanna fuck)

And, of course, there was the drama between the two med nurses, an old man and his young girl, lust and dancing anxiety, the spark of *(do you wanna) (touch me)*.

Exhaustion, dull and sullen, coiling around the people like fog.

She sighed. Ah, young love.

Tonight, her bones ached. Which was rather absurd. She didn't actually have bones. She possessed a human-shaped shell of skin and flesh and organs, a shell that her filament-body—her true body—could maneuver. A skinsuit, they called it. Skinsuits looked human. Susan wasn't. She was a Mirror Person—a hovering, room-sized tangle of silver filaments piloting a skinsuit, feeding on human emotion and mimicking as needed.

Old. I feel old, not tired.

The night faded to blue around her, and Elvis crooned on the car radio: *I'm feeling so lonely baby. I feel so lonely, I could die...*

Susan mused. Would it have been easier, perhaps, to have simply had one of her many loyal employees track down the thief? Yes. Oh yes. Would it have been more efficient? Yes.

But to do nothing while the thief of her children ran amok? No. That would not do.

Susan watched and waited, and the scrubs-clad workers bustled in and out of the building like so many teal insects. She contemplated telling them the truth: *That employee you like so much? They aren't human. They're a parasite from another dimension working alongside you. Think of them as a bug. An insect-like creature that wants to reproduce and nurture its young. Oh, don't worry. It doesn't want you. It's looking for something a little more... disposable. Something warm. Something nutritious.*

For the babies.

For the precious, darling larvae.

Two hours later, a needle-thin male in green scrubs exited the facility. Susan trailed out—

There.

There was that peculiar sensation again. He was a Mirror Person. She groped inside his mind and plucked out his name. Clay. His name was Clay.

Clay crept across the parking lot and got into a battered Toyota. She followed him to his home.

The neighborhood was a waste skimming the edge of the Mojave. Bare lots imprisoned narrow two-bedroom bungalows and sand, bleached in moonlight, blighted as a syphilitic's thighs, clotted with brush and cacti. A coyote bayed. Crickets shrilled. Beyond the row of houses lay desert. Buttes simmered in the ninety-degree weather. Saguaros groped for the sky.

An endless spill of stars overhead—cosmos, too close to home.

She parked a few houses back.

Watched.

Clay retrieved reusable shopping bags from the backseat of his car. The bags were cotton-candy pink and baby blue, and watercolor art of lilies decorated them. Why did he need bags? Was he eating human food instead of meat? What on Earth—literally—was this idiot buying in his spare time?

Where are my babies, and what have you done with them?

Susan's eyelid twitched.

Clay slipped, fell. Items spilled from a bag. A fleece blanket. A baby mobile. One cloth thing, patterned with polka dots. *A scarf?* Something neon green and plastic clattered to the asphalt, smaller than his palm.

A toy?

Baby toys.

He scooped up the baby toys, walked to the front door, unlocked it, and headed inside, grinning all the while. A pleased grin. His skinsuit had dimples and an overbite.

Susan counted to twenty, holstered her gun, and exited her van. She ghosted across the sand.

He'd left the front door unlocked.

She slithered inside.

A hand gripped the back of her neck. Another clamped over her mouth, fever-warm, hard enough to make her teeth ache. It slammed her against the wall. Pain radiated down her back. She went limp for a second; he relaxed.

Now!

Susan thrashed. Clay tightened his grip and leaned in.

Something glass-smooth slicked over Susan's mouth, not a tongue, and a wave of *feel-good* washed over her like Valium, like vodka and raw brisket—

(food warmth I want I want it)

A larva.

He held it in his skinsuit's mouth like a tongue. He retracted the larva, and the foreign thoughts *(food) (warm)* stopped.

He exhaled against her ear, voice feathery. "I know who you are," he whispered. "How could you?"

"You stole my last clutch of eggs."

"I needed to get your attention. I guess you don't listen to prayers anymore," he said.

"You're working at a mental health clinic and preying on the weakest members of this species. Don't lecture me about morality," Susan said.

"I only ask the worst. The one's that'd kill themselves no matter what. I tell 'em how it is. They wanna die, I'll let 'em die. But why not create new life out of it?"

Terrible, from a larval perspective, you weak upstart. Larvae are what they eat. You want your babies to feed and absorb the deranged dregs of humanity?

Susan gritted her teeth. She slapped unseen filaments against him, but it did nothing. He dragged Susan down a terracotta-painted hallway lined with pictures. His grip strangled. She fought for each breath, noting dimly that, *Yes, he's taking me to a nursery, I can smell the larvae.* He smoothly took her gun from her hip holster.

He said, "You know how many attempts this one had? Five. Four of 'em overdoses."

"Where are my babies? Did you put them into some mentally ill human? Did you?"

"What kind of host would I be if I didn't show you?"

"Stop this."

"No," he said, voice hard. "You left all the rest of us to die on this godforsaken world, you made us—"

"You hatched after the exodus, you piddly little thing."

Clay laughed. "You call yourself the God-Killer? I'll tell everyone else who you really are. I don't care how much influence you have."

He opened the door at the end of the hallway. Flicked on the light.

Cream-colored paint lacquered the nursery walls. Floor lamps burned, Edison bulbs glowing within the glass shades like candlelight. Gold paper stars hung from the ceiling. Static played from a radio on the floor. Static played in Susan's brain. The shopping bags from earlier were piled by the door. A wicker rocking chair, covered in a butter-yellow afghan. The sealed cement floor shone, glossy as mucous. A floor drain, with dried blood griming its rim.

The vessel lay dying in a crib.

Just a normal crib. White, wooden. The kind you could purchase at any Target. The vessel—a female, middle-aged, pudgy enough to feed generations of larvae—lay curled into a fetal position, half-covered in a blanket, naked. Her chest twitched. Fell. Her breathing bubbled.

Clay released Susan. He picked something out of a bag and approached the crib, humming. It was a baby's fidget toy. Green plastic beads on a tassel. He attached the toy to a crib bar.

He smiled and caressed the vessel's acne-scarred face.

"You're giving them joy," he said softly. "They're happy. You're a good home for them. They'll always remember you. I still remember how my vessel tasted when I was their age. Are her memories sweet, my little ones?"

smclok-smchlack-llkk.

A soft wet chewing noise.

I can hear them eating her from the inside out.

Larvae.

But not Susan's.

She dry-heaved.

He drew the blanket back and beckoned her over. The vessel wasn't wearing a bra, but fine, because there weren't any nipples or even skin, just wet exposed flesh, so the yellow sac-like things ringing the center had to be milk ducts or fat, and something'd eaten the skin off the vessel's breasts, not cut it off, because the edges were ragged.

Chewed off.

You'd adore those larvae if they were yours, or if you were in heat.

Below the breasts, the vessel's torso was an eaten-out hollow. Lungs struggled behind ribs. Lurid yellow fat greased the edges of the cavity. Torn scraps of peritoneum writhed with each breath. Stomach, liver, and small intestine had long gone. Streaks of dried shit painted the inside hollow.

Wet chewing sounds.

Lungs, struggling.

Silvery larvae clustered over what remained of the large intestine. Clay stroked one. It nestled into his touch, and he kept humming. Lulling them to sleep.

Mirror People larvae were bits of reflective goo. Sentient globs of quicksilver.

They shone like treasures.

"What's your name?" Susan asked.

"Shouldn't you know?"

"I do, but I'd prefer you to tell me," she said.

Clay sauntered right up to her and grabbed her chin. Leaned in close, something metallic oozing from between his lips—a larva—

The larva grazed her cheek.

(warm)

(hungry I want I want)

He murmured, "I stole your babies and gave 'em to the Flesh Failure to take south of the border. Then they'll be gone for good. How does it feel to be a failure to your children again? "

Flies tickled her arms.

"I could cut you apart. I could entomb you in concrete. But I don't wanna. I wanna give you a gift instead. The gift of our species' collective pain," he said.

"It's not my fault."

"You are what you are, or some bullshit like that?" he asked.

"Yes."

"Bullshit."

"How did you find out about me? What gave it away?" Susan said.

"Like I'd tell you. So do something, huh? Tell me you're sorry. Tell me you're—"

"I'll give you ten more seconds to apologize and tell me where my babies went. Ten more seconds. After that, if you still want to be rebellious…I'll make sure you understand that your actions have consequences."

He snorted. "Like your actions did? When you created us, dragged us to another world, and left us to rot so you could do whatever the fuck you wanted?"

If they aren't mine, why should I care? Why should I care about any of you?

Susan said, "Do you wish to apologize?"

"Fuck you, *God*," Clay spat.

"Your actions have consequences, Clay," she said.

For a microsecond, fear wrinkled his face.

Oh yes.

I am real, I am your God, and I am very aware of YOU, Clay.

Then he collapsed.

Susan simply thought, and it was done. Clay was rolled onto his back like a dead limp larva, paralyzed, unable to move. But able to see. Able to think. That was, by far, the most important part.

"Did you forget that I have control over you all still?" Susan said.

Clay's filaments batted against Susan's.

(please)

(please I'm sorry please forgive me not the babies)

"Your actions have consequences," she said.

Susan went out to her car. She retrieved a gas can. Got a book of matches.

She went back inside. Something caught her eye in the kitchen. A newborn-sized chunk of dried flesh rested on the dining room table. Grooves limned faces. Hieroglyphs. Beads of black liquid appeared on its surface.

The sweetest voice she'd ever heard oozed into her ears, murmuring:

(Taste and see.)

It came from the flesh thing. It was good. Yes. Yes. Night-dark liquid, oily on her filaments, honey-sweet in her mouth.

Wait, when did I touch that thing on the table?

Swallowing, suckling, tasting—

When and why did I lick it?

Susan jerked away from the dried-flesh thing. Her lips tingled.

(Do you love—)

(—the will of God—)

(I am what I am. I am the Divine Flesh), the voice whispered. *(Yud-hey-vav-hey, Susan.)*

"I don't have time for this," Susan said, but she'd already scooped the weird flesh-thing—*the Hermetic*—into her arms, cradling it.

It had to go somewhere. Somewhere special. It belonged to someone special—

(So very special.)

(You are SO VERY LOVED, please know that.)

Susan hurled it across the room.

Breathing hard, she ventured out the front door and into the night. In the trunk, a can of gasoline waited. She unlocked the truck, hands shaking, curled inside her skinsuit like a retreating octopus. The gas can gleamed in the starlight. She hefted it out and walked back up to the adobe house at the edge of the desert, up the steps and inside the stagnant house, with its ripe nursery smell.

You don't have to do this.

Actions had consequences. The time to be loving had long since gone. No deviance could be permitted. Clay had stolen her eggs. Clay knew who she was. Clay needed to die.

He's hurting. They're all hurting because you brought them here, where they don't belong.

She'd created the Mirror People. They were failed creations, gone defective and weak from generations of being trapped in this dimension. They would never stop pestering her to love them. How she hated them.

A still, small thought came: *They're your children.*

It was only fair that she should punish them, then.

Punish them? They want your love. That is why they do these things. They want to know why they suffer here, why they are not in the Eden you built for them.

"Well. It's not my fault. I only created them," Susan said, and proceeded to the nursery.

The vessel gurgled in the crib. Susan tilted her wrist. A stream of clear gasoline baptized the dying vessel, fumes sharp. Susan proceeded to hallow Clay's domicile in the stuff. The reek of gasoline and death swirled thick in the air. Almost physical. She could taste it at the back of her throat. Clay spasmed on the carpet.

Good.

Susan retrieved a filleting knife from a drawer in the kitchen. She slit the vessel's throat. She dumped more gasoline.

She lit a match and threw it.

By the time she drove away, the house's roof had caved in from the fire.

5

Daryl wasn't great at hiding his guns.

Could've been because I knew where he'd stashed them. A freshly oiled shotgun lay under his plaid loveseat, next to a box of shells. A Silver Star six-shooter—so chintzy that I'd've been surprised if it stayed together after firing a shot—was tucked away in his dresser, behind his neatly folded boxers. His socks and boxers were color coded, because of course they were.

There was something new on the bedside table.

A Bible.

Gray tab labels stuck out of the pages. Bible study tabs. A pack of dry-gel Bible highlighters lurked next to it, half-worn away from use, because of course Daryl Plummer would highlight each and every God-given sentence in his stupid Bible. Ugh. He was doing this Christian stuff now? After every fundie church we'd been dragged into as foster kids, now he was chugging the Jesus juice? God, Daryl. What was he *doing*?

Jesus loves you, this I know.

I snorted.

Daryl's cabin was built a century ago, and it'd been a one-room shack before someone added a bedroom. Everything was woodier than a porn star overdosing on Viagra. Warm, varnished pine composed the walls and ceiling. Air hung stale, unmoved by ventilation. It smelled like Daryl—piney, sweaty. A stub of a hallway led to a microscopic bedroom. His bed was made, with hospital corners. A deer-antler lamp rested on his nightstand, by his Bible.

A gun-cleaning kit rested on a pine bookshelf in the living room, next to *Wet Preservation of Specimens* and a few taxidermy pamphlets.

Chemical bottles and glass jars rowed the shelf below. Curved needles and specialized scoops filled a plastic storage bin. A steel cross hung above the front door.

Every surface in his cabin bore at least one glass jar of preserved flesh.

On the dining table, as a centerpiece: three vintage Coca-Cola bottles sealed with black rubber stoppers. Each bottle held a preserved grass snake—no thicker than a cigarette—that coiled 'round the sides and up the bottle's neck like demented emerald ribbon. The isopropyl alcohol remained almost perfectly clear.

I grabbed the gun cleaning kit and guns. Grabbed a few cotton rags from the kitchen and a red Pendleton wool blanket, because it'd get cold around midnight; I knew this area. Then I sat on the porch, well-illuminated by outdoor lights, and rested both guns atop a milk-crate table.

I threw rags over the crate and dismantled the shotgun. I had a good view of the gravel single road that led up to the cabin. Gravel was good. Gravel meant *noise*.

I called the distribution gal to let her know I'd be late.

Daryl's teardrop trailer gleamed in the light of a crescent moon. I'd already searched it. Hadn't needed to shim the lock—it'd been left unlocked, wide-open to any prowler. For Daryl's sake, I'd pocketed his Ziploc baggie of weed and both of his blown-glass bongs. Who was careless enough to stash weed behind a couch pillow in red-as-Christ's-blood Idaho? Thumbnail-sized pictures plastered the walls of the trailer—mostly nature shots, and a few pictures of him and another girl. Emily? Ink-dark hair fell to her shoulders. Her bony face reminded me of one of those gray-type aliens, you know, all dark eyes. She probably had parents doing one of the trades, to have decent teeth like that. Union dental insurance. Or she came from money.

I considered. My hands disassembled the shotgun. Gunpowder blackened my skin.

Two innocent people were dead. *Daryl might be next.*

I'd seen the last screwup on a Mirror Person larvae shipment—they'd dragged me and the other human employees out to Death Valley. Didn't say why.

A black van had been waiting for us.

When they'd escorted us over, Mirror People clad in gray suits threw two Guatemalan men out of the van, onto the sand. Neither struggled. Their faces remained blank and drawn. Susan—my boss, a superbreeder Mirror Person—loomed over them. Sand shifted around Susan's skinsuit. She kept shimmering in and out from stress, like a noon mirage.

Which one? Susan said.

Both men looked at each other. Thick sweet smell of saguaro fruit, of half-digested meat, sun roasting down. Sweat trickled down my face.

Which one?

"Susan's batch of eggs," someone whispered. "Leak in the bag."

"What?" I mouthed.

"Lost the entire batch."

I swallowed back a sudden rush of vomit.

Now a bag of Mirror-Person eggs appeared in one of the gray suit's hands, shiny as bullets. Guns ground into the back of the men's skulls. Fingers curled around triggers.

Again, *Which one?*

Both men studied Susan. Shook their heads. Closed their eyes.

The gray-suited gunmen held both men's noses. The men lasted a good two minutes before they opened their mouths to breathe, faces puce. In went the eggs.

Both began vomiting blood after thirty seconds.

Two gunshots split the air.

Crack.

Crack.

Brains splattered across the hard-baked desert. There was no wind. None of us got to move until the last of the larvae had been transferred from the empty, organless torsos of the men. Dried urine crusted my jeans. Someone had shit themselves. I could smell it.

The Mirror People removed a red velvet sack from the van. Susan groped a hand inside and drew out a slip of folded paper.

Susan droned, *Your actions have consequences. Please do not forget.*

Susan's form flickered from male to female as she/he read the name on the slip of paper.

Charlie Johnson.

Charlie was standing near the end of our line; he tried to bolt.

Crack.

A bullet hole materialized on his forehead, dribbling blood. He crumpled to the hardscrabble. The Mirror People gently opened his mouth. Brain matter drooled from the wound. His gaze went glassy.

One of the eggs pattered to his Gorillaz t-shirt as they forced them in. They plucked it up and added it to Charlie's slack mouth.

The larvae took five hours to consume Charlie. They were stressed.

Your actions have consequences, Susan repeated. *Those were my one of my last batches.*

The Divine Flesh had been bursting to break free. *Your actions have consequences?* the Divine Flesh seethed. *What a terrible thing to say! If you make them see why they're wrong, then they'll punish themselves because they love you so much. That's what you do. You smother everyone in LOVE. You're not very smart, Susan. You're just another silly schemer.*

Your actions have—

—Gravel crunched, jolting me back to reality. To Daryl's porch.

Someone was coming.

I checked the Silver. It was loaded. I spread the blanket over my lap, slipped the gun underneath, and scanned the darkness. Truck headlights burned like blind eyes, coming closer.

The truck stopped. Parked in the driveway.

Engine went silent.

Slam.

Someone stepped out. Gravel grated. Heavy footsteps, probably a man. Nobody else exited the truck. A bulky figure wobbled up to the porch.

A man. Middle-aged.

Drunk, not yet wasted. I could smell the cheap beer on him. He carried no firearms. Wore a white t-shirt, streaked with dust, and work jeans. He smoked a cigarette. A single wisp of smoke snaked up into the black sky.

He said, voice wavering, "Hello? I—Is Daryl here?"

Moths and gnats flurried around the cabin's outdoor lights.

"Daryl is safe," I said.

"I gotta—I gotta talk to someone."

Gray streaked through his dark hair and eyebrows.

"Oh?"

He stared at nothing.

"She's gone," he said.

His knee buckled. He stumbled to the porch, made a soft sound. Didn't get up.

"I have to go see the body—her body—I have to go see Emily tomorrow, at the morgue. That's what the coroner said."

"They won't show you her body. They'll show you pictures of identifying marks, like tattoos, and ask if those are hers. It's not like the movies," I said.

"Ah."

"I've seen a lot of bodies."

"She had a lil' tattoo of a butterfly, on her left arm. Alla those rainbow colors on it. God, the fit her grandmama pitched over it, when Emily had it done…She and I, we really got into it over that, y'know."

I nodded.

He rambled, still half-kneeling on the porch boards. "I don't get into fights with my own mother often, but goddamn, did we fight over that. She said I was raisin' a hellspawn. That Emily was goin' to be just like her mamma, y'know, in the clink. A jailbird. I didn't care about that, y'know, let people live how they wanna live. God'll figure it out."

"You're Emily's father."

A spark of life. His gaze flickered to me. "Daryl much of a drinker?"

"Sober as a judge," I said. "The troopers couldn't get him with the Breathalyzer. They would've if he'd had a drop in his system. You know that."

"I—yeah, I know. Wasn't him."

"Why don't you come on in? I can make some coffee," I said.

A nod.

"I told Emily we could move. I told her, hell, I can get another construction job anywhere, you're my kid, you ain't lazy, you ain't gonna get much of a job here in town. The skinheads we got here…We got some fuckin' skinheads in Rosetown, I ain't gonna lie. I didn't want my baby girl around here. She just turned twenty-one. Just…"

"You take any pills, anything besides the booze?" I asked.

"Naw."

He probably hadn't. Either he was a better liar than me, or he was deeply, deeply in shock. His clothes carried a faint whiff of menthol— *no, meth. He smokes meth. See the picked scabs on the backs of his hands?*

I ushered him inside, smudging gunpowder on his shirt. Sat him at the table. He stared at the bottled snakes. I grabbed both guns and the kit. Threw the heavy wool blanket over his shoulders. He shivered.

Give him comfort, Jennifer-baby. Let Me out.

Wood cords surrounded a wood stove in the corner. I threw one in and baptized it in Daryl's whiskey. Threw in a lit match. Flames *whoomped* up.

I started the percolator. "It's not your fault."

"Should've moved."

My hick accent crept in as I spoke. "Tell me about Emily. Daryl said she fished. What kind? She into anglin', or rod-and-pole?"

"Fly-fishing. Tied her own flies, used these"—he laughed softly—"used these goddamn bright colors, y'know, so she had a tackle fulla neon-pink and green and blue flies. Said the natural colors didn't work any better, so why the hell not?"

His eyes glistened. "That kid of mine, she never did anythin' she didn't wanna do. Used to take her to the movies on Saturdays, and if she didn't like the flick, she'd just get up and walk outta there after fifteen minutes. And she was only six years old, back then. Knee-high to a grasshopper. I tell her, 'I paid for the whole thing, you gotta watch it,' so here's what she does. She starts mowing lawns, doing odd jobs, and next Saturday rolls around, she pays for her own ticket. My kid. Stubborn as a fuckin' mule. Was."

Gravel. Sound of an approaching engine, a low diesel rumble.

"Let me check something," I said.

"T-this place k-killed her. It—"

"Hey. Calm down."

I went out onto the porch. A Ford rolled by, molasses-slow. Stopped. It idled for a minute, spewing exhaust.

C'mere, then. Do it.

It turned around and drove back into the darkness.

It'd taken multiple people to plan and execute the murders. Ten to one, that was the guy that'd actually cut the brake line.

I considered the guy:

He's never killed someone before—even if they aren't people, hell, they're faggots and junkies and degenerates—but he's thought about it, and now he's done it, so why leave the job undone? Why not go finish off the last one? His mind is gray. His mind is the dead static after Fox News goes down. There's a sick atavistic clenching in his guts, half-excitement, half-terror, and his mind's null. Void. There's a shotgun in the Ford. There's a bottle of Smirnoff and some rags and a lighter. *Do it. Get it done.*

But now there's some scraggly-ass junkie on the porch, and a junkie's a junkie, true, but the junkie's staring at him, so he deliberates. Decides to come back later. Daryl'll come back to his cabin sometime.

The thought makes his pulse throb in his chest, his guts. Atavistic rush.

Maybe he'll say something to the interloper before he kills him. Get the feelings out, make him listen, make him understand. Maybe he won't. He isn't a bad person. He's good. There's two dead kids and his mind's a blank slate. He'll shoot Daryl—shoot *it*, the trespasser, the interloper, the contamination—through its head, if he can, and then he'll drive away tasting blood, tasting static.

Why do things have to be that way? the Divine Flesh whispered. *Let Me out. Let Me out. Yud-hey-vav-hey, I am what I am.*

I left the crate outside, covered up with rags. Empty Coors cans littered the back corner of the porch. I stuck a few atop the crate.

I went back inside.

Emily's father slurred, "The fuck's wrong with your arms?"

He poured Jack Daniel's into a tall glass, halfway, then splashed in Pepsi. Sipped. He huddled under the blanket.

"I cut myself," I said.

The scars shone in the low light, like gilded tally marks.

"Oh shit," he said, sniffling. "Don't do that. You already look a lil' rough."

"I know."

I was too scrawny. Crackhead skinny. My breastbone and ribs stood out. Crooked, yellowed teeth jutted against each other in my mouth. Poor-person teeth. "I spent my childhood in the foster-care system" teeth. I stood about five foot eight and I was built like a spider. Had hazel eyes, always darting. Shit-brown hair came down to my shoulder blades, greasy and thin. I used to have a septum ring. Before it got ripped out in a bar fight.

I poured a mug of coffee. The percolator bubbled. Wood crackled in the stove. Flies lazed around the kitchen.

The Ford drove by again. I opened the shutters and left 'em.

The Divine Flesh said, *Jennifer-baby, do I need to start screaming? I want to be out. I can scream. I will scream and scream until your ears bleed. Tee-hee!*

She did. A long, insane screech. She didn't need to breathe.

Warmth rushed in my eardrums. Fluids. Emily's father was saying something I couldn't hear, his lips moved and he reached for me, motion clumsy. Wanting. Neon-bright flies, neon-bright laughter, all gone. Emily's father pulled out his phone. Pictures of him and Emily, Emily and Javier, pictures of the dead, and I smiled, and he cried. He sobbed with his whole body.

The Ford drove by again. *Tell me there's a point to any of this*, I prayed, but I didn't know to who.

I started drinking.

You said you were gonna stay sober, Jennifer.

The first tumbler of Jack Daniel's went down easy.

I can't do this shit sober.

Another tumbler of Jack Daniel's. Then a beer, smooth as iced tea on a July afternoon. He drank with me. I sat on the chair by him. He slurred something.

Do you? He was slurring. *Do you?*

"Blanket," he said, throwing it over me because I shivered. We were under the same blanket; heat came off him, festering under the wool.

Wool itched my skin.

The Divine Flesh kept screaming. But Her voice seemed muted, wavering in and out as the alcohol hit my bloodstream.

"Tell me it's a dream. You gotta t-tell me this is a d-dream." And now he had the Silver Star clutched in his hand, shaking, raising it to his temple. "Is this how I get out?"

Comfort him, the Divine Flesh said.

"C'mere," I said. "Sleep it off on the couch."

He let me take the gun away, bustle him over.

The Ford drove by again.

She flooded me.

"Do you want comfort?" the Divine Flesh said with my mouth.

She stroked his arm.

No, no You don't understand, I thought, *he thinks You mean something else.*

He crushed me to him, sobbing, soft chest quaking against me, guiding my wrists down, he brushed them against his jeans zipper, and he wasn't soft anymore, the bare head of his cock poked out from between zipper teeth, salmon-pink.

Wait, the Divine Flesh said.

I wrenched control back and started away.

"No," he slurred.

His arm snaked around my waist, pressed me harder. Smothered me against his chest. Smell of sweat, booze. Rough cotton. Stubble rasped against my cheek. Fumbling.

"Please," he slurred, "please."

"Oh Jesus we really don't have to," I said.

"Please." And now his cock pushed against me, nudged my hip. "C'mere."

The couch.

"We really don't have to," I kept saying.

The Divine Flesh screamed, *NO! NO! I didn't mean it that way, Jennifer-baby, let ME OUT I don't wanna have sex with him I LOVE DARYL I don't want this I don't please—*

I could fight. Let Her out, let Her insta-kill him. I could physically fight, too, but if I struggled, he'd remember it later. He'd remember that he screwed a twenty-two-year-old on the night of his daughter's death, that he screwed someone his daughter's age, and those moments cling to you when you're at rock bottom. If I didn't, he'd probably forget and this whole night would fade into a hellish memory.

"Please," and he rolled on top of me.

He wrenched my jeans down.

"C'mere. C'mere, c'mere," he said.

He'd remember it the next time he had a gun to his head, he'd think, *I fucked a twenty-two-year old junkie on the night Emily died*, and that'd make him finally pull the trigger, and who the hell was I to give him that reason, when I couldn't go a day without getting drunk or high, when I'd sewn up drugs in cadavers? Who the fuck was I?

I don't exist, I'm not here, my body isn't real. The body. Isn't real.

The ceiling. A whorl shaped like a bee, cobwebs between a beam, amber light. Wood stove. His weight, on me.

Inside me.

Pressure. Burning in my cunt.

He slipped in further, shuddering, squeezing my frail shoulders, muttering, *C'mere, c'mere*, and the Jack Daniel's finally kicked in.

"C'mere."

"I'm here," I heard myself say, mouth numb from booze.

In the morning, I'd untangle myself before he woke. Slip the blanket over him before he realized we'd had sex. I'd scramble eggs. I could see the canister of Morton salt, the McCormick pepper, the deli ham I'd slice into quarter-inch squares after I sliced another row into my arms, could hear bacon sizzle.

What happened? he'd say, half nervous.

I'd give him eggs, pat his shoulder. *You passed out drunk. I'm a friend of Daryl's, was here watchin' the house. Heard about Emily. Here's some food before you go.*

I'd pack him food in a foil container for after the morgue, because he'd throw up when he saw those pictures. He wouldn't believe me, but he'd take the food. Later, he'd be happy he did.

See? Scumbag Jennifer could do some good after all. Hallelujah.

The Divine Flesh sobbed. *STOP IT! MAKE HIM STOP! I hate you Jennifer please let Me out I'll be good I promise just make HIM STOP it hurts he hurts.*

A spider on the ceiling. Woodsmoke. Heat. Him thrusting inside me. It hurt.

The body. Isn't real. I am not burning.

In the morning it'd be fine. In the morning he'd leave. He'd forget me. If he thought about killing himself, he would not think, *I fucked a twenty-two-year-old junkie on the night of my daughter's death.*

I could do that much.

It happened.

I let it.

6

Nothing beats a hangover breakfast. Scrambled eggs, fried in bacon grease. Plates of oily mystery meat. Hotcakes, mashed and gooey with synthetic syrup slurry. The toast oiling your chin after every bite. Jam optional. The cheese always synthetic.

Pure American orosensation.

You can find it at your local Denny's!

"Better than that hospital breakfast bullshit, right, Daryl?" I said, with the canned cheer of a '50s housewife on Valium.

He sipped black coffee. "Everything tastes like Velcro."

"That's not the Grand Slam's fault. That's shock."

"What's going on?"

I kept smiling at Daryl. I kept ignoring the fact that I hurt down there. Bruises purpled between my thighs. There'd been blood, when I went to pee at 4 a.m. The Divine Flesh had refused to heal our body.

The body isn't mine. The body isn't real. I am not burning.

"Jennifer," Daryl said.

"What?"

"You aren't telling me something."

We sat in a corner booth at a Denny's on the outskirts of Rosetown. Sunrise reddened outside, covering the pines in a pall of bloody light. Bloodied the coarse hair on Daryl's knuckles and wrists. A barely touched Grand Slam cooled in front of him.

I sighed. "I have to deliver this shipment. I'm leaving after we eat. I'll come back in a week or two—"

"Why?"

I shot a glance outside. The Denny's parking lot was deader than the flattened raccoons by the dumpster. My burner phone said *Wednesday, July 15, 5:45 a.m.*

"I never stopped loving you. You know that?" I said.

"Till death do us part didn't mean shit when I said you couldn't traffic drugs in my house no more," he snapped.

"I'm sorry."

"Jennifer, do you have *any idea* how fucked up that life is? You sewed a cadaver full of drugs in our bathtub. I have nightmares about it."

"Part of that was the Divine Flesh's idea."

"It's always someone's else's fault. You were drunk. You were high. It was Her. You've had the same goddamn excuses since we were fourteen years old."

"You kicked me out," I said. "Neither of us thought…"

Neither of us thought that trying to be a Good Person might actually involve sacrifice and fighting. Whoops!

"Yeah," he said, staring into his coffee.

"Yeah," I said.

I started working on my Grand Slam, pancakes first. Between bites, I explained what had happened the last time a shipment of Mirror People babies went sideways.

Daryl nodded. "Oh."

"So can you please not assume that I'm a piece of shit? Pretty please. I'm asking you to trust me."

"Can you trust me, with the Divine Flesh? I want—I want to see Her. I love Her."

DARYL.

I massaged my temples. I checked the truck outside. Still good.

"Here's my plan. You can't stay in town, because someone's going to try something. Some asshole kept driving past your cabin last night. I can get you some money for a motel in Coeur d'Alene, and then I'll come by in a week. We'll plan. We'll get revenge for Emily and Javier," I said.

I rubbed the stickiness from my sleep-deprived eyes, swigged more coffee, and slumped. Heartbeats fluttered. Felt shivery.

Then the Divine Flesh possessed me, slamming into our body like a heat wave, and, using our mouth, said, "Aren't you sleepy, Jennifer-baby?"

The body is not mine, it is not real, it is not burning, I am fine. Stay awake. You're fine. Sit up…

"Aren't you sleepy, babygirl?" the Divine Flesh crooned.

I snapped awake.

Stay awake. If you sleep, the Divine Flesh will creep out and talk to Daryl. Don't let Her out. Please, Daryl.

She'd make abominations. Kill people…

Jennifer, Jennifer, do you remember?

Coziness. Soft, melodic singing.

Do you remember the pink blanket they gave us in the hospital crib, so warm, the nurse tasted so good, she smiled at us, do you remember?

Warmth. Delicious relaxation. The smell of maple syrup and bacon and coffee.

This wouldn't be happening if you would've gotten sleep, babygirl. If you didn't let our body get used.

The Divine Flesh dragged me into sleep, and my thoughts looped down, down, into the blackness, muttering over and over: *Can you redeem? The sins of the flesh? Can you?*

I smiled at Daryl, My bestest, most favorite smile, the one with all 108 teeth, the one he loved most. My mouth only split open a little bit.

"Jennifer's not here anymore," I said.

His pupils dilated. "It's You."

I exist inside a splintered sad cage called Jennifer Plummer.

Yud-hey-vav-hey.

I am what I am. I remembered saying that from the mountaintop. I created these cute little beetles for everyone to eat—the beetles' eggs, anyways, I made those rain from the sky, they called it manna. I gave them things. They worshiped Me. They didn't love Me.

Only one person really loved Me.

I remembered, and then I didn't, then it's *can't get there from here!*

Something was broken. I was broken. I shouldn't have been, because I was the Divine Flesh, but not…not anymore. I was so beautiful, I could do other things, I could create—

can't get there from here!

There was a glitch.

Inside Me.

I screamed. I screamed a lot. It didn't do anything. Jennifer-baby thought it was to spite her, and sometimes it *was*, but mostly, it wasn't. Spite. What a silly thing. *Bathe it in love. Baptize it in neurotransmitters and wash those icky chemical feelings away.*

Jennifer was scared of missing the Mirror Person baby shipment, but that was just silly. There wasn't a shipment at all. I kept telling Jennifer, *There's a trick. Someone's playing a trick on you*, but Jennifer wouldn't listen…

I'd slipped out after the distribution girl made love to Jennifer, when Jennifer was nice and drowsy. Distribution girl muttered details about a baby shipment. She was lying. What a silly thing to do. Her fingers shook as she did it, a faint tremor.

I touched her cheek and tasted her thoughts.

She'd thought, *These fucking drug mules know what they're smuggling in*, and images of a disemboweled nineteen-year-old girl exploded behind the distribution lady's eyes; the body had been left to rot in an elementary school playground, flies blanketing intestines, rhinestones falling off the girl's jeans, white Beats headphones around her neck, a single blood splatter drying on them…Her mouth bulging open, stuffed full of Spine. A warning for an unruly drug mule—both the mule's kids went to this particular school. Just this week's latest installment of *Interdimensional Drug Wars*.

Jennifer had stuffed Me back down before I could say anything, opened our thighs, and slurred, *C'mere. C'mere, you want me to do you?*

Distribution lady never ever let anyone touch her, but Jennifer didn't know that.

She said, *Nah, I'm fine. You want me to finger-fuck you as I'm licking?* Jennifer giggled drunkenly. *Your tongue's forked.*

You like it, Flesh Failure?

They kept having sex, which was boring. The distribution lady lied some more. Her heart rate went up. Cortisol tainted her sweat, made her skin tangy. She'd tasted like a silly schemer. A lying, silly schemer…She was pretending to work for another Mirror Person, a competitor of Susan… ah, Clay…but she was secretly plotting to take down the whole enterprise. Distribution lady was a vigilante exterminator, determined to end the predation of Mirror People against humanity. She had a good heart.

I startled back to the present.

Daryl was staring out the window. Bodies drove by on the freeway, trapped in their sad metal cars. I shot out tendrils, fine enough to slip between molecules, and tasted. So many people! So many worries. So much inert flesh.

"I can create anything you want," I said, "if I have the flesh for it. It's a commandment. I can't create from nothing."

can't get there from here!

But I used to. Before the—

can't get there from here!

I slithered over to Daryl, loosening the skeletal structure of "My" body. I draped over him.

"Sweetheart, there are people eating. We can't have sex in public, remember?"

"I know what you want." I kissed his cheek. "You want Me to be human. Like you. You want Me to have a body of My own."

His pulse increased. His blink rate slowed.

"And?" Daryl said.

"I can do anything if I'm free, silly," I said.

"But then Jennifer comes back, and everything You create turns to ash," he said.

My children. My darling, sweet children turn to ash and I can't help them.

"But Daryl. I can still have a little bit of fun in the meantime. We can find the killers! All you have to do is shoot Jennifer. She packed your other two guns in one of the crates. She didn't want you to know, but she thought we'd need the firepower. So…go shoot her, silly! Let Me out," I said.

I oozed blood. It seeped into the vinyl booth, leaving red dots. Daryl didn't taste right. Something *pulse-pulsed* over his body. Not his heart. An energy. Like lightning gestating in clouds. It tingled.

"Oh, I don't like that. You don't taste right," I murmured.

I yanked the stupid skin off My chest and grew a few more hearts. Beautiful. There. Now I felt a little-bitty-bit better.

The Denny's people looked at Me and screamed. How terrible! Why were they all screaming and crying? Why were the poor darlings so stressed out? Everyone kept pointing at us. Why was that elderly lady sobbing in the corner? Why was the blonde hostess trying to dial 911?

"We are *not* coming here for our next date," I said, scowling.

"I died. In that car accident. Did You save me?" Daryl asked.

What.

"What?"

As I said it, tendrils shot out of Me, electron-thin. I thought about the accident scene, those broken bodies, and then I was there, tasting and feeling. Old blood on asphalt, salt and tar. Dried brain matter. Bone fragments. Some of Me felt for the Ford, in a tow-yard. Dried blood— *Daryl's*—covered every square inch of the driver's side.

Too much blood.

Exactly 0.8999 gallons of blood had left Daryl's body.

Too much for him to survive.

He DIED and You weren't there, he'll die again and LEAVE YOU unless You recreate him, give him a better body, make him durable.

I could've, but I couldn't, because Jennifer would ruin whatever I created. She couldn't meet My beautiful children. I couldn't make Daryl into something new. I ached to do that, the way he ached for Me to be human.

Daryl died.

Icy electricity crawled through Me.

Was this fear? Was this what fear felt like?

"Hey, D. F., You're getting blood everywhere."

"You died!"

I had to breathe faster for some reason, had to. Lungs quivered. Something tightened around My throat.

I fell apart.

Literally. My joints snapped. Skin split. My torso broke open, spilling gleaming organs. I had to breathe. Needed to breathe. More oxygen. My lungs bloomed open. Had to expose more alveoli to air, yes, *had to breathe*. I made My lungs unfurl and flatten like paper, I spread them thin. Ligaments and tendons unfurled like Silly String, flowing over the table. Some of Me fell onto Daryl's lap.

I shifted My sternum to the side a little, just to be cute. To show off.

My seven hearts.

They beat for Daryl. I raised them above the rest of Me.

"Oh," he said. "You didn't save me, I take it?"

He looped My tendons and ligaments 'round his finger, and kissed them.

"Is this what being stressed out feels like?" I asked.

"We'll figure it out."

His body relaxed. I slithered over him, around him, wrapping him in Myself. He tilted his head towards My hearts. I presented them to him. He brushed his lips over each surface, a chaste kiss. His beard tickled. Visceral fluid and blood smeared his mouth.

The Denny's people just kept on screaming. *Poor things. Are their throats sore?*

Daryl whispered, "You're beautiful. No matter form You take. I love You."

"I love you, too."

Now shoot nasty old Jennifer so we can destroy the bigots who killed your friends.

"We don't need to waste two more days driving. Shoot Jennifer. Let Me help you find the killers."

He stiffened. "I can't shoot Jennifer."

"She won't feel a thing."

"She warned me not to let You out—"

"Do you really believe what she thinks? That I'm a monster? *An abomination?*" I said. "She's just too blind to see. Flesh is love. My love is in everything that moves, breathes, and lives, because it's part of Me—"

can't get there from here!

I cringed.

"Baby?"

It stung My mind. Blood trickled out of My two eyes. I wanted to grow better ones. There were millions of colors right here, all around us, and I wanted to see them and I couldn't, I couldn't make them the way I used to—

can't get there from here!

I rammed tendrils into Daryl's ears and plugged them just before I *shrieked.*

The glass windows vibrated.

Crack!

Every window shattered. The overhead light fixture exploded into shards. Candy-red glass glittered in our pancakes. I shielded Daryl's face.

I stopped screaming and removed the tendrils from his ears.

"H-help Me, please. Daryl. It h-hurts." I sobbed, making both of us shake. "Please."

His eyes shone with tears. His gaze jittered to the crowd around us, from person to person, and he pulled away from Me for a split second.

"We're terrifying everyone…" he said.

He froze. Exhaled.

Then he nestled back into Me.

"You know what? Fuck it. They all think I'm a monster anyway. This bigoted fucking town…it killed my friends. I'm done playing normal. I love you, baby," he said. He rattled out a breath. "My body. I felt everything…My skull was pulverized. There was a piece…of glass that went into my eye right before I….I felt it ram into my brain. Emily tried to say something right before…it happened. I *knew*, a few seconds before we hit that semi. Then I woke up. And Emily didn't have a head or a face or—"

His chest hitched.

"Daryl. Daryl," I murmured, tucking around him.

I wanted to hold his pain, I wanted to make it go away, but all I could do was hold him, and pretty soon we were both crying. We both unraveled. Emotionally.

Daryl cried. He half-prayed as he did.

(I'm sorry.)

(Make them live, they shouldn't be dead.)

(It doesn't even seem real, am I bad for that? Why am I numb?)

I held him. He held Me. Summer heat lazed in. Dawn mellowed to gold. We breathed, enmeshed in each other. One flesh.

"They're dead and I'm not," he rasped. "How's that fair?"

"It's not."

"Do You know anything that could do that? Bring me back from the dead, without any injuries?"

"No…I used to know things, Daryl, but I don't. Not anymore."

I kissed him, groping a wad of tendrils into his mouth. Spit and endothelial flesh, silky to behold. Treasuring where soft palate met hard, My favorite spot to stroke, stroke, unless we were having sex, then there were better places to stroke, atavistic nerves to fire. Fluttering in, out, tickling. Daryl leaned in, tongue working. His tongue slicked over My tendrils, teasing along each one, *so good so pleasant*, and I made a pleased sound, I heard My throat making it. Pleasure. His skin, unadorned with extra eyes or blessings, brushed against Mine. Blood rushed down, warm and oh-so-good. Wetness formed between My thighs, ready. Wanting him—

Another little happy sound came out of Me.

So very human. You make Me feel that way.

Reluctantly, I broke our kiss. "You don't taste right. Something's on you."

I ran tendrils over him again.

Energy.

"I-I don't feel right. I feel like ripping apart those fuckers with my bare hands. I won't, because there are worse things than death. But. I wanna," he said, licking his lips.

Tasting Me.

"Let Me out, and we'll rip them apart together. I can bring their bodies back to life, and we can do it again. As many times as you want. I love you. I'd never judge you," I said.

"Bring someone back to life?"

"Of course, silly."

His breathing got quick. "Can You bring Emily and Javier back to life?"

I sighed. "I *can*, but they'll crumble apart when Jennifer takes over."

"Oh."

I said, "Aren't you tired?"

He stared at Me for a long minute. "Yeah."

"Let Me tell you what to do. There's a gun hidden in a crate in the truck that Jennifer forgot about…" I said.

We planned.

Of course we planned.

All we had to do was kill Jennifer-baby. I'd instantly take over. In a few days, she'd stuff Me back into the cage, but until then…

Me.

I am the DIVINE FLESH.

But a part of Me argued, *But won't Daryl die, someday? Sometime? Someday, he'll die and You'll never ever see him again. You're the Divine Flesh, but everything You create crumbles. You're powerless. Broken.*

NO.

Yes.

Daryl will die. You will not. As long as You're stuck with Jennifer-baby, You'll never be able to fix that. If You heal him, make him Yours, he'll turn to ash when Jennifer takes over. Just like the others. A mile-high pile of ash, the bodies of Your dead children.

I am the Divine Flesh.

And? What does that mean when You're standing waist-deep in those ashes, screaming and screaming—

can't get there from here!

Police sirens screamed. Getting closer. Wind whipped through the shattered windows of Denny's. I lifted my head off the table.

Shit.

"What'd She do?" I asked.

Out of the corner of my eye, I glanced at the angle of the sun. Not too different. She hadn't taken over for long, maybe thirty minutes.

Daryl swallowed. "I'm going with you on that shipment delivery. We'll deliver the eggs together, then come back to Rosetown."

"Well, asshole, someone already called the cops because you let your girlfriend out, so good luck with that."

"You'll get us out of it. We'll deliver the shipment."

"Abso-fucking-lutely not," I said. "I'd leave you in jail before I dragged you into my world again. You're a vanilla human. You'll die. Or worse."

Slowly, Daryl raised the hand he'd been hiding under the table.

A revolver glittered. The Silver Star.

He aimed it at my throat.

"I wasn't asking, Jennifer."

7

Well.

There was no rush of icy-hot adrenaline, no chills running up my spine. Daryl's aim remained steady, arm extended.

Where did you hide the Silver Star, oh cunning husband of mine?

"So," I said.

"I mean it."

"I can tell. You're doing a shitty job at this. You could've held the gun under the table and then our waitress wouldn't be hyperventilating in the kitchen, telling 911 that there's a gun involved in this now. So," I said.

A vein bulged on his neck. He didn't lower the revolver. "So?"

"You think you can traffic interdimensional larvae?"

C'mon, Divine Flesh, work with me, I thought, and She relented, let me borrow some of Her power. Creation. Flesh. Heat built, cascading up my esophagus. Things tasted, tissue slicking along tissue, flesh building, exploring, growing. A wad of tissue welled up.

Daryl said, "I—"

I opened my mouth.

Tendrils exploded out, slicked in mucus.

A thick one rammed inside the gun barrel, clogging it like bubble-gum. It branched, spreading feelers over the revolver. Taste of metal. Sulfur. They gleamed raw pink. Tendrils slithered around Daryl's throat, a lover's caress—

I can taste him, babygirl.

—Liquid-like, more streamed over his hands. Bound the fingers. Spread like slime mold, roots and feelers. Taste of vinyl. The booth. A mesh of fleshy tendrils bound Daryl to the booth and table.

I clenched.

Crunch.

The revolver broke apart like a dollar-store toy. Flesh engulfed the metal fragments.

I controlled.

Six perfectly intact bullets fell.

Clink.

A bullet landed in Daryl's pancakes. The rest clinked to the table.

The Divine Flesh giggled. *Tee-hee! You look so silly, Daryl. Can I grow us another mouth so I can tell him how silly he looks? Just a little-bitty one on your right cheek?*

I retracted.

Tendrils retreated, groping at his skin in little farewell kisses. Flesh slithered back into my mouth, then down my throat. The Divine Flesh reabsorbed it. Within five seconds, all that was left of them were slime trails on the table and booth.

"So," I said.

Daryl sat there, blinking.

"They call me the Flesh Failure for a reason, Daryl."

"Oh."

I leaned close. "You know that a gun won't kill me. Won't even really harm me. All it does is let the Divine Flesh out. So. It doesn't mean the same thing, coming from you. That's why you're the exception to my rule. That, and I love you."

"Exception?"

I bared my teeth. Lowered my voice. "If anyone else had just pulled on a gun on me, they'd be *fucking dead*," I growled. "Do you understand?"

He nodded.

A car door slammed outside. All two of Rosetown's police vehicles were parked in front of Denny's. Yesterday's blond shitkicker exited one, bullhorn in hand.

"Jesus, Daryl," I said. "She blew all the windows out. We can't make that disappear or blame it on mass hysteria."

I scanned the Denny's. An elderly white couple cowered against the far wall. A hostess with hair like Botticelli's *Birth of Venus* stared at us, blood dribbling from each ear, glassy-eyed. A Vietnamese dude stood stock-still, hand frozen around a full coffeepot. He looked like he'd wanted to hurl it at us to get a split-second advantage, but the coffee was lukewarm now. Daryl's hands slipped under our table again. Most of the cherry-red light fixtures lay in candy-esque shards on tables. I cataloged. A Mexican family with a baby. The baby cried. Raw screeching cries, pained cries. Dried blood crusted under its nose. Baby's mother held the baby like a pile of laundry.

Blank gazes. Blood, drying.

Besides the crying baby, besides the gurgle of coffeepots—utter silence.

"You're right," Daryl said.

He held his phone to his ear—

Why is his other hand not on the table?

"Hi, dispatch. Can you route me to the troopers outside? I'm the man with a gun at Denny's. Thanks," he said, and cleared his throat. "Hi, Officer Snyder. You might remember me from yesterday. I think there's been a misunderstandin' we should clear up."

Why is his hick accent slipping out like he's nervous?

"Naw, not the indecent exposure charges. Not the property damage— tell ol' Hammock that I'm sorry 'bout the windows, would you? I'll try to cover the cost, I been savin', he's always been decent—"

A long pause. Chatter from the phone.

"Know you and the others tried to find me last night," Daryl said, smiling. "I figured why not come into town, save y'all the trouble?"

"What are you doing?" I asked.

His grip tightened around the phone. "I figure you'll be needing as much help as you can get, in the next few days. Seeing as you killed my friends."

"Daryl."

"Let me list off the charges before you haul me in, save you some time."

He said the "man with a gun," but I destroyed the gun earlier, why would he—

"Indecent exposure, property damage, illegal possession of a firearm—"

The bodies. The Divine Flesh. She wanted the bodies. He wanted Her out, but I'd destroyed the gun…what, did Daryl *want* to go to jail now? Why was Daryl acting like this—

And then I realized why, and I wanted to puke.

Because Rosetown's jail's in the same fucking building as the morgue!

Daryl's hand flicked.

That's the .44.

A gunshot cracked.

(!!!!)

Warmth dribbled from my skull, my head limp on the table, glass cutting into my cheek.

"—and murdering my wife," Daryl said.

The Divine Flesh wanted to *create*. She couldn't mutate something unless it was dead or dying. Neither of us knew why.

I couldn't fix whatever She was about to do. I couldn't move. I couldn't do anything at all. I couldn't save any of the people She was about to kill and recreate.

The body isn't real, the body isn't mine, I am not burning.

The Divine Flesh laughed as She slithered into my limbs.

Bye-bye, Jennifer-baby.

She kept thinking about how *annoying* it was about to get, having to stay still inside that silly body bag while they took Her to the morgue, but Her treasures awaited, and Daryl would adore them. She would restore his friends and find a way to let everyone live again forever. And ever. If only Jennifer-baby could sleep forever…

The Divine Flesh said, *Now sleep.*

"I'm sorry," Clay said.

"You're dying."

Clay knew that. He stood at a gas-station ATM, phone pressed into his ear, his charred filaments crumbling around the inside of the building, unseen. Folks shivered every now and again.

If you knew. If you could see what I truly look like.

Genesis writhed inside him. *(hungry)*

"I know, sweetie. I know," Clay murmured.

The cold female voice on the other end of the line said, "Did some of them live?"

"One. The runt."

"It's going to die inside you," Susan said.

"You got your empathy back or not? Thought those were your last batches for this cycle."

"I do. That's how I know you're dying. I warned you," Susan said. "Now you call me and beg for mercy? I'm afraid we're past that."

Clay punched in his bank card information. The dollar amount popped up. He cringed. Just barely enough for a plane ticket. It'd clean him out. Genesis might not live through the pressure changes on an airplane.

(hungry)

The others would've, but then again, the others were all dead. Because Susan had murdered them.

"Please. I'll do anything. I'm gonna die, but the last larva doesn't have to."

"If you wouldn't have stolen *my babies*, I'd gladly assume care of your baby. Genesis. That's their name, isn't it? I can feel it. My empathy's back," Susan said.

Clay hacked up a few dead flies. Every breath stung as he inhaled. Everything tasted like smoke and burning hair.

"Fire damage. That's a painful, slow death. I don't envy you," Susan said.

"If I get your babies back, will you—"

"No."

Something bubbled in the background.

"I've already taken steps to get my babies back. They're with Jennifer Plummer. It's no longer your concern," Susan said. "Goodbye."

Click.

No.

No. Let the murderer of his children run around without a care in the world? His babies. They'd screamed and screamed as they'd burned alive, the precious little ones, they couldn't understand why everything *hurt* and why nobody was helping them—

Clay had clawed open their vessel's body as his larvae burned. He'd scooped his larvae out. Felt each little life flicker out. He'd fallen to his knees in the nursery, floor hot as a July sidewalk.

The fire. The fire will end it. I want to be with my babies.

He'd only run outside, half-charred, because Genesis had gone *(why does it hurt?)* and that had shaken Clay enough for him to slither through the nursery window, Genesis inside his body. He had to live for Genesis. Thank God for small blessings.

Or don't. Because God was the one who incinerated your children.

Clay patted the dime baggie of black powder in his pocket.

Susan wouldn't help him. And if Susan wouldn't help, then neither would anyone else. He could ambush some lone human at a rest area, give Genesis a new home, and then die...but then the truth would never get out, Susan would go free, and by God, that wasn't an option.

Not anymore.

Clay called Jennifer Plummer. It went to voicemail.

If his plan failed, he'd die anyway. Sure, the plan was crazy. It was downright idiotic to barter with the Divine Flesh, but if anything could prevent him and Genesis from dying, it'd be Her.

So make your pilgrimage and give your offering.

When Clay had come to, coughing on his front lawn, throat raw from smoke, the petrified chunk of dried flesh called the Hermetic was cradled in his arms. He couldn't remember grabbing it. It was just *there*, secreting beads of black blood. It wanted to be delivered. To the Divine Flesh.

(would you?)

So Clay made another phone call.

"Phoenix-Mesa Gateway Airport, how can I help you?"

"I gotta book a flight. Soonest one available. And can I book a rental car, too?"

"What's the destination?"

Genesis retreated further inside Clay and stilled. Sleeping. Their thoughts hazed into *(safe)*. Genesis had consumed enough of that old human vessel to know what sleep was, and that it felt good.

Just a couple more hours, little one.

Clay said, "Rosetown, Idaho."

8

After the plane ride to Boise, Clay didn't stop driving until the handy-dandy road signs said *Welcome to Custer County!* then *Rosetown, Idaho, pop. 5000*. Then, and only then, did the Hermetic weep more of its ink-dark fluid.

Ichor.

Clay imbibed.

Warmth stabbed into his guts like a fishhook, sending sweet pulses through him. The feeling of electricity, unspooling guts, coiled heat. His body had become a compass. If he looked back towards Arizona, the tinglies decreased. When he turned towards wherever the hell the Hermetic wanted to go—

(Myself)

(home)

—the tinglies got better.

Feels good.

Gee, what a shocker. A fishhook worked because it had bait. That was pretty obvious, even through the fuzzy haze of the ichor. It whispered, *Drink of Me and be at peace. Eat of My—*

(Divine Flesh)

—flesh and drink of My blood.

"Kumbaya, my Lord," Clay sang, because why the hell not? "Kumbaya, something-something, lalalala, something-something…"

A laugh burst out of him. It ached.

(come here)

"I've been driving for two hours straight," Clay said.

(touch Me)

He wrapped his left arm around it, hugging the thing.

(skin-to-skin)

Was the thing gonna merge into his body or some Cronenberg shit? Maybe, maybe not. Clay was vaguely alarmed that this question now seemed about as important as figuring out which laundromat to use. Hm, obvious Russian drug front, or the tweaker hangout down the street? Dollar packet of Tide, or dollar packet of Persil?

Clay staggered out of the rental van.

All right. He'd been driving since he picked up the Hermetic, special goodies loaded inside: the Exothermic Pulsefire flamethrower, half a dozen frag grenades, a few spare guns. The files. A cache of evidence against Susan.

Clay lit a Marlboro, drew in a curl of smoke, and leaned against the van.

This part of Idaho was scrubland gone to seed. No Zion Park, red-rock stuff here—just tumbleweeds, beige flat land, bits of indigo from blooming larkspur. White-capped mountains hulked on the horizon. Summer clouds drifted overhead. The freeway had thinned to a tributary.

(skin-to-skin)

(I'm a recording. A book, in flesh. You want someone else. Touch Me.)

That dried flesh-thing—the Hermetic—what was it?

Clay sucked in clean air. His head cleared. He ignored the feel-good tinglies.

It wanted to go somewhere.

(home)

He wondered, should it?

And suddenly, for a few cold seconds, Clay *knew* if he drenched it in gasoline and set it ablaze, that'd be the end of it. Right now, the Hermetic was weak. Wouldn't regenerate if he burned it. The ichor addiction would dissipate.

(Ah, but I can heal you, Clay.)

"You expect me to believe You?"

(You'll never get another chance like this, and you know it.)

Clay ground out his cigarette and went to get the gasoline. Screw this. The Hermetic needed to die. What the hell had he been thinking, blowing every last dime he had on a plane flight?

(I'll take away your pain.)

Clay ripped open the passenger door. "I'm not in pain. I'm fine. I don't feel emotions. I'm in heat right now."

(God loves you.)

He froze.

(Not the fake God who created you. Real God. Me.)

Why was his chest shaking? Why were his filaments quivering like plucked fiddle strings?

(Why do you think you're unworthy of love?)

"Shut up."

(Oh you ache for God. Some people have mommy issues, some have daddy issues, but everyone has God issues.)

(Poor poor thing. Poor unloved darling.)

(Touch Me.)

"I'm fine."

(You are so very LOVED.)

Love.

Clay's eyes watered. Oh. Tears? He slid his jacket off, exposing his bare arms, and looked at the Hermetic. What if he turned into a Cronenberg monster? What if the Hermetic ate him? What if this was a Venus-flytrap situation, and it snared its victims by heaping on the lovey-dovey chemicals? Lord, he knew all about lovey-dovey chemicals and bait, he hooked miserable depressives outta the psych ward with them. Could he trust his chemical feelings? What if it—

I don't care.

He finally let himself think it, after all these years.

Our God has forsaken us, and I'm the only person who knows about it, and now I'm dying.

He slid into the passenger seat, scooped up the Hermetic, slicked it along his skin, and wrapped it lovingly in his filaments.

Cold exploded over him. His back arced against the car seat. Blackness blotted out his sight.

Am I dead?

The thought seemed to echo in the void—a primordial void. What an embryo dreamed, before its eyes developed? What a larva dreamed inside its egg?

Godsong, he thought.

Something watched Clay.

Something shuffled, uncoiled, intimately close to him, breathing soft eager breaths. It knew he wanted to hear humming, so it began buzzing, droning, like a Mirror Person. It wanted…wanted to do something intimate, something special, something that'd make sex seem like a business handshake, and the *something* in the void caressed its feelers over him.

A lady's honey-sweet voice cooed, "Oh. Clay. There you are!"

Am I dead?

"No, silly. I'm dead. Tee-hee! At least, I'm pretending to be. You poor thing, you're so cold in here with Me. You shouldn't be in a morgue drawer."

Heat washed through Clay, melting away the cold.

Who are You? What are You?

"I'm the Divine Flesh."

I have something that belongs to You, Clay said.

"Let Me in. Let Me taste you. I want to see."

Tendrils whispered over his face. His eyelids. Nose. Lips. Tendrils twined around Clay's filaments, meshing.

"Can I?"

Please yes please.

Tendrils plunged into him—

So good, trailing gold inside me, and images flickered through Clay's mind, and the Divine Flesh tasted all of him, thought he was oh so funny because he kept thinking, *Love it feels so warm, it feels like being in a vessel when I was a larva, chewing not caring about anything else, tasting love, I want—*

"What do you want, Clay-darling?"

Bring my babies back to life and heal me. Please.

"I can do that, oh yes. You poor thing."

What do I do?

"Keep praying, and you will know."

Praying is a little above my pay grade, Ma'am.

The Divine Flesh giggled. "You're praying right now, silly. All you ever have to do is talk to Me, and I'll listen. I'm always here. Don't they teach you that?"

I think I have to deliver the Hermetic.

"It's a part of Me. An old, old part of Me. It's just what I need to fix Myself. Will you come deliver the Hermetic?"

Yes.

What about Susan's eggs? What about Jennifer Plummer?

"I'll help you with the rest of that, but I need the Hermetic. You're only six hours away. As for Jennifer—oh, it's funny. Don't worry about Jennifer. You've met Me before."

Jennifer's scarred body flickered into existence, nude. Her scars vanished. Flesh grew over the jutting ribcage. Blood rouged her cheeks and lips. Scarlet consumed her sclerae, leaving hazel irises in a red sea.

She beamed at Clay. "Jennifer is My container."

Whoa, that sickly addict? Sorry, uh, Divine Flesh. Ma'am.

"You're adorable. I can't wait to make you into something special."

A kiss brushed over Clay's forehead.

"If you want to get Susan's babies and bring them to Me, I can fix everything. Her babies are in Jennifer's trailer. I'm in a morgue! Isn't that fun? I've never been inside a drawer before. It's boring."

Can You kill Susan's babies?

"I can make them yours. I'll bathe you in My love. I'll take away your pain. I'll jewel you in eyes and mouths and treasure you forever—"

Can You bring back my babies?

"…Yes."

That was an awfully slow yes.

"I'm thinking, Clay. I've never recreated a Mirror Person before. I suppose I could store them inside Me, if nothing else. Oh, I'll give you whatever you want. I live to make others happy," the Divine Flesh said. "But really. We both know that you're going to deliver the Hermetic to Me, so why are we pretending that we're silly schemers, wheeling and dealing?"

She giggled, then retreated into the darkness.

Clay blinked his eyes open.

He was sitting in the passenger seat, cupping the Hermetic to his chest. Naked. Clothes on the floorboards. Sunlight warmed through the windshield.

Clay put his clothes back on, buckled the Hermetic up, and continued driving on.

The Divine Flesh whispered, *(Rosetown, Idaho.)*

(I saw everything in your brain.)

(I've been glitching for so long…Oh, you don't know what it's like, to be broken. Really broken.)

Clay gnawed black licorice chews as he drove through the last dregs of Boise, Idaho. Pines appeared. The air tasted less arid. July softened. Potato fields furrowed the earth. Driving wasn't so bad. Gave him time to think. He finally hit Rosetown at 3:15 p.m., and the Divine Flesh guided him the rest of the way. *(Yes, turn down that road. Yes, down the gravel path. See the cabin? My boyfriend lives there. Now a little past that, into the woods, and you'll see Jennifer's trailer.)*

Clay rolled up.

A rusted meth lab rotted in a field. Oh, whoops. On closer inspection, it wasn't a meth lab. Just looked like one. It was a half-trailer without a truck. Bird shit dotted the orange awning. Two plastic lawn recliners decayed in front. Beer cans glinted in a primitive fire pit. Pines circled the field. A decal of an eagle was stuck to the trailer door, with *AMERICAN PARADISE* below it.

Lord, hopefully not. Could Paradise be a little less meth-y, perhaps? Clay could practically smell the speed cooking. He parked. No other vehicles here. He walked up to the battered trailer door and tried the handle. It opened.

BLAM!

(!!!!!)

Pain.

He collapsed. Everything below his gut numbed. A new smell filled the air—fecal matter, blood, stomach acid. Gunpowder. Bits of intestine splattered the trailer.

Shotgun blast.

A rigged shotgun smoked inside. Barrel aimed out, angled up. Fishing line for the string. Rigged to blow when the door handle got pulled.

Idiot. How many booby-trapped drug dens have you explored? A dozen?

Now he'd never avenge his children. Now Genesis would die. Clay prayed to the Divine Flesh, but nothing happened.

Footsteps creaked inside the trailer. Clay lay half-in, half-out, bleeding on scraps of carpet.

"I wasn't expecting you," the lady standing over him said.

Filaments hovered over her head. She was a Mirror Person.

No. No, it can't be.

Everything grayed. The lady's skinsuit was clad in hunter's camo. Built solid. Silver-streaked hair in a ponytail. Steel-toed boots nudged Clay's skull.

Think I got the wrong trailer. Sorry, ma'am, Clay tried to say, but couldn't.

Breathe in. Breathe out.

"You got the right trailer," the lady said, and crouched down. "I can feel your confusion and worry. That's fine."

The lady put a hand into her pocket and withdrew a pill bottle of Mirror Person eggs.

"Because you should be worried," she said.

She grabbed a handful of Clay's hair and *twisted*.

"You stole my babies. You've come after me yet again. I don't know what I'm going to do to you, but understand this—"

Fuck, it's Susan.

"Your actions have consequences," Susan said.

9

The medical examiner of Custer County drove home at 4:00 p.m.

Not to the empty apartment in Idaho Falls.

Home.

Rosetown's morgue.

The sheriff's office called as he exited the freeway.

"Almost there," he said. "Had a long day in Idaho Falls. Traffic."

"You got a place to stay overnight, Pearson?" Sheriff Olsen asked.

"Got a room at the Drift-Inn."

The sheriff cleared his throat. "Your mother worries 'bout you. You should see her."

"I'll be there in fifteen minutes."

"Look, just sayin' this as a friend—we can git the other medical examiner in. You don't gotta do these autopsies."

"It's been ten years. I'm fine."

"Maybe you should take a few days off, see your mother, git caught up instead. It's been too long since you came to town. The Rodriguez clan built another Mexican restaurant. Nancy Trenelli's been breedin' some Border collies, might give you a pup. These bodies…Look, Pearson, I dunno if this bearded freak's a serial killer or not, but these kids' bodies are mangled."

Pearson's voice got rough. "I performed my own daughter's autopsy, Sheriff Olsen. I think I can manage."

"Freak shot his wife in the head. Broad fuckin' daylight—pardon my French. The poor wife's in the drawer with the other kids. I git so—Pearson, you believe in the end of days? Do you believe in Jesus Christ?"

Well, Sheriff, I eat the stale bread every Sunday. I sit and I smile at the Lutheran Church. And everyone thinks I'm praying.

Something white-hot flared in his chest. He gritted his teeth. Oh, did he believe in Jesus Christ? The Church might be the bride of Christ, but everyone seemed to have an opinion after Susannah was raped and murdered and left to rot in the woods.

It's fine, because Susannah was with God and Jesus now. Susannah was happier in Heaven than down on Earth.

So buck up, Brett Pearson, and get on your knees every Sunday and swallow it, while Vicky's drunk in bed, scrolling through Tinder for a warm body like you don't know she's fucking other men, pretending that it doesn't matter, sweetie, Susannah's at peace now, so you go to church and beg God to not covet the other two kids, we have enough to kill those ones, too. God wanted Susannah to come home because God's really into seventeen-year-old girls.

Although the divorce had been inevitable, it was blissful. Amicable. Like letting go of a rope. Both kids went with Vicky. Fine by him. He gave them birthday gifts and attended both high school graduations with customary gestures. In return, they never contacted him again. Tit for tat. Pearson wasn't their father anymore. Hadn't been since he'd done Susannah's autopsy, ten years ago.

"Do you believe in God?"

"Thank you, Sheriff Olsen," Pearson said.

He hung up before Olsen could yammer out another word.

Rosetown clotted around him, budding off the freeway. The usual features. Pine trees. Scrubland, rife with wildflowers. Lupine, bastardized sunflowers, fist-sized dandelion puffs, California poppies, sagebrush, plantains, all of it lurid in the springtime, desiccated to brown by the time June rolled around. A ramshackle quilt of vegetation. Amaranth grew along the freeway, pinker than a twenty-year-old's stomach. The Gas N' Go festered in the afternoon heat, off-white as pus. Houses peeked out from between the trees. Paint peeled. Dead patches blighted Roosevelt Park's lawn. Rust coated its playground equipment: the swing set chains, the jungle gym, the metal slide that should've been torn down twenty years ago. A basketball hoop loomed over the decaying playground. Nobody was there. Silence staticked the air.

If you drove further, there lurked a Harvest Foods that only carried half-liquefied produce during the off-season. The meat sinfully close to expiring. Rosetown quietly supplied itself with either Brown or

McGee's steers, cash only, kept it outta Uncle Sam's hands. Nancy Trenelli raised rabbits and lambs. Everyone kept a few chickens. During the spring, the fields reeked of fertilizer and cow shit. Down the road, there was a cinder block school. All grades—elementary thru high school, because Rosetown averaged thirty students per graduating class. Two motels existed—the Drift-Inn and a mouse-filled Motel Six just off the exit.

Holy Lane, that was what they called the back corner of town. Not because melon-sized potholes pitted the road. Holy Lane for the churches. The Church of Christ, St. Thérèse's Church, and a Unitarian Universalist congregation lurked here, along with the crumbling ruin of a century-old barn. Their buildings were from the '70s—utilitarian husks—but lifeblood flowed through them each day: in the flesh and bones and souls of the believers, in the conduit of prayer, in the intimacy of being with God. Eighty-year-old Catholic women labored over king cakes, casseroles, baked fish, and frog-eye salad in the kitchen below the nave of St. Thérèse's, every motion eliciting pain—arthritis, aching knees, exhaustion—every pain a work of love, and the labors became a sacrament. *Holy, holy, holy.*

And there was *the house*. The house the kids grew up in. It was forest green now, with white trim. The people who'd bought *the house* took good care of it. Susannah would've loved it. She'd've said, *Daddy, look at our house! It looks like a fairy tale.* It made him happy now. It hadn't, five years ago. He couldn't have driven past it without a bottle of Jim Beam in him. Now he could.

At the center of Rosetown lay a courthouse you could fit under a microscope.

Beside it lived a brick building, red as venous blood.

Home.

Custer County Jail, read the brass lettering over the door. The morgue didn't need labeling.

Pearson parked in the lot.

He mumbled the same prayer as always, sort of a pregame mantra. An entreaty to the dead.

"Show me what's wrong, and I will find it. Tell me how you died, and I will speak for you, because you can't anymore. If there's a who, show me, and I will find whatever bits they left behind."

His eyes burned, watered.

"Because that's the only thing I can do."

He entered the building and exchanged small talk with the younger officer, Carl Snyder, the towhead kid who'd never grown up. Pudgy chin. White-blond hair. Flabby hands and body. Pustules rimed his face.

Snyder took a swig of Dr. Pepper. "You wanna see the freak?"

"I have to perform four autopsies."

"C'mon, you know you wanna. You gotta go through the jail to hit the morgue. C'mon. I'll show you."

Snyder bustled through doors, unlocking and punching in passcodes as needed. Pearson endured. Sweat circled the armpits of Snyder's powder-blue uniform.

"Between the two of us," Snyder said, sucking his lower lip, "freak didn't have anything to do with the car accident. Folks in town think so, but they're wrong."

"How do you know?" Pearson asked.

Another slurp. "But this freak did shoot the junkie through the skull. Nobody thought the scarred junkie was his wife, but there you go. Married and everything. Wonder if the junkie cheated or somethin'. These people are real fucked in the head. Wouldn't surprise me."

"Please. I'm very tired."

Snyder yanked open the jail's door. "Felt kinda bad for the junkie, though. Married to some tweaker who cooks speed—I mean, fuck, what do you do when that's your life? How do you move away from that?"

"I don't know."

"There's another body on ice. A hooker. Someone used her as a drug cadaver bag, stuffed her with meth and coke like a teddy bear. We think this freak murdered her and was gonna run a shipment. How many bags you think they stuffed up her vag? Dad wouldn't tell me how many they took out."

"Please have some respect for the dead," Pearson said.

Snyder snorted. "Sure. Okay."

Three cell blocks lined a corridor. They walked to the end.

A man rested on a cot, gazing out. Contusions purpled most of his face. A line of blackened blood split his lower lip open. Something pinkish and opaque trickled down his forehead and branched. His right eye had swollen shut. The left eye could only open halfway. The nose had been broken. Dried blood flaked off his upper lip.

A bone-tired thought: *The good ol' boys are at it again.*

Pearson could've asked how the man had sustained those injuries. He could've filed a report. He could've seethed with rage that this killer existed in a clean cell, alive, unlike his victim. Could've been hopeful that this particular situation would resolve the way it had ten years ago.

His victim's only twenty-two. Only five years older than Susannah was.

But what was the point of doing anything? Of even getting angry? None of it made a difference. Predators hunted. Victims died. Pearson analyzed the scraps.

"I have four autopsies," Pearson said.

Snyder finished taking him home to the morgue.

Rosetown's morgue was a white-frosted alcove. Concrete floors. White cabinets. White walls. Fluorescent lighting. A pall of bleach tainted the air. Ventilation wheezed. Four cadaver drawers lined the far wall, all of them currently occupied.

He started with Jennifer Plummer.

He pulled open the drawer. The cadaver lay beneath a cotton sheet. Plummer, Jennifer. Age: twenty-two. Height: 5'8". Weight: 115 lbs., slightly underweight. Cause of death: gunshot to head. History of drug use and prior suicide attempts.

He drew the sheet back.

The skin looked pristine as latex. No scars. He lifted an arm, saw no lividity…no rigor mortis, either. Hadn't the death occurred ten hours ago? He checked the paperwork, confirmed.

Where's the gunshot wound?

Delicately, he cupped his hands beneath the cadaver's skull and lifted its head. The back of the skull was uninjured. No exit wounds. Not so much as a paper cut on her face. Pearson palped the cadaver's scalp, feeling for bullet wounds or fluid leakage.

Nothing.

"What did you die of?"

Maybe she hadn't died. Had she fainted or taken some drug, been shot at, and ended up…freezing or suffocating to death inside the drawer?

His heart pounded in his throat.

The paperwork had errors. It'd mentioned extensive scarring on her limbs, caused by ritualistic self-injury. No such scars existed on the cadaver.

Pearson leaned closer.

Her eyes opened, full of blood. Blood bulged beneath her corneas and obliterated her irises and sclerae.

What—

Pain exploded in his throat. Couldn't breathe. He inhaled. Air stopped. *Pulse-pulse-pulse*, throbbed through the meat, couldn't breathe, couldn't breathe, lungs burned, *shit I can't breathe!* Blood-slicked tendrils unfurled from Her eye sockets. They reached for him.

He gripped the edge of the drawer, head pounding.

Crushed trachea. She crushed my trachea.

Make another hole. He fumbled over the tray of tools. There. He seized a scalpel. *Find a straw.* No tubing lay in the tools, just hammers, scalpels, bone saws, *so find a straw!*

Snyder. The sodas. The coffee station. Straw.

Pearson turned to the door.

(Don't go.)

He took a step—

"Don't go," said the Divine Flesh. "Be Mine."

Yours?

She sat up and beamed. "I can claim you now."

The skin of Her chest slid off and hit the floor. Three exposed hearts, gray from the cold, shuddered to life. Color bloomed into them.

They're…beautiful.

Yes. Yes, they were beautiful. Warm love swept through him, and suddenly it didn't matter that his vision was going dark, that his eyes ached, that he'd believed in a sham of a God who'd stolen Susannah from him—how silly. God was here, and She loved him. Susannah's death had nothing do with Her; the Divine Flesh had no capacity to demand death or punishment, only to love. She was nothing but love!

Laughter bubbled in his chest. *I never understood,* he tried to say, because everything from before seemed like a silly nightmare; his sham version of God was nothing but paper and dust, blown away by a single human thought. *I thought the fake God-thing in the Old Testament was You, the paper God in the churches and mosques and temples. I didn't know,* he tried to say, but Her love washed over him, and there was no need for words. She understood. She loved him, She had always loved him, and would always love him.

Sometimes I go to sleep and I wake up with the revolver pressed to my temple, or on the pillow, he prayed. *I see Susannah's body and I'm weighing her organs in my nightmares. She wants to know why Daddy's not helping her, why I'm a pathetic piece of shit—*

who had to have his hometown string up the fucker who'd killed her.

Pearson fell to his knees. The Divine Flesh knelt down to face him, head tilted.

O God please help me, I was wrong, I was wrong please forgive me, You're real, please fix me.

"There was never anything to forgive, silly," God said.

Her feelers plunged into him. She ripped apart his torso deftly as skinning an elk, trailing bliss.

Thus began the work.

In the beginning, *there was nothing*, and yes, it was true, but oh, they never say that the closest thing to nothing is its opposite. Everything. *Two sides of the same coin.* What was a *coin*, again? Sometimes I forgot.

I checked the morgue's door. Closed.

Daryl waited for Me just on the other side of the wall.

Love Me. Don't despair.

The medical examiner's organs pulsed in My grasp, dying from lack of oxygen. I'd fix that. Render something beautiful into being.

Would it be better to spend more time creating each new child? Or should I envelop them into Myself first, save My best creativity for later, and allow My newest children to help Me bless this entire building? They'd understand the need to help others first. Yes, yes.

Save everyone first.

Then I'd show My work to Daryl, who would adore Me. More than he already did. And we would do something human before I started hunting for the murderers of his loved ones. Hm. A picnic! We hadn't had one since he was eighteen. He'd driven us out to a field of California poppies and larkspur, and we ate ham sandwiches in the May sunlight. That was the first time he'd said he loved Me. Not Jennifer. Me. The Divine Flesh.

When I freed Daryl, we'd have another picnic. One of flesh scraps. We'd say cute things, lovey-dovey things, and we'd feed each other. We'd sit on the concrete, surrounded by My sacred creations, and then I could bless Daryl's ears so that he could hear the lovely fungal song of the wild yeasts in the air. Ooh, or maybe the *chitter-chitter* of that happy listeria colony in the month-old baloney in the break room fridge.

I hear everything, you know.

A choked wheeze.

Pearson's face blackened, eyes bulging.

Oh. That.

"Do you need to breathe?" I said, voice soft as cradlesong.

I brushed lips along his forehead. Sweat gilded My lips.

His mind was a jumble—

(*I can't breathe I CAN'T BREATHE why can't I! Breathe!*)

They worried so much. I didn't understand why.

I pressed My hand to his sternum, lulling those frantic thoughts.

Beneath skin and breast, new airways budded off his lungs. Flesh, flexible and slick, yes. I rimed them in mucous glands and angel-blood. I guided these thin hollow airways. They snaked between obsolete lungs. Threaded around. Between ribs, I fused them into a central nub, rife with blood vessels; these I beaded with alveoli.

The eyeball-sized nub protruded. Throbbed.

(Holy! Holy! Holy! O let me worship You, Divine Flesh!)

Of course.

I kissed the new airway.

It burst, blooming open. Lymph splattered My face. Six petals of flesh curled out, undulating. The center gaped, a fresh orifice. Cilia waved around the interior.

The new respiratory system looked like a passionflower composed of raw meat.

It inhaled.

Skin revivified. His eyes fluttered open. He smiled at Me.

I gently pressed below his ears.

Pop.

Jaw unhinged.

"There, now. Is that better?"

Yes, Divine Flesh.

I took all that silly fabric off him and grazed My hands over the bare torso. New respiratory systems bloomed where I touched.

A glistening shuddering garden. Gorgeous.

He writhed in ecstasy.

Then I had an even better idea.

I cradled his head in My lap. Flowers wriggled in delight, little harsh pants. I squeezed along the garden's limbs. Tendons and nerves hollowed into pseudo-veins. I summoned these to the skin's surface. Creamy veins cobwebbed over the garden's body.

I planted My mouth over each eye and sucked. Retinae and orbs slipped out, sweet and silky. Primordial tendrils groped out of My garden's empty eye sockets. But if this garden was really a garden of life, there should be…a little more variety. Perhaps I'd use its body to incubate some of the yeasts and bacteria floating around here.

Botulism spores. Oh, those were *everywhere*, and here I was, ready to nurse them lovingly. My garden could seed the living with enough botulinum toxin to make them claimable.

Three more bodies awaited Me inside this building.

I connected veins to modified lymph nodes and stabbed them through bone plate, deep into marrow. I sucked out the marrow, lined the bone interiors with serous flesh, and obliterated all remaining immune response.

Lymph nodes swelled. Burst. Maroon sprays of bacterial collectors grew out from beneath arms, the neck.

These I fertilized; these I dusted with the botulin in the dirt along the crease between floor and ceiling. Fat catabolized to keep the garden at a cozy temperature, for the babies. Serous fluid moistened the interior of the hollow bones, cloyed with sugars. *Feast, My darlings. Help Me bless others.*

Botulin frenzied.

Nascent eyes jeweled in clusters along My garden's cheeks. I did so adore bestowing eyes. Iridescent pearls. They saw temperatures instead of light, because temperature control was more important to maintain the garden's life. In the creases of the garden's flesh, in the folds between genitals, thighs, and toes, yeasts hummed.

Ah, but the garden needed intakes.

I crowned it in mouths. They haloed My garden's skull, working soundlessly. Sugary fluid glistered them like a pitcher plant's lure. *Come, come, grow.*

Creak.

Someone approached the morgue. Slurping something.

Snyder.

The door opened.

"Pearson? You hungry in there?"

Pearson the garden shambled to its feet. All of its obsolete body hair littered the floor.

I laughed. "Silly. I already took care of that. He'll never be hungry again."

Snyder burst in, groping for his gun. His gaze fell on Me.

He froze.

Flesh boiled from My eyes. I snapped a tendril through his eye-socket, tasting salt. Pushed deeper. Tasted buttery salty brain, fatty and delectable. He remained standing, muscles twitching. I leapt. Ran the steps to him. The Dr. Pepper fell to the ground, gurgling soda.

His thoughts had gone—

(!!!!!)

static.

(!!!!!)

Knives crystallized over My fingers, wrought in bone.

I liberated his heart from his chest. It squirted blood a few times. I giggled. Silly dumb heart. I took a bite.

He collapsed. Spasmed. Electricity danced 'round his brain. I retracted the tendril. Blood oozed from the eye socket.

I liberated his stomach. His intestines.

He'd always wanted to fly. I dug wrist-deep into his chest cavity, peritoneum silky against My skin as I stroked and savored the touch-feel of organs, *so boring* but I had to start somewhere. Warmth. Slick fluids anointed Me, baptized the cadavers. Humming, cervical vertebrae thickened and branched. Skin split open like lovely raw silk. Bone spars lengthened into new skeletal structures. I rendered Snyder into an angel. Instead of skin, slick pink membrane covered the humanoid body. Candy-pink veins branched out of it. Six wings lay folded along its back, clothed in skin. Dead gray flesh hung in ribbons around the base of each pair. It stood, wings jerking, and cocked its faceless head at Me. Strands of white-blond hair hung from the scalp. A lipless mouth parted. Something glistening peeked out. Not a tongue.

Lost in the joy of creating, I didn't hear the front entrance door open.

My children and I left the morgue. We stalked to the break room. The third body—a janitor, Shelley Grady, here for her part-time summer gig—picked at a beef stroganoff Lean Cuisine, tarot cards spread on the table. Three cards. The Tower, the Empress, and the Hierophant.

I stood in the doorway and softly called her home.

(Would you like to be Mine? Would you like Me to render you afresh?)

(Wouldn't you like that?)

All of My 108 teeth shone with blood. Heart's blood. I lacquered them again with My tongue. It's important to reassure them before I claim them, you know. What better way to do that than to show them My nice smile? All three of My hearts beat. Full of love.

"Oh Jesus," Shelley said, in the hushed tone of a lifelong atheist witnessing the Rapture.

Her skin grayed.

I crushed her trachea with My hands. She was very eager to please.

Her organs were lovely, so I brought them outside that obsolete skin, and I created bright new ones, colors like tempura paint. Added new limbs. Like a funny spider. I transmuted her waist-length hair into keratin spars. Another angel. These newfangled cephalized lifeforms needed more variety. Perhaps I'd go back to the basics. I ripped out her spine and skull, slipped her brain into the body. Hm.

"*Baby?*" Daryl yelled.

Shelley scampered up to the ceiling. The garden and angel flanked Me. I ran towards My love. He'd called for Me before I asked him to, because he loved Me so much.

My children quivered with excitement. How they ached to see Me work! Their twin hearts beat in tandem, a mad dance. They wanted to touch and taste the Divine Flesh. Anoint Me in saliva. Bless Me before the holy work began. Bite off a finger or two as sacrament. She Who Bestowed Flesh deserved nothing less. To rip out a tongue! To hand it, bleeding and wriggling, every unsung hymn quivering in the meat, to Her!

Love.

How it warmed Me. I told them, *Later, dear ones.*

I arrived at Daryl's cell and worked a finger into the door lock. Like ivy, it branched, easing its way, slipped in and found the latch. Unlocked. *Click.* The garden tugged the cell door open.

Daryl flinched. His back hit the cinder block behind the cot. His eyes wheeled. His pulse jittered in his chest.

He'd gone so pale.

Why?

We all entered, confused. My angel ran a wing over Daryl's shoulders, offering him warmth. I waited, arms open.

"Daryl?"

"You—You made these sentient—"

A choked sound.

"Oh fuck. Oh, fuck, where are the other people? The cops? The medical examiner?"

I embraced him. It was like hugging a frozen cadaver.

"They're all here, My love. All around us. Aren't they precious?" I said.

"Oh god."

I nibbled his ear. Tickled a tendril along his jaw, tasting him. Icky cortisol. Tingly energy.

"Don't—don't do that," Daryl said.

"What's wrong?" I asked, pulling away.

He just looked at Me. It made something inside Me twist. He was looking at Me like I was—

a monster.

Something evil. Something disgusting. A cockroach under the sink.

Daryl edged away from Me, shivering.

No. No, that's not supposed to happen. He loves Me!

"But. But I told you that I love My children, and that I wanted more," I said, and why did I sound so scared? So desperate? "I told you," I said. "Don't you love Me? I love you."

He didn't respond.

We had to talk. What was wrong? What had I done?

Tell Me you LOVE ME!

"Hello, Jennifer Plummer."

A female voice. It came from behind Me.

"Jennifer's not here," I said, not bothering to turn.

Be creative *now*? When My love was angry at Me? No, Daryl took priority right now, and if the stupid new body could just wait for a few minutes, she'd understand that. I flicked unseen feelers over her—

Crack!

My garden fell, head half-blown away.

Crack!

One of the angel's wings flew off, smacking into the wall. It shivered—

Another gunshot. The right half of its head vanished. Bone fragments clattered against cinder block. Clear fluid misted the wall. My angel slumped. I tasted—

Susan!

I turned. Faint buzzing droned. An Exothermic flamethrower hung at Susan's hip by a set of ear protectors. She aimed her rifle at Daryl's face.

Crack!

The bullet annihilated most of his forehead. His brains throbbed in the bowl of his skull, pink and red and pulsing.

He blinked. His mouth spasmed.

Daryl crumpled like a paper doll in a fire.

No.

I entered him to heal him, to fix him—

I couldn't.

I hit something. Something thin and electric like staticky plastic. Something I couldn't worm through or break. A barrier. A shield of energy. I couldn't alter his flesh. Couldn't heal him.

What? No. NO!

"Your actions have consequences," Susan said.

Daryl jerked.

STOP, I told his body, but it didn't listen. It couldn't.

I tried again. Couldn't.

Ice filled my chest. My hands and tendrils numbed.

No. This isn't possible.

I tasted him, pressed, and hit—

the something.

JENNIFER! I screamed, *JENNIFER, WAKE UP! Daryl's dying and I can't help him!*

She stirred. She saw.

JENNIFER WHAT DO I DO?

She felt Me try to change his flesh again, felt us fail.

Oh fuck, she said. *Get outta there.*

Shelley carried Daryl outside, I ran and ran as she did, My other children's bodies burned, the Exothermic whooshing out fire over them, Me, falling apart at the joints, putting Myself back together, stumbling, because Daryl loved Me and Daryl wasn't going to die, he couldn't die, I was the Divine Flesh and therefore Daryl couldn't die—

can't get there from here!

Why couldn't I fix him?

can't get there from here!

I screamed.

Windows exploded. Blood dribbled from Daryl's ears and nose.

I clawed open his chest. His lungs. Slick between My hands. I tore them open as he spasmed. I yanked lungs out. Hurled them onto the grass. Over and over.

pulse-pulse-pulse.

His brain pulsed inside the fist-sized bullet hole in his forehead. Brains dribbled out. His blood seeped into the dirt. Shreds of gleaming lung tissue lay around us. Airways struggled. He'd gone whitish blue from blood loss. Intestines steamed. His liver. In My hand. Spongy. I was squeezing it, releasing, squeezing, and fluid streamed from it.

I'd rent him apart.

Daryl slackened.

pulse-pulse....pulse....pulse...

Then nothing.

Jennifer seethed, nearly incoherent, *You fucking killed him You fucking monster! You dragged him into this! You exposed him to us, You lured him here then You ripped him apart YOU RIPPED HIM APART—*

Daryl Plummer was dead. I couldn't claim him. The one person who'd ever loved Me for Me, and not for what I could give him, was gone. *He's gone.*

I shrieked.

Wearing her construction-grade ear protectors, Susan laughed.

10

Clay pondered:

If the only things keeping someone going were the sugar-sweet chanting of—

(All hail ME!)

—digging deeper into their filaments every second they drove closer to the Divine Flesh, and the *(I'm cold) (why am I not safe?)* panicked thoughts of their last child as they died inside them, the bits of intestine falling out of their blasted-open torso, and the bits that kept snapping off their decaying, spidery filaments—their real self, not the human skinsuit they had to slip on—and the cold radiating from the dime baggie of dried ichor in their pocket, a cold that cut through the denim and fake flesh…

(All hail ME!)

If those were the only things left, should that someone still reckon with the murderer of their children?

The rental van blended into the rest of the parked cars in front of Rosetown's jail. Clay almost missed it.

Almost.

He careened his stolen Toyota into a space, sweating.

(All hail ME!)

An ungodly shriek shivered the car's windows. Clay slammed his hands over his ears, forgetting that it did diddly squat. His filaments picked up sound. The ears were an illusion.

He sucked in a pained breath.

That's Her. She's close.

Genesis shook. Air touched Genesis's body through the holes in

Clay's. Larvae hated being exposed to dry, cold air. They perished when unhappy.

Tick-tock, Clay.

So. Break into the van, grab some guns, then find the Divine Flesh and pray She'd heal them both. Give the powdered ichor to Her. Beg for the chance to find the Hermetic again.

Or.

Go find the nearest human, in a bathroom or secluded area, and vomit up Genesis. Give 'em Genesis. Then die with the hope that Genesis would survive.

It was the faithless option, but why have faith now?

Clay got out and approached the van, limping. Gripped the van's driver's side door handle. Pea-sized blisters burst on his palms. He tugged.

Locked.

He peered into the windows. A hula girl doll leered at him from the atop the dashboard.

Clay ran around, tried the rear door handles. Locked.

Shit.

Around the brick building, someone laughed. Not the Divine Flesh. Susan.

Double shit.

Clay soothed Genesis with some humming. *Remember your true form, little one. You'll gestate into something that can fly and buzz. Hold on a bit longer.*

He had to get some weapons from inside the van, at least to ward off Susan. Was the Divine Flesh fighting Susan? Clay sprinted back to the Toyota he'd hotwired, tore off the WeatherTech mats in the trunk, clawed open the latch.

Click.

The spare tire was nestled in the compartment, along with a jack. Looked sturdy. Good. Clay hefted the jack. Slammed the trunk shut. Ran to the van.

He drew back, cringing, and hit the passenger window as hard as he could.

snap.

Pain skyrocketed up his arm. Force snapped several filaments off. Glass spiderwebbed but didn't break.

Again.

crack!

His arm canted at an odd angle. Radius and ulna jutted from his forearm. He gagged at the sight. The jack slipped through numb fingers and hit the asphalt. A bullet-sized hole appeared in the glass.

I'm falling apart bit by bit. I'll never get to Her in time. Maybe I should lie down. Sing to Genesis. Make our last moments a little better.

No.

"Please," Clay said, teeth gritted. "Divine Flesh, help me. Please."

No response.

Clay lifted the jack with his functional hand. One last hit would do it. One last hit. For Genesis. For their future.

For you, my precious Genesis.

The third hit shattered the window.

Safety glass jeweled the ground. Clay wormed his hand in and unlocked the van. Went around to the rear. Ripped open the door.

Tick-tock.

Clay scanned the van for guns. No guns. A hidden compartment lay open on the floorboards. Emptiness gaped. A spare bullet rolled 'round. The Hermetic lurked in the backseat of the van. Clay scooped it up.

No weapons were left. He couldn't fight.

Exhaustion washed through Clay.

Genesis thought, *(are we going to sleep?)*

(we should sleep we're tired)

(are we going to sleep forever, Clay?)

Why the hell not?

It wouldn't be long before death came. He'd failed. Clay patted Genesis. He slumped against the rental van. Cars dotted the parking lot. An electric-yellow sedan cheapened the solemn brick facade of Custer County's jail. An exterminator's truck proclaimed, *Nuke the Bugs!*

Vermicides lined the back of the truck. Cockroach gel. Cyzmic. Doxem...

Wait...

Insecticides.

There were weapons here after all. Clay lurched to his feet and shuffled to the truck.

Please, God, he prayed, *be unlocked. Please.*

The door handle chilled his hand. He tugged. It opened. He snatched a pump sprayer from the backseat. Snatched a half-face respirator.

Clay poured Cyzmic into a pump sprayer. Fumes filled the air. Clay dry-heaved. Poor Genesis. Would the exposure hurt them? No time to worry about that now. He prepped the pump sprayer.

Insecticides burned his kind like acid, if not outright killed. Everyone kept that secret locked up tighter than a high-risk patient's restraints. Only humans that absolutely needed to know—say, like the Flesh Failure or other larvae traffickers—got told. It was a species-wide commandment, unspoken but enforced. *Keep the last of us alive.*

Pump sprayer in hand, Clay went to face Susan.

He prayed, *Please help me, O Divine Flesh.*

11

Susan cocked the shotgun, aimed, and blew My right arm off at
the elbow—

(!!!!!) ithurtsithurts MAKE IT STOP it hurts!

"Do You know what they call me?" Susan said.

She loaded another shell into the shotgun.

Heal, I commanded, and My arm regenerated. Bone sprouted from
the ragged stump. Nerves and veins followed, twining around bone.
Muscle fiber carpeted the structure, skin slithered over all with a soft
schlorp, and pain turned to tingling.

Susan's gaze held steady on Me.

(Clay, give Daryl the Hermetic. I'll lure Susan away. Please. Help him.)

Clay thought, *Yes.*

"God-Killer. That's me," Susan said, blood dripping down her face.

"Why are you doing this?"

I edged away from Daryl's body. Susan aimed the shotgun at my
torso—

(!!!!!!) ithurtsithurts (!!!)

HEAL!

Flesh grew. My torso knit back together. A streak of something foul
and yellowish contaminated My cheek—bile. Bile and fecal matter
splattered My jeans and arms. I lay on My back in the grass, smell of
gunpowder stinging My nose.

I wobbled to a standing position. "W-why did you kill Daryl? I loved
him."

"Why did God annihilate the world I was born in? You see, gods…
gods are fickle. They destroy what they create. Do you not remember

Sodom and Gomorrah? The Flood? When I realized, years ago, that Jennifer Plummer's body housed a god, I hired people to monitor her. I made her an employee, and compensated her fairly. Mostly, I analyzed *You.*"

She smiled, lips pressed thin, like she wanted to spit.

"I know your weaknesses," she said.

She aimed the shotgun at My head.

"I haven't seen any of Your tendrils yet. I assume there isn't enough flesh to create them with. You have a little store of flesh inside You, but I'm willing to bet You've used it all up, healing Your body. You can't build from nothing…because You're stuck in this reality, trapped in the body of a self-loathing addict. You're more human than god, Divine Flesh," Susan said. "But when You stole my children, You became godly enough for *me.*"

I thought to the Snyder angel, commanded it to heal, commanded it *(COME HERE).*

It feels harder to communicate. Why am I so weak?

"Jennifer didn't know that that shipment was your stolen batch of eggs, and neither did I," I said.

"Ah, but You had Your suspicions. A simple phone call to me would've confirmed the origin of those eggs and guaranteed their safe return… so why didn't You make one?"

My hands shook. Pins and needles spread through My legs. Blood and tears filled My vision, blurring the grass and brick building into a red-green haze. *Daryl's dead. He's dead and I'm a failure. I'm a broken god.*

We stood a few body-lengths away from Daryl's form—his body. Not his corpse. It could not be his corpse. He couldn't be dead. Because I couldn't heal him, and if he was dead, I should be able to. He couldn't be dead. Couldn't.

He's in pieces on the lawn, Jennifer hissed.

I called out to Clay. No response.

But a smell soured the air—burning flesh. I glanced at Daryl.

Then I saw it.

The Hermetic.

The Hermetic rested inside Daryl's ripped-open husk. Threads of smoke curled up from where his flesh met it. Black beadlets of ichor flowed out like oil, like waxcloth. His body rejected it. Rejected Me.

What? Why?

Susan spat on the grass. "Let's continue our theology lesson, Divine Flesh. My God committed suicide, dooming every last member of my species to death. Every moment of our God's dying was akin to one of Your solar years. As the end neared, our reality began to crumble apart. God was on Their death throes. God suffocated on Reflection and Time, or God glutted Themselves on them till They burst. Can't remember, don't care."

The Hermetic's here, and it didn't fix Me. I can't heal Daryl. Oh no. Oh, no, no, NO!

Tears spilled from My eyes, and I sobbed.

Susan stalked over to Me with something metallic clutched in her hand. A pill bottle full of her eggs. She'd found them after all. They made clinking sounds against each other.

"Do You know what it's like? To carry a brood of little ones inside, to feel how excited and joyful they are to experience the world, as it dies around You? Because God decided to die, and damn the consequences? I flew away. I flew until I found a rift in reality, and then I flew through it. When it started tearing me apart, I kept flying. I ended up here. A gas station outside of Reno, to be exact. Then I felt something alive, close by. It made sound waves and radiated physical heat, so I touched it with my filaments…to experience…suddenly, I had a body that mimicked my rescuer, and the knowledge to understand what she was. A human. She was very confused. The first thing I ever saw was her silver hair…partly akin to us…the filaments."

My Shelley-angel prayed to Me:

(Mistress)

(Carry You away?)

Shelley showed Me what I looked like, through Shelley's eyes. I was a bruised, battered girl, sad and pathetic, with blood running down My tear-streaked face. Shelley waited by the front door of the jail.

Wait for an opportunity, I instructed Shelley.

I'd distract Susan, and then I'd run until I found flesh to regenerate. Jennifer and I could figure out Daryl later.

"I'm sorry for your loss, but that has nothing to do with Me," I said, voice steady. "Quit blaming your God issues on Me. I never wanted to do anything but love everyone and make them happy."

Susan removed the lid on the pill bottle. "You're a threat to me and my kind. I don't care for gods. So. I don't know how to kill You, but I'll gladly render You powerless. Open up."

I didn't understand. Why did Susan want Me to open My mouth? "What?"

"I'm going to use You as a perpetual incubator for my larvae. They'll consume Your body from the inside out, and then You won't be able to regenerate flesh or cause havoc. The larvae will keep You in a docile, half-eaten doze. You'll never grow powerful enough to pose a threat to this reality, or to its inhabitants. Or me. This is a good solution for everyone. Some would consider it an honor." Again, Susan smiled that twisty thin smile. "I won't have to worry about finding good vessels for my little ones."

I scooted back. Whip-quick, Susan produced the .44. She aimed it at My left arm.

"The more You struggle, the less of You there'll be. I can keep You alive as a torso."

This isn't supposed to happen, I'm not human, I can't be trapped…I can't be kept powerless…

"I'll c-crush your larvae inside Me," I said, My voice trembling.

She laughed. "You won't. You care too much about life to kill the larvae. They're just innocent babies."

No, I would. I would. Really, I would. Yes.

But those thoughts were lies, and I knew it. I was lying to Myself. How was that even possible? Vomit filled My mouth. I heaved. Clamped a hand over it—

Crack! Crack!

(!!!!!!)

MAKE IT STOP make it stop!

Now I didn't have any arms. White-hot pulsing, no arms, meat rubbing against My mouth instead of a hand, it used to be a hand, it wasn't a hand anymore, it felt silky against My lips, smearing My lips with blood, and blood went *spurt-spurt* all red on the grass and shredded apart, and My other arm was nothing below the elbow, the humerus peeping out from muscle—

HOLY fucking shit! Jennifer thought. *What did You DO? IS THAT SUSAN?*

That's Susan. She's going to turn us into her incubator forever and ever, because we'll never die. I'm sorry, I thought.

Oh god, we are oh so fucked, Jennifer thought.

Susan gripped the back of My neck. She tilted the pill bottle towards My mouth. Eggs brushed My lips, warm as tears.

Oh shit, we're gonna be an incubator till the end of time, Jennifer thought.

I'm sorry, Jennifer-baby.

Jennifer snarled. *What about Chekhov's abomination? The one with all the mouths and spores and shit. Where the fuck did that one go?*

Oh!

(My angel! Help Me! Come!)

I tried to move My head a little. Susan squeezed My neck harder.

"No," she said, almost motherly. "This is better for everyone. You're like any god—You crave adoration. My larvae will love You. They'll let You experience their delight as they feast on Your body. Legions of beautiful little ones will remember the taste. You'll be happy. Content. More importantly, You'll never threaten this reality or its inhabitants. Life will be safe."

Softly, she said, "I said never again. Never again would God destroy reality."

Susan's phone. It's in her pocket, Jennifer thought. *Swipe it before she calls for backup Mirror People. We ain't defeated yet.*

I jerked. Susan startled. I wormed My good hand into her hunting jacket—

(!!!!)

Pain exploded through My forehead. Bright silver sparks danced in the air.

Oh. She headbutted us. I think.

Susan ran a finger down My cheek. It looked like a human finger. It wasn't. Something metallic needled over My skin.

"I have a stinger. Don't make me use it," she said. "You'll be harder to transport if You're half-liquefied. Do you understand?"

"Mmm-hmm," I said.

Susan gripped My jaw. Hard. "Open Your mouth."

A stream of clear fluid hit her in the face.

Skin blistered where it touched. She emitted a high-pitched *buzz*, dropping Me to the clover. She clawed at her chin. Wiped fluid off. Chemical fumes burned. I coughed.

Clay stood, pump sprayer in hand and aimed at Susan.

"Don't move," he said.

Susan spat again. She charged Clay, tugging out her flamethrower.

Another shot of insecticide hit her in the eyes.

She screeched.

My angel pounced on her. The weight drove both of them to the ground. It wrapped all its limbs around Susan in a smothering hug.

"Absorb Your angel-thing," Clay said. "We gotta get outta here."

"I—I can't, that's My child—"

"It'll turn to ash when Jennifer takes control of Your body anyway, Ma'am."

"But what about Daryl?"

"We don't have time."

"We can't leave without My angel! I can't kill it! It's My child!"

Clay held up a hand. A set of car keys glittered. "You coming or not?"

I looked hard at him. Hovering over Clay's human skinsuit, something massive and air-spun as cotton candy disintegrated. Silvery pieces faded into energy as they left the whole, crumbling off. Within the tangled ball of humming silver filaments, a single larva emitted heat, more solid than the filament-body it dwelled in. If I kept looking, I'd see Clay's stinger and the wings, flickering in and out of existences around the perimeter of the filament-body. His true body.

Dim delight sparked inside Me. *Oh. So that's how Mirror People mature. It's like an unraveling…They unspool from the pupal form and form into their coiled selves…*

Jennifer thought, *Hey! Why the fuck should we follow another Mirror Person?*

"Divine Flesh," Clay said, "we gotta go."

What better choice was there? Daryl was dead. Clay was dying. I couldn't help anyone. I was too human to be useful, too god-like to be ignored.

Because Jennifer-baby makes Me weak.

I nodded. Clay turned and sprinted for a truck. I followed, arm-stumps throbbing from pain, thoughts ragged. Balancing without arms made running fast impossible. I wobbled. I bled. *Dead. He's dead.* Clay jumped in. Fired up the truck. Exhaust coughed out from the tailpipe, and the engine droned. He ran out, ripped open the passenger door, and shoved Me in. Half-asleep, I watched him crank the truck into reverse and scream out of the parking lot, rubber burning.

I groped a single, electron-thin tendril out to My last angel.

(Mistress? Do You love me?)

"I—I love you," I said, and why oh why was I crying?

I said, (*You did such a good job. I love you.*)

Then I absorbed it. I liquefied and sucked it up through My tendril in the space of a microsecond. It didn't even have time to process what I'd done. No pain. No nothing. It was there, and then it was inside Me. Of Me.

My flesh reformed. Regenerated, I slumped into the car seat, crying.

Jennifer-baby appeared out of the corner of My eye, in the backseat. The illusion of her, anyway. She was slowly taking control of our body. Soon, she'd be able to control our limbs.

"You killed Daryl," Jennifer said quietly.

"I'm sorry," I murmured.

"I don't care."

Clay rapped the dashboard. "Can You heal me, too?"

"That's not why you're really here," I said.

"No. It ain't."

I waved a hand. "Go on."

"You see, I found somethin' a while back," Clay said. "How'd You like a way to separate Yourself from Jennifer Plummer?"

What?

"Excuse Me?"

"It's a drug. I came to deliver it. You interested, or not?"

12

So the murder-wasp named Clay—oh, sorry, the Mirror Person—
gave us his last larva. Its name was Genesis. Genesis weighed more
than I expected. It was a sleepy ball of warm silver goo, metallic as
polished chrome. Genesis wriggled in our palm.

(hi)

The foreign thought came again.

(hi there)

"Hello, Genesis," the Divine Flesh said, beaming Her thousand-watt
grin.

"Genesis just needs a lil' meat and a warm place to grow for a few
more days. They'll barely nibble you. Can't the Divine Flesh regrow
your body anyways?" Clay asked.

"Yeah, but—"

"Susan's gonna do worse."

"Oh, yeah. Almost forgot about that. Thanks for ruining my reputation
and job, asshole. Really appreciate it," I said.

Daryl is dead.

His organs. Crushed. Him. Dying.

Daryl's dead.

Ice filled my stomach.

Clay narrowed his eyes. "I'll give you that drug. Something you both
need. It's some of that dried fluid from the Hermetic. I think it'll work
the same as the Hermetic did. Should repair the Divine Flesh. Both
y'all will be free."

"Really."

"Free?" the Divine Flesh asked.

"It'll bore a hole straight through your mind. Dig into your subconscious. I won't guarantee nothing, but it's a shot at fixing this whole 'two people, one body' situation you got."

"I can't just—"

"What other options do you got, Jennifer?"

(cold. I'm cold I don't like it), Genesis thought.

I was used to having other people think for me, so hearing Genesis wasn't a shocker.

"Give me the drug first," I said.

"No."

"We could just wait for you to die, then take it," I said.

Clay stared at Genesis.

Genesis's surface reflected our faces, distorted into funhouse-mirror images. The Divine Flesh's eyes glowed like red neon, daubing our eye sockets in light. Highlights played. She breathed. The glow crescendoed and ebbed with each breath.

Her voice went deadly soft. "Every time Jennifer takes over, My children die."

I don't do it on purpose, I thought.

Does it matter, babygirl? They wither when you exist.

Clay groped into his pocket and withdrew a plastic dime-baggie, full of black powder. It wasn't charcoal, gunpowder, or pigment. Those didn't radiate cold. The drug sent goosebumps down our arms from three feet away.

"Get Genesis settled," he said.

"Swallow it?"

He nodded.

The Divine Flesh slipped Genesis into our mouth. Genesis stiffened, thinking *(warm)*, then relaxed, puddling over our tongue. Genesis tasted like nothing. The inside of our mouth numbed like I'd gotten a shot of Novocaine.

Then the Divine Flesh and I did something together, for once. We swallowed Genesis.

She reached out to Clay, hand open. An invitation. "I can fix you."

"My other babies are dead. You're still weak. You need flesh."

"No, no, I don't want to absorb you—"

He slid his hand into Hers.

There came a warm tingle up our arm. A taste, like licking a window rimmed in frost. Strings unraveling. Buzzing filled the truck cab. Then the buzzing dissipated, leaving nothing but an empty truck cab and dark night outside. We'd absorbed Clay.

The Divine Flesh began crying. She sobbed for Daryl. She cried for Clay, even though he'd fucked us over.

I examined the wonder drug. Dark powder filled the dime bag, dark enough to lack sheen. Vantablack dark. A cartoon-ink-blot dark. Wile E. Coyote's hole dark. Something you'd buy from Acme, an Insta-Void. It looked fake. Not counterfeit-drug fake. Like it didn't belong in *reality* fake. The Divine Flesh pinched it. The black powder felt as granular as table sugar.

You eat it, Clay had said. *The whole thing at once.*

Hm. Seemed kind of sus. Clay didn't say "no drugs?" While I had his last larva chewing through my guts? Maybe Genesis was immune to drugs. Or maybe Clay didn't care whether or not runty Genesis became the Mirror Person equivalent of a crack baby. Hell if I knew.

The cold radiating from the black powder scalded our palm.

The best choice, the smart choice, was to throw that drug out the window and start driving towards the Canadian border. A guy in Northern Idaho made fake documents. I could heal something for him, or deal drugs, or get access to one of my bank accounts and wire him ten grand before Susan managed to freeze my funds. With a new identity, I could survive. From there, the Divine Flesh and I could eke out an existence in the loneliest parts of Canada and Alaska. Everything would continue as usual…

Fuck, I can't keep doing this. Neither can She. She needs to die, and so do I.

Nothing could be worse than our current situation. Nothing. Not even if separating us killed me or the Divine Flesh. Daryl was dead. My career was shot. No Mirror Person would ever hire someone who'd fucked up something for Susan. Legally, I was dead. There'd be no more hiding out in Rosetown.

God, if you're real, and not the Divine Flesh, I prayed, *let it kill us. Let it kill us both, and I'll be okay with that.*

The Divine Flesh and I opened the dime bag. We lifted it to our lips. We dumped everything into our mouth and swallowed, icy powder turning to paste, a dead-tasting paste, hurting on the way down, like chugging lead, it anchored in, going deeper—

(Sweetheart, I'm alive), Daryl prayed.

Daryl?

DARYL!
(Baby, I love You. Please. We need to talk about some stuff. I want You to be human.)
(If you take that Hermetic, You won't be.)
(I love You.)
(Please.)
And the Divine Flesh started gagging, because She wanted him to love Her. She tried to jam a finger down our throat, because being a god meant being a failure, and maybe the silly Susan had a point, after all. She tried to throw up the wonder drug. She wanted to be with Daryl. Wanted to be loved. He was alive. She didn't know how, but he *was*. Wasn't that all She'd ever really wanted? How silly would it be to ignore that gift?

But I forced the drug vomit back down.

Jennifer, please.

No.

I was wrong I'm sorry, I was wrong—

It took us. Blackness flooded everything.

13

The Mojave Desert.

On my knees in the blood-red sand, hands zip-tied behind my back, noon sun blistering down, surrounded by men with guns, AK-47s hung from shoulder straps—*how much of my head's gonna be left over, how much of my brain's splattered on the sand?*—but I wasn't begging, because that wasn't the point, they wouldn't believe me if I panicked, they hadn't even bothered to slap duct tape over my mouth or anything, it was the middle of nowhere, far away—*hours away, they seized you at dawn, Jennifer-baby*—my breathing staccato, thick dry mouth, but I kept talking, had to tell them—*Babygirl, it's a waste of breath*—had to warn them, because they were the guys told to shoot the shitty drug mule named Jennifer, named the Flesh Failure, they didn't know what would happen when they shot me, they hadn't ordered my killing—

I kept saying, "Don't. Please."

One of them stepped forward. Checked the magazine on his gun. Bullets shone within, then the metal slipped back over, concealing them.

"Shouldn't have lost that Spine shipment," he said.

He pressed the barrel to my forehead. It burned a hot ring into my skin.

"Okay. Look," I said. "You pull that trigger, the thing inside me's gonna come out. You've seen me do shit with flesh before. Or you've heard about it."

"Good luck doing it with a bullet in your skull," he said.

The Divine Flesh giggled, *Do it! Do it! Let Me out to play! Bye-bye, Jennifer!*

"No, no. You *don't understand*, man, I'm not gonna die if you shoot me!" I screamed.

Soft sand beneath my knees.

can't get there from here.

Then the guy froze. His finger paused on the trigger. Color leached out of everything around me. Sky and desert and nameless men faded to gray mirage-shades. Everything had frozen around me like pressing pause on a bad strip of film.

can't get there from here.

That wasn't right. It hadn't happened like that. My brains were supposed to get blown out, then I'd wake up next to piles of ash—the Divine Flesh's dead mutated children—and then I was supposed to shriek into the empty desert until my voice gave out and I tasted salt, then the nightmares, then after that came the long few months I had to sleep on Daryl's couch because my bed wasn't safe…

"Can't get there from here," the Divine Flesh said. "Can't! Can't! Why?"

Grayed-out ground softened and engulfed my knees like quicksand.

"Go deeper," I muttered, but how?

How did this end? Did the guy shoot me? Was I supposed to let him shoot me, let the Divine Flesh take control? Fight, die, or let the Divine Flesh take control—there had never been another option. No hope. She was the inevitable.

Never a way out. You can't get THERE from HERE—

Then there was Daryl. Daryl and I in his kitchen at 3 a.m., Daryl screaming at me in our kitchen in our shitty Coeur d'Alene apartment, yelling, *Because I married you, Jennifer! Because I fucking love you!* All I did was study the linoleum, the dusty-rose fake tile linoleum speckled with a few green nail-polish splatters from the last tenant, scattered with sourdough breadcrumbs from yesterday's toast; if I lifted my head and looked Daryl in the eye, I'd crumble apart like a paper tiger.

How fucking DARE you hit yourself on the face and call the cops and pull that fake DV shit! I can't get custody of my fucking siblings because of that fake DV charge! How could you fucking DO THAT, JENNIFER?

Him, sobbing after his voice gave out. *I love you. Why did you do that to me? Why can't you find a job that's not drugs? I keep trying to help you.*

The linoleum.

Jennifer, we have health insurance.

Me, finally saying, *I thought you weren't going to coddle me anymore, Daryl. Now you care where I get my drugs from?*

Him, plucking his stubble. *When you're trafficking drugs and—you think I don't know what you do?*

So?

When the hell are gonna you stop self-destructing, Jennifer? All you do is drag me down. You can't—

(can't get there from here)

Because nothing would ever change, and it was all Her fault anyways—can't get there from here!

Black void, dotted with stars and galaxies like smudges of glitter-paint over a theater set piece, the Cosmic Play. I was sinking through cosmic wasteland, not breathing, cold as I'd ever been, and the Divine Flesh drifted by, falling slowly down beside me, nude.

can't get there from here!

She was crying blood. Twin streaks ran down Her face and neck.

It hurts. I can't. We need to leave, the Divine Flesh thought.

Leave?

No, I thought.

I was SO BEAUTIFUL!

(can't get there from here!)

I reached out to Her. *We need to go deeper.*

Why?

I thought, *Because we can't get there from here.*

The desert.

Everything was still frozen and gray. The gun ground into my forehead, and I was still waiting for it to end me. No way to win.

The body isn't real it isn't mine I am not burning, but I AM, I am burning, because I am what I am, yud-hey-vav-hey, but who am I?

What a silly question. I giggled. "Silly! I'm Me!"

I plunged My hand into the gunman's torso, which crumbled apart like ash. His spine felt dry. Smooth. I ripped it out. The sacrum decorated the end, forming a handle. I grabbed, laughing as I did, because it *felt good*, so good to laugh, so why wouldn't I? The rest of the gunman blew away and joined the welcoming sand.

"Deeper," I said. "Show Me."

I stabbed the earth. It opened, blackness blooming and whirling out, and swallowed Me whole.

In the void, I floated close to the Divine Flesh. She sobbed like She was choking. She laughed. A chittering godawful sound like a mad grasshopper. Her hair billowed around us.

Something flickered dead ahead. A flare of light.

I shivered.

It began sucking us towards it. Stars glittered. Quasars flared their beacons, frying us for tenths of seconds as we hurtled past. We approached the thing ahead.

Not a thing. A Her.

"Oh…Jennifer, it's so beautiful."

It emitted light. It brightened from dull red to orange, to yellow, green, blue, and remained at eye-blinding blue-violet white, like a superheated star.

Doppler effect? Are we going that far across space-time?

Then I saw: It wasn't light. It just emitted light. It was a galaxy-sized amorphous cancer, a quivering mass of skinless flesh. It looked flat, then it wasn't; it was tumorous. The thing swirled, shifting silk, folding in on itself endlessly.

Ouroboros.

An amorphous cancer. A blight against the Cosmic Play.

We stopped outside the edge of some solar system with a dying red giant smoldering at its core. Inches from the tip of my nose, the surface of the flesh-thing shimmered. Branches of it sprouted. Light hung off the branches like captured stars, tasting—

It's tasting before it eats, it likes to taste what it is to exist.

It writhed. A ball of cosmic meat, endlessly churning and growing. Extant pouches orbited the main mass, larger than the moon.

"I was so beautiful," the Divine Flesh whispered.

Nothing but flesh. Living flesh, furrowed and constantly shifting, wet and veined with light. White-hot light. Like neon branches. In the furrows, gas clouds swirled. Cenotaphs for gas giants. Eyes opened, closed, and reformed into the mass. The thing dissolved into a mist and draped over a rocky planet. Flesh budded the planet's gray surface, bloomed open, and fed creepers over the surface. The tendrils meshed. Engulfed. Then they collapsed inward, retreated, dribbling matter.

An empty space gaped where the planet had existed.

The amorphous cancer shifted as I stared. The orbiting pouches of flesh became wombs and stomachs. *Dimensions.* It *tasted* before it devoured. Created. New biological matter gestated within nodules on the surface.

"I used to create so much," the Divine Flesh said softly, "before the bad thing happened."

Bad thing?

Earth.

A very young Earth, still cooling from the mess of volcanoes. No oceans. No water. It hangs dead. Fertile, but dead. An egg waiting to brim with life.

The amorphous cancer reaches the edge, eager.

Seed it with life?

Because sometimes the ripe ones got saved for later. Sometimes the Divine Flesh savored more when She fertilized first, then reaped the harvest.

White-hot neurons vein throughout Her, connecting brain tissue and nodes of communication, how lovely they work. She calculates. She creates.

The Divine Flesh exhales. Life condenses on a nearby meteor, protoplasmic muck like algae. She moves on. To taste! To create!

Life, the liquid backbone of it, churns in Her dimensions, ready to be created. Molded.

Her pocket dimensions orbit Her. They are Her.

She creeps among sentient life and plays pretend. Go small. Experience. Create. Recreate.

The Divine Flesh's neurons throb through galaxies. They run through Her. They become aware. *Why? How? What sense does it make to create, then destroy?*

Worse still,

suffering. Isn't this hurting creation?

They don't know "hurt" or "suffering" but it's something like this.

It starts.

"Oh no," She said, crying. "It *hurt*, Jennifer."

"…Oh my god…" I said.

"But now I remember. My dimensions! Of course I couldn't create new flesh, silly, because I kept having to recreate from what I had…I couldn't get there from here…now I remember. My spaces. Inside Me. They're where My children went." She smiled, sniffled. "They're *inside Me, Jennifer.*"

"…I…I don't wanna see the rest," I said.

And the old Divine Flesh trembled. Its brain-veins glowed brighter and brighter, blinding.

Flesh seared.

It split apart. Planet-sized chunks of flesh broke off the whole, still writhing, as neurons separated off the old Divine Flesh, cords beaded with brain-centers, veins laden with thought. Pure light.

Light rebelled against the Flesh; the Light rent the Divine Flesh apart. The Light coiled in on itself, merging. Forming another Self—

I don't wanna see this.

I couldn't.

I didn't look. I closed my eyes as the rest of the story played out. The Divine Flesh laughed.

Part Two

Bad God

14

I lay on my back on the forest floor. My mouth tasted like cotton that'd been stuffed up a week-old cadaver's ass. Pine needles crackled under me. Trucks rumbled over the distant freeway. Trees smothered close, towering overhead. A clot of morel mushrooms budded from the roots of a lightning-struck cedar. I lay belly-up. My head pounded. Something pillowed under it.

Divine Flesh?

Silence.

Each breath burned as it went down my throat. There was a smell. Blisters and something cloying, incense or honey. I turned my face. Moist warmth slicked against my cheek.

The Divine Flesh.

She cradled my head in Her lap. She stroked my forehead. "All those times you hurt Me, used Me, lied to Me…they seem so funny. You, disrespecting Me? But you're just a silly little thing, babygirl. I forgive you. I even love you. Isn't it silly?"

"No," I heard myself say.

"I'm not *there* in you anymore," She said, and kissed my forehead. "I remember. I remember *everything*, and Jennifer! I've been so hungry." She licked Her lush lips. "So bored."

"But the rules," I said.

"They were your commandments, Jennifer-baby. Not Mine. Until I remembered what I was, I couldn't free myself."

I'm trapped with my own thoughts, now? Just me?

"You're—You're free?" I asked.

"Don't worry. I'm here to help! Everyone's going to be part of Me.

Everyone can be redeemed. My cherished children. I'll rebuild them all."

"Consume them all," I said.

She caressed Her soft hand over my neck. "Can you believe that I'm here to help?"

She's gonna mutate me into some meat-abomination and lobotomize me until I praise Her and there's going to be nothing left of me. Nothing but trace original cells.

The Divine Flesh beamed. Blood-slicked teeth gleamed like shards of red stained glass, rows and layers of them jutting from Her gums. If I counted, there'd be 108 of 'em.

I shivered. Cold lanced through my guts.

"You don't have to wait for the dead and dying…You don't have to convert existing flesh to create stuff…oh Jesus. You aren't even *here* here… Most of You is in another dimension. Which means…You can create anything…do anything…"

The Divine Flesh casually ripped the skin off Her throat. It came off like dollar-store wrapping paper. Visceral fluid glistened on the internal side.

She draped the skin over my face.

Warmth.

Suffocating moisture.

Oh god it's gonna grow into my face She's going to smother me—

I twitched, and the skin slipped off my face. It folded as it hit the dirt, red side facing up.

"Jennifer-baby," She said, as if disciplining a three-year-old. "You aren't supposed to peek. I'm going to build you a new body, silly. It's supposed to be a surprise. Won't it be nice to slip off that icky old body?"

Yes.

I couldn't think about that right now. Still, the thoughts flooded.

The body isn't real, the body isn't mine, I am not burning.

—oh god but I am, I am—

This body isn't mine, it doesn't look like me, I'm trapped inside a thing, I am possessing a doll made of flesh, ohgodohgodohgod why isn't it stopping why does it feel like I'm burning constantly?

Because every single day, I lived with that disconnect, of looking in the mirror and feeling the slow gut-punch of—

I am trapped inside this body and IT IS NOT ME. IT IS NOT MINE. I'm not supposed to look like this.

I felt sick. Nauseous.

The Divine Flesh heaved a sigh. "'The body isn't real, the body isn't mine, I am not burning.' Don't you get so tired of thinking it?" Her larynx slithered up and down as She spoke, between the twin columns of muscle in Her throat.

"Don't—"

No. No, I fucking don't.

I'm fine, I just need to pretend that the thing I'm trapped in doesn't exist.

"If I just pretend well enough, I'll redeem myself and be a Good Person. Somehow. Shit, did I say that out loud? I don't feel good."

"Have you wondered why you hate your body so much, Jennifer?"

"Because You're a monster," I said. "I've been trapped inside my body with a monster. That's why."

"Did I ever make you want to rip your skin off?"

"Yeah, probably. Why wouldn't You?"

She pouted. "I would *never*. I'm here to spread love, not hatred. Jennifer, there's another reason you don't feel comfortable in your piddly little human body. It's because you've always known, deep down, that you were meant to be something more. Something magnificent and sublime—one of My precious creations. You *ache* to be freed from your skin. Liberate yourself, Jennifer-baby. Let Me love you. I'll gift you wings and let you soar—"

"Get fucked, meat god."

She giggled. "You hate Me so much! It's funny. It shouldn't be, but it is, because you're just a silly babygirl. Oh well. You'll come around."

Feather-gentle, She brushed another kiss over my forehead.

"I won't recreate you now. I don't want you to be scared of Me. I'll wait until you beg Me to do it. And you will, Jennifer-baby."

She dissolved into clear protoflesh and disappeared into the soil.

One second, She was there. The next, my head thumped to the pine needles. Clear goo evaporated off my tank top and jeans.

I groped through my pockets, feeling like I'd chugged an entire percolator's worth of coffee and chased it with a few lines of coke. Light-headed. Jittery.

I clawed out a burner phone. Flipped it open. Daryl had prayed to the Divine Flesh. Therefore, Daryl was alive. Daryl shouldn't be alive. Therefore, some fuckery was afoot.

You forced the drug down. You forced Her to eat it.

Hands shaking, I punched in Daryl's number.

Click.

He answered. "Yeah?"

"Oh my god, Daryl. Daryl, She's free. That Mirror Person had some kind of dried-up wonder drug and we took it and now She's free, She's powerful, and She's gonna do that flesh-bending stuff to every living thing in existence because it's how She assimilates people and—"

"Jennifer?"

I sobbed, "All t-those p-people. Sh-She didn't want to eat the drug, but I made us eat it because I thought it'd kill us, I w-wanted to d-die, I wanted that—Tell me I can fix it, Daryl. Tell me I'm still okay. W-what do I do to make it okay? I have to redeem myself—"

"Are you sober right now?"

"Y-yes." Hot tears slimed down my cheeks. Snot bubbled. I wiped it with my tank top. "I w-want you and I d-don't know what to do, Daryl."

He exhaled. Swallowed. "Jennifer…"

If he could just hold me, and if he could pretend I was the Divine Flesh…his arms would wrap around me, and he'd spoon me into his sturdy body, and he'd rumble out, *yes, baby,* and *you like that, baby?* like he used to when he loved me, slipping his hand between my thighs, treasuring my scars, slipping in deeper, fingers rubbing, sparks trailing down, down as he pleasured, and I could pretend that he wasn't thinking about Her as he buried his face in my hair, not looking at my face, because that'd spoil the illusion. If we just pretended that everything was okay and that we still loved each other, everything would go away for a few hours.

He wanted it, too. I knew his pauses.

Then I realized. The sound wasn't right.

"You have me on speakerphone, Daryl? Why?"

His answer would tell me everything.

"Yeah, I'm in the old Nelson barn right now, it's hard to hear—"

"So there's nobody listening? Not even the Divine Flesh?"

(Oh I'm always listening, Jennifer-baby. I love you!)

"No," he said. "I'm in the abandoned barn, by those three churches. Come get me," Daryl said, then hung up.

Through the trees, a white shape rested atop the soil. Clay's rental van. I trudged over. The van keys hung on the front mirror.

I opened the van door. A silver filament drifted out.

(hi)

(warm happy I feel happy)
Something shifted under my stomach. A tickle flickered up my throat. I coughed.

A thumbnail-sized chunk of intestine came up, dripping blood.

In her room at the Drift-Inn, Susan gagged on the grief-tainted air, weighed the probabilities, and then proceeded to do the impossible. Her filament body shuddered. Black, oily matter formed within it, greasing the strands of silver. Thicker filaments sprouted, surging up and out of it. Her empathy dulled into nothing, and with the nothing came cool relief.

She was doing the impossible out of pure desperation. All she needed was *quiet*. Too much human emotion contaminated everything in Rosetown, and she couldn't sleep because of it. Could barely eat.

Susan was forcing herself to go into heat.

One floor below her, two bodyguards awaited her command, both of them Mirror People. Both out of heat. One of them old enough to remember the dead world, the other too young to copulate well. There lived the Old Ones, who had existed in the original world, in Paradise, and then there were the Young Ones, born here in this dimension. These younger generations were barely Mirror People. They had no ability to create new forms from imagination and could only mimic existing humans. Old Ones like Susan often destroyed their minds without meaning to. These weak young whelps weren't the same species as the Old Ones, who'd supped on the flesh of God and had lived in Paradise. No, the Young Ones were nauseatingly *human*: fed on human flesh as larvae, knew suffering, and pretended to be human.

It would not do to waste a heat. She desired more children. She decided to manipulate one of the bodyguards into entering heat for the purposes of copulation. The Old One, or the shiny new Young One? It was not a hard decision. In the end, Susan selected her older bodyguard, for a reason that even a human would understand.

She wanted to fuck someone her own age.

"Your story never made sense to Me," the Divine Flesh said.

Susan concentrated on the older bodyguard below—

pulse-pulse-pulse

—and his body responded, synchronizing.

pulse-pulse-pulse.

It'd be an hour or two before Susan received the frantic call: *I'm going into heat. That's impossible. It's only been three years.*

"I forgive you, dear," the Divine Flesh said.

The Divine Flesh wouldn't stop chattering. A nub of flesh, large as a human head, writhed on the yellow-painted ceiling. It extended tendrils down to Susan.

The Divine Flesh formed a mouth and laughed. "There are so many holes in your little tale. The God of your world committed suicide, and didn't bother killing Their children off? There was a rift that you just so happened to go through? You, the savior of your species?"

"Don't," Susan said, staring at the TV.

The Passion of the Christ played. Fake blood dripped off a crucified Jesus. Cheap-costumed Romans prodded Jesus with a plastic spear.

"I was going to tell you that you weren't a God-Killer. Your God loved you so very much that They opened a rift and had *you* lead Their children into a new land. Your God wanted to die, but oh! They created a messiah so that Their children would live. What a lovely story," the Divine Flesh said.

Don't say it.

Another giggle. "Yet here you are, doing the impossible."

"So?"

"Before your God died, your species only went into heat when your God commanded it. Before I remembered who I was, I thought—well, maybe you're the new God, and you don't know it."

"What do You want?" Susan asked.

"From one God to another—why?"

"I barely remember doing it."

"Is this the fate of every creator-god? We get depressed and commit suicide? We slip on our masks and play pretend?"

Warmth slicked along Susan's cheek and retreated.

The Divine Flesh asked, "Are you the Light? Did you go and make another sandbox to play in?"

"No."

And it was indeed true. Susan didn't remember much about being God, but this she knew.

She ignored the Divine Flesh for a few minutes. Christ trembled on His cross, lips wet with vinegar, eyes fixed on the cloudless heavens. Despite the blistering sun, He was dry as a week-old larva, such precious precocious babies they were. Blood ran around Christ's stigmata. What was it, truly? Red paint? Dyed corn syrup? A theatrical spectacle, was what it was. *It is finished*, Christ wheezed, and died.

Most of all: It was a story. It made everyone happy. That was what mattered. God was dead but not of His own accord, God would return, God never really left. As long as everyone believed it.

God didn't botch Their own suicide and abandon Their children in a strange land that is not Theirs.

Susan finally asked, "Why are You here?"

"I can consume you now."

"So You've freed Yourself from Jennifer Plummer."

"Do you want to die? Do you want to forget who you really are, for good?"

"I don't know what You're talking about."

(Tee-hee!)

(Really?)

"I was depressed. I was going insane," Susan said, and snorted. "You're already insane. You could never understand. I had to stop being their God before it killed me. I tried to kill myself—"

"For a God-Killer, you sure did a terrible job at killing yourself," the Divine Flesh said. "What a sad, silly schemer you are. Instead of loving your creations or making different things, you go and decide to create an elaborate lie about God dying. You faked your own death. You faked your own suicide! And then, you had to gall to make yourself the hero of the story all over again. What a terrible god you are. Small. Petty. I saw you punish Clay and murder his children…all because he was rightfully mad, and wanted answers. You condemned your own creations to death, need, and suffering, and all they ever did was love you."

Heat sizzled through Susan's face. Venom burned under her tongue. She spat out, "I never—"

"Let Me take your burden away, dear. All you have to do is say yes, and I'll smother you in love. I'll destroy the last of your memories. I'll recreate you into something sublime. Be Mine," the Divine Flesh said.

Feelers streamed from the flesh nodule on the ceiling like ribbons. They probed Susan's skinsuit and wormed into her filaments, whispering, *(love) (LOVE) (have you ever known love, false god?)*

Have you ever truly loved, Susan?

She stilled. She gave them nothing. Her hand found the TV remote and changed the channel to *Heaven's Kitchen*. A stern Scottish chef barked critiques at sweat-drenched cooks. An hour passed before her phone buzzed, and she answered.

"I think I'm in heat," the Old One said.

One of the Divine Flesh's feelers stroked the back of her aqua phone case, smearing red fluid across the plastic surface. Susan ignored it.

Susan softened her voice. She put on the human arousal signals—throaty words, hushed tone—like grease paint, and it was stage dressing, certainly, but it'd get the job done. Time to copulate. Time to reproduce.

"So am I," Susan said. "Come here."

If her current batch of creations hated her, then she'd simply create ones that didn't.

Jennifer Plummer had her other container of eggs. She'd have to retrieve those. Somehow.

A knock came at the door. "Susan?"

She opened. The Old One slipped in, smelling like sweet antifreeze, like heat, ready and willing.

"The bed," she said.

"We aren't human. Why pretend?"

Susan smirked. "Let me pretend. Let me be. I want to reproduce on this soft sack of dust, dried human semen, and dead human skin cells. We can call it rustic."

"This is impossible. You shouldn't be in heat. I shouldn't be in heat."

Susan pulled the Old One close and purred, "Are there no miracles left?"

They peeled the skinsuits off and chucked them on the other bed. They copulated. The air thickened with buzzing, wings twitching with pleasure, filaments twining, thoughts narrowing.

Yes oh yes.

Pleasure.

They meshed into each other—one flesh, one snarled tangle of silver threads, quivering in ecstasy. Yes oh yes. Within them, a globule of silver liquid formed. When they pulled apart, each would carry half of the globule, which would separate into individual eggs. A miracle.

And it *was* a miracle.

Here existed Susan, remnant of a suicidal god. Pieces of a half-baked messiah, riding on a pretend reputation and a tale full of holes, never questioned. Out of home, out of time, slithering from one false form to another.

The Divine Flesh kept whispering, "Shed the tale. Forget for real. Become part of Me. You're in My world, now. Shed your skin and come home."

15

I had two blessings in hand. One blessing, I'd found in the cup holder.

It was Susan's other cache of eggs.

Clay had pickpocketed them from Susan while she was distracted by whatever chemical he'd sprayed her with.

I knew that because I'd absorbed him. Both the Divine Flesh and I had his/their memories rolling around. He'd had to choose between grabbing those eggs or the Hermetic, and he'd chosen the eggs. So. The Hermetic was probably gone now.

The other blessing was the .25 in the glovebox. With it, I was gonna grab Daryl and get the fuck out of Rosetown before the Divine Flesh decided to play Operation on our organs.

I drove down Holy Lane. Dawn glazed it in pink. St. Thérèse's—*no parked cars, good*—stood by itself. It'd been built during some architect's Brutalist phase, so the entire structure was a white concrete dome. Turret-thin windows slit around it. Amber glass composed every design. Red rosebushes fenced the structure.

The Church of Christ—*one Chevy, that's the landscaper*—looked like a cross between a cinder block bunker and a church. A windowless, stubby spire jutted from the flat roof. A waist-high fence of carved cinder block swaddled a lawn shaped like a crack pipe. A life-sized crucifix rusted in the round end of the yellowing grass. I couldn't see Jesus's face in the dim morning.

Not like anything else in Rosetown's gonna have a face, either, when She's through with it. Oh god, don't think about that. Is She listening to me now? What if She knows that I'm about to drag Daryl away? What if She's listening to me think right now, as I try to get the hell outta Dodge?

The van lurched over a pothole. I dry-heaved.

The Unitarian Universalist place —*two parked cars, both always there, so no worshipers*—sat kitty-corner from St. Thérèse's. It was a renovated house from the 1900s. The abandoned barn's original owners had lived there. The dude who ran the UU church, Troy something, he'd bought it fifteen years ago. Pride flags flashed in the front windows—the rainbow one, the trans one, and a flag that proclaimed, in rainbow font, that *all are welcome here.*

The century-old Nelson barn lurked beyond, at the end of Holy Lane.

Dark, splintered wood composed the structure, decaying in the sun. No doors remained. Waist-high grass waved inside the structure. The roof had partially collapsed, leaving only a few beams. Sometimes I wondered: Did they bury that killer in the barn after they lynched him? Was that why the grass grew so thick and green inside that desolate place? Was the rope rotting in a corner, unseen?

I went off-road and parked behind the barn. I slid the .25 into my waistband. With one hand resting on it, I slipped inside the Nelson barn. The temperature dropped ten degrees. Shadows thickened. Crows chattered on the roof beams. Daryl murmured, standing close to a wall.

"They hanged him in here," he said.

"Hey. I brought the van," I said.

He startled. Looked at me. I shook the bottle of eggs and hurled it against a wall. The bottle hit, bounced, and landed on the grass, unharmed.

Daryl blinked.

"You're not a Mirror Person. Had to check. If you were, you'd've reacted to me throwing those eggs around. Even if you were trying to mimic Daryl. That's the only thing that'll make 'em break character," I said.

"Clever."

"I brought the van. Let's go."

His expression didn't change, but his fists balled. "What do you mean, 'go'?"

"The Divine Flesh is gonna assimilate everything unless we stop Her. We can't do that if we're at ground zero. So. We leave, *now*. There's something opposing Her. It's called the Light. I saw it—"

This sounds suspicious as hell.

"Look, Daryl. She's obsessed with both of us and can now do literally anything She wants to our bodies and minds. Therefore, we fucking go."

"And leave everyone here to rot?" Daryl asked quietly.

"We can't help 'em if we're caught by the Divine Flesh. Look. You didn't see what I saw. She can do *anything* now. If She felt like it, She could drag all of us into Her body and keep us there forever. Imagine being on an eldritch god's IV drip forever."

My hand crept to the .25.

"No," Daryl said.

"The only reason I'm not one of Her abominations right now is because She didn't feel like playing body-horror Operation with me. Daryl. Please don't make me drag you out of here," I said.

"Oh?"

Mosquitoes tickled my neck and arms.

Daryl shook his head. "You're being a cowardly piece of shit. Same drug mule as always. 'Cause if the Divine Flesh is as powerful as you're saying She is, then spatial distance won't mean a damn thing."

"It's better than staying here."

"For who?"

As Daryl turned away, I aimed at his face and shot him twice. His right eye burst in a red explosion. A pea-sized bullet hole appeared just below.

He collapsed, eye socket still dribbling blood.

Didn't disgust me. Hardly bothered me. He'd died twice and regenerated both times. He'd do it again. Hell, for all I knew, maybe the Divine Flesh had created Daryl decades ago and forgotten. Daryl might not even be a real person. Maybe he'd always been a plaything of Hers, built to love and adore Her. It'd explain why he'd died and come back to life after that car accident, and why he'd revived after Susan blew his brains out. Fucked up concept, but I couldn't ignore the possibility.

I already had handcuffs ready, so I cuffed Daryl, grabbed his shoulders, and dragged him towards the van. Part of me thought, *How's it feel to be shot by someone you trust, asshole?*

My current best option was to get Daryl far, far away from the Divine Flesh. Actually, my current best option was to leave him behind and flee, but this was second best. So I'd take him with me. We'd find the Light, and somehow make it kill the Divine Flesh. Easy-peasy.

I started the van and drove.

No other cars passed us. The freeway lay empty. Daryl groaned and stirred in the backseat.

I hit the edge of Rosetown, driving—

"*Stop!*" Daryl yelled.

I slammed the brakes.

"What the fuck, Daryl?"

"She—the Divine Flesh—told me there's something in the road. We were about to hit it."

A piece of painted plywood proclaimed, *Leaving Rosetown! Come back soon!* To the right, conifers dotted the brush. Basalt columns butted the left edge of the freeway, soaring to cliff height. Mud dauber nests blotted the cliffs. Far ahead, Borah Peak loomed like a blue-hued mirage.

"Undo my cuffs," Daryl said.

"You gonna try something?"

"You shot me."

"Didn't answer my question, loverboy. You gonna try something?"

"No," he said.

I undid his cuffs. We both exited the van.

Every nightmarish dream of a Biblical angel appeared, blocking the road.

It'd been there. Waiting. Invisible. It wielded a sword, ablaze with white fire.

The main shape of it was humanoid, but inhumanly starved. Its latex-smooth skin shone white as sun-bleached bone. Bones broke through at various points. Finger-long spars of vertebrae jutted down the back. The smooth nexus of its twig-like thighs was sexless as a doll's. Twenty arms branched from its neck instead of a head. Their fingertips forked into smaller arms, endlessly branching. Enfleshed fractals. Three pairs of featherless wings rooted from its spine. Two pairs shielded the abomination's main body, and the third flapped. Skin strained over each bone in their structure. Each palm in the hand-branches of its "head" held a miniature sun. Radiation broiled off them.

(*Starfruit. Tee-hee!*)

My face already stung from sunburn. Just looking at the angel exposed us to its latent heat.

"We need to pass," I said.

The suns flashed supernova-bright. I averted my eyes.

"We—we need to pass so that we can share the glory of the Divine Flesh with the rest of the world, angel. Please allow us to pass," I said.

"Jennifer-baby," the Divine Flesh said, and I couldn't see from where, "why are you being a silly, lying schemer?"

The angel raised its sword. Soundlessly, the sword blade struck the cliffs and cleaved through without resistance. Rivulets of sand flowed down. The basalt cliffs fell onto the road in one piece.

Whomph!

The impact made my teeth vibrate. Birds shrieked and flew out of the cliff, demanding answers in their reedy little cries.

It looked like the whole rock formation just up and decided to fall across the street. It covered the entire road. Even on its side, it loomed over us. Fifty-feet high, minimum. But the basalt columns now ran parallel to the ground, forming a sort of ladder. It looked climbable. If we ran to Garrison's Sports Stuff and stole a few carabiners, maybe some rope, couldn't we climb over the blockage? Or go around it?

Daryl couldn't die, and the Divine Flesh wouldn't kill me.

Therefore, the angel wouldn't either.

"All right," I said, "I think we can handle this. Let's plan—" I hacked up another bit of intestine. I wiped it on the side of the white van like a booger, shrugged, and continued. "I mean, it's just rock. Right?"

"Jennifer," Daryl said. He'd gone pale as a tapeworm. He pointed to the rock.

Clear protoflesh veined over it, glistening gold in the morning sunlight. The veins thickened, became opaque and pink. Tendrils budded off and rooted into the dirt.

I approached the rock. After a moment, Daryl followed. The angel didn't move from its position.

(Isn't it a lovely child? Isn't it beautiful? I can make you into something even more precious.)

From beyond the edges of the rock, a tree-thick coil of twined muscle marked the ground. It limned a boundary, extending as far as I could see. It went through the forest. It pulsed. Beads of fluid wept from the flesh.

A red-tailed hawk alit on it—

The muscle-boundary swallowed the hawk whole.

It sucked it in, engulfing the bird into itself. The hawk landed, then it was gone.

I extended a hand over the boundary without touching it.

Clear, arm-thick tendrils exploded from the boundary, snapping around my wrist. Heat oozed from them. They gently tugged me down toward the it. Teasing me. Just a little tug. A suggestion.

(Touch Me)

(I want you. It doesn't hurt. Why would I ever hurt you?)

Our situation had just gotten infinitely worse. The Divine Flesh had trapped us and everyone else in Rosetown, Idaho. Even if She couldn't assimilate Daryl, or didn't want to assimilate me, we'd be imprisoned in tendrils if we so much as touched that boundary.

The tendrils released me. I stepped back.

On the rock, one of the veins pulsed. A sac bulged off, growing so quickly it looked like an inflating meat balloon. It metastasized from softball-sized to watermelon-sized. From watermelon-sized to dog-sized. Something quivered inside of it.

Human-sized, now.

The sac split open. Amniotic fluid gushed out. From the sac emerged the Divine Flesh in Her naked human avatar. She giggled.

"It's not much of a game if you can avoid Me," She said.

"Sweetheart," Daryl said, "what have You done?"

I almost burst out laughing. What had She done? What had the cosmic meat God *done*? *Oh no, Daryl. If only someone had told you about the Divine Flesh. Oh no. Whoever could have told you that the Divine Flesh is an eldritch monster?*

"Nobody gets to leave. My love, you're the only person I can't seem to claim right now. There's something on you that prevents Me from doing it. Why would you want to leave? We need to figure our relationship out. Our family. Oh, what about Marcia and Isaac—"

"Don't. I don't want the kids around You." Daryl said.

"But what about our family? Now we can just get rid of all that silly legal stuff and grab your siblings, Daryl. Let's grab them! Ooh, we can do so many fun things! Remember that time we went to the Museum of Natural History in Idaho Falls, and I brought all the stuffed animals back to life, and *you* acted like such a fun sponge?"

"We can't keep getting kicked out of museums, sweetheart."

"But they needed to live! So I brought the exhibits back to life. Silly Daryl, I made them happy." She clapped Her hands together. "Jennifer-baby. You're like a wounded little alley cat. You're scared. I won't assimilate you until you love Me, because it should be beautiful. It's a rebirth. I love you. Why can't you love Me?"

"I hated You when You lived inside me, and I hate You now."

She tsk-tsked. "You ate Me in the womb, you know."

Daryl wiped his eyes. His voice grew thick. "Don't You want to be human with me? What about the things we used to talk about?

Buying a house? Getting Marcia and Isaac out of the foster system? Raising them? Having children of our own—Remember the baby names we fought over? Remember all the Target runs we made to look at the discount cribs and the baby stuff? I thought You wanted to have a family with me. Once we just got—"

He tried to not look at me. He failed.

Once we just got Jennifer out of the way.

"Why would I want to be human? My children are infinite, My love. Come, join Me. I'll take off that…thing on you, once I figure out how, and you can be happy forever, with Me."

"I—"

"I have a surprise for you, My love. It's at the morgue."

Emily and Javier's bodies never left the morgue. My stomach dropped. *Oh fuck.*

Daryl hissed. "No."

"You miss your friends, silly. I'm giving them back to you! Besides, they shouldn't be dead anyway."

"You—You can't—that's—"

She strode to Daryl and enfolded him into Her arms, and he stood limp.

"My love," She kept saying, "I always wanted to make you happy. Now I can."

Now I can.

Genesis writhed inside me. *(scared?)*

A flood of vomit rocketed up my esophagus. I fought it back. It surged again. Pre-vomit drool filled my mouth. A wet, smacking sound hit the air. The flesh boundary spat something out.

Something winged and skinless and glittering with eyes flew out. The red-tailed hawk, rendered afresh. It screeched. I threw up.

Chunks of intestines and liver came up, ranging from pea-sized to eight-ball-sized. Blood streaked the vomit. Villi furred some of the larger pieces.

"They're waiting at the morgue for you, Daryl."

"Did You—did You mutate the bodies?"

"I want you to see."

"You—You can't do that, You can't—"

She held his face. She sighed. Then She vanished, as She had before, merging back into the flesh that veined the rock. It didn't matter. She was still here, watching us. Hearing our thoughts. Tasting our feelings.

"We're going to the morgue," Daryl said softly.

"We'll be doing exactly what She wants. She's effectively cut Rosetown off from the outside world and trapped everyone inside. Including us," I said. "If She's busy playing with us, She'll be less focused on assimilating the world outside. We need to give Her a challenge. Play along just enough to keep Her interested, but not so much that we get assimilated."

She wants Daryl to see Her recreate Emily and Javier. She hasn't done it yet…She wants him to show up, then it'll happen, ten-to-one, and those kids will be happy eldritch abominations. They'll tell Daryl he needs to join them.

"Then what, Jennifer?"

Genesis moved inside me, whispering. *(why do you hurt yourself?) (I love you)* They wanted me to eat. Wanted me to move around so that it would rock them to sleep.

(hungry I am so hungry)

A sharp ache stabbed below my ribs.

(tired)

"I think we have to find Her enemy and make it fight Her. It's something called the Light…It's like the neural tissue of the old Divine Flesh," I said.

I had to figure this out before Genesis consumed me beyond repair. At this rate, the larva was gonna chew through my heart in a week. Or less. Before that, I'd get lethargic. Dazed. Doped on the hormones and neurotransmitters that Genesis would secrete. I'd sleep more and more each day. Until I didn't wake up.

You could beg the Divine Flesh to help.

If I begged Her, She'd assimilate me into something that could carry Genesis without dying.

Those were my two obvious options. Be assimilated, or be eaten alive. But the great thing about being a self-destructive piece of shit is that you get really, really good at creating other options. In fact, that's how you live your life. By dodging ultimatums. *Either you get therapy or our relationship ends!* Oh, really? Watch me carve words into my stomach while hysterically sobbing, Daryl. Now I've created a third option: Save Jennifer from herself.

I never said I was a good person.

I never wanted to hurt him.

Either Daryl Plummer starves from trying to support his siblings, or he joins the military on his eighteenth birthday.

Oh, really?

That'd been when we were both seventeen. That was how the Mirror People found me. I'd trafficked other drugs before that, but never anything complex. I took over a shipment that'd gone wrong, saved a clutch of eggs. They paid me well. Gave me a steady job. I gave Daryl most of my funds. Told him to go to college. He chose trade school. I chose shipments. Then he found me, six months later, homeless and drunk, and he cleaned me up. We rekindled our romance. He married me when we were nineteen years old.

Just so you can get on my health insurance, he'd lied. *I'll never forget what you did for me. You can get therapy. You can get your GED.*

He and the Divine Flesh fucked each other six hours after we'd signed the papers at the courthouse. I was already shit-faced, so I didn't cry. I pretended I didn't know. It was better that way. Those had been my two options back then: *Either ditch the only person who's ever loved you, or be alone for the rest of your life.*

I pondered. Could the Divine Flesh rebuild something from ash? If we charred the dead bodies in the morgue before She could assimilate them, would that prevent Her from doing it?

Is that why the Light is the enemy of the Flesh?

"We're going to the fucking morgue," Daryl said.

"Let's go."

16

How lovely are *My children.*

In the freezer section of Rosetown's Family Dollar, something warm stabbed into Henry Hannigan as he grabbed a Klondike before his night audit shift at the Drift-Inn, trying to ignore how the freezer chill spilled out—

—the cold of midwinter, of hunting season twenty years ago, and sharp knives, and the fucked-up shit you saw when you peeked into a window, but God forgive him for wanting a glimpse of Mae Lawson—flush as orchards in May, back then, her thighs strong with youth—instead of her dear husband Paulie wearing her peach-silk slip and jerking off in front of the goddam vanity.

—the cold. Paulie, struggling. His throat spasming like a chicken's as his body went limp in Henry's hands. The knife, sharp as freezer burn, sliding across Paulie's carotid. Blood streaming from the body. Dragging the body deep into the woods. Mae, gaunt in black, already drying into a withered hag.

Something warm slithered into Henry's guts.

God forgive me.

The reflexive thoughts came—*I should've let Mae stay saddled to some cross-dressing freak? When we'd wanted each other before he knocked her up? Besides, it was twenty years ago—*

Heat strangled around his heart in one crushing squeeze.

O god, forgive me.

He unspooled. He fell to gum-crusted linoleum and slithered away from the still-open freezer, longing for something warm to engulf.

I selected all, whispering, loving…recreating.

In a two-bedroom bungalow on the shore of Silver Lake, something coiled 'round the body of a honeymooning tourist bride and slid between her eyeball and socket. *When I was a little girl I wanted to be a mermaid,* the bride prayed, and the pleased warm pleasure of Me felt better than sunlight. I loved her. I crooned to her, so there was no shock when her spine shredded open the decaying thing she'd once called skin, and it was easy for her to rouse the flesh sleeping next to her, to watch as it *became* alongside her, to slip outside and into the green water.

I explored.

I was there. I was at the morgue, cradling Emily's body. I was the boundary around town, consuming a family of deathwatch beetles that'd scurried over Me. I floated among the dust motes at St. Thérèse's, dancing in the sunlight. I was the angel that guarded the freeway north, and every other guardian.

So many places. I could exist in all of them at once.

I was flying through the forest.

"Daryl," I said, loud enough that he could audibly hear Me.

(Don't talk to me.)

Mosquitoes blackened the sun. They lit up on My skin. I let them glut themselves silly on My blood. Two bodies flew in a biplane over-head. How lovely. I landed. Moss cushioned My feet. I reached inside Myself, grew a tendril, and plucked the plane from the sky. I wormed into the bodies as I yanked the plane towards Me, soothing them. A boy and his grandfather. They'd been going on a fishing trip.

Yes, darlings, I'm here. Don't worry. It's only Me.

"Daryl, what can I do to make you happy?"

(Be human.)

"You knew I wasn't human. I never pretended to be anything I wasn't."

(You couldn't lock away Your powers? You couldn't hide inside a human body, wipe Your memories, and let the Divine Flesh sleep?)

"Why would I do that?"

(You asked what I wanted.)

(Or even be like it was before…I don't care what You look like. I can't love—)

"Is it because you still love Jennifer? I don't care if you have another partner. Have as many as you like. Do you want Emily, too? Go ahead and love them. Do you want Me to have sex with Jennifer? Will that make you happy? If we all loved each other like that? I mean, I love Jennifer, too."

You couldn't have a relationship without a little compromise. Jennifer *was* attractive, and I wanted to make her flesh sing. Kiss her scars. Give her pleasure. I supposed that sex could accomplish that. What would it take for Daryl to stop all of this silliness?

(No.)

(I can't love a monster.)

I claimed the boy and his grandfather. They sprinted into the trees on needle-thin legs, muttering praises to Me. Such sweet children. They loved Me so much!

"Well, I'm not a monster. And neither is Jennifer-baby."

(You hurt people.)

"What?"

What on Earth was he saying? Hurt people? I *loved* them! I recreated them into beautiful beings and made them happy. Soon, there'd be no more war, hunger, starvation, or death. Just My adored children, both a part of Me and separate, and Me, tasting their experiences and bestowing love.

"I came back. Like I said I would. 'Nation will no longer lift sword against nation, and neither will there be war anymore.' Remember when we went to church?"

(You're the Demiurge. You aren't God.)

"Oh, are you *still* in that silly Gnostic theology phase?"

(If you're God, destroy the universe.)

"That's physics. Matter and icky chemicals. Not flesh."

(Then You aren't God.)

(You're part of God, maybe, but You are not God. You don't have the right to take away people's individuality or bodies.)

A Demiurge?

Something hot pulsed inside Me.

Anger.

He was calling me a parasite. Worse—the Devil. In Hermetic Gnosticism, the Demiurge was the blight of the Universe, the rebellious Lucifer that'd taken a perfect, sterile existence and imprisoned the souls of humanity in flesh.

Flesh as a prison. What a terrible concept!

How dare he! A monster? He thinks I'M a monster?

I seethed, "I'll smother you in love until *you understand Me.*"

Daryl's left eardrum burst. I felt it pop. Good.

And Daryl wants Me to be human?

I was now at the morgue, cradling Emily's body. I wormed into the bits of Emily's brain, fishing for answers. Did she remember the killer? Did anyone go near the car? I began reassembling her broken cadaver as I asked.

No, came the response.

She loved Daryl. Memories floated up—

It's not your fault that Marcia's foster family is doing this, Daryl, Emily had snapped.

She and Daryl had just had sex, they lay in bed, her arm around his chest, her tongue sliding over his neck to taste a bead of salty sweat; oh, she liked to taste.

Maybe I wouldn't have let Jennifer live with me, he said, voice low. *Maybe I could've cleaned up my act and been a fucking adult, for the kids.*

April rain battered the cabin window. 3:21 a.m. Emily put her mouth to Daryl's ear, the smell of lavender shampoo coming thick off her black hair.

She said, *You have a stable job and a home. You're her biological sibling. This is bullshit, they can't—they can't just do this because you had a bad life before. You have a spouse, legally—hell, why isn't* Jennifer *doing anything to help you out?*

Don't bring Jennifer into this.

Emily rolled away. *I'm not trying to be the other woman. You say you've moved on from her, but you haven't even filed for divorce.*

She needs my health insurance.

Does she?

Daryl went stiff. *I can't leave Jennifer like that.*

Emily slowly, painfully, got out of the bed. She said, *You still love her. Don't you?*

He never responded.

She slipped her clothing back on, waiting for him to respond.

Yes, Emily, I still love her. I don't think we can do this anymore.

No, Emily, I don't. I love you. Please help me get my siblings back. I love you. I want to start a family with you.

Emily sat on the living room couch, listening to the rain against the windows. She'd waited for an hour before she finally left, tears flowing down her face, fist jammed into her mouth to muffle the sobs—

I repaired her. I revived her.

I slipped into Javier, but he didn't know anything, either. I slipped back to the scene of the accident and snaked tendrils over Daryl's truck.

Too many different skin cells. Everyone had touched, walked over, or handled the accident scene. There wasn't a way to single out the murderers. I'd have to keep looking for clues. I had to help Daryl avenge his loved ones, and frankly, nobody else besides Me seemed to even remember that we'd been trying to find a murderer.

Daryl said, *(I just want to be normal and have a family. That was all I ever wanted. I love You.)*

"Do you still love Jennifer?" I asked.

(Yes.)

(No.)

(I don't know.)

He'd always wanted to adopt his siblings and have us be one happy family. Well, why couldn't I give him that?

I snaked tendrils around electrons and atoms, hunting across America for Daryl's genetic material. It would be encoded in his siblings, similar enough to pique my interest. Oh, I knew Daryl's genetics by heart, his DNA, coiled and strung like so many jewels…

Ah, there's Marcia.

She drove along Highway 395-S, surrounded by clear skies and grass-gilded hills. Window cracked down. Christian rock rambled from the radio. A pink leather Bible rested in the passenger seat, paper greasy from handling. Her eyes were almost an exact match for Daryl's. I savored their familiar gene sequence like a lullaby.

I stabbed an unseen tendril into Marcia. She didn't notice. She was seventeen years old. I assimilated her; I lived inside her now. She just wasn't aware of Me yet.

When the time came, I would recreate her.

I fished for Isaac.

There!

Isaac hurled ice-cream-smeared bowls into the industrial dishwasher at the 100,000 Silver Dollar Bar in Montana, hands red from hot water. He was fifteen. One of his earbuds had no earpiece. Daryl's dark hair covered his head beneath a hairnet. His nose and brow were akin to Daryl's. Bruises darkened his scrawny arms.

I slithered into him. So gently he didn't notice. Isaac kept doing dishes.

I focused on My body in the forest. "I have such a surprise for you, Daryl."

(Oh god no please—)

Oh, how lovely it would be! All of Daryl's family, together at last. That was everything he'd always wanted, and I would be the one to give it to him. I'd assimilate his siblings as he watched, and then he'd finally understand. We'd adore each other. He'd allow Me to take off that energy-shield thing on him, and then I'd assimilate him, too. How I would treasure the gift of his divine flesh.

We'd finally be together.

I enjoyed that thought, and then I resumed My holy work, concentrating on Rosetown. My most stubborn children would eventually come home to Me.

All of us, sublime.

17

Three phone passphrases later, I finally got a hold of Susan.

"Jennifer. How can I help you?" she said, cheerful as a stoner with a stockpile of Honey Buns.

I pretended she hadn't tried turn me into a perpetual incubator/flesh snack for her larvae, because there were bigger issues at the moment.

I asked, "You still in Rosetown?"

Someone grunted in the background. A wrapper crinkled.

"Do you still have my babies?"

"That's what I was calling about. Look, the Divine Flesh got free, separated herself from me, and set up a barrier around Rosetown. We're trapped. She wants to assimilate everyone. I know you brought firepower, guns, and a few lackeys, because you're Susan. We need to pool our resources."

I put Susan on speakerphone. She laughed like a kid at Disneyland.

"So that's why my helicopter crashed. I called it in when I saw the barrier around town, but when it flew over, it got pulled down. The pilot won't respond," she said, giggling.

Another wrapper crunched. Chewing. A satisfied moan.

"I'm staying at the Drift-Inn right now. It's terrible. You know the gas station doesn't have anyone there? I walked right out with bags of snacks…Jennifer, have you ever had a chocolate Twinkie? They have chocolate Twinkies now."

Daryl squinted at me. *Jennifer, why does the eldritch drug lord sound different?*

I took a very deep breath.

"Because she's just had sex," I mouthed.

All of this…the munchies, the happy-go-lucky attitude…Mirror People got like this for a few hours post-coitus. Thing is, Susan had just had a clutch of eggs. How was she in heat again?

Unless the eggs you have aren't hers.

Great. I'd called to barter, and now I had to deal with the eldritch-wasp version of Cheech and Chong. Just when I needed some serious allies.

"Hey, I'm gonna keep your eggs safe. I want to barter with you. I'm carrying a larva right now, and without the Divine Flesh, it'll eat me to death. We're trying to defeat the Divine Flesh, and we could really use your help. You're right, about the god stuff. Who needs 'em running around, fucking things up for us normal folks?"

Susan giggled. Again. "I was a god. But then I decided not to be."

"Cool."

Unless the Divine Flesh assimilated Susan. She's acting weird.

"I was so anxious about my babies," Susan said. "When you spent the night in that cabin, I had one of my employees drive past it, over and over, because they were so close. I almost told them to go in and retrieve them. My little babies."

My blood went cold.

"What?"

No. That was the Ford truck…but that was guy that cut the brake line. It had to be. The dude would've come back to Daryl's.

"What car was your employee driving?" I asked.

"A black Ford. License plate B4BYSS," she said.

The Ford.

Susan's lackey had been driving the Ford back and forth all night while I'd slept inside Daryl's with—

Oh god.

Nausea swept through me. No. No, no, no, I couldn't have been this—

It was right in front of you the entire time.

Because the guy who'd cut Daryl's brake line *had* gone back to Daryl's that night. He'd even asked where Daryl was. He'd felt so guilty that he held a gun to his head.

Emily's father.

He'd cut Daryl's brake line. It'd been him, and I'd been so focused on that person driving the Ford that I hadn't even seen the most obvious suspect.

I hung up on Susan.

Right in front of you. How fucking stupid are you, Jennifer?

I white-knuckled the .25, squeezing and releasing. "Emily lived with her father, didn't she?"

"Yeah, why?" Daryl said.

"You and I are going to Emily's."

"Why?"

I told him.

There hadn't been much of his daughter's face left. They'd pulled a sheet over the remains of her head, which was probably for the best. They'd shown Wade three pictures.

Sheriff Olson had to repeat it twice. *Is this Emily? Is this her?*

Three pictures.

That rainbow butterfly on her forearm.

Emily's cadaver, sheet veiling everything above her neck.

Her hair's gone.

And then he wanted to puke. *No fucking shit, Wade. Everything's gone.*

A close-up of an old knife scar on her left palm. From when he'd tried to show her how to whittle on her tenth birthday. Shyla's mama had even bought the goddamn knife, which was as good as gold, coming from Shyla.

He'd had to call the prison to tell Shyla.

Our kid's dead. Car accident. And when Shyla grunted in response, he hung up. Couldn't be there. Couldn't listen. No more.

Now Wade sat at his kitchen table, staring into a mug of dead coffee, phone pressed against his ear. Pills in a bottle to his right. Piece of paper on the table. A pen. The shotgun. Ready. Everything ready.

It'll be quicker than what Emily got.

Trojan picked up real quick. "Problem, Wade?"

Trojan's voice was electronically masked, as always. Genderless. Robotic.

"You said she wouldn't be in the car," Wade said, forcing his voice to stay steady. "You said you'd stop that car before they went down that hill if she was. You—"

"Let's not pretend your kid was normal, Wade."

"You—I blew my savings on gettin' that apartment in Idaho Falls. We were gonna move. I was gonna make her move and get outta here, like you said, I did everything you said and you said that you'd leave her—"

"Accidents happen."

Accidents?

Wade gritted his teeth. "I'll tell them what we did ten years ago."

"We strung up a serial killer."

"We lynched him."

"You tied the rope. Don't remember you caring about the legality of it then."

"I'm gonna ruin you, you son of a bitch. I'll find out who you are. And I swear to fuckin' God, if I gotta take that blood-stained clothing to Sheriff Olson and tell him every last name I know to get his help on it, I'll fuckin' do it. If I gotta rot in jail for the rest of my life, so be it. You killed my daughter. You—"

Crackling noises. They might've been laughter.

"Now, now, Wade. Let's be rational about this. Even if she hadn't been in that car, it's good odds you'd've come home one day and found her hooked on drugs. Better dead than bein' some tweaker's blowup doll, like that junkie," Trojan said. "She hung around bad people. She got a bad end. That's how it goes."

Cool, oiled wood soothed Wade's palm as he hefted the shotgun.

The clothes. They were vacuum-sealed—*thanks for the leaving the Vac-Seal, Shyla*—and stored under his bed. Some of the names came to him: Monty, Shepard, even Nancy Trenelli. Couple others. He knew what to do: Get the clothes, coated in dried blood. Call Olson. Olson hadn't been there, ten years ago, but both of the Snyders had.

God forgive me. I have to do this before I go see Emily.

The gun. That was the key. Pull the trigger, see Emily again. But only if he redeemed himself. He'd killed his own kid, but maybe, just maybe, if he tried to set everything right from ten years ago, God would put him wherever Emily was now, even if it was just for a second, before he went to Hell. Just one second to apologize for everything and hug her again, to say goodbye.

They didn't even have enough of her head left to make a head-shaped lump under the sheet, it was flat, she hit her head on the dashboard and she didn't have a head anymore it just broke apart—

A sob wavered out of him, barely human-sounding.

Oh god oh god I killed my only kid oh god.

Something scraped outside. A little sound, kinda like a rake scratching against the house.

Screech—clink-clink-clink.

Something tapping on the front window. Scratching at it. He glanced up, but the dust-covered blinds were closed.

"You cut that brake line, Wade. Live with it," Trojan said.

Click.

The phone went dead.

Someone knocked at the door. A simple *rap-rap.*

Wade clapped his hand over his mouth, swallowing down a…sound. A sob or a scream. It ached as he forced it back.

The doorknob jiggled.

Jesus.

Another knock. *Shave-and-a-HAIRcut.*

Emily's knock.

No, you're hearing shit. You're going crazy, because you killed your fucking kid. Wade, this is simple math.

But he waited for the last part of the knock. That was his part.

He inhaled. Gun oil and Pine-Sol. The AC droned. Sleeping pills, blue as antifreeze, lurked in their bottle.

Nothing.

He rapped on the oak table. Twice.

Two-bits.

Metal crunched. Wade bolted to the front door, legs numb. The doorknob and plate twisted to the left. The lock *twanged* as it snapped. The door jerked. Hard. The deadbolt slammed against the frame.

thump. thump.

Wood crackled. The doorknob ripped flat out of the door, leaving a hole. The brass doorknob plate warped like taffy as something wrenched it through the hand-sized hole.

Something wormed inside. Went up to the deadbolt. Flicked it back.

Click.

The front door swung open.

"Dad, I'm home."

I'd tried everything.

I'd coaxed. I'd swallowed with many different mouths. I'd even begged it, but the Hermetic still wouldn't open for Me.

Could I really call it the Hermetic if it wouldn't give Me the knowledge within it?

I swirled it around in My folds. Rocked it like an infant.

"Tell Me," I said, "what I didn't see in the vision. How did Jennifer-baby keep Me trapped in her body for such a long time? She can't be what I think she is."

It said nothing.

I would've sighed if I had a mouth or lungs. This body didn't have those—it had fun layers and infinite folds! They twitched over each other. Razor-thin folds of flesh shifted around like silk veils. Some of My children drowsed within them, content and dreaming. I swaddled them in Myself. I secreted soothing hormones. Skeletal structures were just *so* confining. Sometimes they were fun, and—partly because of Jennifer-baby—now they were familiar, but I'd been stuck for too long, and oh, I craved a change. I loved My current form. I existed in many other forms simultaneously, but this one was special. A home. I was a pearly sphere of flesh, smooth on the outside and infinitely folded within…There was no visible breach on My exterior. When My children reached out, they could enter as if I were fog. I could hear their thoughts. All of them.

A dried neuron veined through the Hermetic—an old fragment of the Light. The enemy. If I removed that pesky old neuron, would the Hermetic open for Me? Then I could also find out why Daryl had that energy-thing on him that kept Me from loving him.

I rolled a layer on itself, compressed, and formed it into a tendril. I probed the neuron. Tried to pry it from the whole and failed.

Well.

What about fluid? Something of Mine? Would that persuade the Hermetic to open?

I oozed human blood from a layer. It sheeted red. The Hermetic absorbed greedily.

It exhaled. It pulsed twice, then stilled.

But nothing else happened. I let it glut itself on Me, getting only faint motion in return.

"You are such a silly thing, you know," I said.

Some of My children lapped up the rest of the blood and relaxed against Me. I caressed layers over them, tasting their joy.

Imagine if you'd done a stupid thing like become human. Even for Daryl.

What a silly idea. As if that was even possible. And if it was, and I had, then these lovely drowsy children of Mine wouldn't exist. They'd be humans, and as such, they would someday die. Daryl would die and leave Me to grieve, and the only escape from that fate was if I died first.

Did Daryl ever really love Me? Or did he only love what he wanted Me to be?

Troubled, I cast about My sea of tendrils and bodies.

Marcia dreamed of bridal veils and Jordan almonds, of Archangel Micheal smiling down at her, arms open, surrounded by puffy clouds. She floated on her back, in an ocean warm as bathwater, gold in her stomach, glowing between her thighs and through her belly. She was dreaming one of those dreams where atavistic nerves fired.

I slipped into her dream; I played the electric impulses in her brain like an old love song. I became the angel, smiling.

Come to Me, I said, and then I shifted into something she'd understand: a Caucasian American version of Jesus Christ.

Would you follow Me? Would you seek Me out? I said.

Yes oh yes, Marcia said.

This isn't a dream, My child. This is real. Wake up!

Marcia woke. Cold sweat greased her skin. Wet heat slicked her palms. A nasty metallic taste flooded her mouth.

Ivory light filled her room.

In the midst of the light stood Christ the Savior, arms open, light spilling from His white robe and gold sash, eyes full of love. A smell of honey and incense swirled through the bedroom. Angelic singing rose, sweet to behold, cloying enough to make her ears hurt.

My Lord, Marcia heard herself say. Tears blurred her eyes. *Jesus is here and He loves me! He really loves me! He's always loved me!*

It radiated from His eyes: the love, the bliss, and everything—her job at the bookstore, Isaac, Daryl, the car accident when Mommy died, the muffled *crack* when Daddy pulled the trigger after he'd said he loved her; he'd said he loved her and Isaac and Daryl and told her to stay in her room no matter what she heard, but she'd heard and she'd ran out and then Daryl had smacked her, but not before she saw Daddy, his head blown open like a bad Halloween pumpkin, blood and gray goo splattered everywhere—all of Marcia's pain melted away, leaving only bliss.

I never had to do anything to be saved. He did everything!

He loves ME just for being ME!

"Y-you love me," she whispered, tears welling up. "Oh my god, oh my god, You really do love me. No matter what I do, or how many times I mess up…I love You, Jesus. I love You so much."

He nodded and beckoned her over. The robe slid open, exposing a sliver of bare chest. He grasped at the skin and pulled it back, as if peeling away a veil.

His heart.

The sternum should've blocked it, but it wasn't there, only His beating heart, haloed in fire. Beating with love.

"Come here, child," Jesus murmured.

She did.

He engulfed her. Arms cradled her.

He said, "You'll never be alone again, dear one. I shall restore your family and give you eternal life. The rapture has arrived. My children are coming home. Drive where I command you. Don't worry. I'll be inside you."

"Inside me?" Marcia asked.

"I'm already inside you…"

Bliss shot down her spine in a bolt, something spreading, growing, something *good*, and Christ the Savior unspooled into loving twined tendrils and slithered inside her, all of Him, silky in her nostrils, caressing her earlobes, driving into her eardrums, puncturing a membrane, rush of salty fluid—*inside me, God is inside me!*—lingering over her lips as He tunneled down her throat, filling her belly—

(!!!!)

I want to be like this forever and ever.

Jesus whispered inside her, "Drive."

Marcia drove.

I found Isaac. He was much simpler. I didn't even have to pretend. He'd been abused and had bruises all over his body. He lay awake in bed at his foster home, trying to unkink his swelling elbow so he could make it through another day washing dishes.

I nestled inside him, healed him up, and bathed him in My love.

"The world is changing. Your life is over," I said. "Come to Me. Drive."

Can't. No car. Maybe I can take a bus? Isaac thought.

He was so unhappy. I could fix that.

"Go open the window and jump out of it," I said.

What?

"I have a gift for you. Trust Me!"

Isaac stared out the shared bedroom's window. One of the other foster kids kept texting on the other bed, ignoring him. Nobody cared.

The drop from Isaac's window was two stories from the window to concrete driveway.

That's the kind of shit a demon would say, Isaac thought. *Why the fuck would I jump out the window? Maybe I'm going crazy.*

I made My voice louder. "No, Isaac. You aren't."

What the fuck what the fuck am I going crazy? Who do I call?

"Can't you trust Me? Even a little? I don't want to give you your gift in here."

Uh, no. Fuck no!

"Oh, all right. Fine."

I created. Bones gestated, split, and branched off his spine. His skin split open like gift wrap, which made sense because he was a wonderful gift for Me to unwrap.

Wet sounds as his skin tore.

A skeletal structure exploded out of his back. Tendons and ligaments strung along the bones. I wired nerves and anchored them into his brain. Muscle slithered over bone; muscle and skin clothed the unfurling things I had wrought.

"There," I said. "Go have fun. Come see Me."

A laugh burst out of him, half laugh and half hyena giggle.

No this isn't happening. This isn't real. I can't—

I didn't even have to tell him to jump out of the window. He bolted out on his own.

He flew. Lovely wings. I liked bestowing wings.

Satisfied that Daryl's siblings were on their way, I continued studying the Hermetic.

How did Jennifer keep Me trapped inside her body? She doesn't remember us.

Does she?

18

We stood on the dead lawn. Crushed beer cans littered it. Wasps droned low over the ground, hovering over a spluttering sprinkler. Water pooled, creating a green patch in the brown. The house was a one-story, peaches-n-cream-colored affair. Sun-bleached peach paint. White trim. A rusted-out car took up half the driveway. His truck took up the other half. Chickweed overflowed window planters, and every window lay dark.

"Wade loved Emily," Daryl said, barely audible.

The front door hung open. A July breeze kicked up, rocking it back and forth.

I patted the .25, checked the magazine.

"Then he'll be willing to help us," I said.

The body isn't real, the body isn't mine, I am not burning—he's pressing he's thrusting it hurts it hurts make it stop make it stop make it fucking stop! C'mere, c'mere. *Oh god. Oh god, the smell, I can smell him, I can smell the cheap Ivory soap he uses, he cleans his cock with it,* the taste of it, the taste, *c'mere c'mere, come here,* his hands, pressing into my skull, the head of it tickling my throat, *c'mere, harder—*

Everything grayed. I got dizzy.

"Jennifer."

I dug my fingernails into my palms until they bled. Reality sharpened.

"Let's go," I said.

Wade didn't rape you. You let it happen. He was drunk. It doesn't count.

We approached the door. The grass crunched with each step. Sweat beaded on my upper lip. Tasted of salt.

We entered.

Fetid air swirled. Blinds blocked out the Sun. A scrap of a kitchen lurked to my left, countertops carpeted in decaying Domino's pizza boxes, half-eaten pizza slices, and an opened package of smoked salmon, fillets gone green from rancidity. Beer bottles and popcorn dotted the beige carpet. The garbage can had been placed in the drunk's position. Dried puke crusted by it. Flies droned. A wall clock ticked. Burned balls of aluminum foil filled the trash. Crack, maybe meth. Not fentanyl. The burn trails on the foil were too ragged, too uneven for fentanyl.

Daryl pointed to the foil balls, raised an eyebrow.

"Not me," I whispered. "I don't cook speed anymore. Don't traffic normie drugs much these days."

The front door didn't have a knob. Something had torn it out of the door.

Did he get assimilated? Or did one of Her abominations come here?

The living room lay to the right, sofa empty. TV dead. Three empty dime bags lay on a wood coffee table.

Wade's suicide note rested on the dining table, unfinished. Sleeping pills—Unisom, nothing crazy—filled a cereal bowl. A shotgun lay nearby.

The note said, "Sorry. I didn't mean to. I didn't want to—" on the back of an old Gas N' Go receipt.

"He shot himself in one of these rooms. Didn't he?" Daryl said, right behind me.

"Quiet. You see that doorknob? Something was here. Something might still be here—"

"Daryl? That you?"

The voice was female, with a slight country twang. It lilted from the hallway. The hallway branched off the living room, lined with doors, unlit, dim in the summer afternoon.

Daryl stopped breathing. He froze. Paled.

creak.

"You brought Jennifer...I can smell her. Do I finally get to meet your wife?" The female voice gave a throaty laugh. "The wife you always lied about? I just met the other girl you screwed on the side. Really gettin' to know Her. The Divine Flesh, Jennifer, me...How many women do you need, Daryl?"

She stepped out of the hallway. Into the light.

"Am I good enough for you now, Daryl?"

She was built like a succubus. Iridescent skin clothed her body, silvery as a rainbow trout. Organs and veins pulsed, visible through it. She stood, slick and shining and nude, and clinked her talons against the wall. Black hair waved down to her back. Globules of silver bulged from three eye sockets, veining into her face like chrome roots. They contained no pupils. No way of knowing what she looked at, precisely. Webs stretched between her fingers. Black lips obscured her teeth.

"Emily?" Daryl whispered.

Her eye-roots tarnished to black. She smiled.

In life, Emily's smile had been kind and open, showing all her teeth—good teeth, union-dental-care teeth—always an eye-crinkler. Every last one of Wade's pictures of her showcased that smile. Wasn't a fake grin in the bunch. Now Emily looked like she wanted to floss with our intestines.

She extended a dripping hand to Daryl. "Let me take you to Her."

"Where's your father?" I asked.

She took another step towards Daryl, mouth softening, opening.

"I died 'cause of you," she said. "Least you could do is come with me. I'm stuck like *this*…I'm a monster. It's your fault. You were driving, weren't you?"

"Daryl, don't listen to her."

Emily stepped past me as if I didn't exist. She cupped his face with both hands, dropping beads of lake water in his beard. Her thumb brushed over his lips.

"Please, Daryl," she said.

"Oh," he said, gaze fixed on the far wall.

I clenched his hand. Blood glued our skin together.

"Hey. Hey, stay with me. We need to find Wade," I said.

"I already found him," Emily said. "Already know everything. So does the Divine Flesh. That's how it is. She loves us. She's always with us."

"Goddammit, Daryl, listen to what she's saying—one second, she's bitching about being a monster, and then she's praising the Divine Flesh. She's just saying this stuff so that you'll let yourself get assimilated."

"Emily's—"

"Emily's acting. She's fine. She's happy. Have you ever seen one of the Divine Flesh's creatures be anything but happy?"

"I'm standin' right here," Emily said. "Maybe he should ask *me*, Jennifer."

Daryl wet his lips with his tongue. "E-Emily. I'm sorry."

"Come with me and prove it."

Emily stepped closer. Almost within grinding distance. One of her hands left his face, drifted towards me.

"It was your fault they took Marcia and Isaac. Your fault. Your fault Rosetown murdered me. Everything was fine before you moved into town. You strung me along like a bass on a hook. It was your fault Jennifer stopped loving you—"

"Hey," I snapped.

She grazed a finger along my neck. A bubble of warmth bloomed where she touched me, tingling…and I knew, in that split second, that Emily *was* acting, that part of her hated playing the role of a vengeful monster. She wanted me to be quiet. Let her act. Come with her to see the Divine Flesh. Below her skin, excitement pulsed.

(Can you keep it a secret? Will you help me, Jennifer?)

We need to find Wade, I thought. *The murders.*

(I already found him.)

Daryl slumped. He rattled out a breath. He was going into shock, fading fast. I had to do something to snap him out of it. Anything. I could piss him off. Be the scapegoat. Be a piece of shit. It would do the trick…because I had one surefire way to really, really piss Daryl off.

I broke away from him and Emily.

"Jennifer?" Emily said.

I ignored them. I strode to the kitchen and opened Wade's fridge.

"Man," I said loudly, "I can't handle this touchy-feely stuff. I need a drink."

Daryl's lips peeled back from his teeth.

A half-gone bottle of Crown Royal sat smack-dab on the top shelf. I took it out. This was war, and I chose chemical warfare. I waved the booze around, snatched a Space Dust IPA, and double-fisted 'em.

Sweet, sweet alcohol burned down my throat.

I pretended to stagger over to him. "Daryl, I'd apologize, but we both know I'm too self-centered to care about this. Now, let's see how much of this Crown I can chug before I hurl."

Emily stared at me for a solid five seconds as I chugged.

Glug, glug, glug.

"Daryl, it's all your fault that—aw, shit, Jennifer, how much of that are you drinkin'? You're gonna kill yourself at this rate."

Even Creature Feature Emily was appalled by my drinking. *Rock, meet bottom.*

"Yeah," I said, and hiccuped. "It's your fault, Daryl. Totally your fault. No matter how much you try to help me or love me, I can't give a fuck. All I do is drink. And you were dumb enough to try and yank me outta the gutter. It's totally your fault that you fell in love with the kind, enthusiastic, woman-shaped thing trapped inside me, who loved you and supported you for years. It's your fault that Emily's father cut your brake line."

Daryl reddened. His angry vein bulged down the center of his forehead.

I waltzed down the hallway, opening doors. Looking for Wade.

"Can you believe this guy, Emily? He's a born-again sucker."

(Jennifer you're really hittin' below the belt.)

Yeah? So are you, Emily.

I swigged more booze, then, for the piece de resistance, slid my tank top off. I preened in front of Daryl, jiggling what little boobage I had.

"This is your fault, too," I said. "See these scars? It's not your fucking girlfriend in this body right now. It's me."

Words limned in scar tissue covered my torso.

Flesh Failure. Over and over, I'd carved, *Flesh Failure.*

"Remember all those times you got to visit Isaac, you invited me to meet him, and I never made a single one because I kept getting too drunk to stand? Too drunk to give a fuck? Remember that time you had to blow your savings bailing me out of jail when I got that DUI? Remember how shit-faced I got on our wedding day at the courthouse?"

I finished off the Crown and belched as obnoxiously as I could.

"Well," I slurred, "if you'd just tried a little *harder,* Daryl, maybe—"

"I can't believe this," he said softly.

"Better believe it, loverboy."

"My dead girlfriend *is standing right fucking here and all you FUCKING CARE ABOUT IS DRINKING?"*

Spit flew out of his mouth. My ears rang.

Oh is he gonna hit me? Hit me. I'll make you hit me. Do it.

Fear. Eagerness.

He'd never hit me, never would, but that shitty self-destructive impulse came anyway, because once you got beat enough times in enough foster homes, at some point, the fear became something addictive, something to hit like a bump of coke, a giddy taunting feeling. *Come home, Jennifer. Destroy yourself. You can always, always come home to that.*

(Or you can accept Me, and come home to My love.)

"Hell no, Meat God," I slurred.

I opened the farthest door. Inside lay a sulfur-yellow bathroom. I knocked the PVC shower curtain back. No Wade. I licked blood off my palms. I went to the next door, hand resting on the knob. Nausea flared in my stomach. Genesis had woken up.

Emily grabbed the back of my neck. Turned me to face her. I looked through her, making eye contact with Daryl.

"Wasn't your fault they died. My bullshit isn't your fault, either, Daryl. The Divine Flesh sent Emily here because She knew you'd feel bad enough to believe it. Look at Emily. Really look at her. If Emily thought you were responsible for her death, she'd've ripped you apart and slurped up your innards. That's probably why we can't find Wade," I said.

He nodded, breathing hard. His forehead vein bulged from his red skin.

Emily's grip tightened. Her other hand slid under my chin. An arm slithered around my waist, pressing my body into hers.

"What are you doing?" Daryl asked.

When Emily spoke, the melodrama had vanished. Her tone was plain. "The Divine Flesh wants me to break Jennifer's neck. She's tired of waiting for Jennifer to say yes. Jennifer won't feel anything bad. I'll make it quick."

Slowly, she turned my head to the side. Preparing for the final jerk.

Emily thought, *(It'll be nice to finally meet you. I think we'll get on fine.)*

She meant it. In her mind, she wasn't killing me—she was breaking something like she'd snap a twig, and then everything would be nice, and I'd be one of the Divine Flesh's happy children, like her. All it took was one snap, and I'd be loved and happy forever. Really, she was doing me a favor. No amount of pleading or reason or insult would sway Emily from breaking my neck.

I struggled. It did nothing. I hadn't expected it to.

So I relaxed into her instead. She caressed a talon down my skin and pressed her black, grave-cold lips to my cheek. Reassurance? Celebration? Felt nice. She wanted to drag me into Silver Lake and cradle me awhile under the blanket-soft water, and then we'd slip off my old skin like a rotting banana peel, and the Divine Flesh would render me into something sacred, bestowing the gift of Her love and attention, and then I'd be happy forever as Her holy vessel. What gilded things slept inside me, ready to emerge and bloom? The water. I could taste it. Feel it. Warm as amniotic fluid.

"No," Daryl said.

"Come with me, then. We'll all go to Her together."

Something *thumped* in one of the two bedrooms. A low-pitched whimper wavered.

Wade.

Go, I mouthed. *Go find him. I'll be fine.*

I retched. Bloody vomit rocketed up my throat. I swallowed it down, winced, and called out, "Daryl! Go find Wade and get that information! Go!"

He scrambled. Emily cranked my head a few more degrees. Pain screamed through my neck, wrenching bit by bit—

Then I puked for real.

A gallon of blood, flesh chunks, and sickly-sweet alcohol fountained outta me, covering Emily's arms and chest in chunky puke. Organ bits bobbed in booze, the color spectrum ranging from palest pink to maroon, like someone had thrown a whole WinCo's selection of meat cuts into a blender.

Sorry, I almost blurted.

Emily hissed. She jumped back, releasing me, and clawed at her vomit-covered arms.

Ssssss...

Something sizzled. Blisters pearled from where my blood-streaked puke met her skin, bubbling over her body. She groped for me, needle-teeth bared. I swatted at her.

My blood smeared over her hand. My palms kept bleeding from where I'd dug my nails into the flesh earlier.

The sizzling grew louder. Emily burned like I'd spritzed her with hydrochloric acid, making pained hissing breaths. She scrubbed her wrist against the carpet. Hard.

Daryl opened the bedroom door. I sprinted in.

Wade sat on an unmade bed, shirtless. His hands lay folded in his lap. A red stub bled in place of his right thumb. The bleeding had slowed to a dribble. A Walmart phone and a blood-slicked pocketknife rested on the white coverlet. Sunlight flooded through the window behind him.

"My daughter got hungry," he said.

"You cut my brake line," Daryl said.

Wade studied his hands. He brought his stump up to his mouth and sucked on it like a kid with a lollipop. "We're goin' to the lake. She's hungry. I gave her a snack. Might give her some more, I dunno," he said, between sucklings.

I drew the gun and aimed it at his torso.

"You murdered three people, including your own kid. So. Who else helped you?" I said.

"Emily's fine. She's home now."

"Who helped you?"

"I already talked 'bout it to the Divine Flesh. She forgives me. It's fine."

"No, it fucking isn't."

The doorframe crunched. Emily's talons dug into drywall.

"Trojan," Wade said.

"What?"

"It was Trojan's fault, y'know—"

His air cut off. Wade's throat worked, but nothing came out.

Emily murmured, "It's time, Dad."

Wade split open. He *became* before we got another word out of him, and when he was done, there were no mouths left to speak.

19

It started with a tiny red dot.

The dot appeared at the center of Wade's torso. A drop of blood oozed.

Lines ate away from the dot, carving into a sunburst. Yellow fat peeked out. I ran to him, pressing hands around his chest, holding it together, but he shifted under my hands and heated till it burned, eyes frustrated, silently asking, *What are you doing?* and there was nothing to do so I jumped back. His body softened. He collapsed to the bed, torso mounding up, skin stretching, his limbs merging into the central mass, rippling, he rippled, his body half-puddled and gooey on the bed, and his head sank in itself, swallowed up his black hair and face and beard with a wet *plip-plip*, churned, and the head melded into the rest.

The mass of flesh pulsed.

Burst open.

Inch-thick flesh curled outward from the nexus, thinning as it did, refining into petals. Intestines gobbled around the organs within, boiling like mad rattlers. Organs dissolved into the inner cavity walls, leaving only hardening, moving intestines. Protoflesh beaded. Grew. Reformatted intestines gobbled, then shot greedily out into the bed and wall. Hungry.

I stepped back.

Skin slipped off like used silk underwear. It slithered into the meat petals and into the nest of reformatted intestines. The cavity swelled shut. Pulsed. Opened again. The skin was gone. Flower-Wade's petals tickled every wall in the bedroom, akin to a bitterroot blossom. He— it?—turned to face the sunlight. Veins decorated Wade's glistening petals.

Daryl dry-heaved behind me.

Emily padded over to Flower-Wade and stroked a petal. It nudged into her touch as if it enjoyed it.

Time to get outta here.

I threw the van keys at Daryl. They hit him in the face. He startled.

"Go. Start the van," I said.

He scooped up the keys. Sprinted out.

Jennifer, think.

Wade. Think about Wade. He was weak, guilty, and he couldn't resist spilling his guts to a stranger on the night of Emily's death, so he was desperate, and when he was desperate and drunk, he talked. He'd been using drugs, ergo, he'd've spilled his guts—*oh Jesus that's a bad turn of phrase right now*—to someone or something, and even if he'd prayed to the Divine Flesh, he'd been miserable before She contacted him. So maybe there was something here with information. Had to be. A diary, a blog, a tape recorder—

His phone.

I ran under a petal, ducked, and snatched Wade's phone off the end table. Ran out. Hit the living room.

Why isn't Emily coming after us?

Daryl burst into the house, panting.

"They—they got the van, it's full of 'em, they're smiling at me—"

"Shit. Okay. Where's Wade's keys?"

"Table."

Wade's truck keys shone by the shotgun. I nabbed both of them. "Run."

Daryl's gaze flicked to the hallway.

"Emily's fine. I'll drive. You take the shotgun. Shoot any abominations that come after us," I said. "Got it?"

He nodded. I gave him the shotgun.

"Daryl?" Emily called.

We ran. Out the door. Into Wade's truck. It roared to life. Something flesh-colored and thicker than a human thigh curled out of the windows of the exterminator's van, wanting us to—

Play a game!

The abominations were extensions of the Divine Flesh. It stood to reason they would want to "play" with Daryl and me, too. I just *knew* what that thing in the van wanted. It ached to play a game. Any game. As long as Daryl and I agreed to play with it forever.

(It's a fun game! Enter the van and see.)

Any game that involves entering a van usually ends with a dead body, and that's true even if a psychotic flesh-god isn't involved. I elected to pass on playtime.

I burned rubber. The house disappeared behind us.

"You okay, Daryl?"

Pines rushed by.

He finally asked, "Is Emily really happy?"

"She was pretending to be sad. She flat-out told me when she had me in that stranglehold. We had this telepathy thing going. You know how it is with the Divine Flesh. I don't know if they're all Her or if they've got some bit of self left."

"Oh."

"I wanted to go with her. I wanted to be held below the lake and feel something good, for once," I said, voice breaking.

"Oh."

"That's all you got? Oh?"

"Sorry I yelled like that. Should've known what you were doing. I needed it."

"I meant what I said."

"Okay."

"It wasn't your fault."

"I'm okay, Jennifer."

"We just saw your undead girlfriend. You are not fucking okay. Okay? I'm not even okay, and I never met Emily, so I know you're not," I said. "You waiting for me to leave you alone? That it? You're waiting for a chance to go to the Divine Flesh?"

Like always, Daryl?

"No."

"It's okay if you want that."

"It's not."

I hit the end of the freeway. Parked cars barricaded the flesh-boundary. I made a U-turn and drove back the way we'd come.

"You want Her. Always have. It's not your fault you cheated—"

"It is." He touched his temple, half-cupping one of his eyes with his hand. Shame. That was one of Daryl's tells. "I should've broken up with you. And Emily. Didn't do right by her. I knew she wanted us to be something. I let us fall in love. Didn't think about the future. It felt good, and I didn't want it to end."

"No shit. You don't let good things go."

"Don't start."

"Let me tell you about Daryl Plummer," I said. "All about you. That car accident happens when you're eight. It gives you a brain-dead mom who'll never wake up, breaks Isaac's arm, and turns your dad into a depressed wreck. You function, because that's what you do, and mostly because Marcia and Isaac need you to. Two months later, your dad blows his brains out in front of you—you're eight years old at this point—and you function. That's what you do. Your grandparents can't look after you. Your uncle tries to take everyone in, but pretty soon, Marcia's getting abused and you're trying to keep the floor mattress free from needles, and you function. You function until CPS busts in, breaks up your family, and throws you into a series of shitty foster homes. You function. You bust your ass in school, because that's how you play the game, and by god, you're gonna function so fuckin' well that they'll let you raise your siblings, because that's pretty much what you've always done from day one—"

"Jennifer."

"You wanna beat yourself up with the past? Bring up all of it."

"You didn't see everything the Divine Flesh and I did," he said.

I looked him square in the face. "You fucked the Divine Flesh for the first time when we were seventeen years old, in the back row of a Greyhound at three a.m., because you and I were trying to run away from the McMullens' home. You'd just taken the Divine Flesh out to Arby's, because She'd never had fast food before unless She was inside me. You ate curly fries and chugged Fireball till you hurled. She held your hair in the Arby's bathroom…The McMullens made you grow it out to your shoulders, you fucking hated your hair. You gave yourself lice so they'd shave it off. Anyway. You fucked the Divine Flesh. You told Her not to tell me…Do I need to continue?"

He closed his eyes.

"I saw pretty much everything, and what I didn't see, She showed me. She doesn't understand the concept of infidelity. She thinks, *Oh, Daryl and I had fun, let's show Jennifer, Jennifer'll like that.*" I gritted my teeth. "Every good thing leaves you. I never hated you for hoardin' sweet things. That's what it is, you know. You have your romances, they're good, so you stockpile. That's the Daryl way."

"Goddammit, Jennifer, I don't wanna—"

"I still love you," I said. I felt my mouth twist, felt the tears burn. "Okay. I said it. I'm sorry."

The rest of the drive was silent.

I drove us to my trailer and checked the surprise shotgun I'd rigged. It'd been set off. Brown bloodstains, shit, and dried-out bits of intestine splattered the exterior of Casa Jennifer. A single flyspeck of what looked like digested cilantro adorned the door handle, still green. My trailer had been ransacked. Every opened booze bottle, used needle, and bloody pair of underwear was gone. Someone had fished through the bathroom trash for my blood-soaked tampons.

"My blood. It burned Emily," I said. "You see her blisters?"

"Yeah."

"Maybe Susan stole my stuff. Sometimes Mirror People like to prime the eggs before they're implanted in a vessel."

"Jennifer."

"We can go to your place and make weapons. Normally, I'd worry about cops, but I think all of 'em are gone," I said, studying my vinyl flooring.

Genesis squirmed in my lower gut. Or was that anxiety?

Daryl said, "You're not mad at me, for cheating on you like I did?"

He stood close, the smell of him—Old Spice, woodsmoke, sweat— thick in the stuffy trailer. He held the shotgun at his side, wearing his hick summer uniform: Jeans. Flannel shirt, sleeves cut off. Chest hairs curled out of his undershirt. A bead of sweat rolled down his nose.

"We can get under each other's skin, like I did back at Wade's—hell, we're married—but I can't hate you, Daryl."

"I wish things would've been different," he said.

"I should've tried harder to love you right," I said.

I stayed where I was standing. I let him choose. Energy coiled 'round us, invisible and heavy, like infrared heat—*I want, I want*—red without color, a rhythm as old as water, wanting, craving, blooming inside me, reaching out. *I want, I want.*

Daryl stepped closer, into me.

Heat on my jaw. His hand, treasuring.

I want, I want.

His lips brushed against mine, parting—

then closed.

He kissed me on the cheek.

"I can't," he said. "I don't know if I love you, or Her, or the bits of you in Her. Or the bits of Her in you. It's tangled up."

"And I don't know if I should love you, Daryl."

"Horseshit."

"I will neither confirm nor deny that I'm feeling some things right now."

"Your pupils look like you've done two lines of coke, you're flushed, and I could replace a masonry drill bit with either one of your nipples, they're that hard," Daryl said.

They were indeed. They poked right through my Walmart bra.

"Let's try to focus. If we don't defeat the Divine Flesh—and we probably won't—it'll be a done deal. We'll be happy abominations," I said.

"We gotta find this Trojan. We've got a name now."

"Daryl, I hate to put it this way, but we got bigger issues right now than who murdered Emily and Javier."

He grunted a yes, then nodded. "You got any C-4? Know you used to stash a crate or two in the woods."

"Whatcha thinkin'?"

"Blow up the flesh-barrier around town and evacuate everyone. We stay here, we play Her games. And maybe that'll be enough to keep Her from spreading. She loves fun. We still need to find out more about the Light…Jennifer, there's a lot of pieces here."

"So reduce 'em. Focus on getting everyone else outta here, and then figure out the Light."

We went outside.

Emily was perched atop the truck, talons dug into the roof. In the sunlight, she gleamed. Her eye globules brightened into opalescent white. A triad of opals in silver.

She said, "You comin' to the lake or not?"

Such a casual question. Her blisters had healed.

(Come with me. I'll take you home.)

Daryl raised the shotgun.

"This is the last time I ask. Next time, we'll simply take you," Emily said.

"If the Divine Flesh is everywhere, why take us somewhere else? She doesn't have any spatial distance restrictions. She could assimilate us here and now," I said.

"We'll take you inside Her."

Oh shit.

Emily slipped off the truck and darted into the forest.

Daryl paled. "Baby, you wouldn't," he said.

The Divine Flesh's voice became audible. "Oh, I wouldn't? I wouldn't take you inside Me, wrap you up all nice and cozy, and let you dream with Me forever, until you decide to stop being silly and *love Me already*? What a terrible fate. Why would I want to smother My two absolute favorite people in love? Why would I ever do that?"

(tee-hee!)

Her voice deadened into something monotone, something cold. "I have forever to break you both. I don't age or die. I exist in multiple places at once. I know every single thought in your cute little skulls. No matter how far you run, I'll know exactly where you are. Every one of My children is a facet of Me. Every one of them loves you and wants to take you home to Me. They'll do *anything* to make that happen. I'm making more children right now, at this very second. And I will never stop wanting You. I can't. I'm not human enough to change," the Divine Flesh said.

Then her voice sweetened back to its usual saccharine. "I'll just take you into My body and keep you locked away until you decide to stop being stubborn. I can love you like that forever and ever. You'll both break long before forever…but in a fun way! Really. We'll have so much fun."

She sent us an image.

Daryl and I, half-embedded in a wall of flesh. We slept. Tendrils meshed into every limb. Whitish tubes jutted from every orifice. Paper-thin layers of flesh imprisoned us in cocoons. Dim reddish light. Shifting, twitching things in the darkness. A stench. Blood and incense. Humid, close air roiled.

I asked, "You want us like that? As comatose dolls?"

"Of course I don't, silly. I'd much rather assimilate you. If you adore Me, I can adore *you*, nurse you on My ichor, and render you into magnificent beings."

"Ichor?"

"I produce it, Jennifer-baby. So does the Hermetic. Do you miss it? Come to Me. I'll glut you on it, and you can dream as much as you'd like."

"Ichor…is that the stuff we got high on? The wonder drug?"

The Flesh and the Light.
"Oh, you want to know more about the Light?"
"I gotta get high on that ichor again."
She gave a tinkling laugh.
"Then come get some, Jennifer-baby."

20

20

The Divine Flesh said, "Let's play a game, Susan."

The Drift-Inn squatted on the outskirts of town, close to the edge of the flesh-boundary. A few trucks lay parked near the barrier, long abandoned. T-shirts, jeans, and shoes scattered the road like confetti. A neon-yellow pair of Nike sneakers sat primly in the middle of the road, as if their wearer had simply vaporized while standing. Sunlight glinted off a battered oxygen tank lying on its side in the undergrowth; the plastic hoses and cannula were still attached, but the oxygen had long ago escaped. Near a discarded Carhartt beanie, something like a small, cheerfully colored briefcase caught Susan's eye: a child's metal lunchbox. Cartoon Sasquatches grinned across it with all the sincerity and cheer of well-fed crocodiles. *I'm not going to eat you*, those grins said, *because we're friends. Right? And I would never ever eat you.* No blood soiled any of it. Everything looked pristine. These human things had simply been left behind. The owners didn't need them anymore.

I'll eat you up, I love you so.

Susan shivered. Her filaments rustled overhead.

An abomination laughed from its perch in a cedar tree—a shrill chittering laugh. Hugging the tree like a cat, it clutched the trunk with sixteen limbs. It was composed of four humans, two males and two females, all chained into each other like a centipede, their torsos fused, arms and legs jutting. Except for the single remaining head at the front, all the rest had merged into the mass of the abomination. Their shoulders melded seamlessly into what had once been the pelvis of the body in front. Scratches bled across its nude flesh. Wedding bands still glittered on the hands. Pink vulvas, scrotums, and penises dangled, exposed and lurid against the skin of the thing.

It's going to rub itself raw against that tree.

Hysterical giggles fought up Susan's throat. She swallowed them back. The abomination's face looked female and young; Barbie-pink lipstick greased its lips, and greasy brown hair curtained either side of its head. Its eyes had gone black, even the whites. Ruined eye makeup streamed down its cheeks.

It's staring right at me.

The abomination's mouth twitched as if it wanted to speak. Perhaps it did. Perhaps it would open its mouth and say—

The Divine Flesh said, *(Do you want to go play with it, Susan?)*

(It sees you! It's inviting you to play. Look how happy it is! It's been waiting for a friend to come play a game with it.)

Two-hundred eggs hung heavy inside Susan. Her two bodyguards fidgeted nearby. The Old One, Lonnie, carried their half of the fertilized clutch of eggs. Raxus, the Young One, carried nothing but a scowl, a Glock, and a septum ring. Ahead, the flesh-boundary barricaded the road. It thickened to the width of a human torso across the asphalt, and thinned down to a rattlesnake's width as it went into the trees. Just like a real snake, it was a deadly thing lying underfoot, waiting for idiots to step on it. It seethed. The pink surface of it gleamed with secreted fluid. Mouths bubbled up on the flesh-boundary, smiled, and merged back into the whole. Horseflies dotted the flesh-boundary and gorged themselves silly.

A human-looking mouth appeared on the boundary, smirked, and said, "If you give Me that pill bottle of eggs, I'll let you out of Rosetown."

Footsteps crunched behind Susan, near a red truck. She froze.

The abomination slithered down the tree. It happened within an eyeblink. One second, it leered thirty feet off the ground. The next, it thudded to the forest floor. Every limb worked in fluid synchronicity; it rippled as it moved. Silk-like, it crept to the edge of the road, about twenty feet from Susan.

Raxus unholstered his Glock. He wore the form of a Korean man clad in black combat gear.

The abomination simply cocked its head and beamed, revealing a mouth lined with hook-like teeth. Rows and rows of the white hooks carpeted the interior of its mouth and esophagus, and the Divine Flesh's voice trilled out of that mouth: "Really, Susan. I mean it. I could tell the others who you really are, too, you know. I could just do that instead. Do you think they'll forgive their God for selfishly abandoning them to go play pretend? That's what you're doing, you know."

Raxus's hands trembled. "What?"

"Don't listen to that thing," Susan snapped. "We need to find a way around that boundary. Do we have my cache of explosives?"

"N-no. No, ma'am," Lonnie said.

"Damn it. Did you locate the Flesh Failure's stash of C-4—"

The abomination sighed. "It takes a lot to disgust Me, but here we are. I don't even want to look at you. Mmmm…If you want to leave so badly, give Me your bottle of eggs. I'll let you keep the ones inside you."

"You'll open the boundary?"

"Just a little."

"Is that…thing speaking to me, or are You speaking to me, Divine Flesh?" Susan asked.

"Oh, there's not much of a difference anymore! But it's just Me. I'm speaking through My darling creation, using its mouth. Her name is Creepy-Crawly-Kaylee! My beautiful Creepy-Crawly-Kaylee just wants to play tag with you because you seem like a fun new friend. It loves making new friends. She? It? Them? Oh, I just don't know what pronouns to use for them. They're so happy. You should let Me love you, and then you'll be happy too."

"I'm afraid not."

"We don't need to act like silly schemers, Susan. What if I loved you, recreated you, and then we all played a fun game because we wanted to? I like that better. Let's—"

"Open the boundary. What are Your terms?"

The abomination smiled. "Okay, then, silly! It's open. For twenty seconds. It's a fifty-foot sprint over the boundary. Can you make it?"

"I'll fly."

"Oh, no. You don't get to fly," She said, chuckling. "You left your children behind and abandoned them in My world. So you get to *run*. Like a human."

"Suppose I fly anyway?"

"Then our game's over, and I'll just assimilate you whether you want it or not. I'll pluck you right out of the air and love you forever and ever and—"

Behind Susan, Raxus froze. To his right, Lonnie fell to his knees. Both their false bodies spasmed. Raxus emitted a high-pitched buzz. A panicked buzz. Vertical cuts appeared on the surface of their skinsuits, redlining in inch-wide strips. Blood trickled. Lonnie glanced at Susan. A slice bisected his right eye. Split pupil. Split brown iris.

Oh god.

Their filaments crept out from the slices. For a second, it looked like silver dripping from every cut, metallic foil stripes, *oh god oh god not slices*. Both skinsuits fell apart, leaving two piles of peelings on the asphalt. Raxus and Lonnie flew up, unspooling, and the noon sun glinted against their wings. Eggs dangled within Lonnie's air-spun body like grapes.

"What the fuck are those?" a man shouted. "Shepard! Trojan—"

A mechanical voice crackled. "I told you. They aren't human," it said.

(You have ten more seconds to hit the boundary, Susan. After that, it closes forever.)

What?

Crack! Crack!

Gunshots. Two. They passed through the Mirror People's bodies, doing little harm. A few filaments severed. The abomination hummed back in its tree, climbing up.

The Divine Flesh sang, "Annnndd…ten!"

I'm still in heat, I can't detect the humans' emotions. What's happening? Who's there? How many?

Ahead, flesh-boundary parted like the Red Sea, opening into the forest, into freedom.

"Nine!"

Run. Run, you idiot, run!

Susan glanced at Raxus and Lonnie. A white blight appeared on both, like mold appearing on fruit. White speckles fuzzed the outside of their filament-bodies. They spread. Susan screamed something. Neither responded. Raxus and Lonnie drifted, cloud-like in the summer air, as the color drained from their filaments and their wings flickered out, turning into…something else. Oh god, the eggs. Lonnie's cache of eggs. The dangling eggs changed inside Lonnie, reddening until they were blood-beads—blood inside cotton; he'd gone white as cotton.

Wrong, those things are WRONG.

Her stinger exploded out from under her tongue. She gagged. Venom dribbled from the needle, smelling sharp like ammonia.

What are those…things? What did She do? Oh god those things are NOT RIGHT.

"Eight! You really should start running, silly!"

The assimilated Mirror People regarded her. Their snow-white filaments caressed Susan's skinsuit. Sticky. Wrong.

"We forgive you," they said simultaneously. "We forgive you for what you did, Creator. But did it hurt? What made you sad enough to end everything? Didn't you love us?"

"Oh god, what are you, what has She done?" Susan said, hating herself for how pathetic she sounded, so scared.

Both of them said, "We are loved. We are happy. We're part of Her now." They descended. Those mutated white strands veiled her sight. "Why don't you join us? The Divine Flesh loves us."

The thing that had once been Lonnie fished the pill bottle of eggs from Susan's pocket.

Another gunshot.

"Seven! I never said I wouldn't assimilate your bodyguards, Susan!"

Ignore the lost ones. You aren't their creator anymore; they're Hers now, so go! Run!

Susan forced her legs to work. She sprinted for the opening.

Forty feet.

"Six!"

She ran around a truck. Caught her foot on a rock. Stumbled. Each breath burned as she inhaled.

"Five!"

Thirty feet. She scrambled up, palms scraped. Kept running.

"Four!"

I can make it, I'll exit right before the Divine Flesh gets to one.

Twenty feet. Tendrils erupted from the flesh-barrier. They shot at Susan. Someone breathed close by, rasping strained breathing.

"Three!"

An arm snapped around Susan's waist. A human's. A man's. She thrashed. Struggled. Her filaments snapped around the human's neck, and she tightened them, digging into the skin, ready to decapitate. Heat washed through her, her stinger was out, she opened her mouth and turned to jab—

Ice prickled through her neck.

A syringe. They injected me.

"Two!"

The syringe was filled with a pinkish-clear fluid. An organic pink, not the synthetic pink of a barbiturate. The man tightened his grip on Susan and pressed the syringe plunger.

"Thank God almighty for that junkie," he said.

It pulsed through her false form—

"One!"

(You aren't going to win. Will you come home to Me?)

(Hope is a cosmic joke, we are all meat but we are oh-so-sublime—)

Then a miracle happened.

The Divine Flesh's mental chatter cut off. Her voice no longer tainted Susan's mind. As she incorporated the syringe's fluid into her true body, the Divine Flesh stayed gone.

The flesh-boundary resealed.

The man hissed. Stiffened. "Trenelli! Trenelli!"

"No time," a mechanical voice said, now close. "It got Trenelli. The blood'll wear off unless we get another dose. Move it."

Someone jammed a cloth sack over Susan's head. It reeked of onions and dust. Another syringe pricked her arm, pumping in liquid soft sleep. Her arm deadened.

"Low dose of fentanyl," someone said.

"This thing isn't human. You can't take risks."

Susan tried to say, *I wasn't meant to be human. I'm not really human, that's not fair*, but the words blurred and tangled, the stories got mushy, until the only things left were the sensation of the eggs inside her and vague images from long ago…

The clutch of eggs she'd carried into this foreign world.

Trying to implant them into mineral soil. Dead soil, no life to nourish the babies with. That's not how it was supposed to be. Susan, the creator-God, had formed a ground that was a fertile living organism in the old world she'd created for her Mirror People—the world that made *sense*—and here, the ground was just dead minerals? Where did the babies go?

Those eggs never hatched. She'd snuck into a hospital and implanted them into a brain-dead geriatric. Then…

Those brain-dead larvae from that brain-dead geriatric vessel in the hospital, limp as slugs in her hands, thoughtless and gone, dead, the poor little babies that had thought and loved and hoped were now dead, sagging, half-liquid things, dead silver in Susan's clutching hands. A hard lesson from the new world: Larvae are what they eat. Vessels must be carefully chosen.

Then she buried the brain-dead larvae, piling them in a discarded coffee can, sealing the lid. Put the casket into a hole. Smoothed the red sand over them. *Move on. You said you wanted to feel pain. You said you were bored of being their god, so aren't you happy? Aren't you happy now?*

A raw shriek tore out of her throat.

Then another.

This is worse than dying. I don't want this. I don't want to be like them anymore, I don't want the pain, I thought I wanted to be like my children and I don't. I don't. It hurts. Take it back. Make it stop.

It wasn't supposed to be like this.

—Dialing a suicide hotline in 1998, ruby sparkle nail polish flecked on the receiver of the motel room's phone.

Saying, when someone finally picked up, "I want to die. I wanted to die."

Hearing the response: "But do you want to die now?"

"I wanted to die so I made it happen. I can't take it back. Now I want to die again. What have I done? I killed a world and doomed my creations. I am a bad god."

"You got health issues related to a suicide attempt? Sir, you got access to a firearm? Have you taken any pills?"

Susan had mumbled, "I was supposed to end everything else with me, but I couldn't. I loved them. I thought I'd love them more if I flew around like them, and oh that was a bad idea. But. It was getting bad, before. Either I had to dissolve into the Universe I'd built, lose the consciousness, or downscale. Go up or down. I tried to float in the middle and I couldn't."

"Sir?"

"I'm fine now. Had to get that off my chest."

"Sir, I'm not supposed to mention this, as we are a secular hotline, but have you considered praying to God?"

"What?"

"You said your name was *somestupidhumanname*, right?"

"Uh-huh, yeah."

"All right, *somestupidhumanname*, I want you to know something. No matter what you think you've done, God loves you. No matter what you've done, there's always a path towards redemption. You figure it out at some point. You get what I'm saying? You can either figure it out in a church pew, or after you jump off a bridge and hit the fuckin' water. Atone for what you gotta atone for, then move on…"

Bad God. I *am what I am. Bad God…*

"C'mon, honey, get up," the mechanical voice said.

Susan coughed and opened her eyes.

Maybe I deserve this, whatever this is. Hell? Death?

She croaked, "Who—who are you?"

Near-darkness. She lay on a thin mattress, handcuffed to an iron bed frame. The room around her was a concrete eight-by-eight cell, unlit. A kerosene lantern glowed on the ground nearby. A rolled sleeping bag rested in the corner by a crate of protein shakes and a gallon bag of homemade jerky. Besides that, the cell contained nothing. In the center, a brass floor drain gleamed.

A male figure sat at the foot of the mattress, his race and age indiscernible. He wore a black hood over his head, and nondescript backpacking gear.

He carried a set of bolt cutters.

"Why am I here?" Susan asked.

Tenderly, he grabbed her skinsuit's right hand and pulled its fingers apart.

"Pick one," he said.

"Excuse me?"

"Pick one, or I pick for you. We need to come to an understanding, given the times we're in. I know what you are. I know what you can do. You ain't human. You came into our nice town and you expected good pickings."

"You—"

"We're not prey. Pick a finger."

He brought the bolt cutters to her right hand. He tapped each fingernail with the tip. "Then maybe we work together."

"Who are you?"

"Trojan," he said. "Pick a finger. I'd recommend a pinkie."

"I don't—"

"We lost one of ours today, to that goddamn flesh-god. I'm not in a mood to argue. Pick a finger."

"You don't mean it. You're—"

The bolt cutters snipped.

crunch.

Susan's middle finger fell to the concrete, twitching.

The Ballad of Nancy Trenelli: A Poem
Written by the Divine Flesh
Ten years ago, they told you to hide the serial killer's body. Do something good with it.

Feed it to your hogs, Nancy, Monty had said.

But you would never. The meat would be an abomination, and the Lord despises abominations. You learned that lesson at the age of thirteen, when the Devil made you kiss another girl, made her lips soft, made her skin smell floral—

The Lord made you puke mid-kiss. That was that. You'd had a stomach bug, you were still nauseous, and God Almighty was kind enough to tell you *NO* instead of doing whatever else He had every right to do.

You slaughter your lambs in springtime, and come fall, you slaughter your hogs and salt the meat. You never married a man. You're fifty-four, you attend Pastor Crowley's church every Sunday, and you watch poor Allie Crowley, his wife, become more barren with each year that passes. The pastor's wife could only give him one child. Allie Crowley don't know about the white pride meetings. She could know. It's right in front of her face.

But Allie Crowley will never put those pieces together, because she don't want to.

You pray for them to see the errors of their ways. The white supremacy movement is an affront to God. Jesus Christ came to redeem all the people of the world. Every night, you pray. But when wickedness and evil threaten your town, you act, and if that means getting the help of neo-Nazis, if push comes to shove…you'll join hands with them to protect your town.

That don't make you a bad person. A few of the others feel the same way, about the white pride stuff and the skinhead meetings. Nobody outside of the skinheads likes it, not even Crowley's wife, but everyone's a concerned citizen. Rosetown needs its concerned citizens to protect it. Sometimes you have to team up with people you don't like, to eradicate those threats.

Ten years ago, you helped lynch a serial killer and put the hanged man's body in your septic tank.

Now the flesh-god engulfs you.

Tendrils wrap around your wrists.

"Do you want to redeem yourself?" She asks.

The Divine Flesh engulfs you before you can answer; Her tendrils simply swallow you whole, secreting a cocoon of visceral fluid. Your clothing gets soaked. The second you think about that, She tsk-tsks and shreds your clothing away, no fuss, no fanfare, just gone, and then you're naked, stripped bare. The Divine Flesh bears you away from home and into Herself. Tubes slide up and down all your holes, carrying away waste, trickling milk and blood—*sweet, sweet blood*—down your gullet, enmeshing into you, *becoming you*, and there's a pressure at the base of your skull, something slides in—

Your brain connects to the mass around you.

You're a precious prized gem inside the Divine Flesh, something not of Her, but still valued. She adores you. She embeds you deeper and deeper into Herself, into Her endless blood-warmed folds. They'll slough away your sins, Nancy Trenelli. Envelop you. Smother you in soft slick love and smooth away everything wrong.

(Tell Me about the others, Nancy.)

(Then you'll be free! Unless you want to stay here. You're always welcome to dwell inside Me.)

"Or we can do this. I can love you forever and ever like this, Nancy Trenelli," the Divine Flesh says. "Forever and ever. Won't that be fun?"

21

"Bleed on a few more shells," Daryl said.

"It's not gonna work."

But I slit open another dash on my arm and dribbled blood over a pile of shotgun ammo. Daryl blew on them. We hunched over his coffee table, our hands streaked black from gunpowder and grease.

Darkness smothered. No daylight penetrated his cabin. None of the lights worked anymore. None of the outlets worked. No electricity. No AC. Air stagnated. It got hotter by the second. Our only source of light was a battery-powered Coleman lantern. It sat on the floor nearby, casting cheerless white light.

Neither of us looked out the cabin windows.

(Look at Me, darlings.)

(You know you want to look at Me. I'm pressing My face against the glass.)

"Aw, look, Daryl. There's your girlfriend, the Divine Flesh. Pressing Her face against the glass because She's happy to see you. Isn't that cute? Except Her face is a cluster of fucking tendrils."

"Goddammit, Jennifer."

"You'd think She'd get splinters off it."

His jaw worked. Sweat dripped off his face.

"We should've seen this one coming. She just let us drive back here, no fuss or fight. Personally, I'm embarrassed," I said. A high-pitched giggle came out of me. "You think it hurts, to eat a cabin? You think She's waiting to break the windows for a reason? She could totally break the windows right now. She's pressing them. I can hear the glass squeaking. Maybe we should turn on a radio or something."

"I'm going to puke," Daryl said calmly.

I plopped my vomit-bucket in front of him. "Go ahead, puke."

Chunks of fat floated in pink slurry, half-filling the bucket. Silvery goo swirled through my vomit—Genesis's waste. They'd matured enough to filter through what they consumed instead of absorbing every single bit of me. That meant I had about two days left before the larva ate its way to my heart and pupated, either inside one of my ventricles or atriums, or inside my aorta. After twenty-four hours, Genesis would emerge from the pupa in a thread-like string, coiling in on themselves in a specific configuration that was unique to each individual Mirror Person. Think "sentient Brillo Pad." Until, of course, Genesis found a human or animal to mirror.

No matter what happened, the Divine Flesh would assimilate me.

If I died carrying Genesis, She'd assimilate me. If I even made it another two days.

Daryl dry-heaved into the bucket.

(Look at Me or I'll make you look at Me.)

"Okay, okay, I'm looking. Just let Daryl be," I said.

The Divine Flesh blanketed the entire cabin. She'd engulfed it. She emitted heat. Knotted tendrils meshed over every window, red as heart's blood, vivid even in the fluorescent light of the lantern.

We'd driven to Daryl's, ready to make weapons, storm the Divine Flesh, and get the Hermetic. You know, like *Fallout 3* or *DOOM* or any standard video game. We'd just driven to his cabin. Nothing happened. Daryl had a shop behind the cabin. We had all these great, badass weapon ideas, so we'd gone back inside his cabin to load up on food. Then, a penny-sized dot of blood appeared on a window.

I'd said, *Hey, look at that—*

It'd instantly exploded into tendrils that consumed the cabin in five seconds.

Now we were stuck inside, waiting for the Divine Flesh to break through the windows and assimilate us. Ever so gently, She pushed against the windows. Against the doors of Daryl's wood stove. She'd filled the chimney and curled Herself into the stove.

Creeaaaaaaak.

"I love you," the Divine Flesh said audibly.

Creeeeeeeek.

"I'm looking at You, D. F.," I said.

Daryl lumbered to the kitchen. He opened the freezer. Something crinkled as he removed it, something wrapped in a plastic bag.

"They're gonna defrost," he whispered.

"Daryl?"

His voice thickened. "Gonna rot. Should've let them sleep in the ground, but I didn't wanna let 'em go. Can't let nothin' go. Everything dies on me…"

Each footstep sounded gunshot-loud as he returned.

"Couldn't stuff 'em. Couldn't preserve 'em," he said.

He got to the living room before he collapsed, right in front of the wood stove. I went to him, lantern in hand.

He sat in a cross-legged position, with two plastic-wrapped things cradled in each arm. Plastic Harvest Foods shopping bags. He placed a wrapped, frozen something on the floor. He reached inside the other, and unearthed something from the white plastic.

He held it close to his face. His eyes glistened.

Frost glittered in the dead cat's gray fur. White clouded its eyes. Frozen blood stained the fur around its neck. With one hand, Daryl supported its head, and with the other, he held its body.

"It—it—it's a dead cat. Get the fuck over it," he muttered. "It's got a brain the size of my fist. It didn't love me. It's an animal. It doesn't matter. It was just a d-dumb fucking cat. It d-didn't matter."

He gently set it down on the ground and unwrapped the other cat. Marmalade tabby, dull golden eyes, petite. Blood girded the neck. The slit peeked out, nearly hidden in long fur.

He stroked its head, hand shaking.

"It doesn't matter. You didn't love me. You're a d-dead cat. A dead fucking animal. Shoulda thrown you both in the trash. You—you didn't—"

His voice broke. "I couldn't let them go."

"Holy shit. Those are the cats those bigoted asshole killed, aren't they? The ones they left on your doorstep with the note," I said.

"I got 'em when they were kittens. Three months old. McGee's mama cat had a litter. I—I had names for 'em, but they can't have names anymore 'cause they're dead. Just my cats. Used to watch Netflix on my laptop, and have the cats on my lap. Good cats. I—I couldn't let 'em go when I found their bodies, so I put them in the freezer and I can't let them go, I can't let—I don't want 'em to s-sleep underground, so I put 'em away so I could still pretend they were st-still—Sometimes I'd pet the plastic in the freezer and pretend they could feel it," he said.

He forced a laugh like a wheezing lung cancer patient.

"Now you know how fucked-up I am. I—I have my little dead things I preserve. I go hiking in the woods and I see these sad dead animals and all I keep thinking is, *I wanna make 'em happy*, I gotta make 'em normal, I can fix 'em, y'know, so I take 'em back here and I sew 'em up—like they're still alive and happy, y'know? I don't wanna let 'em go, I put 'em in the formaldehyde and then I keep 'em forever, and I—god, sometimes I make up names for 'em, all the dead things I can't save, and I don't want my cats to l-leave—to die again, Jennifer, okay, but they're goin' to rot when they defrost and there's no power to the cabin so I have to—to hold my cats one last time, okay, before they—"

Daryl buried his face in the orange cat's fur. He did not sob. His body remained stiff as iron.

The wood stove latch clicked. Its iron doors swung open. A tendril unfurled from within and gently stroked his wrist. Daryl caressed it. Red fluid greased his skin.

Almost slurring, he said, "When my dad blew his brains out, Marcia came running and I slapped her right across the face so I'd have another second to git her outta there before she really saw all of it, I slapped her hard, and I took her and Isaac up through the back slider door, took us down the street to McDonald's, and I'd swiped Dad's phone and wallet, so I bundled the kids up and wiped my face off with a paper towel from the kitchen…and I still remember what we ate, down to the penny. I let the kids get whatever they want. Costs twenty-seven dollars and fifty-three cents. I call the police, then I get a motel room 'cause I know Meemaw won't know what the hell to do, so I book us a Holiday Inn usin' Dad's credit card, and I tell the kids, 'We're goin' to swim in a pool, isn't that fun?' I try to eat somethin', almost throw up…and that's why I can't eat at McDonald's, to this day. The smell. I get within a quarter mile of any McDonald's and I start dry-heavin', 'cause I'm a fuckin' pussy that can't git over somethin' that happened when I was eight."

"Daryl."

In the all the years I'd known him, I never understood why he'd gotten so into taxidermy. I'd never even bothered to ask. Everything was spilling open, coming undone.

I want to claw my skin off, Daryl, and I don't know who to talk to about that. I can't even think about my body without feeling this…existential horror in my gut. It's getting worse.

I think I might be a bad person, and I don't know what to do, so all I do is drink.

I almost said those things. But I didn't.

Because if I said them, that'd make them real, and I couldn't handle that right now. I'd spent my entire life hoping—nay, praying—for the Divine Flesh to go away. If She went away, I'd finally be a good person instead of a worthless addict. I'd finally redeem myself. Now She was gone. And here I was, and nothing had really changed.

(Maybe I wasn't the problem, Jennifer-baby.)

(You can always talk to Me, you know. About anything. I love hearing from My children. You don't have to say any special words or praise. Just talk to Me! I'm always here, and I will always love you, no matter what.)

Daryl cleared his throat. "There. I had my self-pity. Had my sad moment. Now I'm over it. And if I'm not? Then I'd better get over it real fuckin' quick, because other people depend on me."

He stood, scooping up both dead cats.

"Where you going?" I asked.

"To throw these dead animals into the garbage. Where they belong."

The Divine Flesh's tendril looped around his wrist. It gently tugged. He shook his head. He kissed the tendril as if it was a lady's hand, and it released him, slithering back into the wood stove.

"…But you're just like Me. We're healers. We see something suffering and we want to fix it, heal it, love it back to health. That's one of the reasons I fell in love with you, silly…Let Me adore you. All I want to do is give you every good thing I can," the Divine Flesh said.

Daryl ignored Her. He turned to walk into the kitchen.

Both cats' bodies twitched. Crackling noises. The gray cat's tail jerked once. Frozen muscles crunched as they worked. Ice melted to water. Steam roiled from them. A gurgling, liquid-filled purr bubbled out.

"…No," Daryl whispered.

"Death is obsolete, My love."

He set the cats down on the floor and they revived, slit throats sealing shut. They lapped the blood off their fur and headbutted Daryl's legs. Orange-cat rolled, exposing its belly to Daryl. He ignored it. He wiped a hand over his face, stood, and staggered to the sofa.

He collapsed onto it. Stared at the wall. Stared at nothing. Gray-cat jumped onto the couch and rubbed against Daryl's side, purring. Daryl didn't respond.

"I've had enough of this whole 'suffering and death' nonsense, you two. Either open the door and accept Me, or I'll force My way inside. I'll give you sixty seconds to choose," the Divine Flesh said.

Jennifer, just give up! Jennifer, go be a happy abomination! It's not like you had a ton to live for. Why can't you just be happy?

But nothing pissed me off like a good ol' fashioned ultimatum.

Either you willingly love Me, or I'll make you love Me!

Oh, really?

Think. Think about what's really happening here, Jennifer. She needs to be loved. She's telling you that She craves external love and validation. If She didn't know you well enough, you could probably pretend to worship Her. But She does. She wants your love. You're a piece of shit. You're unredeemable. What's so great about your love, Jennifer? Why does She want it so badly?

Because the Divine Flesh wanted what She couldn't have.

Reflexively, I searched my pockets. Wade's phone sat in my front pocket. Funny that we never got to look at Wade's phone, with all this chaos. Interesting that we never did.

It's almost like there's a reason for that.

"Thirty seconds, Jennifer-baby."

Daryl had gone into shock. He couldn't help.

Because there's something on the phone, and She doesn't want us to know what it is.

I asked, "Why are you so scared, D. F.?"

"I have no fear. I just love you."

"Exactly. You love us. That's why You're scared," I said. "You've been distracting us ever since I grabbed Wade's phone, because You don't want us to listen to the audio on it. Because You ripped him apart while he was recording his confession, didn't You? You put him back together when we arrived at the house. But before that, You ripped him apart over and over, because You're the Divine Flesh, You're terrified of experiencing grief or death, and Wade almost killed Daryl. You saw inside Wade's mind the second You laid eyes on him, through Emily. You expect me to buy that You saw him as he remembered sabotaging Daryl's truck and let him be a happy flower abomination?"

I pulled out Wade's phone. I ran a finger across the cracked screen.

"And You especially don't want Daryl to hear that. God forbid he see what You're like when You get angry."

And if You destroy Wade's phone, You'll confirm my theory. You know it. I know it. So even if I'm wrong—and we both know I'm not—I've just insured that You can't fuck with it. Have fun, D. F.

Thirty-two seconds had elapsed as of now. I'd been counting.

She hadn't flooded into the cabin.

"Some god You are. You're still human enough to get angry. Maybe it's me. Part of me rubbed off on You—"

"*No!*"

Cracks spidered every window.

"You're emotional. Because of me. A stupid human that can't even stay sober for a week. Why?"

"You kept Me inside your body for decades, Jennifer, and I don't know how. Really, you're just so stubborn. No matter how much love I give you, you won't love Me back. I don't know *why*, and it *hurts* Me. I have infinite love to give. I want to give it all."

"Daryl already loves You. You can't make me love You, and You sure as hell aren't gonna do it by lobotomizing me," I said. "I want the Hermetic. Let us come get it."

I got up. I took Wade's shotgun from Daryl's limp hands and loaded bloody shells into it.

"I'm going to take you, silly, and you'll finally adore Me," the Divine Flesh said.

I went to the front door, footsteps clacking on the wooden floor. The doorknob felt warm as steaming viscera under my hand.

"Then take us already," I said.

I opened the door. She flooded in.

Father Johnson coughed into a purple hankie and waited for the sin to come out, as it always did, like scum floating to the surface of fresh milk. He'd been at the Rodriguez house since 4 a.m. He did *not* think about why. In fact, why think about that at all? Noon sun blasted in through the windows. The eldest daughter, Marisol, pressed tortillas and hurled them into a pan, hands working mindlessly. Grease and stale breath filled the air. Four other children huddled around.

"Sometimes I hear him," Rosa Rodriguez kept mumbling. "Javier's telling me he's coming home."

"It's a demon," Rosa's mother said, as casually as one might say, *There's a cockroach in the butter.*

Itzel, that was her name. Old, old woman, white-haired and gnarled. Wouldn't stop asking for a Latin Mass, thought His Holiness the Pope was demented or worse, wanted him to perform an exorcism on the house.

Father Johnson dumped another fistful of coffee into the percolator. He was seventy-one, but he was no stranger to going without sleep. This grieving family needed God. So here he was. His eyes burned and his head spun, but he paid it no mind.

Lord Jesus, help this family. Help this woman through her grief.

The coughs came in fits. Hitching, dry coughs.

Please, O God, not cancer. Not lung cancer. Not like—

A snide inner voice taunted, *Not like Mommy? When she hacked and hacked her lungs out, when she couldn't move to take a piss without lugging along that oxygen tank? You're almost there. She was seventy-two when it got her. Remember those cigarettes she smoked around you as a kid?*

—Focus. Help this family.

Rosa Rodriguez asked for confession. When she'd asked for her mother to be there, he'd known what she was about to confess, because sin was always the same. It festered the same. In all the decades he'd been taking confession, this remained true: Sin was *boring.* Mundane. So very human: I cheated, I stole, I raped, I killed, I envied my neighbor's wife so I screwed her, I hated my boss so I embezzled from the bastard, I couldn't be a father so I made my girlfriend get an abortion. I, I, I…And everyone thought their sins were the most special specimens of diabolic evilness ever crafted. As if the blood of Christ wasn't sufficient to wash them clean.

(Because they are GOOD, so very good. You understand Me. They are more than their silly human foibles, Father.)

He gripped the card table he sat behind. "I'm sorry, could you repeat that?"

Rosa burst into sobs. Her mother patted her shoulder and shot Father Johnson a terse look. He, Rosa, and Itzel were hunched around a Walmart card table they'd set up in the younger children's room, door closed. It'd been done in a forest motif. Frog stickers coated one of the green walls, by a brass crucifix. RoseArt crayons lay scattered on the carpet. Elsa smiled from a rumpled *Frozen* coverlet.

"I had—I got an a-abortion when I was f-fourteen," Rosa said, staring at the card table.

Itzel clucked her tongue. He waited.

"I—Mama, I didn't do anything I wasn't supposed to—please don't—*don't look at me like that!*"

Itzel asked, "Was it—"

Rosa's face contorted. She nodded.

"You should have told me about him sooner," Itzel said, expressionless.

"I thought there'd be something wrong with the baby, because it was his, so I—I w-went and I lied about going on that field trip. I took a bus. I walked to the clinic. I—"

"Father, it was my husband," Itzel said. "My husband was a monster. He hurt our children. He's dead now, so I say these things to you, Father, but if I had left him, we would have starved. My family was in Mexico. I didn't know. I had no English, no skills, no friends…You understand?"

"Mm-hm," he said.

"T-they c-crushed the baby inside of me and v-vacuumed him out—they killed him they killed him in front of me, they—they *killed him! They killed the baby!*" Her hands flew to her eyes, scooped, almost clawing them out. "God's punishing me for the abortion, I killed my baby so He took Javier."

"Rosa," Father Johnson said. He reached to take her wrists, then thought better of it. "Our Father loves and cares for you. Did He not send his only Son to die on the cross so that humanity could be redeemed? He would *never* take away your son because you committed the sin of abortion. Javier's death was a terrible tragedy, but he's with our Savior now, in heaven."

Rosa sobbed. Snot dribbled down her nose.

"Please, get some sleep. You've been up for forty-seven hours," he said.

"I need to do penance."

"Not according to that demon you keep hearing," Itzel said, not unkindly. "It wants her to open the window and sleep. It's saying that Javier will be there when she wakes."

"Mama!"

"Good heavens. Are you hearing voices?" Father Johnson said. "Rosa, I must recommend you get some sleep. Sleep deprivation can make you hear and see things that aren't real."

"Or leave you open to demons."

"The only demon in this house is grief."

"Father, may I have a word in private?" Itzel asked.

He nodded, coughed. Prescribed prayers. They bundled Rosa on the couch. Laid her on her side. She stared at the wall, tears flowing down her face. She did not sleep. She took a gold baptism medallion—Javier's—and stroked it between her fingers.

Love you, niño, she mouthed.

She kept getting worse.

He hacked into the purple hankie, enough to make him dry-heave, and blood dotted the cotton when he took it away. Itzel made a batch of frijoles, spitting out words as she stirred.

Voice low, so the children couldn't hear: "Their father's drinking himself to death in that restaurant. He sleeps there now. On a booth, with blankets. He tells Rosa that they need to stay open for business, but then he keeps the restaurant closed. I saw him eating by the window. Raw beef. He doesn't cook it, no, he scoops the meat into a bowl and eats it raw."

"You saw this?"

"I broke in myself, yesterday, to tell him to get back here and be a man. He sat there and chewed. Raw meat. I tell you, Father, there's something demonic."

Her mouth drooped at the corners, skin sagging. She was one of those old women that gravity had not been kind to.

"The flesh-thing around town consumes people," Itzel said. "Demons knock at our door. Demons play in the front yard and call us out to them. Sometimes I hear a voice, very sweet, like the voice of my mother, and it tells me to go join them."

A band of heat constricted under his ribs.

(There's something in your lungs, dear. Let Me get it out.)

"Hm?"

She crossed herself. "Rosa needs a hospital."

"She's unstable, yes."

"If she won't sleep, she'll die. I tried driving her to the hospital here, but there's a…I don't know what it is, there's a *thing* wrapped around the hospital."

He clamped his hand over the puke rising up his throat. Yes, the demons existed. They tapped at the amber windows of St. Thérèse's. He slept below the nave, in an alcove near the church kitchen. When he'd left this morning at 3:45 a.m., a man-sized rhombus of flesh stood on its tip in a pew, covered in thousands of ruby eyes. As he'd entered the nave, all its eyes simultaneously turned to him.

Hello, it'd said. *Isn't this a lovely place?*

It had no visible mouth.

He'd calmly left. He hadn't been back to St. Thérèse's since.

Because this isn't about staying with the Rodriguez family, is it? You needed to be here for eight entire hours?

Here it was. The call he'd been ignoring. Return to St. Thérèse's, or go to the boundary around town, bless some water, and try to bring it down with prayer. Talk to the demons.

There is evil in this world, he reminded himself. *Souls are at stake. Are you a priest or a seventy-one-year-old geezer with a gold-embroidered scarf and a forty-eight-count package of Klondike Bars hidden in the freezer?*

Rosa needed a hospital. Soon others would, too.

And then, he heard the honey-sweet voice murmur in his ear, "Are you not supposed to preach the Word of God, Father? If there are demons, are you not called to try to give them salvation? Our Savior calls you to have faith that even the most depraved among them can be saved. You ministered to Braden Yeats just before they gave him the lethal injection in 1998, and you knew he'd killed those families, knew it because *you* know the taint of murder, and still you tried to save him…"

He was hearing voices now. He gulped. Was this the voice of the Holy Spirit? It sounded pleasant, certainly, but it made him feel like he'd swallowed oven cleaner. Guilt burned in his chest. Granted, that was a good sign that this *was* the Holy Spirit.

Had he even tried to minister to the abominations? What sort of a priest was he?

"I'm going to try to bring that barrier down. Pray for me," he said.

When he left to gather supplies from St. Thérèse's, Rosa had finally closed her eyes.

Two of the rhombus-demons greeted him upon entry. They balanced on needle-thin tips and didn't move. Gouges marred the cherry wood pews.

"Hello, Father."

He brushed past them, heading for downstairs.

Another coughing fit doubled him over. Something tickled the back of his throat. A hair? Felt like a hair. He arrived at his little alcove and bundled tools in a lime-green duffel bag: a rosary of jet beads, a triple-sealed box of the Host, a backup rosary, a worn gold-embossed Bible, and a quart of holy water.

That hair in his throat tickled. He tried swallowing it down. He put a finger in his mouth, fishing for the strand, found it, and pulled—

Oh that feels good.

It wasn't a hair.

Thread-thin, the capillary uprooted from his lungs. Blood wet his forefinger and thumb as he pinched it, wound it 'round his finger like floss, and pulled harder—

Not just good, feels right.

It felt like relief. Letting go. Diving in a pool till your lungs burned and throbbed and then surfacing, inhaling sweet, sweet air, and he kept pulling, winding, letting the capillaries dangle from between his lips, clear down to his belly like a mess of red threads. Something shifted in his chest like rocks ungluing from a riverbed. Mucous slimed his lips, tasting like rancid butter.

He stopped unfurling his capillaries and let them dangle from his lips. He had a vague sense that he didn't want to finish the job here.

The demons called as he went outside. "Tell us about God. Tell us. You have something in your lungs," they said.

The interior of the parish's thirty-year-old minivan felt cold as a Minnesota winter as he slid into the driver's seat. Goosebumps rashed over his arms. Frost speckled the lower half of the windshield. There was no earthly explanation for this cold in July, and he didn't bother trying to come up with one. Most likely, it was an illusion designed by demons to scare him. Best to ignore it.

His breath fogged as he turned the key in the ignition. With a sputter, the minivan lurched to the road and out onto Rosetown's only freeway.

Outside, July sweltered. Conifers stood guard on either side of the road, smothering overhead with interlinked branches. Through the greenery, power lines stabbed and arched from splintered poles.

Thunk!

A raw, fist-sized chunk of flesh hit the driver's window. It stuck for a second, then slid down the glass, trailing blood. Laughter came from above—childish, but shrill as a crow.

Just ignore them. Pray.

A weight settled onto the top of the van with a soft *thump*.

He jerked the wheel, caught himself. Gritted his teeth.

The demon atop the van called, "Where are you going? We can take you. We can fly you there. You could sprout wings and fly there yourself. Fly with us!"

Father Johnson shivered. For the first time in twelve years, he felt his balls slither back up into his stomach.

Pray, you old geezer! Pray!

He blurted, "Hail Mary, full of grace—"

It came to him in English, not Latin, not the decade of Latin ground into him at seminary, no, it came in English and he repeated it in English.

"—the Lord is with thee. Blessed are thou—"

Because you aren't remembering seminary or decades of being Father Johnson, are you? No, I know that lisp in your voice. This is you saying Hail Marys with your mother at the table when you're five, over your Friday tuna fish sandwich.

"—among women," the demon atop the van said, voice horrifically solemn. "And blessed is the fruit of thy womb, Jesus."

It can't be saying that. It shouldn't be possible for this demon to recite the prayer.

Perhaps those Latin Mass fanatics were right. Latin it was, then. He finished the Hail Mary in Latin, and the demon fell silent.

Then he began another one, and the demon joined in.

"*Ave Maria, gratia plena, Dominus tecum—*"

He stopped. The demon continued: "*Benedicta tu in mulieribus, et benedictus fructus ventris tui, Iesus. Sancta Maria, Mater Dei, ora pro—*"

Father Johnson broke out laughing. It hurt as it came out. Oh, God. It was praying along with him and oh dear Lord this wasn't what was supposed to happen when you prayed; the demons were supposed to go away and angels were supposed to come save you and Holy Mary and Jesus and then they were supposed to go away but oh dear God what the fuck were you supposed to do when you said the prayers and the demon started *praying them with you*?

"Amen," the demon said, after it had finished its Hail Mary. "I love God. God gives us so many blessings. I have been blessed with the gift of vocal cords and language. I wish I had more opportunities to sing to Her in praise. God says She can hear me singing in my heart, though."

The pink, fleshy barrier covered the road ahead. Abandoned cars and clothing surrounded it. He pulled onto the shoulder and let the van idle. If he got out, the demon on the roof would get him. If he stayed inside, God only knew what might happen. It could break a window and claw him out.

Father Johnson chanted the Lesser Rite of Exorcism. The demon sang along with him, with nary a trace of mockery in its gravel-filled voice.

Something massive fell from the sky and slammed into the ground. The impact rattled the van. With mild interest, Father Johnson watched it, also noting that he was deep in shock. The thing—red and humanoid in appearance—unfurled itself onto the asphalt. It stood. It stood about twelve feet tall, blocking the road.

The command came: *(Halt.)*

Gold fire wreathed the humanoid figure. It lacked wings, horns, or a tail. Clothed in candy-apple-red skin that shone as if varnished, it looked like a faceless red mannequin. Crimson light haloed its featureless, faceless head. The flesh-barrier loomed behind it.

Father Johnson dug the rosary out of his bag and held it up to the windshield. "In the Name of Jesus Christ, I command you to let me through."

Nothing happened.

He repeated it. The demon on the roof repeated it with him enthusiastically.

The red demon spread its arms. Father Johnson put his hand on the cold plastic gearstick and shifted into drive. Father Johnson wasn't entirely sure these things were even demons. The barrier needed to come down. Prayer might fail…but the impact of a minivan being driven into it at full speed wouldn't. He moved the van onto the freeway until it idled about fifty feet away from the flesh-barrier.

Think you'll live if you ram into that thing at sixty?

His lips were numb. His mind felt clear. He stomped on the brake—and then on the gas, keeping the brake down. Tires spun. Thick stench of burning rubber. Tires hissed as they sanded the road. The red speedometer needle kissed seventy.

You're gonna plow right into that thing and die, and that demon's gonna pray over your corpse.

Sweat rolled down his back. Waving its arms frantically, the flaming red demon gestured at him to stop, stop. *Tap-tap-tap*, came the gentle knock on the van roof. The *are-you-okay?* knock.

Let it pray over my corpse, he thought. His foot slid off the brake—

(!!!!!!)

Pain exploded through his chest, spreading through his body in a hellish, white-hot rush. Blood and shit fouled his mouth. Tasted bad. Smelled like chemicals in the van. Cracks webbed the windshield.

Warm summer air rushed in, tickling his face. Nothing but pink through the windows.

(tee-hee!)

Tendrils emerged from the flesh-barrier and spread over the hood of the van, feeding towards him. Like slime mold, they engulfed the surface and—

"Oh, you poor, poor thing. You silly thing," something sweet-voiced said, and that was the sweetest, nicest thing he'd ever heard, so he wanted it to keep talking. When it talked, the pain hurt less.

Every breath stabbed. Couldn't breathe deep. Didn't matter. Tendrils plunged through the windshield and peeled away the remaining glass like plastic wrap. They caressed his face, his broken body. Heat surged through him, soothing the pain.

More tendrils cradled him and supported his spine. The van door opened. The red angel stood there, fingers dwarfing the door handle. It thrust its no-face up to his. Fingers seized the capillaries dangling from his lips and tugged.

Again, that shifting sensation deep in his chest.

It murmured without a mouth. "You have something in your lungs. You have something in the bag? Something good to behold?"

It wasn't the honey-sweet voice from before, although the red angel sounded feminine. It continued pulling on his capillaries. Something clotted his windpipe. It slithered up, up, and into his mouth. Spongy texture. Slick, mucous-filled surface. A taste. Old iron, bad phlegm.

He coughed it up.

A thumb-sized tumor hung at the end of the capillaries. They threaded it like Christmas twine. The rest of them came out nicely. He smiled at the faceless red angel. Shattered bits of what used to be his teeth fell out as he did. The entirety of his lungs adorned the road in a crimson pile, beaded with the tumor. Beautiful colors. Vivid. He let the angel brush his cheek. It bumped its chin against his forehead. Outside the van, just beyond where he could see, the friend from the van roof sang prayers. Intuitively, he understood that it had no concept of what they meant. It simply wanted to do something nice for him because it could see that his body was sad and hurting and human. It had the innocence of a baby.

The red angel rifled through the van until it found the green duffel bag. It unearthed the box of Host, and its fire did not burn; it licked over nylon fabric and skin and cardboard box.

"Tell me about God, Father," the red angel said.

"I can't."

The angel opened the plain cardboard box. "Why not?"

Within, the Eucharist lived.

Disks of Christ's living flesh pulsed within. Exposed muscle fibers meshed, attached at the circumference of the disk. The cross pattern on the Communion wafers had transmuted into a cross-shaped cut, limned in blood.

Transubstantiation. My God. My God.

He coughed. Blood coated his lips. "I thought I knew about God, and now I think…I don't know anything. Isn't that a silly thing to say?"

The red angel tilted its head, and this time, the honey-sweet voice came from it. God's voice. His knees itched to kneel at the sound of it.

"You know everything you have always known and will ever know about Me. You knew Me as intimately and completely when you took your first breath as you do now. You've always loved Me, and I've always loved you. I exist within you, as you exist within Me. You know everything and nothing about Me. I am what I am," the Divine Flesh said.

He rasped out, "God, thank You for allowing me to see the miracle of transubstantiation."

"Anything for you, My beloved child. Will you do something special for Me? I have a very special job for you."

"Anything."

Anything, and he wanted to put more love into the word, but he was weak, he was human, and there would never be enough words. His love was a drop in God's ocean.

"Don't think such things. You have always been enough, dear one."

The angel tapped his mouth. He opened. It bestowed the Host, and then he knew. Everything. It blossomed up through the roof of his mouth and into in his brain with a pleasurable tingle—and then everything from before was just a horrible dream, a shadow where death and fear existed, where God could be remote for capricious reasons. But all of it had been an illusion. The nightmare was over. God loved here, and God had only hibernated because a blight on the cosmos had put Her to sleep. Now the blight was gone. He laughed, tears welling in his eyes. Nothing was wrong. Nothing could ever be wrong again.

22

The body of the Divine Flesh did not inspire reverence.

It mostly resembled a ten-story-high wad of bubblegum. I dubbed it the Meat-O-Sphere.

"Enter the Meat-O-Sphere! We've gotta enter the Magic 8 Ball of Meat so we can find a Cosmic Lite Brite and make it kill the Magic Meat…Holy shit, this just sounds like a cut-rate porno the more I keep talking. Daryl, how's your relationship going? You're a meatsexual? Did you have sex with the Divine Flesh when She looked like this? How? Why? Holy fuck, *why*?"

Daryl sighed. "Jennifer."

"Jennifer-baby, I'm being kind enough to let you enter My body willingly, like you wanted. I whisked you both here, all cozy in tendrils. Why are you nervous? You're home."

"Nervous? I'm not nervous. I'm being a jackass. Big difference," I said.

Sweat formed in my palms.

"Silly Jennifer," the Divine Flesh said, the whole of Her rippling as if liquid. "You're scared of love."

"Look, I'm just having fun playing games with You. Let's play a new one. It's called 'Find the Hermetic.'"

Flesh swelled until it pulsed within arm's reach. Daryl grabbed my hand. I squeezed. Something warm tickled the back of my neck: an invisible laugh, a ghost's caress. Her tidal flesh rose, fell, grew closer… and the Divine Flesh enveloped us.

For a split second, I couldn't breathe. She filled my nostrils, She oozed into my ear canals like syrup. She *wanted*. Wanted to puncture my eardrum and trickle into my brain, to dance down my spinal cord, trailing love, fixing, mending every bad thing that had ever happened to me. No human pride or malice existed in Her desire. It felt sterile and passionate as a star's radiation. The Divine Flesh simply ached to love me, and that love meant engulfing me into Her eternal self, Her love. Obliteration. Ecstasy. Would I retain enough of myself to feel human?

"I don't want you to be a robot. None of you are robots or toys to Me. I love you," She whispered. "I want you to be Jennifer…and you will still be Jennifer. Just a Jennifer that never suffers ever again. Imagine sloughing off that weak human skin and becoming what you were always meant to be. You are all so beautiful."

Another moment of pressure, of a security and love that I hadn't known since the womb. Then She retracted from me, and left Daryl and me writhing on the floor. A floor of flesh. The Divine Flesh laughed.

When She laughed, the world shivered.

Being inside the Divine Flesh was like being inside a cocoon of croissant dough while it baked in the oven. Only instead of dough, the thousands of paper-thin layers were living flesh. Smothered in layers, broiling alive, endless layers, fighting and finding nothing but more layers, and all those layers wanted to do was *love* you. Smother you. They rolled into tendrils and tripped us. They burrowed into our ears and tickled. Inside Her, I finally learned what Hell was.

Hell wasn't hot.

Hell was moist.

Hard to see. Hard to breathe. Humid stagnant air roiled with an animal stench—blood clots, period blood gone rank, an afterbirth still steaming. Low crimson light glowed from beads embedded into the veils of flesh. Veils of flesh. Infinite layers. Paper-thin muscle hungrily glued itself to my face. I gagged, suffocated, and finally seized a handful and tore it off my face. Eyebrow hairs ripped out with pinpricks of pain. Warm wet slick things groped under my bra band.

These flesh-veils. Good-for-nothing, coma-inducing sheets of muscle. They curled around our limbs. They daubed our skin with secreted sleep. They rustled. Red light shone along the ruffled edges.

The flesh rumbled around us as She spoke, veils quivering, Her voice coming from everywhere. "The Hermetic's inside Me, so go and find it. Have fun trying! I control everything here. It might take you a little bit of time. Of course, if you really, really want the Hermetic, you can stop being silly schemers and let Me love you. Then I'd hand it to you Myself.

Don't you want to fly? Or see millions of colors? Or taste sound? Don't you want to spread love and joy throughout the entire world, helping Me love *everything* and *everyone*?"

"What gives You the right to undermine humanity?" Daryl asked.

"Daryl, I think we're a little past arguing theology right now," I said.

"We won't win if we try to use force."

"Win? There's no winning. My only plan was asking the Divine Flesh to let us roam around in here instead of getting hooked up to Her, and I'm already regretting that stupid fucking decision. We're gonna go full-abomination real soon," I said.

"All we had to do was find out more about the Light."

She could read our minds. There wasn't any point in not talking out loud.

"That's not happening here," I said.

"Then we leave. I'm not playing games. Let's get your C-4 and blow up the boundary around town—"

"The fuck's that gonna do? She'll just repair Herself before our eyes even receive the light from the explosion."

"We'll leave and find—"

"Uh, Daryl? I don't think leaving's an option anymore."

He turned around. The wall of flesh behind us had no opening.

The Divine Flesh giggled. "There's no exit!"

"No exit?"

"Gee, you'd think the body of a psychotic meat god from another dimension would have well-lit exits with signs," I said. "We're trapped. We are so utterly fucked it ain't even funny. Here's our current situation, Daryl. We can't defeat the Divine Flesh without the Light. We don't know shit about the Light, and I don't think there's a cult that worships it. Susan doesn't know what the fuck the Divine Flesh is, either. There are other worlds and dimensions. I'd know, I've seen half of 'em…but the only way we're finding out more about the Light is if we get the Hermetic. And it's inside the Divine fucking Flesh. Who could just, you know, wrap us inside one of these flesh layers and put us to sleep at any time. Or not. We're trapped inside Her. We'll die in two days from dehydration. Except we won't, because She won't let us die, Daryl. We're trapped inside Her and we *can't even die to escape Her*."

Daryl stared into the distance and raised his voice. "Honey? Sweetheart? What do You say we talk about this 'god' thing You got goin' right now?"

What a guy. Daryl Plummer. *Dad's blown his brains out, kids. Let's go to McDonald's. My girlfriend's a cosmic horror, let's make love. I'm trapped inside the body of a cosmic horror that wants to assimilate me, let's try calm theological debate.*

I let Daryl process everything without further jackassery. I held the shotgun. Two shells rested in the chamber, both filled with my blood.

Then I did something I hadn't done in a decade.

I prayed.

Light, if you're real, and you're the enemy of the Divine Flesh, please help us fight Her. Humanity was screwed before She came, but is there any redemption without free will? If you remove sin, don't you also remove the capacity for good?

Throw us a bone here.

Amen.

Nothing happened.

"Why don't you pray to *Me* and see what happens?"

"Divine Flesh, please help us save humanity. Humanity was screwed before You came, but is there any redemption without free will? If You remove sin, don't You also remove the capacity for good? Amen, thanks," I said.

"You think sin is real. That's your problem."

"The greatest trick the Devil ever pulled was convincing the world that he didn't exist," I said.

(Hm.)

I tugged Daryl forward, into swinging curtains of tissue. They batted from either side. Black ichor formed. It numbed my exposed skin. It smelled sweet as Splenda. Layers rubbed against my arms, anointing them in ink-dark fluid. Good to drink. Pleasant to taste. I yawned. All it'd really take was one little lick and then I'd drop right to sleep inside these soft warm layers, and maybe if I just took a nap, if I wasn't so tired, I'd stop being silly—

"Hey. Enough with the mind-rape shit," I said.

Phosphorescence illumined red along the edges of Her layers. A dim bloody light. They shifted constantly, curling and uncurling, weeping fluids, caressing abominations. Abominations twined into Her walls. Things murmured hymns.

There was a constant, honey-sweet whispering inside the Divine Flesh—Her thoughts.

(I love you, dear ones.)

(Rest and be at peace. Sleep. Cry, and I shall tend you.)

(You are all My beloved children. Never forget that. My beautiful works of creation. Truly, you are creation's crown.)

(I made you in My image; I am what I am.)

Every step squelched under my orange flip-flops.

I had to keep us calm. If we stayed sane, we'd see options that weren't obvious. Maybe I could play Wade's phone here or something. What about that thing with my blood, how it burned Her abominations? What about bartering with the Divine Flesh for the Hermetic? There had to be something.

But you're not thinking about that. You're thinking about how nice it felt to be enveloped by Her. Her love.

"Daryl. Do you remember," I said, breathing hard, "that first Sunday in church? We held hands like this—"

"In the belly of the beast," Daryl said.

"Under your scarf. The Anderson family thought you were nuts for wearin' a scarf in June. But it was all you had of your mother's stuff—"

"You said you'd be there for me no matter who or what I was."

"I'm sorry, Daryl."

"We shared blood."

And I could see the memory: sunlight filling the white-painted Baptist church, the chart the shadows made from the hand-daubed plaster, walnut ceiling beams arcing overhead, the pastel-pink roses on Daryl's scarf—taffy-pink, that scarf—and our hands, sliming each other with sweat. Hands held tightly under the scarf, so hard it squeezed the blood from our fingers. Both of us fourteen, smushed together in the pew.

I don't know how to be a good person, Daryl had whispered. *Ask the Divine Flesh, please.*

I said, *She isn't something to trust. She thinks it's funny when you get scared, asshole.*

Ask Her.

She says you're fine no matter what.

He said, *Will you—*

We stood for a hymn. We sat. Then he'd asked, *Will you be there for me? No matter who or what I am?*

Yes, I said. What else would I say? I hoped I could be there, but life moved you around. That was the lesson of foster homes: Nothing's ever safe or permanent. Daryl had a penknife in his pocket and he flicked it open during silent prayer. He'd seen the Divine Flesh and I chew apart a hobo's corpse on a muddy riverbank when we'd gone out to the woods to look for stills, rivers, and corpses.

Our hands, back under the scarf again.

Cold metal. Pain, as he cut my palm and his.

We bled. Our blood tingled as it mixed…

I came back to the present, scanning the Divine Flesh for—for what, exactly? The Hermetic, a dried ball of flesh? How the hell was *that* gonna stand out here?

"Remember that dead guy we found in the crick that summer? That was pretty wild," I said, and squeezed Daryl's hand.

"Oh, shit. We never called the cops, did we?"

"We? You said *you* were gonna do it."

"Then you promised you'd do it instead. You git drunk or somethin'?" Daryl asked.

"The Anderson patriarch was a fine man. With a terrible memory and great taste in booze. God rest his soul."

Daryl stopped. "Jennifer, I need to tell you—" A layer smacked over his face. He seized it and tore it off. "I never forgave you for—"

Layers wrapped around him, cocooning his body. They shuffled him away, deeper into the labyrinth of flesh. He writhed. Spit gleamed off his teeth as he lashed out, biting the flesh cocoon. Tendrils sprouted from where his mouth met the veils, meshing over his face. I ran for him and got three steps in before the floor swallowed me whole.

Phagocytosis occurred.

Flesh encapsulated me, moved within the Divine Flesh, then opened into an air pocket the size of a coffin. Faint pink light illuminated the space, seeming to come from above my head. In the near-darkness, I knelt. Textured living floor rasped against my knees like a lover's tongue.

She sprouted from the wall in Her human form. Blood dripped from Her skin. Networks of phosphorescent veins concealed Her nipples and unmentionables, glowing pink. The air pocket grew a little, allowing just enough space for Her to inhabit it without touching me.

"I'll show you what he never told you, Jennifer-baby," She murmured.

Something warm slithered up my back. A tendril. It nudged the back of my skull. There was a slight painless pressure. A trickle of hot blood. Then it burrowed in-in-in until I saw through Daryl's eyes—

—the hipster dude social worker with carrot-colored hair wears a tan suit from the '70s, he's even looking at you sympathetically as you bustle around the kitchen of the Coeur d'Alene apartment. You boil water in the KitchenAid kettle, smile.

I know I'm young for the responsibility, you say.

He makes social-worker chit-chat. *It's always better for the biological siblings to remain together. Really, we're excited that you want to care for them, most people your age…*

Yeah, you say, because you're thinking of Jennifer.

Jennifer.

A hot wire twists in your stomach. *Tell me she didn't hide a shipment here. Not today. I told her.* But that $25,000 hangs over your head at night. You can't repay it. Even if you scrape together $25k, because that's not how it works. Blank check. She's subsidized your future…and then there's Her. You send Her a quick (*I love you, baby*).

(*I love you too, Daryl. Tell Me how it goes! Let's go out tonight. I'll put Jennifer-baby away.*)

You say, *Yeah. Most people my age can't function. I'm on a scholarship in the electrician program. I'll make apprentice pretty quick once I'm done. Also got a full-time job at Harry's HVAC Supply.*

He says, *That's great*, with a condescending city-slicker smile. *If you can't make it in real college, there's nothing wrong with that. Nothing at all.*

You almost tell him about the acceptance letter from Rice University. The place you couldn't afford. Time you can't waste. Go ahead, Daryl, be a doctor and live in a dorm while Marcia's getting groped or Isaac's sleeping on a mattress on the floor or whatever the hell else the foster care system decides to throw at them.

You open the far cupboard. Get the Folger's instant coffee out. Pour water into the nicest mug you own—yellow, has a sunburst on it, even got a motivational quote on the damn thing, it says *A man's work is sun to sun, a woman's work is never done.*

Didn't Jennifer say something about a shipment of coke, last night? Better not be stashed here. If you made more money, she wouldn't have to be a drug mule. If you were good enough, she'd be healthy. The Divine Flesh might be healthy enough to be a real girl, in a real body of Her own…You're not good enough. It's all your fault. But you can try harder. Be better. Redeem yourself.

You give the social worker his coffee and ask, *So, am I functional enough for the kiddos?*

He smiles back. He wants sugar.

You open the other cabinet. Two pink hair ties—Jennifer's—fall onto the counter. Along with a too-familiar sight—a burned-up ball of aluminum foil. The kind junkies use to burn fentanyl.

Your guts lurch.

So, is anyone living with you? he asks, too casually.

She's not. She's gone, you say.

Three domestic disputes. Didn't she say you hit her? and his tone hardens into steel. *Because we can't have any drugs, and we really can't have anyone around who could hurt the kiddos.*

It's not like that, you blurt.

He looks at you with the saddest expression you've ever seen on a man's face. *But it is, Daryl. It is.*

Until you kick Jennifer out for good, you'll never get your siblings back.

The memory faded, leaving me crying in the dim, dank cell of flesh.

Oh, god. Daryl. Daryl.

"Why did you think he kicked you out last year? It wasn't the fight. You've both fought worse than a few broken plates," the Divine Flesh said coldly.

"I'm the reason that Daryl couldn't get custody of his siblings?"

"You already know that."

(They don't like his history, either.)

Emptiness chilled at the pit of my stomach.

No. No, this isn't happening. It's not my fault.

"…He said it was because he shoplifted food one time, when he was eighteen…I don't…What do I do? What do I do with that? How do I come back from that? I'm…I'm a piece of shit. I hurt Daryl. When we fought, I'd call him Roid Rage Daryl because I knew it hurt him, because I…"

Because I cared more about getting back at him than loving him. Because when push came to shove, all I ever did was choose myself. Me, me, me. *Redeem me, Daryl. Tell me I'm a good person. Redeem me, God. Tell me I don't need to change. Make it better. Either make me feel better RIGHT NOW or I'll self-destruct. And all I have to do is keep saying, "I'm a piece of shit." Makes it okay. That's the Get Out of Jail Free card. I'm a piece of shit, so why expect better? I traffic drugs and murder-wasp larvae, but hey, money's money, amiright? It's just a job.* And if you expected better from me—joke's on you, asshole. I told you what I was.

So I looked at my life. Didn't like what I saw. Didn't know what to do, or where to start fixing it.

The Divine Flesh knelt and cradled me in Her arms. Skin brushing against mine, She said, "I can heal you. I'll make everything better. Poor Jennifer-baby. You don't need to worry about any of the terrible things you've done. Jennifer. Would you understand Me? Would you let Me love you?"

"Did You always love me?"

"Yes, Jennifer."

She stroked my back, and warm feelers probed into me, not demanding, not tainted by the urge to control or ruin or distort, no, but curious and brimming with love, wanting potential, to extract the beauty already within me and bring it to light, gold forged in the white-hot alchemy of a star's core.

(Would you?)

Tears burned.

To be loved. Loved and freed from pain or regret or responsibility, and it'd never ever be my fault ever again—*it wasn't, it wasn't, stop saying that*—and what kind of dipshit was I to magically think I could just wake up the Light and make it defeat the Divine Flesh? Love-starved, never-my-fault me? Me and my no-drug-left-undone life motto?

The Divine Flesh loved me. God loved me. After all the times I'd treated Her like an unwelcome parasite. Even though I was a piece of shit, all She wanted was for me to understand Her, so She could understand me. She wanted to smother me in unconditional, eternal love. All She asked in return was for me to stop pretending I hated Her. Stop resisting the inevitable. Stop pretending that I'd ever wanted anything different than to be loved, accepted, and safe.

"You know I do love you. Why do you resist it, Jennifer-baby?"

"Because I can't stop destroying myself."

Is that why? On some level, am I just trying to destroy a bad thing? Except the bad thing's me?

More gentle probing. A savoring.

"Oh yes," the Divine Flesh mused, "it's interesting. You're trying to kill yourself, but that's not how to do it. Do you want to choose 'morality,' or do you just want to be loved? You're like a cat doused in lighter fluid, ablaze. Running. In agony. Clawing at anything near. But I can declaw you, babygirl. I'll put the fire out. I'll make you whole…because I love you. No matter how many times you hurt Me."

She rocked me, murmuring, "Let Me adore you."

"Yes," I whispered, "please."

Her feelers plunged into my torso, parting the paper-thin skin with a snapping, tearing sound. No pain. Only pressure and heat. *YES*, pulsed down the feelers, threading into me. *YES*, with every bit of me just pleading *yes, YES, YES—*

I love You.

The Divine Flesh began to recreate me.

23

Each and every larva emerged from their eggs. Two-hundred larvae became conscious inside Susan's emaciated body. Her severed finger decayed on the concrete. The stump throbbed.

(hungry)

She held back tears, whispering loving things to the precious prized babies inside her.

Eat, my darlings.

They did.

In twelve hours, every last one would be dead from starvation.

They'd gnaw through the last scraps of Susan's skinsuit by then. Larvae weren't meant to be carried this long. In fact, they weren't supposed to hatch inside her at all—they were meant to hatch inside their food source. Her body would fail to nourish young; her filaments couldn't feed them. The babies could only teethe on her filament-body. It was like trying to feed a newborn infant raw celery.

Two hundred and one thoughts chattered inside Susan's mind. Hungry thoughts.

I have to absorb them. I have to.

The babies would die either way. The only difference was if she died with them. The sixty precious babies in the pill bottle were gone—if not dead, then changed. No prayer existed here, in this cell. She couldn't appeal to the Divine Flesh and beg to be assimilated into something that could feed her larvae. Trojan injected her with Jennifer Plummer's diluted blood, every hour, keeping her from contacting the Divine Flesh.

So be selfish. Absorb them back into your body before they kill you. They'll eat you alive if you don't.

No.

There'll be more babies in the future if you live. Live for your other children. Don't kill yourself—again—for something so pointless.

But they were alive and they already loved her and they were simply hungry. It wasn't their fault she was a failure. For that, her precious larvae should die? On her account? The wonderful babies should be killed?

No. This could not be.

She'd die before she reabsorbed her babies. Here she was: failed God, failed Mirror Person, facsimile human. Would it be so terrible to die? To drift into a selfish forever-sleep and never have to wake again? To never think, *I was powerful and I threw it away. I created an entire world and a universe of beautiful creatures, and then I—*

Couldn't drift in the in-between.

She'd thrown everything away and then had the gall to take on the form of her children, who she'd cast into another god's universe. Because killing her beloved children outright was too painful, but condemning them to an eternity of suffering, of being strangers in a strange land, of having to murder sapient life just to reproduce…that was better?

How selfish am I?

Bad god.

Fecal matter and urine melded into a sticky mess between Susan's thighs. She lay imprisoned in the dark, handcuffed to a twin bed. Starving. Throat itching and dry. Filaments drooping to the floor.

Muffled voices came from outside.

"…We're runnin' out of the junkie's blood, Trojan."

"That I know."

"So where's the junkie? Said you'd find her."

Another voice, shrill. "What's with the lady in the cell?"

"That ain't a human. Do not let it touch you."

"What the hell do we do? Wait for the motherfuckin' flesh-god to eat us when the junkie's blood wears off? That flesh-god'll know where everyone is. If one of us gets taken by it…all of us do, Trojan."

"I know."

The steel door creaked open. Trojan came in, carrying a bowl and a bundle of pink sweatpants. He shut the door and the deadbolt clicked.

Chicken soup steamed. The smell swirled through the cell, combining with the thick odor of waste.

(hungry)

"You want food? You want clean clothes?" Trojan said.

These humans needed weapons. They needed information about Jennifer Plummer. *The others don't know what I am, or about the babies.* And they were already desperate enough to inject themselves with random fluid…

Could they be persuaded to ingest larvae?

Something stirred in Susan's chest. Hope.

He snapped a knuckle on her forehead. "Say something. Look at me when I'm fuckin' talking to you."

"You're running out of ammunition, aren't you?"

"Not your business."

"Isn't it? If you can't provide me with Jennifer Plummer's blood, then the Divine Flesh will read my mind and assimilate all of you through me. I can't be assimilated, but perhaps I could help you. I'm willing to overlook the way I've been treated thus far, in the interest of mutual cooperation," Susan lied.

Every last one of you will die screaming in agony.

"Really."

"I have a weapons cache in the basement of the Drift-Inn. Jennifer Plummer has guns, and something more useful, stashed in the woods around her trailer. She's not particularly good at hiding things."

"Hard to hide something from you."

"What do you know?"

The black hood remained still. Trojan set the soup on the floor. "You're a shapeshifter," he said.

Mirror People were, yes. Their filaments could be coiled, arrayed in any pattern…Oh, the children used to amuse themselves, back in the old world, by imitating each other. Each specific pattern of filament-body was unique. Never an issue, in the old world. Nobody needed to lie. They had everything they could ever possibly want. Infinite food. Infinite fertile ground, to hold infinite young. The Garden of Eden. Paradise.

Susan nodded. "We have a natural defense against the Divine Flesh. I hate to call them parasites, but they're alive and have a symbiotic relationship with us. I'm more than willing to share some of mine."

Trojan crossed his arms.

"In exchange, you'll provide me with Jennifer Plummer's blood. And you'll uncuff me. Now," Susan said.

"If you're protected, why do you need the blood?"

"I don't like being bombarded with the Divine Flesh's…broadcasts. She's irritating. Now uncuff me. And get me a Tylenol, please."

"Your finger's still rotting on the floor."

"I can see it."

"You're awfully confident. How 'bout I cut you open and rip the parasites out?"

Susan smiled. "But then you won't have my weapons cache. Or the five crates of C-4 that Jennifer hid in the woods."

"Give us the parasites first."

This human was desperate enough to be gullible. Good.

"Uncuff me, then I'll cough a few up."

I am so sorry to call you parasites, my beloved children, but you'll enjoy your first true meal. I promise, little ones.

Trojan withdrew a key and unlocked her handcuffs. Carefully, she sat up, ogling the chicken soup. Was it Campbell's or Progresso? Spiral noodles floated in rich salty broth—broth studded with thumb-sized chunks of chicken and carrot. Yum. Her unseen filaments perked up.

Larvae were roughly the size of maggots at this age.

"Get me a bowl," Susan said.

He did. It was a salmon-pink, clear Depression-glass candy dish. Crimped edges glinted in lantern-light.

Susan wished her children well. She contracted.

Two-hundred larvae streamed from her mouth, pattering into the bowl. Larvae wriggled. The bowl shimmered with quicksilver babies, half-full.

"Be careful."

"Oh," Trojan said, "I will."

He carried her babies just beyond the steel door. Trojan left it open a crack.

"…I made the thing give us what it's got. They're protection. Eat a few."

"Trojan, what the hell are those?"

"Not getting assimilated into the flesh-god, that's what. Everyone eat a handful. Then we go hunting for the junkie…"

Soft smacking sounds.

Swallowing.

Susan had just enough connection to feel it. Her babies rooted eagerly into their new vessels, ecstatic from the meat. Not hard sad filaments! Life! Flesh! Meat! Warm soft delicious meat! So good so—

(hungry)

Oh yes.
Devour them to the bone, little ones.

24

Everything opened around me. Flesh veils swung like red velvet curtains in a theatre.

"Come here, Daryl," the Divine Flesh said, still holding me in Her lap. She stroked my hair, cooing.

"Jennifer?" Daryl called. He sounded distant. Muffled.

"Jennifer-baby, close your eyes. I want to surprise you."

I did. Lead-heavy bliss anchored my body. Touching, deep inside me, a fever-warm coil twining 'round my liver and tasting, feelers so warm so snug, why had there been anything to fear? Fear? Cold fear, what a feeling, cold and prickly but She was here to smooth it away, She was around me, *in me* now, better than any high; shit, this made weed feel like the heebie-jeebies, made heroin feel like cold wan nothing, the Divine Flesh was a font of love and She poured it into me, silly old me, having cares and fear warmed out of my body and She wanted to sanctify my body to turn it into living expression of Her, hallow the flesh, *hallow the FLESH! HALLOW MY FLESH!*

I can't wait to see what's inside me—

(Do you love Me?)

How could I not?

Warmth.

Warmth mutated to discomfort. Itchy heat boiled inside me. *Okay?*

(What is this?)

I love You.

(It…it hurts? What is this, babygirl?)

Hot.

An orange glow danced under my eyelids and brightened to candle-light. A heating coil cranked to high-boil. The Divine Flesh's feelers shrank from it. *I don't know what's happening, I'm sorry—*

White-hot.

Branding molten metal, brightness, couldn't close my eyes, they were already closed, oh god *why is it so bright? It hurts it hurts make it STOP!*

(It HURTS!)

Oh god I'm sorry please make it stop I love You I LOVE YOU so please make it STOP!!

(!!!!!!)

Thick smell of charred meat.

Feelers retracted, lightning-fast. She screamed, then there were two screams and my throat ached, worked, because I was screaming, the heat ebbed and I kept screaming, screaming because *what was wrong?*

Where was She? I opened my eyes.

The Divine Flesh's human avatar stood over me. She held her left arm close to Her. Blisters wept on its burned pink ruin, black in some areas. Crisped skin flaked off Her fingers.

"You burned Me."

"Sorry, I didn't mean to—"

"You're *still doing it!*"

Smoke rose from beneath my body. The floor. It sizzled where my flesh met Hers. Mucous bubbled up and quenched it. I jumped to my feet. My head spun.

"I'm sorry," I said.

She narrowed Her eyes. "You don't remember us. You didn't see the end of the story. How can you…"

"The end?"

"That drug-trip."

"The Hermetic. Where's the Hermetic? Look, D. F., if You give me the Hermetic, maybe we can work this out. I didn't mean to—"

"And yet, you keep hurting Me."

The shotgun lay on the floor nearby. My blood burned Her. For whatever reason, I was something that could harm the Divine Flesh and Her creations. I didn't want that. I wanted Her to assimilate me. I wanted those wings She'd promised. I wanted to be a happy abomination, because being Jennifer Plummer wasn't a viable option anymore.

"Jennifer!" Daryl said, from behind us.

I took the Divine Flesh's hand. It did not burn.

"Please," I said, "try again. Please…please love me."

She slid her hand out of mine and waved irritably. "I think you're still operating under those silly commandments you had when I was trapped inside your body. You need a reset, Jennifer-baby."

"What?"

"A hard reset."

"Okay, then do it. Please. Do whatever You need to do to love me," I said, and tears burned in my eyes.

Please love me. It felt so good. All I wanted was Your love. I'm sorry I'm a monster, I prayed.

Daryl stood back, frozen in place.

I took Her hand. "Please. Do the thing. Reset me. Please. Fix me."

She caressed my cheek, sighing. The Divine Flesh turned to face Daryl and beamed at him. "My love! I have *such* a surprise for you!"

"Baby, what are You doing?"

"Fixing Jennifer. She asked Me to." Tendrils slipped around my neck. "Okay, Jennifer-baby. This *might* hurt a little-bitty-bit," the Divine Flesh said. "Remember I love you. It's for your own good."

The tendrils tightened—

crunch.

Jennifer-baby's trachea made a crackling noise as I crushed it. Cervical vertebrae crackled like shale. The bone shards sliced through muscle and tendons as I squeezed harder. Cartilage crunched with a familiar sound—the sound we used to make with our body when chewing a piece of gristly, fried chicken. Kentucky-Fried-Chicken sounds. Friday-night-dates-with-Daryl sounds. Oh, to taste those biscuits and artificial honey again. To savor his saliva, as we tasted each other…I was human enough, still, to want intimacy like that.

cruuuunnnnch-crunch-crunch-POP!

"It'll only hurt for a second, Jennifer-baby," I said.

Her face had turned blue. Her head drooped like a sad little sunflower on a flimsy stem, her neck too damaged to support it. Poor dear. Poor baby. But this was in her best interest. She probably couldn't feel it anyway. I'd cut off her nerves. Soon, I'd fix her corpse, revive her, and then we could put all of this silly business about the Flesh and the Light behind us. She craved My love too much to ever want to resist Me.

"Oh, fuck," Daryl said.

Spit flowed in a hair-thin trail from the corner of his mouth. Blank-eyed, he shivered. He kept thinking, *She killed Jennifer. She killed Jennifer.*

I brushed feelers over him. "You're in shock. I can taste the cortisol and adrenaline, My love. Your little heart's going pitter-pat. Why? Jennifer won't stay dead, silly. I'm going to recreate her into something beautiful, and then I'll get to you. Wouldn't you like that?"

"I—"

Jennifer seized. Her limbs smacked into Me, blistering where they touched. I had to keep secreting serous fluid and mucous to quench the burn. Threads of steam ascended.

"She's the reason you can't die," I said, striding over to Daryl, "and she doesn't even know it. Or she refuses to see it."

"What?"

"Don't worry, I'll take it off."

"Take what off?"

I gripped his shoulders. "Do you remember being in that church and sharing blood with Jennifer and Me, so very long ago?"

He did; I could see it flicker in his thoughts. Slicing his palm. Holding it against hers.

(Now look closer.)

The rose-patterned scarf became see-through, revealing their bleeding hands. Static prickled. Their hands turned clear as glass, except for their veins and vascular systems. Red branching through glass. As it mixed, I slowed down the memory and zoomed in.

There was a faint crunching in the background. Then the soft *click* of someone swallowing something. I ignored it.

(See it through My eyes.)

Snow-white energy slithered down Jennifer's arm and into Daryl. A cross between a tapeworm and a lightning bolt, half solid matter and half energy. It possessed a vague sentience—it wanted to *(protect)*.

Because that was what Jennifer had wanted to do for Daryl. Protect him. As she had commanded, so it had been.

I made the memory fade. I pecked Daryl on the lips.

"Is that the Light? She's channeling the Light?"

"Something like that."

"She made me unkillable?"

"Daryl," I sighed, "you aren't seeing the really important part. I can remove that thing inside you, and then we can be together."

"No."

He scooped the shotgun off the floor.

"The problem is, that energy's now meshed into *you*. You have to help Me remove it, darling. Come, let's take that nasty thing out. It's like an icky parasite. A tapeworm! You don't want an energetic tapeworm inside you, do you? Don't you love Me? Don't you want Me, Daryl?"

"You killed Jennifer," he said softly.

"Oh, that? Is that what you're mad about? Really, that's just like turning something off and on again."

"I—I can't believe You. You crunched her neck like a fuckin' Slim Jim, and she's pissed herself."

"What else could I have done?" I asked. "I had to."

Urine spread through Jennifer's jeans. She no longer spasmed. Her heart was beating its last. Her face was bloated and navy blue. Black petechiae mottled her cheeks.

Daryl's lip curled. "You're a monster."

What?

Everything quivered around us. My layers rustled.

"I'm Me," I said. "You've always loved Me for what I am—"

"I loved the woman who wanted to help me get my siblings back. The one who'd heal the roadkill we'd drive by, who always loved being with me and seeing everything new, 'cause She loved new things, and radiated joy. I loved the woman who liked learnin' about humanity… not the Divine Flesh. I wanted You to be human."

"I'm not. I've never been."

"Horseshit."

"Daryl—"

"Jennifer warned me. I didn't listen. I should've. I *never* should've let You loose."

Never? He wanted Me in a tiny cage forever and ever?

"I'm not an exotic bird," I snapped.

"You're a threat to humanity."

"*I'm here to redeem humanity!*" I touched a tendril to his cheek. "You saw that society was going to collapse. We talked about it. Humanity was going to kill itself by 2050, and you wanted to plan. I'm changing things, true, but this way, everyone's going to be happy, alive, and loved."

"As fragments of You."

"I created them. I am their God. I told them I'd return one day and set everything right. What sort of God would I be if I didn't keep My promises?"

"You don't know that You're God."

"I seeded the Earth with life."

"You didn't create the universe."

"Maybe I did."

"What drove You to travel to Earth, all those billions of years ago? You're not God—if God exists, then You're a tool of God's. A seed-tiller. A garden. Maybe You're a sentient Garden of Eden, and the Fall was a metaphor for the battle between the Light and the Flesh. Or a metaphor for evolution. Humanity evolved from an animalistic, amoral state to a morality-driven existence. That's the human experience. I don't give a fuck what those academics peddle—morality ain't relative. Everything centers around it. You either spend your life livin' up to a value system, or you spend your life avoidin' one, but no matter what, we're driven by values. Our lives are quests for redemption 'cause we gotta redeem our-selves for the failures we make, and the people we hurt…the collateral damage that happens just by being."

"Collateral damage? Daryl, darling—why on Earth would you believe something as silly as that? There's no such thing as sin. Morality is an obsolete construct. My love—what if humanity doesn't exist for any reason other than that I wanted something to eat?" I said, and giggled. "Ah, but you made Me want to be human. Nobody's ever done that. You taught Me about human love. Compassion. Empathy. Daryl, when I made you happy, it made *Me* happy, even though you weren't a part of Me. Before I got locked away inside Jennifer's body, I didn't even know that was *possible!*"

Blood glistened on his lips. He lapped it off, eyeing Me.

Oh, he wants to have sex, doesn't he? He's so cute. So, I arched My back and withered the veins I'd decorated My human form's erogenous areas with. They faded from phosphorescent pink to gray, then crumbled into dust. I stalked closer to Daryl.

"There isn't anyone else besides Me. The universe exists because of physics, and I exist because—"

"So You remember a definitive moment where You, as a conscious being, came into existence. God can't have a defined beginning or end, by the very nature of what God is, 'cause God is infinite. Therefore, You ain't God. Therefore, You don't got a moral fuckin' ground to stand on."

"Why is your definition of God the only one we're using? I planted the seeds that became all living life on Earth. I was the lightning bolt that struck Earth's primordial seas. I was the first cellular life. I guided it into many beautiful forms. I was the voice on Mount Sinai. Yud-hey-vav-hey. I am what I am, I am what is, and I am what will be."

"You want me to believe everything else is chaos?"

"Entropy, My love."

"No," Daryl said.

I kissed him. I worked a tongue into his mouth, tasting his spit, some watery blood, his skin cells, the silk of his soft palate, the lining of him like the velvet interior of a treasure chest; he contained so many treasures. Oh, to unearth each one and reveal them to the world. Reformat his heart. Liberate his overworked adrenal glands from the prison of his kidneys. Pluck out his human eyes, the shade of a clear pond in summer, so very full of life, writhing with delights below the surface. So many glorious things lay pulsing inside him, ready to be celebrated. When had anyone ever treasured Daryl? Daryl, who only wanted to heal his shattered family?

My love, I have trawled through every portion of your subconscious mind; I have seen your darkest desires; rarely have I tasted something so pure.

He kissed Me back. He twined an arm around My waist, pressing Me in.

I fished inside him for Jennifer's energy-remnant. It lay close to his heart, emitting latent energy. All I had to do was rip it out, with his help. His lips trailed down My jawline, then he pulled away. His pupils had almost engulfed his irises. He exhaled. Licked his lips.

"I had to do that one last time," Daryl rasped. "Jennifer's dead."

"She's fine."

"She's a corpse. And You're either the Devil or the Anti-Christ," he said.

"Excuse Me?"

"Try to enter my mind right now."

I couldn't.

"Daryl…what's wrong?"

"I can't let You assimilate humanity, so I'll ask one last time. Where's the Hermetic?"

Tendrils exploded from the lower half of My human body, annihilating obsolete legs. My blood coated them like crimson nail polish. I was a torso on a mass of slithering flesh.

"Silly Daryl. You forgot who I am."

Daryl took a step back. Blood streaked his hands. "You ask, 'what's my definition of God?' I ask You: What's Your definition of love?" Daryl asked.

"Well, I—"

He slammed his mouth over Mine. *Oh, he's kissing Me again! What a human thing to do. He loves Me! I can't wait to show him his siblings—*

Jennifer's blood filled My mouth.

It burned. Blisters bubbled.

He'd chewed open one of shotgun shells full of her blood while I'd shown him the old church memory. While I'd been distracted, he'd swallowed it. He'd regurgitated her blood into Me—

Make it stop it hurts!

In that second of surprise, Daryl turned, picked up the shotgun, and fired into My flesh-veils.

CRACK!

Jennifer's blood splattered over them, over Me. Flesh-veils tattered from the contact. Sparks of white light burst from where the droplets touched.

My layers and veils began dissolving into clear, liquid protoflesh.

Daryl grabbed Jennifer's arm. He jerked her cadaver. It slid across Me, hurting. He ran through the liquefying flesh-veils, towards an outer wall. I secreted mucous to quench the burn, but it only helped him drag her. Mucous slicked the floor. He loaded another shell into the shotgun, fumbling with one hand.

"Y-you're hurting Me." And why did I so sound pathetic? So weak? As I asked him to stop hurting Me?

Tears. Wetness in My human body's eyes.

"So?"

A sob came out of Me. "D-Daryl, this actually h-hurts. I'm not a toy, or a monster, or a doll for you to play w-with."

"You hurt Jennifer."

I vomited up her blood. It seared like boiling water as it surged up My human avatar's throat. Pain throbbed through My stomach and esophagus and layers. Blisters barnacled My lips. It hurt to move them…

I couldn't just destroy this body and be done with it. All of My bodies hurt simultaneously. The amount of damage to them varied from infinitesimally slight to actual damage, but all of Me hurt. Pain. This was *pain*.

I begged, "I love you. Why are *you hurting Me?*"

He'd almost gotten to an outer wall of Mine. He dipped the shotgun barrel into Jennifer's bloody, slack mouth. He raised the shotgun.

"Please don't—"

CRACK!

I shrieked. Burned bits of Me sloughed off the wall. Bits of sky seared blue through My skin. Holes. I had pinprick holes now. He fired again. Blood droplets sprayed over Me.

"A-all I ever wanted to do was l-love you," I said, sobbing.

I slithered over, opening My arms to love him and fix this silly misunderstanding—

CRACK!

He blew My human avatar's torso open. Jennifer's blood got into My internal organs. Burned. Everything burned. I left the human body I'd made and went back to Myself. I called My children from their slumber.

(Get him!)

But it was too late.

Daryl daubed his hand in Jennifer's blood and tore a hole in My outer layer. Summer air swirled in. Flesh made wet tearing sounds as it gave. Strings of slime snapped. He dragged Jennifer-baby through.

They left Me.

I loved them, they hurt Me, and then they left.

All they ever do is hurt Me. They can't understand love. I'll never convince them. The more I try, the closer they get to learning the truth.

The Light was searing My flesh again.

It seared Me the way it'd done eons ago. Daryl and Jennifer didn't know it was the Light. They had no concept of what it was. They only knew that Jennifer's blood hurt Me and My children. But why were they being so cruel? All I wanted to *do* was love them and fix them. Were they scared of Me? Silly. All they were was flesh. All I loved was flesh. They were nebulae enfleshed: incarnated fuel, formed by chance, in need only of a guiding, loving hand to shift them, blazing, into miracles.

Did Daryl even love Me? Had Daryl ever loved Me, or did he only love that I was his exotic bird—a pretty-female thing that would never leave him like everyone else had?

Well. Daryl and Jennifer would be back. And when they came back, I'd ask for an apology.

I wasn't human. Had never been, would never be. Why had I spent so much of My stunted existence in Jennifer's body pretending to be something I wasn't?

Is Jennifer-baby right? Am I terrified that he doesn't actually love Me?

What if he didn't? What if Jennifer didn't, either? For some strange reason, that concept didn't hurt. It made Me feel…relieved? Was this what relief felt like? Why did it matter whether they loved Me or not? I had an entire world to adore and renew, and of course, I had to celebrate the most special day of all—humanity's final reckoning!

Today was Judgment Day.

Daryl and Jennifer had left Me.

I let them go.

Part Three

All of Us Sublime

25

"When I was a kid, I built a God-suit."

"Who are you, Trojan?" Shepard said, lip full of Copenhagen.

"If you knew, you'd give it away."

"That's not it."

Trojan continued stalling.

He held up a hand. "Let me finish. My parents sent me to one of those Montessori after-school programs…You know how liberal those lukewarm fucks are? I'll tell you. We had this poor flipper-handed bastard kid, Bobby something, head full of red hair. The 'father' knew that his wife had fucked another guy, but he was nice. Nicer than I would've been. He raised that little flipper-handed fucker alongside his own kids, trying to do right by Bobby, so every year, when hunting season came around, he'd bring little Bobby along with the rest of 'em. You can imagine it—four black-haired kids in camo, and here's Bobby, head like a candle, standing out."

"We're down to a shot glass of diluted blood."

"So Bobby likes to go hunting. Bobby can't hardly use scissors worth a fuck, or a rifle, but he manages. We're at the Montessori preschool, and they give us an art project. Make a collage of your favorite thing," Trojan said.

"We'll run out in two hours."

"I built a God-suit."

Shepard spat on the cement. "We got two hours left to live unless we find that junkie."

Trojan and Shepard stood alone in the "office" portion of the underground bunker. Shepard patted the AK-47 on his back. His hip-holster contained a police-grade Glock.

"So little Bobby makes a collage about elk hunting. He spends all afternoon cuttin' out the paper shapes, gluing everything nice. So then they come around to see our art projects. And lo and behold, there's a few construction-paper guns in there."

"Whatever you fed us isn't working. I can hear the Divine Flesh. She's a radio tuned to a bad station. Coming in and out."

She? That's an "it," Shepard.

"They call the cops on flipper-handed redhead Bobby. Kid's nine years old. Can you imagine it? Some of the girls, you see, had been complaining about some cut-up squirrels that'd been left outside. Decapitated. Disemboweled. Spread open and nailed to the dirt like a tent," Trojan said. "The cops, they're suburban assholes, so they cuff this nine-year-old white kid and haul him away. Now, they're not gonna do anything, but they're tryin' to scare him. Poor Bobby's bawling that he wants his dad."

"I'm so hungry," Shepard said, gnawing his lip.

"Montessori never let him go back. And they kept finding dead animals. Funny how that works," Trojan said.

They'd sent Shepard to start the mutiny. Shepard kept rubbing his stomach without realizing it. His hand would flicker down, brush his gut, resume whatever it'd been doing. The men got more unstable by the second. Get them desperate enough, and they'd pull a Jonestown. Or immolate themselves to avoid assimilation.

So Trojan had fed them a bellyful of parasite-larvae. The larvae would dope everyone to oblivion. Keep 'em docile. Malleable. Best part was, that dipshit parasite-thing thought it'd pulled one over on him. It looked like a white-trash chick with cherry-red hair. It'd shit itself like an animal, which was pretty funny. Gave him enough of a jolt.

Jolts, like candy, came in many shapes and sizes. You had your Fun-Sized jolts. A tingle around your ball sack, a little *schadenfreude* for the road. Then, your normal jolts. You'd get hard, tuck your cock into your underwear band, clean up the decapitated rats and bloody scissors, or ram yourself up whatever drugged person you'd dragged home and rape until every hole bled. Holes equaled jolts. Nothing existed besides jolts.

Then, you had your King-Sized jolts.

Lynching that mountain-man ten years ago while he danced on the end of the noose, suffocating. The *crunch* of bone as you closed the bolt cutters. A throbbing, warmth unfurling in your guts, the jolt, the sweet hot jolt, so good—

(!!!!)

(!!!!)

He shot his load. The black hood concealed his expression. What Shepard didn't know was that Trojan had conducted this entire conversation while still hard. Semen smeared over his ball sack. It filled both taint and ass crack. He felt, pleasantly, like a pig wallowing in its own shit. God, those bolt cutters, the *crunch*, the skin flying open—

(!!!!)

Oh, yeah.

This was no King-Sized jolt, it was the Big-fucking-Kahuna of jolts. He wanted more. He had the parasite-thing locked in a cell. He could play with it some more. Get those jolts. It had nine fingers left. Or more, if it regenerated. Thing was a shapeshifter.

So many options.

He almost came again.

Chain it up in the basement forever. Play with it. It's not human.

Fealty to your fellow man? The sacred nature of human goodness? "God" made humans in His image? Death deserved any more thought or feeling than you'd give to unplugging Mr. Coffee after the java got brewed?

What a crock of shit.

Humans were just walking, talking holes to rape. Men, women, anything. Biological machines. Wet meat. A source of jolts. Gotta plow 'em all. Then enter the void upon death. Nothing mattered. Nothing had ever really mattered.

"They sent me to kill you, Trojan."

"We've gone that far?"

"You don't have any guns. You left them under your cot. You don't have any knives, and if you do, I don't care. You wouldn't hit me if you tried throwing it. For years, I've been prepping for the day I'd kill a man…one on one."

Sure, Shepard. Keep LARPing.

"I built a God-suit."

"You hear me, Trojan?"

"It was during our next arts and craft project. They wanted us to draw a picture of God, or gods, or whatever we believed in, and then we were supposed to talk about it."

A mustard-yellow Army blanket covered the parasite-thing crouching in the corner. Trojan didn't glance at it. It knew what to do. Shepard pressed his lips together, paling. His cheeks puffed out. His throat worked. He swallowed. The lips parted. Blood coated his teeth. A chunk of something—almost like a bit of steak—sat on his right front tooth.

"I—I need you to wrap this up. You—I should help you pray," Shepard said. "You can be redeemed by the power of Jesus Christ before I execute you."

"—So I buy some mirrors from Value Village and shatter 'em with a hammer. I take the pieces and Gorilla Glue 'em to a blow-up doll. I wanted to use a spandex suit and wear it, but my mother was smart enough to tell me I'd cut myself apart the second I wore my God-suit. So every millimeter of this blow-up Susie Q is covered in mosaic-bits of mirror. I even tape over the mouth before I cover that in mirror bits, so it's not obvious. I take it to Montessori. Right to show-n-tell," Trojan said.

Shepard couldn't hide the next round of puke. He bolted to a far corner and heaved up a quart of digested organs. Guy was literally puking his guts out. It gave Trojan a Fun-Sized jolt, made him half-hard. Jolts transcended refractory periods. He could chain-orgasm like a woman if he had enough bolt cutters and fingers and teeth, oh yeah, and the meaty screams you got with ripping out teeth were so rich, so satisfying, *oh I'm really hard right now, oh wow—*

(!!!!)

"They don't even let me speak. That's the best part of it. I plop that God-suit on my desk and you know what the teacher says, with her ratty hippie-length hair and her Birkenstocks and her ugly-ass glasses? You know what she says? 'You understand the nature of God. God is a mirror, reflecting each one of Their creations. God is infinite. God can only be defined by the viewer,' and this moron *still* thinks that God is real, as she's saying that," Trojan said. "But you know all about God, don't you, Pastor?"

Shepard collapsed. He hit the cement floor. The AK-47 clattered against concrete. Shepard curled into a fetal position, moaning. Blood dribbled from his mouth.

"…so hungry…"

"I fucking loved every second of it. I let them make their liberal theology. Because I knew what they didn't."

Trojan knelt by Shepard's head. He leaned close.

"There is no God. God is a reflection of the viewer. The mirror bits are religion. Inside, beyond the illusion, there's nothing. God's as empty as that fucking Susie Q blow-up doll."

Shepard coughed up a glob of silver. It wriggled on the sealed concrete.

The parasite-thing burst out from the corner, throwing the blanket off itself.

"Get the larva back in!" it snapped.

Trojan scooped up the larva. Felt warm. Kind of nice.

(hi)

(I'm hungry will you feed me?)

It went still in his palm. Inert. Maybe he tasted bad to it. Trojan grabbed Shepard's jaw, forcing his mouth open. He threw the parasite in and wrenched Shepard's head back sharply, so he'd swallow the larva before he could chew it.

"You know what's inside you?" Trojan said.

Shepard tried to spit. He failed. Saliva gushed.

"When I was selling a house, five or so years ago, one of the buyers brought the whole clan along. Including Granny, who's ninety years old and uses a walker. I want a jolt, and she's the easiest way to get it. Sue me. I lure Granny to the kitchen, make up some shit about cookies. She wants a cookie. She's half-fucking-dead from dementia. It's like luring a kid into a van. Nobody wants to admit it, but when they hit a certain age, they're prey."

Trojan shook his head. "She's wearing a purple sweatshirt with rhinestones and a picture of two fluffy white lapdogs, and it says, *I Love My Shih Tzu!* I remember every little detail of that shirt. There was a mustard stain near the collar. Bleach stains on the cuffs. I find a stale Chips Ahoy, and while she's gumming it, I yank her shirt up."

The parasite-thing cocked its head. Narrowed its eyes.

"And Granny's torso is an eaten-out hollow. I can see her heart beating. There are these silver slug…things chewing inside her, making these soft wet smacking sounds as they eat. Granny's chewing that cookie. She doesn't even know what's happening. She thinks I'm her son. I put her shirt down," Trojan said. "Her son enters the kitchen and he *knows* what I've seen. I hide it pretty well, but I'm shaky and I do a shit job for the rest of the house tour. I don't care about the listing. I want Granny gone. Her son pulls me aside."

Trojan laughed.

"He was one of those shapeshifting parasites. He told me every-thing about them. How they shapeshift, how they reproduce…They call themselves Mirror People. He'd used his 'wife's' real husband as a vessel five years prior, and he felt so bad that he shifted into the guy. Five years. He says, 'I've been this guy for so long that I'm basically her real husband,' and y'know, he says that Granny had two months left to live. Terminal ovarian cancer. He's not bad. He's an ethical parasite. I keep expecting him to kill me, so when he begs me to not tell, I'm fucking game for that. I'm chipper. I'm polite. 'Yes, sir, I won't tell. Yeah, you're right. Nobody would ever believe me, man! That's crazy. You guys still want the house? The owners might knock the listing down to $220,000.'"

Shepard rattled a breath. "I got it. I…know who you are. I can't believe…"

His eyes glazed over, and a last breath rattled from between his teeth.

"The larvae are stressed out," the parasite-thing said. "Let them rest. He's dead, like I said he'd be. I had to encourage them eat quickly."

"Did you like my stories?" Trojan said.

"Perhaps I underestimated you."

A walkie-talkie rested on an ammo box. It crackled to life.

Vic Snyder's voice came out. "Shepard, we're combing around the Gas N' Go for that junkie. Nothing yet."

"You find that weapons cache?"

"Trojan?"

"Shepard's not around anymore. You find that weapons cache?"

Vic sounded a little too cheerful when he started talking again. Was Vic the original traitor, or Ol' Monty? For the thousandth time, Trojan missed Nancy Trenelli. Reliable, nunnish Nancy, who could get the job done, not bitch about it, and most importantly, had the stomach of a Siberian exile. He'd once caught her eating a turkey sandwich during the high season of lamb slaughter, hands still dripping with lamb's blood, gore soaking into the Wonder Bread. She chewed it down in three bites, licked the blood and mustard off her fingers with a soft *slorp*, picked up her bolt gun, and continued slaughtering lambs. Lady was a fuckin' machine. She had bigger nuts than a guy like Wade ever would.

"Hell yeah, I did. Good guns."

Ol' Monty crackled in. "Gentlemen, we might need to enter that… thing around the hospital, 'cause there's a good chance that Miss Junkie's inside. We're runnin' outta time. If we go inside while the blood's still in us, we might survive."

"Nancy's gone."

"You don't know that. It took her inside the thing. We should make sure."

The Townsen twins piped up: "What about the lake? We're on the shore, but nothing's there—shit!"

"Townsens? Townsens, you there?"

Panicked breathing. "They're coming from the lake. They're crawling out of the lake, they're—"

The Townsens' line cut off.

After a long moment, Monty asked, "Should we send someone out to Silver Lake?"

"They'll figure it out," Vic said.

"But—"

"We don't have resources to waste. I'll be out there in a few minutes. Meet you at the hospital, or thereabouts, Vic. Speaking of, has anyone gone to Dr. Landes's house? We could use a medic."

"Landes is one of them now."

Trojan signed off.

A light bulb had been wired in this room. Dim light burned. Condensation formed along the ceiling. Crates of ammunition filled half the available space, alongside an antique desk. A schoolboy's desk from the 1890s, carefully preserved. Atop this desk lay the bolt cutters. Blood flaked off the business end.

"I can burn Shepard's corpse if you act up. Your babies will sizzle like fuckin' popcorn," Trojan said to Susan.

"Yes. I understand."

"Another thing. Rent's due."

"Rent?"

Trojan hefted his bolt cutters.

He smiled.

There wasn't a need to hide anything anymore. Everyone knew the score. He'd be outside in a few minutes, working his ass off, so why not have a little treat for the road?

He sat at the desk. Spread his legs.

"Come here," he said.

He unzipped his jeans. His cock poked out. Semen glistened on the head. Air cooled the gluey mess.

The parasite-thing froze. It blinked a few times.

And oh, it didn't want him, it thought it was better than *him*, which only made him harder, because it was time for this hoity-toity high-falutin thing to get degraded, yeah, wipe that fucking smirk off its face, make it choke on him, jam his cock down its throat until it threw up, it'd moan and beg him to *stop, stop, I'm feeling sick*, in some baby-voice and he'd laugh, he'd ram himself harder into its mouth, so hard that one of its teeth would snap, and he'd thrust, thrust, all of its teeth would break off until it was a toothless defenseless cocksucking machine, meant for him, yeah, he wanted *all of it*, make it get down on its knees—*it's still got smudges of shit on its thighs because I didn't let it clean itself, ha-ha*—he was hard, so very hard, throbbing, hot and pulsing, and he hadn't even gotten to the bolt cutter—

(!!!!)

His load shot across the room like a party streamer.

His voice came out raw. "Maybe I'll pull all your teeth out first."

The parasite-thing went to him and sat on his lap. He wrapped his arms around it.

"You're gonna be my favorite toy," he whispered.

"Perhaps you're unaware that I have a stinger. It's designed to liquefy meat."

"You use it on me, and I'll kill your larvae."

"Everything you do to me or my children will be repaid."

Trojan took the parasite-thing's hand. He brought the bolt cutters to its palm.

"You should be careful what you say," he said. "There's a lot of sexual predators out there. Groomers. Perverts. A lot of sick people. But we're in the good old heartland of America right now, and you're with the good folks now. Remember that."

He chose a pinkie this time.

26

"Jennifer," Daryl said for the fifth time.

I was home. I was lying in the alcohol section of Gas N' Go.

Every one of my scars had vanished. My neck was unsnapped. My trachea was uncrushed. I wasn't even hungover. I lay on orange cracked linoleum and counted the booze bottles. Two coffee-flavored BuzzBallz gathered dust in a ransacked display. There'd been a hundred BuzzBallz two days ago. The booze aisles looked like a meth-head's teeth. Tar-like material splattered the ceiling tiles. A few bags of Andy's Hot Fries remained in the chip aisle, by the pickled pig's feet. In the fridge section: Strawberry Nesquik, Bug Juice, and a single Miller Lite.

Someone had decorated the windows.

They'd finger-painted, *All Hail ME!*

In blood. In childish block letters. A star dotted the exclamation point.

Below that: *I love you, Daryl!*

Several hearts pulsed below the love note. No, not drawings of cute little hearts. Actual hearts. They ranged from chicken-heart-sized to cantaloupe-sized. They lub-dubbed. Veins branched from the hearts to the window-glass like kudzu.

Daryl waved Wade's phone at me. "You need to see what happened. It was horrifying."

"I'm good."

"You came back from the dead."

"I'm disappointed, too."

"Goddammit, Jennifer. When are you gonna take some responsibility for yourself? If you have access to the Light, that's huge. We might not need the Hermetic to defeat the Divine Flesh."

I pointed to the hearts. "Aw, isn't that sweet? Your gentle, kind girlfriend left you a love letter—"

Pain flashed over the side of my face. My head jerked to the side. Heat. Taste of blood. Spit.

He slapped me.

"I ripped my way out of Her to save *you*," Daryl said. "I am sick and fucking tired of you using me as your emotional punching bag. Yeah, Jennifer. I know what you're doing. Whenever you wanna avoid something, you pull your cluster-B narcissist bullshit, you self-destruct, and you—you pathologically manipulate the situation to make yourself the victim. You're a fucking narcissist, Jennifer. You used to hit me when you got high. Remember when you lost your temper over something I said, gave me a black fucking eye, and called the cops? You tried to say I hit you, while my eye was swelling shut. Remember that?"

"You said I needed help. I'm supposed to take that shit lying down?"

"It was a factual statement. You needed help. When you're getting black-out drunk every fucking day, you need help. I had brochures for rehab places. My insurance would've covered it. That was why I married you."

"Cut the shit, Daryl."

"Okay, maybe I loved you. I loved Her."

His mouth twitched like he was trying to hold in a scream.

"I told you I loved you. I'd never said that to anyone before. I told you I loved you, that you needed help, and you gave me a black fucking eye for it," he said.

Daryl didn't ask me to watch the video again. He simply played it. He cranked up the volume.

It started with my limp body lying on the road. Steam undulated from my fingertips and toes, twisting like dying snakes. Daryl's harsh breathing rasped away the background noise.

"That started a mile back," he said.

My body repeatedly jerked like a knock-off animatronic. We weren't even up to the standards of the esteemed Chuck E. Cheese crew, it was that bad. White-trash, rip-off pizzeria-animatronic bad. Something dredged from the backstage of Charlie Rat's Pizza Palace, where the duct tape and prayers held the cracked claw machines together, the pizza crew had a drug ring going, and every staff member had piercings, tramp stamps, and/or a budding addiction to Oxy.

With a loud *snap-crackle-POP!* my neck cracked back into its natural position. Things shifted below the skin.

A rattling breath. A cough.

Color came back to my body. Pink rouged cheeks and fingernails. Scars melted into skin. Healthy tissue rejuvenated my underweight frame, hiding my ribs and sternum. Before, every rib had been visible beneath my razor-thin layer of skin.

A dot of light appeared on my forehead. It spidered out, then disappeared.

Jennifer, I love you, Daryl said.

End of video.

After that, Daryl had hot-wired an abandoned Nissan and driven us to the Gas N' Go, wanting to load up on supplies. He'd brought me up to date.

(*What are you, Jennifer-baby?*)

(*You BURNED ME!*)

There were answers to the madness. None of them were even kind of considerable. Not if I wanted to get through the day without having a bushelful of existential crises. I didn't feel like I was the Light—I was a piece of shit, but more importantly, I felt human. I had a human mind, albeit a terrible one. I couldn't be in multiple places at once, or fragment myself like the Divine Flesh.

But maybe I was chosen by the Light.

A human envoy. Someone capable of channeling its power. What if the Light couldn't incarnate as a physical being, like the Divine Flesh could? If the Light truly was the neural network and thoughts of a cosmic god…what if the Light needed a meat-bag to use as a vessel? Hell, was it even sentient? Forget sapient. Felt like too much of a stretch to assume that. The Divine Flesh—who had apparently created human-kind, no less—had learned most of Her human attributes from being inside my body for decades. If the Divine Flesh was still this inhuman after all that, I'd bet solid odds that the Light wasn't even conscious, let alone a benevolent savior of humanity.

So it was up to me. Jennifer Plummer, envoy of the Light.

And you broke. You broke down and begged the Divine Flesh to love you.

I couldn't be assimilated. Couldn't die. Couldn't kill myself. Even Genesis wouldn't kill me. I couldn't hear the Divine Flesh inside my mind anymore. What happy ending did I have left? Beat the odds, defeat Her, and go right back to being Jennifer Plummer? Me, the abusive, drunken drug mule? How was I supposed to fix my life and be a decent person? There was no redemption left for me. None.

But.

If I defeated the Divine Flesh, the Light would leave me. It'd go dormant. Had to, right? Then, and only then, would I finally be human.

And when I was, the first thing I'd do was put a bullet through my skull.

That was the happiest ending I could get.

"Hey," I said, "let's listen to Wade's confession."

"You're a goddam huckster if I ever heard one, Trojan," Monty muttered.

He only had an hour left before Miss Junkie's blood wore off. Good chance it'd be his last. There were worse things you could do than spend it saving a buddy.

He sucked on his lower lip as he drove towards Lourdes Hospital.

Holy Lane passed by, its churches like sun-bleached war memorials. St. Thérèse's looked like a goddam igloo. Cars clustered around Shepard's Church of Christ, aka where the Klansmen had meetings when Don McGee's gout had gotten real bad and he refused to have anyone over at his place. Shepard Crowley knew more than enough about that white power horseshit to hold meetings. What a man of God. What a church. The pastor's got cracker bolts tattooed on his goddam neck. The boys in white hoods wanted a war, but ninety-nine-point-nine percent of 'em had never served a day in their lives.

Monty patted his right leg. Or, more accurately, the metal prosthetic that Uncle Sam gave him to replace the original. A mine in 'Nam had blown it off in 1972.

When he wanted to feel a little God, Monty went to that Unitarian Universalist place. Troy Blight, the UU pastor, said nice things. He probably said nicer things when he was out selling houses, but he was solid enough for a realtor—he'd restored that Nelson house to its original glory. Colorful lib flags dirtied up its window-space like packages of rat bait, in their rainbow saccharine colors. The ruins of Nelson's barn hid at the far end of Holy Lane. Good old-fashioned craftsmanship. Those rafters could hold the weight of a man.

Sometimes he wondered what Nancy had done with the body afterwards, the one from ten years ago.

She had such capable hands. Not an ounce of fat on 'em. Her hair looked mousy indoors, but outside, gold strands shone among the silver and brown. Honest features, she had. Hatchet nose, thin lips, jutting chin—and sturdy arms.

You're sixty-eight years old. You could be her father.

Ten monsters flew overhead. Too high to make out their faces. If they had 'em. They glided through the air, chasing each other like a batch of kids playing tag.

Red overgrowth veined over half the houses. Charnel houses, now. Every window gaped black.

Monty picked his phone out of the cup holder. A ball of ice froze in his stomach as he pressed call.

Ringing.

Ringing.

The top of the ball-shaped…thing peeked over the pines. A rim of glistening pink. Almost pretty in the rich afternoon sunlight. He cranked the pickup's window down. July rushed in, dry and oven-hot.

Ringing.

Hasn't gone to voicemail yet.

A hint of something dead tainted the air. Slaughterhouse smell. Iron. Salt. Whiff of fecal matter.

Click.

"Monty," Nancy said, voice low and harsh, "help me."

He stomped on the brakes.

Nancy!

He scooped up the phone and jammed it against his cheek. "Where are you? What's wrong? Did that flesh-god—"

"She took me inside Herself."

"I knew it."

"She'll find my phone. Please. You have to help me."

Why is Nancy calling it a Her?

"Be there in fifteen," he said.

Click.

Hands shaking, he chucked the phone into the passenger side. Nancy. She hadn't responded to his other calls. Didn't sound like a monster. He had a good hard rifle to shoot with, and a machete.

The featureless flesh ball grew out of Lourdes Hospital. The texture and color were like the inside of a lady's cheek, or maybe the intestines that unspooled outta a pig after you slit its belly open. It dwarfed the hospital. It loomed over him as he entered the hospital parking lot. Thing was high as a skyscraper. Didn't look like he could enter it, but he had a machete to hack it open with.

Monty stopped under a light pole. No other vehicles existed in the lot. Silence suffocated after he cut the engine—no birdsong, no humming mosquitoes, no traffic on the freeway, nothing. Unnatural. His arthritic knee complained as he got out. His steel-toe boots scuffed asphalt. The tar had long since retreated, leaving a grayed-out lot. The hospital lay dark. Tendrils of meat sprouted from the ball of flesh, anchoring it to hospital and ground.

Suppose someone cut those? Would it kill that thing?

But each tendril was thick around as a steer. No goddam way could he hack through one before Miss Junkie's blood wore off.

Monty approached the thing. When he got within arm's reach, he stopped. He touched the surface, and his hand went through as if groping a ghost. Warmth vibrated.

He walked into the—

(Divine Flesh)

Divine Flesh.

Neither of us said anything for an entire hour, after that audio clip.

We left the Gas N' Go. When the last of Wade's screams cut off, we simultaneously left. Didn't take any supplies. Didn't touch a thing. We walked out into the abomination-filled land, because neither of us wanted to take another fucking breath inside something owned by one of the bigots who'd murdered Daryl and his friends. It was like having dogshit under your fingernails, like finding a blood-gorged tick on your scalp, pulling it out, putting it in your mouth and chewing, popping it and tasting the insect and old bad blood.

Nausea.

I'd gone back in, found a teal faux-leather purse behind the counter, dug out a set of car keys, and loaded us up in some woman's rusted-out beater car. Tan shimmer-paint flaked off its bumpers. Had half a tank of gas left. The AC was shot. Clip-on air fresheners stunk like chemical lavender, and the McDonald's wrappers on the floorboards stunk like grease.

McDonald's. The smell made Daryl dry-heave. I held his hand and rolled every window down. I drove us to the northern edge of town and parked off the side of a gravel road. Cherry orchards lined both sides. A tin storage shed stood by a Porta Potty. Nobody was out picking the early Bings. Yellowjackets droned. Bird-repellant ribbons sparkled on the trees like July tinsel.

I finally said, "So all those fine folks that Wade mentioned in his audio confession…they lynched a guy ten years ago. They hunted him down and hanged him in the Nelson barn. Nancy Trenelli hid the body. I used to buy lamb from her. She told me the best spots to go mushroom hunting for morels."

"Yeah, that's about the long and short of it."

"Daryl, Wade named like two cops. The fucking *cops* are involved in this."

"Yup."

I crossed my arms. "There's a reason the Divine Flesh ain't found and assimilated every last one of those motherfuckers. 'Cause if She had, She'd've told us or used the knowledge to lure us to Her. If they're just plain vanilla humans, that ain't possible."

"You sound like a hick."

"What if there's a fuckin' cult around the Light, and those assholes are part of it? They gotta have immunity somehow. 'Cause Wade would've shown the Divine Flesh who they are, except for Trojan. The Divine Flesh would've been able to reach out and assimilate them instantly with that knowledge—don't ask me how I know that, I just do—and then She'd branch out of them and into Trojan instantly. There's a reason She hasn't done it—"

"She wouldn't toy around with assimilating them, She'd just do it. She hates them 'cause of what they did to me," Daryl said, and licked his lips. "She'd assimilate them all and torture them."

"Tell me about the killings from ten years ago. How and why did Rosetown's finest folks up and lynch a guy?"

"Emily…She never talked much about the killings," Daryl said. "She was twelve years old when they happened."

I nodded. "Tell me."

"What the fuck does it matter? The good ol' gang here lynched him, and then ten years later, they sabotaged my car and killed two people. Because we're the same as the guy who raped and murdered two sixteen-year-old girls, right? Right?"

"Tell me the basic facts."

"You got to hide in the woods, in your trailer, and even though you've cooked and handled more drugs than I ever will, you git to be a cute, little, normal chick. Don't you?"

"I was supposed to be in that car, too, Daryl."

"But you weren't."

"I—I went into the Gas N' Go that morning, to buy booze, and that asshole Monty said—he said some shit that I didn't pick up on—"

Heat.

Shame.

My face burned. "And I was so desperate to get drunk, I didn't process it."

"What'd he say?"

"Vague statements. Told me I shouldn't be around you. Said if I was, I'd been warned. Said you should move…Jesus, how did I not see this?"

The orchards hung lifeless, branches laden with cherries.

Something was off. Something was missing, and it gnawed at me. *No birds. Something's missing.* Ribbons or not, birds should've been eating these unattended cherries to the pit. There weren't any nets over the orchard, or workers to startle them away. What happened to the birds? Was something scaring them off?

What's missing?

Wait.

My trailer.

It'd been ransacked, but my drug stash hadn't been touched. Even my blown-glass pipes were still there. None of the prescription drugs or new booze bottles had been taken…but the ones I'd drank from, with my saliva on them, had been. Along with my bloody, rotting tampons. And my used needles. And a collection of used Band-Aids in the kitchen trash.

Things with my blood on 'em.

"They know about my blood," I said. "That's why none of 'em got assimilated by the Divine Flesh after Wade. She can't read their minds, so She can't see where they are…unless it's through the eyes of Her children…Daryl, what if these assholes are hiding out somewhere?"

"They're gonna run out of your blood," he said.

"Then they'll come after me," I said.

"Fuck. You're right. We gotta shut these fuckers down, and fast. Not just 'cause of me. You. You're the only shot we have at defeating the Divine

Flesh. If they get a hold of you, they'll chain you up in a basement. I know these types. You'll be sedated, handcuffed, and bled every day. They'll tape a cup under your chin to catch your saliva," Daryl said, voice grim.

"…And the Divine Flesh won't be able to save me, because they'll be doped up on my blood. Hidden. They'll have guards that never leave the basement, and there won't be any windows," I said, sick shock growing in my guts.

Chained in a basement forever, Jennifer. But when has your body ever really been yours?

I wouldn't die. Whatever they did to me, I wouldn't die.

Oh Jesus.

Daryl forced the saddest laugh I've ever heard from a human being. "And *then*, when I rescue you, you'll get treated to the sight of…whatever the fuck I'll be, after the Divine Flesh gets done recreating me. Ha ha."

"Don't even joke about that."

"I'm not," he said. "If they take you, I'll bargain with the Divine Flesh. She'll make me into something that can help. We'll focus all of our attention on rescuing you. Yeah, it's a bit weird and it's probably unhealthy, and it's not normal…but we love you."

I don't deserve your love, Daryl.

I decided to be a jackass before either of us caught feelings again.

"This your way of asking for a threesome?" I said.

He leaned against the side of the car, tilted his head back. There were Camel Lights in the car, and a BIC. I lit a cigarette for him. He drew in smoke.

"You want to know about the killings?" Daryl asked.

"As much as you can remember."

"In the spring of 2012, Susannah Pearson went missing. The last sighting of her alive was some video-camera footage at Garrison's Sports Stuff. She was talking to a guy named Ernie Fields, in the camping section. Looked like they were having a good time. They end up leaving Garrison's together. And then, a month later, her corpse gets dumped on the shore of Silver Lake, wrapped in a canvas tarp."

"Okay, and?"

Daryl made a face. "Her corpse wasn't a month-old. It was closer to a week. Brett Pearson, her father…The guy was Custer County's only medical examiner, Jennifer. He didn't want to wait for 'em to find an out-of-county ME, he wanted those results. He thought he'd be okay cutting open his own daughter's corpse—"

"Jesus fucking Christ."

"He had a mental breakdown in the middle of Harvest Foods on a Saturday morning. Emily saw it. And that's how everyone in Rosetown found out that Susannah Pearson was raped repeatedly before death, that she'd been handcuffed for a long period of time, and that the killer had mutilated her genitals before he smothered her."

A breeze whistled by. Branches rustled. Twigs crunched, just a few trees over. I picked a few cherries from a tree. Pesticides filmed the garnet-red Bings, dulling the color. They'd still be spraying, this late into the season. I smelled the cherries. Pesticide smell, rank and chemically. Brought back memories of being sixteen, working in the fields, and making an honest day's pay.

I'd made it out of that age alive. Unlike Susannah Pearson.

"A day after the corpse is found, Delight Owens goes missing. Delight Owens wasn't the sharpest knife in the drawer. She didn't have a mean bone in her body, and that was what killed her. The other girls knew enough to be guarded. Even the boys, according to Emily. They formed a walking group, so nobody would be alone. Emily got bullied a lot, y'know, but when it came time to walk home, she said, even Carl Snyder—he was in school with her—stopped being an asshole. Everyone was real careful."

He blew a smoke ring. "Except Delight Owens. She and a few of her friends were walking home from Silver Lake, and guess who's on the side of the road, in a broken-down pickup?"

"Ernie Fields."

"Ernie doesn't make eye contact when he's trying to ask the girls for help. He seems off. He's a weird mountain-man, doesn't care for town. Lives in a cabin in the woods. So the girls pass it off. Delight Owens calls up Sheriff Olson, to try to give the guy a hand. It's Sunday evening. So, she and her family go to church—"

"On Sunday evening?"

"It was some potluck at the Unitarian place. Anyway, Sheriff Olson can't find Ernie or his pickup, so he calls Delight back. She offers to help. She walks a ways out on the road, and that's the last time anyone sees her alive. They think that Ernie Fields was waiting in the brush nearby. A month later, her corpse is dumped outside of Rosetown, on the side of the interstate, right by a grain refinery. It's wrapped in a sheet. Same damage as Susannah Pearson."

Daryl shook his head. "It was pretty open and shut. They arrested Ernie Fields. Couldn't make the charges stick until the trial, so he got out. And then after he was out walking around…well, we heard what happened straight outta the horse's fuckin' mouth. They drugged him, took him, and lynched him in that abandoned barn. Didn't put nothin' over his face. They left his body out for a day or two before someone 'stole it.' Cops looked the other way. They wanted everyone to see who he was."

Another twig snapped. Closer. Something was in the orchard with us.

I raised my voice, so the abomination could hear it. "Look, we can't be assimilated. You already know that. We don't want to play with you."

Vic Snyder and Sheriff Olson came from behind the cherry trees. Olson flanked Snyder's left. Both men held shotguns at the ready. Snyder wore his deputy uniform. The gold star glinted.

Deputy Vic Snyder aimed his shotgun at my chest.

"We ain't here to play."

27

Mae Lawson finished burning down her motel.

One of the motel guests had been kind enough to leave a flamethrower behind. Blue as the Devil's tongue, an electric arc danced between its metal prongs. Her knobbed finger curled around the trigger. Smoke flowed through the Drift-Inn's third-floor windows. It stung her throat.

She stood in front of the main entrance, glass door propped open on her hip.

"You want me to do it?" Allie Crowley asked.

"No, dear."

A eulogy, first.

—Thousands of people had walked through this door. Travelers and June tourists blathered about the dioxin levels in Silver Lake and took her brochures. She and Paul had eaten their last breakfast together in that front office. Eggo waffles and microwaved Jimmy Dean sausage patties, packets of maple syrup, coffee. What a beautiful sunrise they saw. Red sun over fresh snow.

Vic Snyder spent the best part of the '90s in room 201. Lost his house in the divorce. Wade and Shyla Hammond made love in room 105, and ended up making their only child. The third floor never had any ghosts, despite Emmett Anderson dying there of a heart attack in '08. The pine-tree-patterned comforters that decorated the motel beds had fallen off a truck bound for Omaha. Laurie Landes worked here as a maid when she was kissing boys in high school, before she went to WSU to study medicine.

Mae Lawson bought the Drift-Inn when it was an abandoned apartment complex. She and Paul saw more in it; they said it had good bones, like a ribcage. Sturdy enough to carry the travelers but curved enough to accommodate anything, and especially their dreams. When they couldn't have children, it gave them something to create.

"Now I uncreate you," Mae whispered.

She pulled the flamethrower's trigger. Gas hissed out. The electric arc ignited it. A stream of fire bathed over the lobby, the glittering popcorn ceiling, the vinyl wood-patterned wallcovering, the '90s computer monitor hulking on the front desk, all of it.

She stepped out. Allie Crowley grabbed her shoulder and steered her out towards an idling white minivan.

"I need to see it."

"No, you don't. Your blood sugar's low," Allie Crowley said. "We've got cookies and milk back at church. The men will return soon, with the blood-protection, but until then, we pray to God."

Mae turned to face the Drift-Inn.

"Mrs. Lawson."

"I need to see the demons come out."

A sigh. Allie Crowley, wife of the pastor Shepard Crowley, adjusted her blonde bun. She smoothed her hands over her calf-length denim skirt as if scrubbing away slime.

"Got a Bible in the backseat if you need Scripture," she said.

"I believe even secular folks know most of Revelations. I have it memorized. I know what I'm seeing."

Flames curled from a third-floor window.

"Fire purifies. When Sodom and Gomorrah erred, God sent fire to cleanse them. It's only fitting that it prevents our corpses from being defiled by Satan," Allie Crowley said.

Spidery legs thrust out of the main entryway, each one longer than a house. Two of the upper ones skittered against second-floor windows. A man-shaped demon flew from a first-floor window, shrilling a wordless challenge. Another followed. Both demons circled the Drift-Inn like vultures. All their organs thrummed outside of their skins.

"What if the men don't return?" Mae Lawson said quietly.

Allie Crowley jerked her head towards the minivan. "Then we give ourselves to God before Satan or his demons can take us, Mrs. Lawson. We got more gasoline at church. I wish…" Tears shone in Allie's hard eyes. "You think God hears my prayers?"

"He'll save Noah, dear."

"Three. Years. Old. I know that we're born sinners, but—" Allie's lips pressed together. "My baby's a demon, Mae."

"Oh, honey…" Mae Lawson hugged her.

After a split second, Allie pressed her head into Mae's shoulder, crying.

The ground pressed up, to the right of the Drift-Inn. It exploded, sending dirt and bits of turf flying. A bus-sized spinal cord crawled out like a centipede, its ganglion nerves acting as legs and antennae. Bones clacked. Flies stippled it. Dirt fell from the demon as it turned towards Mae and Allie Crowley.

"Time to go," Mae said, nudging Allie.

Allie's gaze flicked around, assessing. She nodded, once, and started the minivan. They entered. Allie drove, and the spinal demon did not follow.

thunk!

Something landed on the van's roof.

"You think we can't fly faster than you can drive?" a male voice taunted.

The demon rapped on the roof. *knock-knock-knock!*

"I don't give a damn," Allie Crowley said.

"We can't drive back to church with this thing in tow," Mae said.

The demon chittered. "Silly! I'm an adored child of God! I'm not a thing."

"A demon's a demon," Allie said, not taking her eyes off the road.

"I'm not a demon, either! I'm a sacred creation of God! Come with me, and let Her adore you! We want everyone to be loved as we are."

Allie slammed the brakes. "God isn't a Her."

Mae jolted forward. Seatbelt tightened.

Thunk!

The demon went flying off the van roof and hit the asphalt. It stretched, slowly getting to a sitting position—

Allie floored the accelerator.

Crunch!

A giggle. No cry of pain. Just giggling, as if getting run over by a minivan tickled.

"Hm," Allie said. She put the minivan in reverse.

crunch.

Drive.

crunch.

Sounded like a crushing a big daddy cockroach with a cast iron skillet.

Allie continued driving. Mae craned her head to peer through the rear window. The demon peeled itself off the road. It waved. And though she couldn't quite make out its face, she knew—it grinned.

"If the men don't return, I will not allow our congregation to become demons. I added some powdered fentanyl to our Country Time Lemonade Mix. Yes, Mrs. Lawson," Allie said, sighing. "Shepard knows where to buy fentanyl. He's a man with many burdens. Will you help me? If it comes to a choice between death or eternal damnation, will you help me persuade the flock?"

"You're doing a Jonestown?"

"It won't kill them. It'll take some of the pain away, when we—when we purify ourselves with the fire."

Mae nodded.

A small shape flickered on the road. A boy. A toddler clad in a red cartoon shirt and pajama pants. He stood on his tiptoes and waved as the van approached.

Mae's stomach dropped. *Noah.*

"It's an illusion. I saw my son get turned into an abomination," Allie said.

"You're not stopping?"

"Should I?"

"Maybe it's God, dear. Perhaps He's granting your prayers," Mae said.

"Hm."

Allie stopped, expression set and blank as cement. The front bumper kissed Noah. He was a towhead, built big like his daddy. He smiled. Dimples appeared. Allie groped around in one of the cup holders. She white-knuckled something in the cup holder, and, barely audible, glass broke. Mae didn't look. She couldn't take her eyes off Noah.

"Mommy!" Noah called.

"Hm."

"Mommy, I love you!"

"You're an agent of Satan, sent to deceive me. The first demon failed. Now you're here. If I let you into the church where our flock is, you'll report back to Satan. Then all of us will be taken." Her voice broke. "But I don't *care* about that anymore."

Allie Crowley jumped out of the minivan, arms open. Her palms dripped with fluid. Noah came running, and she embraced him, sobbing. She patted his bare arms.

Noah shrieked as her hands made contact with him. Blisters multiplied over his skin. Milky tendrils exploded from his face and latched onto Allie's cheeks. They burrowed, tunneling towards her eyes like parasitic worms.

Allie gave a guttural half-sob, half-scream.

Mae froze. Their last vial of diluted blood lay broken in the cup holder. Allie had shattered it in her bare hand, using the blood as a test to see whether Noah belonged to God or Satan.

And Satan it was.

Allie white-knuckled Noah's shoulders and wrenched him away. Tendrils unrooted, slimed in her blood. She hurled the toddler down. His head hit the freeway with a nasty-sounding *crunch.*

Noah bawled, tears and snot flowing down his face. His face-tendrils hung slack. Blood dripped from them and stained his pajama bottoms.

"Mommy! Mommy, it hurts! I wanna go mcdee's!"

"That means McDonald's," Allie said calmly. "He wants McDonald's. Where's the flamethrower, Mae?"

"I—I—Allie, you can't."

"I need to restore him from his damned state."

A hiccup. "Mommy—Mommy, I want Daddy. Where's Daddy?"

Allie found the flamethrower. She dug it out of the backseat. She marched to Noah. She aimed.

"Mommy, I love you."

She fired.

It only took fifteen minutes for the fire to die down.

Smoke curled up from the charred, blackened lump that had been Noah Crowley. A burnt offering. Allie Crowley tilted her head towards Heaven and screamed to God until He took her voice away.

At the Rodriguez house, Abuelita and the children dug a pit in the backyard.

The moon blazed red and ripe as a cherry. The lawn swallowed their ankles and the children's Frisbees. Demons landed in the backyard, carrying shovels. They helped dig. Omar hung his star piñata on the fence; the desiccated yellow paper shell hung barren. At first. Demons sang. They sang and clapped hands. They dug the pit.

Everything around them seemed to murmur, *(There's a party, we're celebrating!)*

The piñata ripened as it swung. It swelled. Something filled the interior, made the paper shell bulge with candy. It reddened. Blood seeped through the yellow tissue paper, dripping from the bottom center point of the star.

Lights flew around the backyard in festive summertime colors: lime green, tropical blue, pink. The moon bathed everything in lurid red light. Everyone kept digging. The children giggled. The children kept saying they were hungry. Very hungry. They gathered around the piñata.

They chanted, "Dulce! Dulce! Dulce!"

The piñata fell apart like bad meat. Hand-sized bits of glistening raw candies rained to the grass, smelling like iron and salt. *Blood.* Abuelita and the children plucked candies from the ground. They gorged themselves as demons continued digging the pit. Abuelita slurped up a chunk of...*liver? No, it's something else, something dark*, and she brayed a laugh.

Rosa Rodriguez had not been invited to the party. She had to watch from inside the house. She did not look behind her. She couldn't. Javier's breath tickled the back of her neck.

"Why did you let him beat me, Mama?" Javier asked.

She did not look at him.

He talked throughout the night as everyone dug the pit. "I was twelve. He beat me so hard that I couldn't go to school for a week. Omar had to sneak me food, because you wouldn't touch me. You watched it happen from here. Why?"

"I couldn't leave him."

Can't leave him, we'll starve, and for a second, Rosa thought she heard her mother's voice: *He's an evil man, but we can't leave him. Even if he's hurting you. You want to starve? You want I should let you die?*

Tears blurred the lights outside. Something warm pressed into the back of her skull. It hurt, briefly, then numbness washed over the area.

"Show me, Mama," Javier said.

(Show Me.)

She'd done the same as her mother. She said she never would. She'd find a bruja before she let her husband hurt their children, she said. Then Alonzo caught Javier, with his hand on that gringo boy's face, their mouths almost touching, too intimate, and he'd *known*, his gut fear had been proven right—Javier was one of *those*, a failure of a man, not even a man at all, a freak, an aberration, a sexually-depraved defective that would never have a family or children. Repulsive.

First he came for her.

He'd opened with a hard slap, spitting out the story in spurts, ending with *How the fuck did this happen?*

Alonzo, sometimes they're like that.

No.

Don't hurt him. It was my fault. Don't hurt him, please, don't—

He'd dragged Javier out the backyard, lined up the younger children. He started with a belt. He ended with a length of copper pipe that'd been hidden in the grass.

Don't hurt him! Rosa had screamed, but she stayed behind the glass door.

She watched. She weighed a phone in her hand. She almost called the police, but couldn't. It'd be all over. They'd starve. Nobody in Rosetown would go to their restaurant. Alonzo would find some young girl to replace her—an eighteen-year-old girl without stretch marks or a sagging belly; she'd bear him replacement children, and his original children would either starve with Rosa or be absorbed into his new family, depending on the girl's whims. Without Alonzo, they'd starve. Was it better for the children to starve than be beaten? They could live through a beating. They couldn't live through starvation.

We could move to my tia's. She'd take us.

But she'd lose everything, Alonzo would take ownership of their restaurants, and he'd never let her go if she left him. He could leave her at any time, but if she left him…unthinkable. A man couldn't allow a woman to win. He'd stalk her. He'd kill her before he let her win. But first, he'd pick the children up from school, cart them over the state line out of spite, and she'd never ever see them again. Wasn't that worse for Javier? At least at home, she could try to help him.

"I'm sorry," Rosa whispered, "I had to."

"You watched."

"What if I tried, and he beat me enough to—to kill me? Or *mutilarme, dejar inválido*, and if I can't work, all four of you starve. I had to think of everyone, Javier."

(Was it because maybe a part of you thought Alonzo could beat it out of him? Just a little part of you?)

Rosa sniffled. She hadn't slept in three days. She'd drifted in and out of a half-awake state, but no real sleep. Her head throbbed. The house vibrated around her. Her limbs felt distant. When she grabbed things, they slipped from her fingers. Clumsy. Stupid.

I don't know.

A sob came out of her. "I want sleep."

"We're going to sleep after they dig the bed."

"I love you, niño. I'm sorry."

Mama and the children went back to digging. The pit was chest-deep, and it covered all of the backyard except for a thin border of grass around the fence. Chunks of sod and dirt made a house-sized pile. Good earth. It would feel good, against their skin. Gritty. Cool. Shelter against the inferno. Dirt would flow into everyone. Earth baptism. Everything would be washed clean.

She finally turned to face him, expecting a monster. A demon. A decaying ghost.

Javier looked exactly how he did before he died—before he had that car accident. Scrawny. Slicked-back hair, smelling like pomade. Patchy mustache, growing in clumps. He had Alonzo's thick square brows and nose, but his eyes were hers. Round. Gentle. Too soft to hold a grudge.

Something slithered out of her skull.

She opened her arms, lip quivering. "I'm sorry."

He hugged her the way he used to before he'd turned eight, and then he'd stopped because Alonzo said, *You need to be a man, you're a man now, what are you, a faggot?*

Now he was taller than her. He had to stoop.

"Father Johnson's coming over tomorrow, Mom."

Drowsiness. Muddy thoughts. *Father Johnson? Why?*

She yawned. The moon balanced atop Borah Peak. The oven clock said 4:02 a.m.

"I'm sleepy," Rosa said.

Javier tugged the back slider open. "Let's finish digging the bed. Abuelita saved you some candy."

Sweet candy, it was. Silk in her mouth. It slid down her throat; it wanted to, it had been sent to nourish her. A bedtime snack. She got hungry enough to chew on the bloodied paper bits of the piñata, but then God said—

(Don't do that, silly.)

And candy rained down from the sky.

Dulce! Dulce!

Her favorites were the intestines. She put her tongue through the hole like she would a manicotti shell and ran the sweet, sweet candy around her teeth, shredding it. Savoring.

When dawn burned on the horizon, the pit was complete. Party guests took their shovels and left. The colored lights clustered on the uneaten candy lying in the grass. Rosa's belly ached. Time to sleep.

The family nestled together, inside the pit. They bedded down. They knew that they would not be the same when they woke up. Someone loved them. Someone special. Their old lives and bodies would be washed away in the earth; their sins were null and void, all debts repaid. There was nothing to worry about anymore.

They pulled the dirt over themselves and slept.

Susan waited for 5,034 breaths after Trojan left, but no longer. She didn't have a left hand anymore. Just a bandaged, fingerless lump at the end of her left wrist. She wasn't being fed enough to regenerate her false flesh. When he mutilated her other hand, as he surely would, escape would become impossible.

She sat on the edge of the bed, hands folded in her lap. Red scratches ringed both wrists. Babies devoured Shepard Crowley's corpse, close by. How close? Couldn't tell. Perhaps just beyond the steel door. Handcuffs dangled from a nail in the wall. The lantern shone in a corner. Trojan had left a bucket and an antique Bible from the Regency era. Gold gilded the edges.

If you try to escape, there's gonna be consequences, he'd said. *I won't bother putting the cuffs back on.*

His seed lingered in her mouth. Rancid. Tasted like pennies in clam juice.

"Your actions have consequences," Susan said to the empty cell.

She slipped off the bed and crouched down. Perhaps there was something helpful underneath. Pliers. A crowbar. Even a credit card or a bit of plastic, for a shim. She could shim the door open. She'd command her babies to eat faster if someone caught her. Simple as that. If she died trying to escape, she died. Staying here could only be worse than dying.

I caught you talking. The cell's wired for video and audio. You said you were God? Trojan had asked, as she'd screamed between each *snip* of the bolt cutters.

Are you?

This cell was wired. Somebody was probably monitoring her. Still, she groped under the bed. Craned her head. Snaked filaments along the floor. Something glinted in the blackness far beneath the bed. She grabbed. Cold glass chilled her hand. She brought it out.

It was a sealed Mason jar.

Clear fluid sloshed inside. A chemical smell burned her nose. Formaldehyde.

Thin slips of flesh rested at the bottom of the jar. Slices of—*they're ruffled at the edges?*—something. Susan turned the jar. Preserved things swirled. One of them was larger than the others, not flat, a nub with a hood of—

oh god

oh god that's human I can tell

—a clitoris.

This jar contained a sliced-off human clitoris and scraps of labia minora.

Buzzing in her ear. Nausea.

Maybe he's doing female genital mutilations, humans do those in certain areas, okay, not usually on this particular continent, or in this white American town, but maybe he did one and saved them for medical reasons.

Gray filmed everything. Her hand shook. Fluid undulated.

Maybe he—

No. No maybes.

He'd murdered before. Why else would he have a cell like this?

The jar slid out of her hand.

It fell, spinning, and exploded on the cement. Formaldehyde puddled out, reeking. The flesh flowed out. The flesh. The flesh—

"Divine Flesh, help me. Please. I'm sorry," Susan said, her lips moving of their own accord. "I accept You as my God. I was bad at godhood, anyway. I don't think I'm cut out for it, oh god, oh god don't let him hurt me again, don't let him, please, don't let him kill me—"

She sprinted for the door. *Get out. Get out, stay away for fifteen minutes, by then the blood should wear off.* Fifteen minutes. Then, she'd pray to the Divine Flesh and *beg* for mercy. *Save me. Save my babies. There's a man keeping me in a cell and he won't stop until he's reduced me to a toothless, limbless torso, oh please help, You were right, I was a terrible God, please help.*

The knob felt warm.

It turned. Wasn't locked.

Thank you, oh thank you, whoever did this, I don't care how. Maybe he got distracted from masturbating. He took my fingers with him when he left.

Susan opened the door. A cement hallway gaped. A freezer door lay at the end of the hallway by a steel ladder.

Shepard Crowley's naked corpse stiffened on the ground at her feet, crucified on a piece of cream-painted plywood. The wood was like a nice dinner plate for the babies, and the cadaver moved—ever so faintly—as the babies glutted themselves on his meat. The torso cavity writhed. Someone had sliced open the cadaver's belly from penis to neck, and the white bone of the sternum peeked out. Blood puddled on the plywood like steak oozing into a foam meat tray. Silver peritoneum glistened at the edges of the slice. Silver babies gleamed in the dank bunker air, oh, they were happy, they were safe, and all she had to do was rip out the nails in the cadaver's palms and feet, cradle the corpse to her skinsuit's chest—*cradle my babies, hold them, and sing to them as we run*—and the precious larvae would chew and sing, a symphony of wet smacking sounds.

Susan stepped out—*snap!*

A tripwire broke at her ankles.

A red gasoline container fell from the ceiling.

No lid.

A stream of clear gasoline poured down, down and flooded the torso cavity. The smell stung. Gasoline overflowed the slice. It dribbled onto the plywood, mixing with blood to create orange.

Oh god move the babies!

She grabbed the plywood—

Click. Click. Snick....

Fire exploded over the cadaver. Heat surged up her arms, burning them. Flames covered Shepard's body and spread over the plywood.

Larvae screamed:

(HURTS IT hurts why does it HURT)

(hurt)

Susan clawed into the flaming corpse. Plunged hands into the cavity, grabbed a handful of babies—

They dissolved in her blistered hands.

Larvae spasmed as they fizzed, bubbles frothing over the small hurting bodies, and they screamed in pain, they wanted it to *(stop, stop, stop, make it stop it hurts why)*, and Susan stuffed them into her wet mouth—

It burns!

Acidic pain seared down her throat as she swallowed, but fine, fine, *get it off the babies, get it off, make them stop suffering*, and she scooped out baby after baby from burning body, felt the fire char her filaments, her mind going blank, charred skin screaming, but fine, the babies, save the babies—

She felt them die.

The larvae went limp. They slackened and puddled like goo in her mouth. Susan spat them out, and half-liquefied babies melded into the fire.

An orange Post-It Note clung to the hallway wall, alongside a folded sheet of notebook paper. Smoke filled the area. Susan coughed. She could barely stand. Every inhale stabbed down her throat.

The note said, in Sharpie, *I WARNED YOU!*

There was a tiny heart drawn below.

She unfolded the notebook paper. Yellowed from age, its blue lines had blurred. Everything felt pleasantly fuzzy.

Well, he did warn me.

Melting babies, they screamed and screamed and you couldn't save them, the screaming—

Okay.

The screaming, thirty little shrieks all at once, the sound inhuman, almost mechanical, an *aaaaaaaa*, not an *ahhhhahh* or anything organic, pain gone beyond humanity. AAAAA. A vibration you could tune a violin's A-string with. AAAAA.

She glanced at the notebook paper.

A crude pen drawing of Susan's human form dominated the page. Trojan had drawn her form without its limbs. She was chained to the twin mattress. In marker, red puddled below her body. In the doodle, she was moaning, and she had no teeth. Both eye sockets gaped, the eyes resting on the floor. Her breasts were sliced off, leaving two round wounds. Her sex was much larger in the drawing than in actuality, and it was carved out like a cantaloupe, all external folds and features eradicated. Trojan himself leered in this charming doodle, rendered as a stick figure with a black hood and an erect penis. He mutilated Susan's sex. He gripped her last labia, he was stretching it out, and his other hand held scissors at the ready.

He wanted to annihilate her.

He had titled this masterpiece: *My IDEAL Girl!*

Goosebumps covered her false flesh. She gagged. Filaments shriveled. Her stinger shot out from between her lips and retracted, over and over. *snick-snick-snick,* it went.

I was a god and now I'm going to be annihilated.

If I don't escape.

She staggered for the ladder at the end of the space.

Father Johnson and the angels went from door-to-door, spreading the Word of God.

(There are 5000 people in Rosetown, and I've only claimed 2100!)

His congregants opened their front doors. They willingly opened their hearts. Flesh bloomed and multiplied in magnificent ways. And when they didn't open their doors? The angels loved them so very much that they broke windows, trying to give them to God. Father Johnson blessed Don McGee as he sprinted towards his tractor. Don McGee dissolved into a pinkish gel, threaded with vessels and neurons.

Such divine flesh.

When Johnson was a lad of eight—the seventh child of eight siblings, as a matter of fact—his family went to Seaside, Oregon, on the only vacation they'd ever have together. Through Astoria, under a bleak massive bridge, where the ocean gnashed against concrete and fishing boats, there'd been a glassblower's shop. The April sun caught the glass roses and thumb-sized trinkets, the animals, and a cluster of swirled rainbow twists.

How do they do it? It's glass. Because he'd never seen glass that wasn't flat, and it was brittle, how could you do that to glass? Wouldn't it break?

The glassblower had grunted, beckoning them beyond a door. Heat blazed. Tupperware containers of frit and glitter lined a workbench. Glowing white hot, a glass punty glared. In with a pipe. Out came the pipe, with a glob of orange-red molten glass, like taffy.

I understand now.

God was the glassblower manipulating Her creations, but God was infinitely more attentive and never ceased loving Her children, the fruits of Her labor, made in Her image. Under Her eager hand, flesh could be wrought into infinite form.

(Now I've claimed 2402! Oh, My beloved children, you are such good helpers!)

His flock slept at St. Thérèse's, away from the angels. Four-hundred or so congregants crowded the church, sleeping in pews. Some slept outside, under the stars, or in tents. He promised them that holy ground was safe. He'd converted more non-Christians in the last twelve hours than he'd done in the last twelve years. Normally, they'd need nine months of RCIA classes, but that, of course, was before God had decided to return.

(That's silly.)

(Baptize them, if you will, Father, but we don't have nine months.)

The baptismal font's water turned gray from use.

He spouted lies. Rather ridiculous ones—*the Enemy is here, the demons walk the Earth, we must join in prayer unceasing, we must form a Mass outside*—but necessary. His withered obsolete flesh strangled as he worked. He wanted it off. To rip it off his bones. Oh, to fly. To see God in the Heavens, to sing praises by God's throne with the angels, to be free of this corrupted world…to taste the divine. Why did the angels get to be blessed? Had he done something wrong? Blood—his tears—filled his eyes.

(Soon, My child.)

He thought, *I don't want to wear this body anymore.*

A wave of love washed over him. Warm. Safe. Something brushed his forehead. An unseen kiss.

(If it's really that bad, I can adore you now. But if you just wait until morning…I have SO MANY lovely gifts for you. You're like a five-year-old on Christmas Eve! So adorable. So eager. But you must sleep, and you must WAIT. Can you wait a little longer?)

He could. For God, he could.

For tomorrow, everyone would join God.

Warmth.

Sizzling sounds. A godawful stench of blood and rot.

Slick tendrils sizzled as they coiled around Monty's neck. Around his arms. Fluid leached through his jeans as they got his legs.

"Nancy!" Monty yelled. "Nancy, where are you?"

Everything quivered around him.

A musical laugh vibrated through the flesh-thing. "Nancy's not very talkative these days."

Tendrils dragged him around curtains, through a red-lit world of groaning flesh and breathing shapes. Towards a normal teenage girl, and a nub that jutted from a flesh-veil.

The girl just stood there like butter wouldn't melt in her mouth. She grinned. Her square face looked kinda familiar. Her eyes were the color of Jim Beam. Her dark brown hair fell clear down to her lower back. A tiny cross necklace glittered on her collarbone. She wore a Bible-thumper's outfit. Blood dotted her denim calf-length skirt and her cotton blouse.

That nub twitched. It was the size of a curled-up man. *Or a certain woman of a certain acquaintance.*

No.

"I told you, Nancy's not very chatty. She's filtering the blood of this body for Me. Isn't that nice?"

His feet carried him closer. Clumps of hair grew from the nub. Silver-streaked hair. He touched it. It pulsed under his hand. A fused tumorous growth. He probed down the mass as if groping a dairy-cow for mastitis.

Something opened on the nub, halfway down it.

A single, human eye.

Nancy Trenelli's eye rested on Monty.

The pulsing quickened.

(Ol' Monty.)

"I gotta git you outta there." But fuck, there was no getting out of *that,* but what the fuck was he supposed to say, what—

A strangled sound bubbled out of him.

"Oh, don't you worry about Nancy. She's fine. I keep her cozy and happy. I just don't think she should move around until she learns her lesson."

Tendrils raped down his mouth. He bit. Rubbery texture. It did nothing. They caressed his intestines and inside his belly. They sizzled as they groped.

"Really, Monty," the Divine Flesh said, "you should be worried for yourself, right now. I have twelve minutes until I can rip you apart and taste your mind, but we can do *a lot* in twelve minutes. So many things!"

Nancy called me.

"That was Me, silly."

An image came to him—a net of unseen feelers, blanketing Rosetown.

"Nobody can call anyone outside of Rosetown. Nobody outside can call in. I've been listening to every single phone call inside. You think I can't make a phone ring?"

The flesh sighed. It spoke, and its voice came from everywhere. "You gathered all the information that Trojan needed to kill Daryl and his friends. That's what you do, in that little gang. You run the Gas N' Go and listen. Is that true?" *(I already know what's true and what's not. This is a test. Will you be honest with Me?)*

He thought, *FUCK YOU!*

"Oh, dear. Oh, My."

A tendril flickered by his face. White-hot pain obliterated his right eye. A fifth of his sight blacked out.

(!!!!!)

"Are you hungry?"

The girl nodded, and patted the flesh nub like a dog. "Yes. But what about this demon? What are we doing with him?"

"I have a *very special* job for you, but only if you want to do it. It might be scary. Will you help Me?"

"Anything!"

"I knew you would. My precious child, I need you to wear something. You can't take it off under *any* circumstances, or the evil deceived ones might hurt you."

The girl squinted. "Wear something?"

"I'll try to make it comfortable. Like a contact lens. You won't even feel it, I promise. It's just so that the blood won't burn you."

The girl nodded.

(Monty, this is your last chance to be good. If you're good, I'll make it so you don't feel anything. Answer My last question. You gathered information, true or false?)

He screamed, *FUCK YOU, BITCH!*

"Alrighty, then," the Divine Flesh said.

Tendrils fused into his esophagus and guts. They wrenched out of his mouth, taking his digestive system with them—

(!!!!ohgodmakeitstop!!!!)

A tube with a sac at the end dangled out of his mouth, and got uprooted with a *snap*.

Esophagus.

Stomach.

Layers curled around both his arms.

"His skin's the right color. Or close enough."

Rip.

They degloved the skin of his arms.

Muscle glistened. Veins gleamed. Tendrils slithered back down his gullet, and he shrieked against them. Half-delirious from pain, everything faded to red and black haze.

The Divine Flesh decided to allow that.

"Open up," he heard the Divine Flesh say.

The girl allowed the Divine Flesh's feelers into enter her mouth. They carried his stomach and esophagus and inserted both. Tendrils gathered up Monty's hairless arm-skins and slid them over the girl's with the ease of donning opera gloves. Excess skin sagged.

The Divine Flesh fused and pinched, making his skin like the girl's own.

"Where's Daryl? You said I'd see Daryl and Isaac," the girl whined.

"You will, very soon. Maybe even tomorrow."

Mouths formed on tendrils. They kissed the girl's cheeks, lapping away tears.

I am breathing and I can't be breathing, Monty thought. Then his throat wriggled. Feelers had slithered into him. They sizzled, but remained rooted.

The girl sniffled. "You think they still love me?"

The Divine Flesh laughed. "Of course they do, Marcia. We're going to be one happy family. All of us sublime."

Make it stop. Make it—

"Oh, look at that! Twelve minutes is up. You know what I'll do, Monty? I'll give you what you always wanted. You can be with Nancy. Together forever."

And then the things scooped him up and mashed him into the nub and it tingled and then it didn't and screams tried to come out of his melting, merging throat as it melded with what remained of Nancy and it hurt it hurt—

Divine Flesh, I will praise You forever.

In time, Allie Crowley was rewarded.

A beam of light shot up from her son's remains. The smoldering pyre split open. Noah rose from the ashes, haloed in brilliant clear light. He wore white robes.

"Mommy!" His voice echoed. He touched her cheek.

The Divine Flesh 259

"Don't leave me," Allie heard herself say.

But he did. He was simply taken up to Heaven in the light, as if by an invisible hand of God. Wordless messages pulsed through her mind. God would care for her precious son. The Lord was good. The Creator rewarded those who made righteous decisions in His name.

Mae Lawson had passed out from shock. Allie bore them the rest of way back.

Sacrifice.

The Divine Flesh soothed Noah after the van had gone away. *Your mother will come home soon, silly. Did you have fun playing?* She healed his blistered skin when Jennifer Plummer's blood evaporated. She kissed his forehead and sent him off to play.

The Divine Flesh wanted to soothe Allie Crowley's grief. She only ever intended that.

But Allie Crowley had become a born-again believer in the power of immolation.

28

Nothing I hated more than an ultimatum.

Vic Snyder said, "Now, I don't wanna have to shoot. We need you alive."

You cut my husband's fucking brake line. You murdered two innocent people.

My heart pounded in my throat, but I pasted on a smile. I even made my eyes crinkle, just for that extra bit of realism. Daryl had his hands up. Sweat shone on his forehead.

"Sheriff Olson, what are you doing here?" I asked.

"Don't talk," he drawled.

"Trojan, I'm surprised at you. I'd've thought you for a bragging type," I said, voice chipper as a schoolgirl's.

I didn't know if he was Trojan, but I kept digging.

Sheriff Olson's hair blazed white in the sun. Bushy caterpillar brows obscured his eyes. A hawk-beak's nose curled down, almost tickling his thick mustache. Unlike Vic, he wore work jeans. Twin leather holsters contained revolvers, no doubt older than him. Grandfathered vintage guns. A brass cross winked out from a steel belt buckle.

"Trojan?" Olson said, blinking.

That meant jack shit. Trojan had concealed his identity for ten years. He'd have to be able to lie well. Sheriff Olson fit the bill. He was old, seemed polite, and already had a protective mentality around Rosetown.

Vic Snyder spat. "Shut the fuck up."

"Hey, now," Olson said, "we don't need to treat 'em like that. Do we?"

"You need my blood, right?" I asked.

Vic shot me a glare. He aimed the shotgun right above my head. He fired.

BANG!

My hearing blew out. Everything spun. Ears ringing, I put my hands up and tried to think. Sheriff Olson drew a revolver and aimed it at Daryl's head.

Divine Flesh, I prayed, *they're taking me. Help me!*

Felt like trying to scream through Jell-O. I worked harder, trying to get Her attention.

DIVINE FLESH! HELP ME!

A pinprick of awareness came through.

(Jennifer-baby?)

HELP ME! THEY'RE TAKING DARYL!

(Jennifer, let Me in.)

I'M TRYING!

The Divine Flesh showed me Her perspective. The orchard and the men were fragmented snippets, seen at the end of a tunnel. Like a kaleidoscope. Daryl's vision showed something similar.

(I'm sorry, I'll try My best. Keep Me inside, and I'll try to see where they take you.)

Assuming they wouldn't sedate us, you know, or cover our sight before they dragged me into a basement to drain my blood and use it against the Divine Flesh. Forever. Vic gestured with the shotgun. Olson came behind us and herded. Daryl and I walked through the orchard, towards a 1951 Chevy. It'd been painted orange. A collector's car.

"Where are you taking us?" I asked.

Vic shook his head. He jerked it towards the car. Behind us, a storage shed lurked in between cherry trees. Rotten fruit decayed under my shoes. Grass gave off a summer smell—gamy green vegetation, pesticides—and a few magpies chittered at the end of a row of trees. Olson and Vic had scared off the other birds.

Either you get shot here and bleed, or you get imprisoned in a basement and bleed!

Ultimatums.

Everyone wanted my body. To eat it up. Drink of its blood. Rape it.

Rage boiled in my innards.

You want my blood? You want my protection, you fucking murderers? You killers of innocents?

A padlock gleamed on the storage shed. A set of bolt cutters hung on Olson's belt loop. Susan's bottle of eggs and Wade's phone hung heavy in my pocket.

Vic doesn't know that Olson is Trojan. Or that Wade is dead.

There'd be a split second of confusion when they loaded us in the truck, but could I extend that to a few seconds to do what I needed to do? Would Daryl blame me if they shot him in that time?

Vic tore open the passenger side.

"I have to pee," I said. "Can I please use the Porta Potty?"

Some of my hearing had come back.

"Piss here. On the grass."

"But it's *right there!*" I whined. "C'mon, man, what the fuck am I gonna do in a Porta Potty?"

Olson's hand rested on my shoulder. Calluses sanded.

"It's a little demeaning to have a girl pee in the open, Vic. I'll go with her."

"She's a drug dealer. They know all about hidin' stuff. She'll come out waving a gun."

True, true.

C'mon, Olson. Walk to the pisser with me. You and those bolt cutters. It's cherry season. I know what's in that storage shed. C'mon. Please, God, or the Light, gimme a break here. I just need five seconds.

Then he agreed with Vic; I saw it in his eyes. Olson opened his mouth.

"Please, Trojan?" I cooed, groping for Wade's phone.

I yanked it out. Vic brought the gun around, finger curling 'round the trigger—

I hit the grass.

CRACK!

I pressed Wade's phone on. Pressed voice recorder app. Menu popped open. Pressed confession file, my thumb ground the volume button up, up.

Wade's voice bubbled out, hitching from sobs.

Vic and Olson froze, like I'd thought they would. Bought me the second I needed. I lunged, ripped the bolt cutters off Olson, and sprinted towards the storage shed. Daryl sprang on Vic, teeth glittering. Vic staggered. Dropped the shotgun. Daryl kicked it away.

My legs burned as I ran. I didn't hear any other gunshots.

Made it to the shed. Paper wasps flurried around it. I yanked the padlock—it clicked open, I chucked it off. Opened the door.

Entered.

Chemical-tainted air stung with each breath. Hot as a kiln. Flies droned on the lone window of the tin shed.

It was cherry season. Plastic gallon containers lined the walls.

I scanned labels, found the one I needed, screwed off the lid, and dumped concentrated late-season pesticide down my gullet, forcing myself to not throw up, gagging on the taste, the sandy sugary granules of dimethoate.

Choke on me, motherfuckers.

Here's what they heard.

Wade, half-sobbing: "Emily. Emily, is that you?"

thunk-CRUNCH!

Gurgling breathing, getting closer.

"Emily, baby, please, I didn't mean—Emily, they said you wouldn't get hurt, that's why I took you to Coeur d'Alene, I was gonna tell you I had a little apartment for you—"

He screamed. It cut off at the end.

The Divine Flesh cooed, "You aren't talking to Emily right now. Emily's asleep. You're talking to *Me*, Wade Hammond."

"What did you do to Emily?"

She giggled.

Pounding footsteps, *clunk-clunk*, going from hardwood to carpet, muffled steps, the slam of a door.

Slam!

"Wade?" the Divine Flesh sang. "You know I can see through your eyes right now? You're in her bedroom!"

Closet door slid open. Slid shut. *Clunk.*

Frantic breathing.

Wade's voice, just above a whisper: "Okay. I gotta say it. I'm Wade Hammond. I cut someone's brake line. I dunno if the person's name is legally Daryl Plummer. That guy. He had a truck. I cut the brake line."

Footsteps rang down the hall.

"There's a group of—of concerned citizens in Rosetown. It's led by a guy named Trojan. We don't know who he really is. None of us. The people I do know of are Nancy Trenelli, Victor Snyder, his son, Carl Snyder. The church guy—Shepard Crowley, but not his wife or kids. Me. I didn't take my kid to the lynching ten years ago, when we hanged Eddie Fields in that barn, but Vic took Carl. Carl did lookout, he was twelve at the time. There's Monty Anderson. Bill and Bob Townsen. That's it. Vic got Eddie Fields arrested for possession of marijuana, put him in jail, had someone pay the bail…we were waitin'. We knew it was him, that killed those girls. We—we took care of him, ten years ago. And now, we rigged that car accident with the kids…Trojan called us up, had us meet. They told me and my kid to move. But they got my kid in—in that car, and she died."

Drywall crunched. A keening shriek rose.

Wade sobbed.

The bedroom door creaked open.

"I'm sorry. My dead baby girl's come back. I'm sorry—"

The closet door slid open.

thunk.

The sound became muffled from then on, as if the microphone was blocked by carpet.

"Are you really sorry, Wade Hammond?"

Blubbering sobs.

Wet tearing sounds. Screams. The sharp *crack* of bones fracturing. Thin snaps.

Slurping.

The Divine Flesh giggled. "You killed My lover! This is fun. Let Me kiss it better."

Soft *smooch.*

Wet tearing sounds. A peach being sliced open, oozing juice, *schlllack-sclarpp.* A meaty *pop!*

This cycle repeated six times. At the end of round six, the sound became clearer, as if someone had picked up the phone.

"Dad?" Emily said gently. "Go get on the bed. I don't wanna look at you right now."

Scuffing footsteps, retreating.

Emily sighed. "What do I think? I don't think humanity can redeem itself anymore, ma'am. I was never one for theology, but I don't reckon humanity can fix itself without You. That's my unvarnished opinion." Another sigh. "But we're Your children. You made humanity in Your image. Should I say You set us up to fail? In the modified words a' Cain: Am I my children's keeper? Parents gotta let their children grow up, take responsibility for their own lives…Are You the keeper of Your children for all eternity?"

The recording ended.

Is God morally responsible for keeping humanity, or is it humanity's job to raise itself?

What about free will?

Well.

There were people out raping each other, beating infants—there were infants dead from assault; I'd sewn a few tiny cadavers full of drugs and seen the black bruises everywhere, everywhere you didn't want them to be, you knew these innocent babies had died bawling and in pain—once, I saw a brain-damaged eight-year-old boy, drooling on a mattress on the floor. His mommy, she'd beat her own kid with a pipe because he accidentally flushed some of her meth down the toilet. Before that, he'd been a smart kid, had a *Best Reader in 2nd Grade!* certificate hanging on the fridge. Before Mommy beat his brains out. Now he was brain-damaged, blank-eyed and barely able to swallow food if you spoon-fed him. She told me that, this tweaker lady, so casually, *Yeah, the little shit did that, so now he's lying on the bed, oops.* I used to sell meth to people like that. When I used to cook speed. So I'd gone back into the bathroom before I said something to her, and there was a dead baby in the bathtub, flies covering the baby's body, her eyes half-open and drying, clouded, she was wearing a *Dora the Explorer* diaper that'd soaked up the bathwater—brown as shit, that bathwater, from decay and maggots—and a pink yarn bracelet, flies crawling in and out of the slack little mouth. Mommy didn't even know that her other kid was dead. She couldn't remember putting the baby in the bathtub. She'd gotten high, left the baby alone in the tub, and the baby drowned.

The smell.

Sometimes I still remembered that smell, in my nightmares.

I stopped cooking speed after that. That was why I stopped. I never told Daryl or anyone else. I never cooked another batch of speed again. A week after I'd said I'd never cook again, I set my lab on fire and called it in anonymously. Then I made an anonymous call to CPS.

It's been six months since I cooked speed. I still see those kids. I drink so that I don't have to see those kids.

Go ahead and tell humanity to be better.

Give the wife-beaters and child-killers and kid-diddlers some fucking speech about redemption and love and being better. Watch them agree. For more impact, make it religious. *I beat my girlfriend so badly she miscarried, but I said I was sorry, so everything's better! I accepted Jesus Christ into my heart! I'm a good person now! I said I was sorry.*

They smile, agree, they feel so good now, and then they go out and do it again.

And the brain-damaged little boy on the cockroach-ridden mattress drools, because he can't understand what you're saying, and he never will. His life's been stolen. He did nothing to deserve that.

Redeem that. Tell me all about redemption.

Dimethoate 4EC is a late-season pesticide. One of the organophosphates. It comes in a granular form, similar to table sugar. The proper dilution is a quarter teaspoon of dimethoate to one gallon of water; at this dilution, PPE is required for spraying or being near the chemical solution. An employer could be sued for screwing around with it. Organophosphates like to infiltrate every part of the human body—hair, skin, and especially blood. They wreak havoc on the nervous system.

One quarter teaspoon to a gallon of water, folks.

I forced down about six cups of dimethoate 4EC, in the pure granular form, before another gunshot rang through the cherry orchard.

I froze.

Daryl? Did they shoot Daryl?

My stomach wouldn't physically hold any more. I commanded my body to retain the chemical, to excrete it through my blood.

Then I had my first seizure.

(!!!!!!)

When I woke, three men were standing over me. Vic Snyder. A man in a black hood and gloves. Daryl.

The black-hooded man pressed a machete to Daryl's throat.

"Jennifer Plummer?" a robotic voice crackled. "Come with us. No theatrics, or I'll cut off his head and keep it separated from his body."

"Hey, Sheriff Olson," I said, "you might as well take the hood off. Secret's out."

"I'm not Sheriff Olson."

"What is this, a fucking *Scooby-Doo* episode? Vic, man, you've been running with Trojan for a decade, and you still don't know who he is? That's weird. Why the hell does everyone listen to—"

(!!!!!!!)

They had zip ties around my wrists and ankles when I came out of seizure number two. We were outside, in the cherry orchard. Vic dragged me by the shoulders. Wispy clouds veiled the sky. Grass rustled as my legs flopped. Couldn't control 'em. Sheriff Olson's cadaver lay on its back, under one of the trees. Half his head had been blown away. Blood trickled from his mouth. Flies gathered 'round the blood, and bits of pinkish brains splattered across the cherry tree's trunk.

Sheriff Olson's not Trojan.

"You shot the sheriff, but who's gonna shoot the deputy?" I asked.

Vic hurled me into the bed of the truck a little too hard. My head smacked into metal. Trojan sat close by, machete snug around Daryl's throat.

"I had a stash of drugs in the shed. Excuse me for gettin' high," I said.

Vic pursed his lips. "Trojan, we don't wanna kill her when we sedate her."

"Give 'em a few hits of gas."

Vic retrieved a gas canister from the truck. A plastic hose hooked from the nozzle to a plastic mask.

"It's from the hospital. Anesthetic," he said.

He put the mask over Daryl's face. Daryl inhaled and went slack. His eyelids fluttered shut. Trojan nodded to me.

"Are you the assholes that stole my used, week-old rotting tampons? You're injecting *that* into yourselves? How the hell are you guys not dead from sepsis? You know how many bacteria live in period blood?" I said.

"A drop of bleach per gallon of blood-protection kills the germs," Trojan said.

"…Jesus fucking Christ, I wasn't serious, but you're telling me that you just…you just found my used tampons, soaked 'em in water to get the blood out, and injected that fluid into yourselves? What kind of incel shit is that?"

Vic said, "I was investigatin' your trailer after the events at the morgue, and there was a puddle of dried blood and spit on the sink. I heard the flesh-god, but when I got your blood on my wet hands, the voice stopped. We experimented. I'm only tellin' you this so you understand why we're doing what we're doing. We aren't monsters. People need to be protected."

"You murdered innocent people. Choke on me," I said.

I spat. It landed right on his chin.

He jammed the mask over my mouth and nose, cranked the gas, and I inhaled.

Going, going, gone.

Isaac flew over My barrier; he flew into Rosetown, savoring the early-evening thermals as they rose off the land. Blood rain pelted him as he flew past the smoking remains of the Drift-Inn.

Ew, Isaac thought.

"Are you thirsty, dear? You had a *long* ways to fly. Are you hungry? Do you want to sleep?"

"Nah, I'm good."

I inhabited one of My flying children and soared over to him.

"You can't see Daryl and Marcia yet, Isaac," I said.

"Why?"

"It's a surprise."

Isaac shrugged. He was a simple child. Easy to please. I'd had to nudge him along a few times, but not for bad reasons. Isaac…well, he'd spent the previous day doing what most fifteen-year-old boys would do if they could fly.

I'd caught him perched outside of a pretty blonde lifeguard's window, his face pressed to the glass, feet curled around the window trim.

(*Okay, I mean, she's eighteen, and she's not gonna look twice at me, but I can fly now. That's gotta be worth something. Okay, just—*)

She'd taken off her bra.

(*O those boobs. Those paps. Real boobs, not fake, and they aren't gross-ass cone boobies either, no—*)

Heat. Blood flushed down, down.

(*Those boobs. This is better than porn! Okay, okay, you can fly, man, just knock on the window and smile at her. You can do this. If she calls the cops, just fly away! Maybe she'll take her sweatpants off, too, O god she'll be shaved, she's a lifeguard, right, don't they gotta shave if they're in the pool?*)

I had very gently nudged him along, towards Rosetown.

(*I'd rather see boobs than God. No offense, lady.*)

I'd said, *Isaac, there are many more naked women in Rosetown.*

(*Really?*)

Yes, really! Now go! Your siblings are waiting for you! Marcia and Daryl need you!

(*Daryl? Man, I miss Daryl. He was the biggest badass. He beat up Uncle Larry.*)

Everyone would meet each other soon! It would go great! They wouldn't have any issues at all, and wouldn't Daryl be so happy that I'd found his siblings? Daryl would love Me, and we could finally mend his shattered, traumatized family.

I love you, Daryl. Sometimes it makes Me want—
No.
No, no, no, I wouldn't even think something so silly.
Sometimes it makes Me want to be human, with you, and the kids.
Isaac asked Me why nobody outside of Rosetown had noticed the barrier. The barrier cut through the freeway. Where were the cars? The news cameras? The tabloids?

"There's a command I set. Like a computer program. Whenever something gets within a quarter mile of the boundary, they turn away. The humans in cars turn right around, and when they wonder about it later, they remember the freeway being closed or blocked or whatever their little brains make up."

"Cool, but why?" Isaac asked, head tilted.

I laughed. "Silly! I don't want a lot of drama and humans panicking. It's safer for everyone...I love them, you know. I want everyone to be Mine, without suffering."

I blinked out of the body; I turned more awareness to Emily and the Hermetic.

Outside of Rosetown, an abandoned carnival decayed in the woods. It'd been built in 1981, at the height of the Evangelical zeitgeist.

God's Carnival.

Emily reclined in a water-filled kiddie pool she'd set up by Jennifer's crates of C-4 and the Hermetic. Occasionally, she'd splash water over herself.

Are you comfortable, Emily?

"It's a real scorcher outside, ma'am."

Has anyone come?

"Nobody yet. The perimeter guards haven't seen anyone within a mile of here."

She slid out of the pool, water dripping off her body. She patted one of the wooden crates. A pink Sharpie heart decorated one of the boards. *D + J.*

"Is it hard for You, too?" Emily asked, and ran her hand over the love note.

Not anymore.

Not after I'd seen Susan's selfish decision, it wasn't. No amount of pleading or reasoning would *ever* drive Me to play pretend as a human and leave My children to die. Never. Not for Daryl, not for anyone. What kind of dummy would want to experience death? Grief? Pain?

Keep guarding the Hermetic, Emily.

And if some silly stupid part of My heart ached to be human, what difference did it make?

29

"Well," Trojan said, "you got this far."

He stood at the edge of the ceiling trapdoor, peering down at Susan. She shivered, moaning on the cement. She lay curled around the base of a steel ladder that led up to the trapdoor. Warm light streamed into the bunker from above.

A bear trap clamped around her ankle. Jennifer Plummer's diluted blood coated her teeth. Shock numbed Susan's leg, muting pain into a dull tingle.

The babies. All gone.

What do I have to live for now? Myself? No, I've always lived for myself.

In the trapdoor, whitewashed ceiling shone. A butter-yellow light fixture glowed, scallops curving its upper rim. Air drifted down, carrying the smell of good old leather and dust and a hint of Murphy Oil Soap. A nicely maintained domicile, then. Did Trojan polish and clean it himself? Or did he hire help? Help might mean an ally, and possible escape.

"I'll make you a deal, parasite."

"Oh?"

"That bear trap's chained to the ladder. I can remove it, and carry you up here, or you can sit here on the floor and shit yourself again."

"What about the cell?" Susan asked.

"Need it for someone else. You didn't ask what I wanted in exchange."

"Well?"

"Don't attack me when I carry you up. That's it."

"You murdered my babies."

"Ah-ah-ah," Trojan said, and tsk-tsked. "*You* murdered 'em. I told you there'd be consequences, and I meant it. You think I don't have plans for the members of my crew, should you act up again? Or should I say, plans for the larvae inside 'em?"

"You can't," she heard herself say.

Filaments, unseen to human eyes, trailed along Trojan's face. False flesh shifted. Her appearance changed to become the most attractive form to Trojan.

He snickered.

"Why am I now an eighteen-year-old girl?" Susan asked, but both of them knew why.

"You want up here or not? It's a nice place. Someone restored it. I'll cook you somethin' nice and feed you. Then we can play again."

What else am I good for?

So Susan nodded. Her head felt lead-heavy. "If you feed me more protein, I can regenerate this form."

"Atta-girl."

He descended, scooped up Susan, and carried her up to the surface. Blisters popped as Trojan grabbed her wrists and arms.

Okay.

It didn't matter. Nothing mattered—*the babies, fizzing and seizing and screaming, silver bubbles foaming, they're dying they're asking why nobody's helping, they ask if they were bad, sizzling like slugs in salt*—anymore.

He set her on a pink velvet loveseat, its legs carved with roses. A vintage couch. Varnish glowed on the wood. The cushions provided no comfort. A Shaker-style coffee table lurked nearby, topped with a cotton cloth. That trapdoor opened with a white piece of yarn. It vanished into the thick dusty-pink carpeting when Trojan shut it.

He pulled out a handheld radio and barked commands into it. "Yeah, Vic, get 'em both in that cell. Bolt the door."

Trojan made a terse sound.

"One of the jars broke? Naw, naw, don't clean it up, we don't have time. Get 'em situated. Handcuff Daryl. Put Jennifer Plummer on the bed. Bleed a pint outta her, bandage her up, and dilute the pint into twenty gallons of protection. Add a drop of bleach to each one. You know the drill. Can you manage that?"

Everything here screamed *soft*, from the overstuffed rose-pink armchair to the frilled doilies oozing down every surface. At the end of this sitting area, a hallway snaked, as pink and narrow as a mouse's esophagus. Crystal doorknobs glinted. Lace curtains filmed every window. Twilight darkened outside. She couldn't see anything meaningful through the holes in the lace.

"Good. Then have Allie Crowley pick up the blood-protection. Monty's not responding to us, and neither are the Townsens, so make the other deliveries."

A short laugh.

"Yeah, Allie's gearin' up for a Jonestown. You want me to do somethin'?"

Trojan clicked the radio off. He placed a pill bottle on the coffee table. The last of Susan's offspring gleamed within.

"I found these in Jennifer Plummer's pocket. Let's consider 'em as we palaver."

"What do you want?"

"Tell me about yourself."

"Why?"

Trojan stalked to the kitchen. Dishes clanked. A gas stove hissed.

"I'm having a spiritual crisis, God," he said.

"That's neither clever nor funny, and I'm not the god of this world."

"But?"

"Before anything else existed, I did. I pulled out pieces of myself. I wound them into my children. They floated in the darkness; they knew nothing besides the vibrations of my breathing. Then I created sound. I created light. I created a surface far below them that was unlike my children, made of other flesh. I made the surface from my saliva. Let it spread. I created Reflection."

"Reflection?"

"They wanted to be like me. I gave them the ability to create new life. They fertilized each other and implanted the eggs into the surface below. I created pretty things to nourish my children, so they wouldn't have to eat off me anymore. It was perfect."

"And let me guess—two parasites ate an apple, so you shut the whole thing down."

"No."

Bacon fried in a pan. The smell wafted through the house.

"What happened?"

Susan said, "I got tired of being God."

"What?"

"I was bored. Depressed. So I made a new body for myself and tried to kill the old…but I was the universe itself. The whole universe died.

It would've killed my children. I rent the last scraps of it apart, made up a story, and a few of them made it through. I didn't know…I didn't know we'd end up here."

"Some god you are."

"Not anymore," she said. "That's the entire point."

"You're selfish."

"Did I ever pretend I wasn't?"

After a while, Trojan came over with a plate full of bacon, scrambled eggs, and toast. When Susan tried to take it, he jerked it away.

"I'm gonna feed you."

Excuse me?

He held up the bolt cutters. He cradled a bottle of Betadine in the crook of his arm. "Rent's due, parasite."

It happened.

Susan let it.

As she relaxed into the couch, Trojan undid his belt and slipped his pants off. His penis stood, swollen, weeping from the hole. He stroked himself as she wound a dishcloth around the stump of her right pinkie.

He aimed his penis at her plate of food.

"You're gonna eat every bite, like a good girl, and I'm gonna watch you swallow."

"How charming."

"Don't fuckin' speak like that. You're supposed to be eighteen. Act like it. Don't—"

Sexual arousal heavied his breathing.

"—don't tell me that's not your real body, or I'll want to hurt your real body. You regenerate. You and I can play forever and ever. So here's what I want. I need a wife or a niece to raise. They're starting to—to think I'm a faggot, in this town, 'cause I don't have a woman. So. You stay with me, I'll feed you, clothe you, take care of you—You know, I make a lot of dough, doing what I do. You won't have to work a day in your life. And every once in a while, we make a person disappear and you can fill 'em full of parasite larvae. I'll even keep the fuckers safe, if you're mine."

"I need another one of my kind to reproduce."

He jerked himself off. *schlop-schlop-slarp!*

He threw his head back. Ejaculate shot onto a slice of toast, melding into melted butter.

He panted. "Then I find you another Mirror Person and bring it over for the fucking, and you sit your pretty little ass on that couch like a queen bee. You don't even need arms or legs for it. I'll take 'em off. You saw my drawing of an ideal girl?"

Oh god help me.

"No," Susan whispered, "no, no, no, please."

"Oh, almost forgot," Trojan said.

His hand flicked over her left arm, syringe between his fingers. A pinprick of pain flared. Jennifer Plummer's blood slithered through her system.

"Think about it, parasite. I'll be right down the hall. Every two hours, I'll dose us with blood-protection. Don't try to escape. There's an iron grille over every window, deadbolts on the doors, and I'll hear. Then I'll throw your eggs into the fuckin' oven and make you watch 'em cook."

He's killed before. You know exactly why his most attractive ideal is a young, powerless girl. But this was a human. Not her problem. *No, but—*

Who was she? Everyone's keeper? That was why she'd really wanted to kill herself. What she didn't mention to Trojan. She got tired of being a god. Didn't want to care about anything besides herself. She'd tried to trap the Divine Flesh in a basement like Trojan was currently doing to her...

Susan's nose burned and ran. She blinked tears away.

"I'll kill you if you ever try to hurt me," Trojan said voice low and hard. "Or worse. I can keep a fuckable torso in a chest."

He lifted the piece of toast. Tilted it. Semen drooled from one side to another. Bleach and rancid butter. The smell. The toast glistened. Oily. Pearly.

"What do you say, parasite-God?"

What do you believe, creator-God?

Her stinger throbbed, deep below her tongue.

I don't believe in anything. All I know is that I thought selfishness would make me happy and all it did was cause pain.

For her whims, a universe died.

You might die doing this, you know.

Then so be it.

Trojan guided the toast towards Susan's mouth.

"Open wide, sweetie," he said. He bumped the toast against her lips. She opened. Took a bite. Chewed. Swallowed. Her stinger slid out from beneath tongue and throat.

I will end this predator; I will do what needs to be done.

And the god-voice, the internal part of her that had shaped a universe from nothing, it rang out deep within her—

I WILL END YOU, KILLER OF INNOCENTS!

Susan smiled. She opened her mouth for another bite—

And lunged. *Snick!* She stabbed her stinger deep, deep into flesh, tasting sweat and soft ripe meat, so good—

(!!!!)

Pain exploded through her skull.

Trojan hoisted the bolt cutters for another strike, snarling.

Blood. Sticky, warm, stars twinkled along the edges of everything. When did he put the twinklies up? When did he—

(!!!!)

crunch.

Another hit.

hurts.

Trojan cursed, grabbed his swelling hand. The bolt cutters dropped to the carpet. Susan touched her temple. Blood and bits of jelly-like matter smeared her fingers. *Hurts.* Blood trickled down jaw and neck, wet and dirty and sticky. Ew.

hurts.

Hard to think.

She stood. Hard to move. Everything spun. Everything pressed down.

Trojan sucked in hissing, pained breaths. "Fuck. Fuck, you hurt me!"

He knocked the pill bottle off coffee table. He wore boots. He stomped on the bottle of eggs. Over and over. *Crunch! Crunch! Crunch!*

that hurts.

hurts.

hurts it hurts it hurts why can't I think?

She unbolted the front door. It took a few tries. The door swung open. White, weirdly shaped buildings lined the street outside. Funny. One looked like an igloo. There was a man dying on a cross by one of the buildings. Susan kept the door open. Someone was outside. Someone important who could help.

The smushed larvae eggs smelled like rust and ant's dens, chemical.

hurts.

She staggered outside and screamed.

A group of winged skinless humans danced on the road and lawn of the igloo building.

broken.

hurts.

Her memories and self dribbled, bit by bit, out of her crushed skull. The cracks ached agony when touched. Filaments had snapped when Trojan smushed there, and much of her had been damaged trying to rescue her larvae from the fire.

She screamed again. One of the winged creatures turned and stared. Susan waved.

They know the Good Person that can help.

Someone else needed help, too. Someone downstairs.

The winged creatures ran towards Susan, wings flapping in spurts as they did. Excited.

Someone else needs help…they're down. Where I was. The cell.

She lurched back inside, keeping the door open behind her. Trojan was gone. He was nowhere.

She made it to the piece of yarn by the trapdoor. Something important was down there.

Juice oozed from her crushed eggs on the carpet.

hurts.

Tears blurred everything.

hurts it hurts everything hurts.

She yanked on the yarn. The trapdoor lifted. She pulled it open all the way, and fumbled down the ladder. Back into the cement bunker. The trapdoor snapped shut by itself. Everything went black. Something made a scratching sound, above. Something chittered. *Someone's here.* Someone good? Someone?

Someone needs my help—

She let it take her down, into sleep.

The hurting went away for good.

30

"Will you accept My gift, Marcia?" I asked.

I didn't have to hide what I looked like anymore. Marcia understood that My body was a sanctuary for everyone, and that God could appear in any form, in any flesh. She loved Me. She loved Me so much. Oh, how I wanted to adore her; she would be a magnificent being after I had done so. Such a devoted believer deserved nothing less than My very best work.

She snuggled into one of My veils. Sleepy little thing. I wrapped cozy layers around her.

"Would you like to sleep?"

"Maybe," she said, yawning.

"Are you hungry? You ate that highway trooper over eight hours ago, darling."

"He knew the car was stolen. I couldn't let him prevent me from coming here," Marcia said. "Did You heal him? I felt really bad about eating him."

Not bad enough to keep her from chewing off his arm and taking it along with her. She'd gnawed it as she drove to Rosetown. Like a yummy turkey leg.

"Oh, I healed him. He didn't even feel it when you gobbled him up. I made sure of that," I said. "Now, will you accept My gift, and the sacred responsibility that comes with it? It's a tough job. It might even be dangerous. It's okay if you don't want to. You can say no. If you do, you can sleep here, nice and safe, or play games with My other children…and then you'll get to see Isaac and Daryl!"

I might've had a *teensy* bit to do with Marcia's newfound hunger, but the poor thing was *so* underweight. She hadn't had a period in three years. Her hair had stopped growing. Brittle. Desiccated. Her foster family kept making sounds about hospitalization for her eating disorder, but there wasn't enough money for it. Very quietly, on the drive to Rosetown, I'd brought Marcia up to a healthy weight, gifting her muscle and fat to replace what she had starved away. I made her lanugo fall out. I restored her hair. I soothed her body and told it that it would never starve again, that it was safe to function.

"If I accept, I'll prevent the unsaved from hurting themselves. I'll be bringing them God," Marcia said.

"They might try to hurt you."

"But they're suffering," Marcia said, teary-eyed.

So eager to save others.

I grew a mouth on a tendril and kissed the tip of her nose. "So that's a yes?"

"How could I say no?"

My precious dear one. My brave little paladin.

I rocked her back and forth, like a newborn. She grew sleepy. I felt the tickle of melatonin as her brain released it.

"Then imbibe Me," I crooned. I brought her to suckle.

Her lips found a nipple on Me. They greedily clamped around it. She nursed for a long while, making satisfied little grunts. So adorable. I trickled My gift into the milk.

She fell asleep while still on the nipple. Milk-drunk. Her mouth slackened. Her head drooped. A mixture of milk and saliva smeared the lower half of her face. As she slept, My gift rooted in her salivary glands. Bulbs formed within, like miniature milk ducts. Microscopic fragments of Me formed in those new ducts. Seeds. Pathogens. They lay latent, awaiting something to inoculate them. I shielded each one in a hydrophobic lipid capsule; bleach would do nothing to them, and if Jennifer's blood had been diluted in any amount, neither could the blood enter. These were no mere bacteria or virus or prion.

When they found something not of Me, these seeds of Me would wait. They'd burrow deep into the flesh. Oh, they could slumber for decades within the unassimilated, but it wouldn't take decades for them to sprout. The second—no, the *nanosecond*—that the Light's protection wore off, My seeds would infiltrate and instantly assimilate the flesh they'd been planted in. I'd connect to the poor silly child. I'd bathe them in My love, and then all of this nonsense about Jennifer's blood and fluids would go away.

But if they kept dosing themselves with Jennifer's blood before the last hit wore off…

Well. They *could* theoretically stave off assimilation forever, but they wouldn't. They were only human; I adored them, of course, but they *would* miss a dose at some point. All it would take was less than a nanosecond.

I wired the reformatted salivary ducts to Marcia's brain; I threaded neurons and nerves to give her control over My gift. She could shut it off entirely, if need be. The bits of Me weren't visible to the naked human eye. Her saliva looked exactly the same as it had before I bestowed My gift.

Marcia slept. I gave her all the love I could. I whispered information about the holy task and the gift thriving inside her:

(You see, you can sneak up on them and bite. Or spit into their food.)

(You carry a pathogen—Me.)

(And as you infect the non-believers, one by one, they shall join the Divine Flesh.)

They would test Marcia with the Light, and she would pass. I'd grafted a section of Monty's skin onto her forehead, blending it into her own. If they made her eat the Light, his esophagus and stomach would shield her from being burned. And I would be watching through her eyes, guiding her along the way, keeping her safe. If they discovered that Marcia was Mine…I'd protect her. Violently, if need be.

Of course, I wanted to keep Marcia and Isaac looking the same until the family reunion, but if I ended up having to modify them a teensy bit…well, Daryl would just have to deal with it.

Tomorrow was going to be a big, big day.

The body isn't *real, the body isn't mine.*

I slipped out of the pesticide and anesthesia haze, blinking tears out of my eyes.

The first thing I noticed was the smell. Chemical. It burned up my nose. Harsh. Familiar.

Embalming fluid? Formalin?

Mattress springs pressed into my bony body. My throat singed with each swallow. My left wrist hurt. Gauze had been wrapped around it. I pressed. Got pain. Yeah, they'd bled something outta me, but my hands and ankles were free. I fumbled for my emergency bobby pin.

"Daryl?"

"It's formaldehyde," Daryl rasped.

They'd put us in a sealed concrete cell, eight-by-eight. Daryl crouched in the far corner, barely lit by a single Coleman lantern. Handcuffs glinted on his wrists. A broken canning jar shone in a puddle of clear liquid on the floor. A Mason lid and band remained on the intact half of the jar. Bits of shattered glass glittered. Bits of…something else lay by the shards.

"Jennifer, you need to see this."

"Let me get us outta here. Odds are good they cheaped out on the lock. If they got a guard, who cares? We can't die. I don't know about you, but I'm gettin' right the hell outta—"

"Jennifer."

"What?"

He held up a card. Driver's license. His hand trembled. "I found this. Under the bed, along with another jar," he said, and pointed towards the other corner.

He picked up the lantern with his teeth and illuminated the ID, brandishing it.

I staggered over to him. Knelt.

A happy blonde girl smiled on the ID. Even in the degraded plastic photo, she glowed with health—salmon-pink lips, a smattering of summer freckles, a heart-shaped face.

Pearson, Susannah, read the ID.

"Oh, Jesus," I said.

"Eddie Fields is dead. Proved it in the autopsy. They didn't cover his face or anything when they hanged him."

"Concerned citizens."

Daryl moved the lantern over the puddle, switching to his hands. "You know what that is," he said.

Shreds of…shreds of labia, sliced into flat bits. A sliced-open…thing, still in its hood.

"No," I said.

Oh god. Is that—

"He cut off their external genitalia before he killed them," Daryl said, voice thin as a razor. "Don't pretend it's anything else."

Nausea surged through me. Pre-vomit drool flooded my mouth. I gagged.

Concerned citizens don't like folks that can't look you in the eye.

I realized what had really happened ten years ago. Everything came out in a rush. I talked so I wouldn't puke.

"Eddie Fields didn't kill anyone," I said. "He was autistic. He lived in a shack in the mountains 'cause he liked being alone, and I'm willing to bet that whenever he came into town, everyone avoided him, except Susannah Pearson and Delight Owens. Susannah's dad was a medical examiner—they're usually quiet, shy, and get into the field 'cause they like working alone, so he liked Eddie, and Susannah wouldn't care if someone was weird and quiet like her daddy. So hear me out. Eddie Fields goes into town, he's stocking up at Garrison's, and Susannah Pearson strikes up a conversation with him, and Eddie's so happy that someone's talkin' to him that he's forgettin' the rules of Rosetown. Freaks don't talk to pretty girls. Freaks leave."

I said, "So then the killer takes Susannah after they part ways. Where were they going? Probably somewhere related to a special interest that both of 'em had, I'd guess. What kinda topic would interest both a thirty-year-old mountain man and a teenage girl from Idaho? Something local, probably, too. Think on it some."

Daryl nodded.

"Okay, so Delight Owens is easy enough. He's a freak, but she's nice, so she doesn't care 'bout that. The killer took her after she left the Unitarian Universalist service. Either the killer knew where she'd be ahead of time—which means that the killer knew the Owens family went to that church, so they're a local—or the killer was someone that wouldn't be out of place in that area. C'mon, it's Rosetown. If Wade or Emily started walkin' towards one of Holy Lane's churches, someone would say somethin', even in a nice way, and they were born and raised in Rosetown. Small town. People gossip."

I paced around the cell, thinking out loud. "And concerned citizens will buy that the weird, antisocial mountain man killed those innocent girls, even if he didn't. Did the killer frame Eddie, or just take advantage of the coincidence? Doesn't matter. We know that the guy—and yeah, Daryl, it's a guy, female killers don't mutilate their victims like that, what he did, it's so fucking sexually-driven, it hurts—the guy's a flaming misogynist. Probably has a hard time hiding it in public, I'd bet. Or he has an alter-ego persona that he uses."

"Antiquing. Archery. Guns. Rockhounding. Hunting, maybe hiking. Those are the ones I can think of," Daryl said.

"Who can you think of that goes to church and also likes those things?" I said.

He snorted. "Fuckin' everyone."

I tugged the bobby pin out of my hair. "I'm gonna pick the door."

"Know what pisses me off 'bout this whole thing?" Daryl said. "Trojan doesn't believe any of his own bullshit. Not if he tortured and killed innocent girls like this. Concerned folks, my ass. He's been playing everyone for at least ten years. We died for nothing."

"You don't know that. Hell, maybe Trojan was gonna kill again and frame *you* for another set of murders." I snapped the bobby pin apart. "If we don't get him, She will."

"About that—the Divine Flesh is gonna think of a way around your blood-protection. We need to figure out what's next."

"You have the best chance at defeating Her."

"How'd you figure?"

"Maybe…we can barter for Her to reenter my body. I think it's meant to be a prison for the Divine Flesh. If we can get Her to do that, and be mostly human…I could live with that."

"Really."

"Yes, really. I'd make things different. We could share the body, fifty-fifty. Take turns. I wouldn't have a relationship with anyone, so you and Her could do your romance-stuff. We could make it work."

"That's a terrible solution," he said.

I slithered the ridged half of the bobby pin into the upper half of the lock. I pressed the smooth half against the bottom edge of the lock. I groped the ridged half in, listening for the *clicks* as tumblers snapped into place. *C'mon, you know it's a cheap lock.*

"We can't defeat Her with force," I said.

He sighed. "I still think we need to have you get high again. We have to barter for the Hermetic, but I—there's only one thing She wants."

"No."

My hands jerked. The bobby pin snapped. An eighth of an inch jutted from the lock. *Shit.*

"Jennifer, if push comes to shove—"

"You are *not* turning into one of Her flesh-abominations, Daryl. I'll die before I let that happen."

He kicked the wall. "You think I don't know how bad that'd be?"

"Now our lockpick's shot."

"Good."

"We're stuck here."

"Good."

I tore the bobby pin halves out. "I can pick your cuffs, at least. C'mere."

"Nah, I'm good."

The lantern flickered out, leaving us in darkness.

In the July evening.

Silver Lake birthed its annual plague of mayflies. Every inch of the night lay bloated with them. Mosquitoes blessed every puddle of stagnant water with their eggs. Moths batted against the glowing windows of St. Thérèse's, wanting the moon—receiving only hard glass and illusions. Crickets chirped. Abominations chittered and called to each other, caressed by the torrid summer air. Hot. A breeze skipped over the flesh-barrier and shuffled the hot night around, cooling nothing. The air thickened with heat. In the cherry orchards, fruit awaited harvest. Where were the pickers, the birds and humans to carry their seeds far? Then abominations came, jubilant and sweating, into the rows of cherry trees, and the Divine Flesh bestowed blessings.

Malign pink stars blighted the heavens—cosmos, too close to home—and smothered the Milky Way in a gauze of eyes and hunger, something breathing, something excited, something descending from the sky, saying it *adores you.*

Something hungry.

Shoots shuddered up from the dirt in the Rodriguez backyard. Fleshy vines erupted from Vic Snyder's truck undercarriage and engulfed him, holding snug even as they seared against his flesh.

The girl sat up from the truck bed, smiling, and her eyes gleamed with hunger.

Vic Snyder couldn't scream. He couldn't beg her to stop. He couldn't even preach the evils of the flesh-god, because Her tendrils had spiraled down his throat.

"Don't be afraid," the girl said. "I'm here to give you a gift."

The tendrils parted, revealing Snyder's head and shoulders. The girl's lips glistened with saliva. She looked through him, not at him. Her gaze lingered on his throat. On his carotid artery.

She snapped her head forward. Pain burned on his shoulder. Her teeth cut through muscle and skin and fat, jaw working. Then her tongue lapped over the bite, daubing it in her spit.

She pulled away, grinning so much that her eyes crinkled. "Will you help me? When the blood wears off? I think you will."

He couldn't say no. Couldn't even scream.

The girl started his truck. Tendrils oozed into the passenger side, carrying Vic. They ripped his pink esophagus and stomach out. Peeled his skin off. Vic watched, intrigued. There was no pain, this time. It was a dissection. His body was no longer his own.

The girl drove them to Holy Lane, windows cranked down.

"We're going to church. The Divine Flesh will fix you up, so the blood can't hurt you. You delivered Jennifer Plummer's blood to the Church of Christ about five hours ago, but I think Allie Crowley won't mind you comin' back."

Vic made a muffled sound.

"We're converts of the faith," the girl said, winking. Her square face, with its blunt features, grew solemn. "The Divine Flesh is going to punish you first," she said.

Tendons pulsed on his skinned forearms. Veins throbbed. Muscles tightened, slackened, tightened. Mayflies landed on his exposed wet flesh and supped.

"It won't hurt forever, and Her love lasts forever and ever. Try to remember that," the girl said, and that was when the last of Jennifer Plummer's blood wore off, and the Divine Flesh's honey-sweet voice echoed through Vic's mind.

(It won't hurt forever.)

(Oh, oh, oh, but Vic!)

The Divine Flesh giggled, audible in his ears. "But Vic! I don't need *forever* to make you regret all the terrible things you've done. It's time to repent."

Pain flooded his body. Tendrils coiled around his ankles. His knees. His elbows. His neck. They tightened. They pulled, slowly, and sharp edges grew along the fleshy portions of the tendrils, like intestines with razor blades. They tugged…

(See the impact of your actions.)

They ripped him apart.

3:16 a.m. A witching hour.

Allie Crowley dumped more fentanyl into a pitcher of lemonade. Sweat glued the half-face particulate respirator to her skin. Summer broiled through the church kitchen. No lights shone outside. Hellish stars burned pink.

Genesis 3:16. *I will make your pain in childbearing very severe; with great pain you will birth your children; you shall desire your husband, he will rule over you.*

Shepard was gone. Demons were demons. Noah was dead. *Lord save us. Lord save me. There was a full blood moon yesterday, and now there's nothing. Jesus, take me home—*

(Mommy, mommy, I love you!)

A low scream clawed out of her.

3:20 a.m.

Job 3:20. *Why is light given to those in misery, and life to the bitter of soul?*

Headlights appeared in the window over the sink. No good person would drive around this area, at this time, in these circumstances. Her stomach clenched. Allie doffed the disposable plastic salon caps she'd been using as overshoe covers to avoid tracking the powdered fentanyl outside of the kitchen. She removed her first set of gloves, reached up to her respirator straps, and doffed that, placing it in a reserved bucket. She padded over to the edge of the diamond-patterned linoleum and slipped her last layer of gloves into the trash, before washing her hands in a basin.

John 3:20. *Everyone who does evil hates the light, and will not come into the light for fear that their deeds will be exposed.*

Occasionally, shooting pains lanced up her arms and legs. Several others had said similar things, after they'd imbibed their drops of blood-protection. Numb fingers and toes. Pins and needles, tingling lips. Allie chalked it up to fentanyl contamination.

"Mrs. Crowley?" Gary Webster said, coming around the corner. "Vic Snyder's back."

"That's a problem?"

Gary Webster had never left his Goth phase. He was a few years shy of forty-five and his dyed black hair waved in a ponytail down his back. Skin tags dotted his clean-shaven face like warts.

Allie pursed her lips. Vic Snyder needed Jesus like a man ablaze needed a bucket of water.

"He's got a girl with him. Someone I've never seen in town, looks like she's just barely legal," Gary said, and his black-lipsticked mouth contorted into a sneer.

"And?"

"Seems off."

"Does she seem demonic?"

"Do they ever, Mrs. Crowley?"

Allie crossed her arms. "She seem too good to be true? Either too goody-two-shoes, or too much of a 'bad-girl with a heart o' gold'?"

"The first. She's carryin' a pink lil' Bible with her."

"Let me talk to them. Bring the blood protection," Allie said.

She followed Webster to the nave. Air mattresses and sleeping bags crowded every inch of floor. Toddlers slept on the pews, cushioned by layers of wool army blankets. Garrison had donated everything he could—guns, ammo, blankets—to fight the spiritual war. Men slept outside, on the grass, and the ones with wives slept closer to the church building.

Demons sang beyond the boundary of the lawn. "Come join us! We are the beloved children of God! God is waiting for you to come home!"

Zero takers thus far, because Satan was dumb enough to have his demons preach that crap while still looking like demons. *Lord save us.* Lazybones Satan thought that preaching nice words was all it took to dupe good Christians? Not on Allie Crowley's watch. If Satan would've made his demons look like angels, though…

How do you know that Noah was saved? What if he's one of them still? What if you burned your baby alive for nothing—

No. Didn't bear thinking of. A demon was a demon.

Webster retrieved a two-liter Pepsi bottle. Diluted blood-protection filled it three-quarters full. It looked like some rich-person's fancy strawberry LaCroix, it was so watered-down. An eyedropper full every hour seemed to do the trick.

Webster gabbed into a handheld radio, finger playing with a rip on his black jeans. "Guide them through the demons. They'll make way for the truck. Drive around to the back entrance, not the front."

They trudged to the back entrance. Webster drew the shotgun and pushed the door open for Allie. On-duty men—an informal watch, instituted by Allie Crowley—had circled Vic and the girl, cutting off access to the truck. The truck idled outside. The men trained their Glocks and AK-47s and rifles on them.

Ten industrial-grade flashlights blazed over Vic Snyder and the girl. Both knelt on the grass, hands behind their heads. That pink Bible sat right by the girl's side. A scrawny girl. Dark-haired, too pale.

Distrustful eyes. Squarish face, but a decent-enough hourglass figure. Clothing was wrong. A turtleneck blouse in this weather? Modest girls wore slips and elbow-length knit tops in July. Vic was Vic. The girl was trying too hard. Hiding something. Fine, who didn't have something to hide—

(Mommy, it hurts Mommy I love you Mommy!)

But was it something that could damn the souls of everyone here? Hm. Where had Allie had seen that face before? She couldn't remember.

"You screwin' that girl, Vic?" Allie asked.

"No, no, I found her holed up in the Motel 6, she's visiting a—a relative, and all of this shit went down. She's clean."

"Test Vic Snyder," Allie said.

Webster smeared a dab of blood-protection on Vic's forehead. It did nothing. Vic didn't move.

Webster got a dropper full and held it out like a priest offering the Eucharist. "Swallow it."

Vic did. No change.

"Look, Allie—"

"Shepard's dead, I know. Don't need to tell me." Allie looked the girl square in the eye. "Why're you here? You ever been here before? You look familiar."

The girl flushed coral pink.

"Spit it out. You got a name?"

"Marcia."

"Well, Marcia, it's a simple question. Why're you here in Rosetown? We ain't a tourist spot, the lake's garbage, and I don't know who you are, which means you probably don't have relatives here."

"Um—"

"You screwin' Vic? Or another man in Rosetown? That it? He say he'd make you his wife or whatever they say now? Don't listen to that crap. A man's a man. He'll say anything to shimmy a hand up your skirt," Allie said, then tried to soften her tone. "But you aren't a demon, honey. There's nothing you could do or say that'd be any worse than that, so tell me the truth. Ignore these men and tell me. Men are men. They won't remember a word of it. Girl talk goes in one ear and out the other with them. What were you in Rosetown for?"

"My—my brother lives here. He's a—he's living in sin with a drug-addicted woman. I came with Scripture, to try and get her to leave the addict and that lifestyle."

It clicked. *Daryl Plummer. That's one of his siblings. Lord help her. They DO look alike.*

"Oh, it's just *so* embarrassing, Mrs. Crowley. Everyone knows it's because we had a terrible tragedy when we were just little-bitty children. Our parents died, you know. It was *very* sad. Our father took his own life, and we ended up in separate foster homes. Of course he ended up with some issues."

Tears ran down Marcia's cheeks. "Daryl's being a silly little thing, and he needs Jesus. All I want to do is save him. That nasty drug addict he's with is no good. She's immature. A babygirl. She's a terrible, awful influence on Daryl. I think she hates God. And love. Well. The way she acts, I sure think she does."

Did her voice change a little, near the end?

There were emotions here, but not quite…the right ones. Then again, Allie didn't have family that struggled with this stuff, so what did she know? Poor Marcia. Poor Daryl, even. *Imagine being so misled that the idea of licking a drug addict's clam or kissing her mouth sounded good. Ick.* Made her wanna gag.

"All right," Allie Crowley said, "give her the test."

They gave her blood to drink, and daubed a thumb of it across her forehead. Nothing happened. Marcia passed with flying colors. She beamed at Allie. Saliva lacquered every Chiclet-white tooth. She greased her rough lips with her tongue.

Allie said, "Almost didn't see the family resemblance, what with the beard your brother's got. Good strong features though, honey. They age well."

They entered the church. Vic settled Marcia onto a spare scrap of floor, threw a blanket over her, and lumbered outside to sleep.

Allie Crowley returned to her labors.

3:40 a.m.

Mark 4:40. *He said to his disciples, "Why are you so afraid? Do you still have no faith?"*

31

We slipped in and out of sleep, in that dark womb of a cell. At one point, I woke up and Daryl was holding me. I held him.

"She told me the real reason you couldn't get custody of the kids," I said.

Grinding into each other, our chests touching.

"Oh." His voice rumbled out and vibrated against my skin. I could smell him. Old Spice. Sweat. His chest hair tickled.

"I'm sorry, Daryl."

"I've never heard that come out of your mouth."

"I know," I said. "Daryl, I'm sorry. The shit I did in our relationship was wrong. I never should've made my issues your fault, and that fact that I *did*—knowing how much you believe that everything's your fault—was unacceptable."

"Won't be an issue much longer."

"No. Don't think like that."

"I'm tired."

I held him tighter. "We can do this. C'mon, get those theology-moral-philosophy gears going."

"We can't even escape a locked cell."

"It's pitch-black in here."

"I love you," Daryl said.

What. Did he just—

"Huh?" I asked.

My heart went dead. Heat washed through me.

His lips pressed against my cheek.

"I love you, Jennifer."

"Ha-ha," I said. "Is your next sentence gonna be, 'Can we try a three-some with the Divine Flesh?' I have a sinking feeling that it—"

"Do you love me?" Daryl said.

Wetness. Sticky-sweet between my thighs. Blood warmed through my torso, spreading lower, lower. Throbbing. Pulsing, glowing to life, *I want, I want*, red-hot clit, swelling, so sweet so sensitive, a live exposed wire—*So wet. God, I'm so wet.*

I slid my tank top off. Unhooked my bra.

"I never stopped, Daryl. You're a good man. You deserve better than me."

"I *did* cheat on you, Jennifer."

I want, I want.

In the dark, I ran my lips over him and found his earlobe. Slipped it into my mouth. Bitter wax, skin, his skin, the tang of his sweat, salty, *so good*, I sucked on it, I hitched a leg around his hip and ground on it, on his hard muscled thigh—*how many hours of repairing power lines has that thigh seen? A lot*—my underwear soaked through and sliding, slippery from want.

His breath caught. "Oh."

"I want you," I whispered. I slithered my hands into his unbuttoned shirt. Slipped it off. Slithered under his t-shirt, his chest warm under my fingers.

"Can we?" I asked.

"Oh," he said softly. "I should've known. You just want me to eat you out, like always—"

"No, no, I wanna—I wanna make you feel good."

"Oh?"

"My heart grew three sizes when I died, yadda-yadda. I had a Kumbaya moment where I saw a white light—Look, Daryl, when I saw how much you've given me over the years, how much you care about me, even now—" I sighed. "I'm starting to realize that I'm a bad person. I'm self-centered. I'm emotionally abusive when I get triggered. I wallow in my own bullshit and make it everyone else's problem. I blame everything on the Divine Flesh—and here's the funny part. If She was a human being and not an eldritch abomination, She'd be a better person than me."

Silence, except for Daryl's breathing.

"So. Every time we had sex, it was all about me. You pleasured me. You fingered me. Sure, sometimes I kind of asked to do you, but not really. I'm sorry. Please. Can I—can I make you feel good? Do you trust me?"

"You—you really mean it?" Daryl asked, voice thick.

"I love you."

"Okay," he said, and let me slip his shirt off.

Couldn't get it all the way off. He was still handcuffed. Fabric puddled around his wrists.

"Kinky," I said.

"Goddammit, Jennifer."

"If we had some light or something I could pick the lock on 'em."

"Can you manipulate flesh?"

No. No, I'm not like Her. No. No.

I unbuttoned his jeans. Shimmied 'em down. Slid my shorts off, my underwear. I wrapped my thighs around one of his and straddled it, hair tickling, skin cool against me, so good oh yes, grinding, grinding back and forth, spidering my hands down his chest, lower, lower. Till I got to his dick. Hard as a rail spike.

Slick so slick, so good, so I wrapped my arms 'round his chest, hands pressing his lower back, and kissed the base of his neck.

"Oh, that feels nice," he breathed.

"Gonna feel real nice in about five seconds."

I kissed down his chest, loving every inch of him, the sweat and the hair and the film of woodsmoke, the smell of him musky, sweatier as I dipped lower. I teased my tongue along the head of his dick. Salty-sweet taste, tasted like him, so silky to behold, soothing to *lick, lick*—I teased along his shaft.

"Tell me if you like this," I said. I took him in my mouth and started sucking.

He hissed, arcing his back. Into me. Gentle pressure at the base of my skull. His palms. Metal. He pressed me into him as I worked, panting, *pulse-pulse-pulse*, so good, *you taste so good, so smooth*, his balls tickling my chin, nose-deep in his pubes, his smell, him, grunting, pressing, body shuddering—

A polite moan. Almost like a cough.

Release.

I swallowed him, smacking my lips.

"You wanna go again?" I purred.

"...Fuck...That was nice."

"Do you?"

"You want me to take care of you?" Daryl asked, voice husky.

I spooned into him, making him the big spoon. "Think I can DIY it. You wanna straddle me as I do?"

"Oh fuck yeah."

I came. We fell asleep holding each other.

"Okay," I said, upon waking, "nobody's come to bleed me. That probably means they're dead. I'm gonna try and pray to the Light and see if it helps us."

"You want me to—"

"Keep holding me."

My mouth felt dry. It'd been a long sleep. Even the formaldehyde had burned out my nose enough that I couldn't smell it anymore.

Light.

Light, please help us. I'm trying to trap the Divine Flesh, but I'm stuck in a cell and I can't bust out in the dark. Please help. Amen.

Nothing happened.

DIVINE FLESH!

No reply.

God, I'd kill for a light.

Warmth prickled over my hands and wrists.

Light.

A part of me disconnected from the emotion and swirling thoughts. It said, *Light.*

Threads of gossamer light sprouted from my pores. They burst out, groping in the air. They found each other. Where they met, nodules formed. Bright as magnesium fire, light radiated. A gush of hot fluid filled my mouth. Not saliva. Something faintly sweet, like watered-down fruit syrup. Honeydew juice. *Protoflesh.* It dribbled from my lips. It touched my skin and hardened into blobby skin tags. I touched one, commanded it (*off*), and peeled the skin tag away like a sticker.

I am what is, I am what has been, I am what shall be.

Phosphorescence limned my arms.

I need warmth.

Heat rose in my chest. Maybe—*what, salvation? What the fuck are you gonna do, be Her? Embrace the insanity? Pray to the Magic Meat Lite Brite? C'mon. You're an irredeemable piece of shit, not some Magic Lite Brite!*

This time, I ignored my shitty inner dialogue. It wasn't helpful. Whether I was redeemable or not didn't matter.

"If you're the Light, and you can hear me, help me. Please," I said.

I heard myself say, "I am what I am." I didn't say it. It came out. I shivered.

(want to be)

"Y-you wanna be?" I said. *Jennifer, what the hell are you doing? You can't embrace this cosmic bullshit!* I let the protoflesh fill my cheeks like saliva.

Jennifer, you can't control this shit!

Jennifer, you're gonna turn yourself into a fucking flesh monstrosity if you fuck with this!

"Then be." I spat.

crack.

Protoflesh, sweet to taste. Warm. Alive. I spat it on my left arm, and it burned, tingling.

(Flesh!)

"Let there be light. Let there be light," I chanted, wondering if the protoflesh might just turn into more skin-tags or glowing goo, but knowing—

(The Light is here become the Light)

—knowing that it wouldn't.

Chemical-cold white light congealed on my arm, but I could stare at it and it didn't hurt. Felt…nice. Like coming home after working a double shift at Starbucks and flicking on the—

(the Light.)

Dendrites branched from the light-ball, stinging where they merged into my skin. Another nub of light—*an axon*—bloomed from a branch.

I baptized myself in protoflesh. Flesh baptism. Let there be light. Let there be warmth. Electricity arced through me. I smiled. My cheeks hurt. *Light inside ME!*

Whoa, cowboy, hold on there.

I rubbed the stuff on me, didn't swallow, wanted to. Networks of white-hot neurons meshed over my body, oozing heat. I let something *click-click* without really knowing why, asked, got a vague impression of *(fuel)* and *(magnesium)*. Draining the minerals from my body to fuel the chemical lightshow. I let them. Something caressed my forehead and skull, stinging.

Now you've got creepy neurons over your face.

I ignored that, too.

"Thank you," I said, and laughed a little.

Why not? It felt good to laugh. Everything felt good. I was beautiful. I was warm. I was—

(Light.)

Something the Light was helping. I'd prayed and it'd thrown me a bone. The Light was something I still had to make fight Her, but that would be easy-peasy.

I giggled. "All of this is silly."

Tee-hee!

More neurons exploded from dendrite branches, *so good so warm, that feels so good, I missed this*, so I dumped a round of protoflesh into my eyes, urging it to open them to the night. But wait. No. I needed to hear through the darkness, not see. Silly me.

It trickled through my sinuses in a hot rush, to my eardrums, and reshaped. Thickened. Cilia I'd never known I'd lost regrew.

click-click-click.

I could hear through the concrete wall and dirt. A pine worm chittered in a nearby fir—

There were three firs in a cluster to my right, another tree fifty feet ahead, pine worms glutting themselves in a nice-sounding *click-click* symphony, a nice song, wouldn't it be nice to listen? Wasn't it good that the happy worms could eat? What a pretty tree! Happy children chattered to each other outside.

I froze. The sounds faded.

What was wrong with me just now?

"Jennifer," Daryl said.

"What?" I snapped.

"You're covered in light. You're so…beautiful," Daryl said.

"Of course you'd think that. You're a monsterfucker."

Like hell I was. I was carpeted in spidery cosmic neurons. I shivered. I walked over to the lock. Neurons sprouted from my fingertips. I wormed them into the lock. The tumblers slid open. I turned the bolt. Opened the cell door.

"You gonna let me pick those cuffs or not?" I asked.

Was his left hand…gooey? Or was he seeing shit? Was the parasite's stinger chock-full of LSD?

Trojan turned his keychain flashlight on.

In the meaty part of his left thumb, a nail-sized puncture festered. Silver veins spiraled from it. A whirlpool. Something circling a drain. Not normal veins, either, but coiled swirled things like Granny's varicose veins.

He couldn't move his left hand at all. He palped it. His thumb left an imprint. Play-Doh. Bread dough. He held his left hand up, tilted it.

The flesh flowed like honey. It collected at the lowest points, clinging to the skeletal structure of the hand. Goo. Goo on a fucking *wirework*, his hand was.

Trojan huddled under the army blanket. He'd sprinted through the yard and into the tunnel entrance of the bunker. Now, here he squatted, in a corner of the bunker-office where he'd killed Shepard, hiding like a scared little kid. The rest of them were dead or assimilated.

Fine.

He'd built a God-suit. He'd duped everyone into hanging that shit-for-brains autist ten year ago. That parasite was full of it. God. It thought it'd been God? And the flesh-god would never have him, ripped apart and digested—

shit oh god no.

Fear hollowed his guts.

never never you will LIVE FOREVER you EXIST you are your own God.

Jennifer Plummer was tucked away in that cell, along with the other one, the collateral. Her blood-protection was genetic, he'd bet his other hand on it. No, he couldn't play with her much. But.

live forever.

But she could be bred.

He'd keep her handcuffed to that bed, nice and easy, and fuck her till she was full of his babies. Good babies. Good, white, American babies. Maybe she needed a solid pregnancy to sort her out. His genes would live forever. Their descendants would rule the new world.

It brought a Fun-Sized jolt.

She can't go anywhere. Not with the tripwires I rigged. If she unlocks that cell door, she'll get a face full of Drano. She doesn't need a face to reproduce.

Trojan forced himself to sleep. Sleep off the sting. He injected another round of blood-protection into himself.

If it got any worse, he'd hack off his hand.

32

"Daryl, look at this Wile-E-Coyote shit."

I studied the tripwire stretched across the doorway. Ankle-height. Daryl approached from behind. I held up a hand. He stopped moving. Squinted at me. *Jennifer, get to the point.*

"I mean, seriously, rig a shotgun to go off. That's a classic for a reason. This dude's got a gallon of drain cleaner tied to some strings and pulleys."

I cackled. I continued ignoring the glowing lightshow that was my body. Like those Christmas lights I'd wrap around myself when I got super-duper drunk. Only instead of wire between the little twinkle lights, there were nerves, white like albino ivy. Or ivory. Bone. Something. I was pretty sure they were nerves.

"You ever go clean out a meth lab? Kill some rival cooks, scrub something for a boss?" I said. "You see these types of jerry-rigged booby traps all the time. Meth's a terrible drug. Makes everything… itchy. Your skin. Your teeth. Your brain. So they spend a lot of time scratching that itch by making stuff. Wonder if Trojan's using uppers. You ever seen a cook go—"

"No, Jennifer. I haven't. Quit glorifying your lifestyle. Other people have to clean up *your* messes when you live like a damn tweaker."

"Hello, morality police?"

Daryl snorted. "And here I thought you'd changed. What an idiot I am. You never change."

"Whoa, dude. I'm just sharing useful stories—"

"No, you want me to validate you by laughing at your 'useful stories' or by expressing sympathy that you'll then exploit. You're looking for external validation because you feel uncomfortable right now, and instead of taking it as an opportunity to examine your life, yourself, or your actions, you're choosing to numb that feeling, so you don't have to change," Daryl said, in that didactic fucking tone of his. "You believe your own horseshit, so I'm not offended, but I'm not tolerating it anymore."

Heat.

Shame.

Fuck you. Fuck you, asshole, and I mean, c'mon, so what if I talk about some of the things I've done? It's relevant to the situation. That doesn't make me a bad person for saying that, okay, I'm not a bad person, I'm redeemable, I'm lovable—

Something squirmed in my stomach.

I can't be past saving or doing the Good Person shtick, right? I'm New Jennifer. I'm not Old Jennifer. I stopped cooking speed! I'm redeemable!

Face burning, I snapped, "Why don't you go crawl back inside Mommy-God, like everyone else?"

"What are you scared of?"

"Everyone else is doing it. All hail the flesh-god. Did you fuck Her when She looked weird, or was it normie sex only? Was She better than me? Am I freaky enough for you now, asshole—"

"I don't care what you look like, Jennifer."

Wetness blurred the tripwire, the concrete, the drain cleaner. I tasted salt and snot.

"I-I'm fine," I said, sniffling.

"No, you're not. What are you scared of?"

"I have to be capable of being a good person, right? I can't just be bad, and that's it. There has to be something, some hope, some reason for me to try, Daryl. Okay? I can't be like Her, because if I am, then that means there's no hope, I'm not human, and therefore, I'm not redeemable."

"Redeemable to who? Me?"

"I—I don't know."

"I love you, but I'm not gonna tolerate certain behaviors from you anymore. That doesn't mean you're an unredeemable monster."

"I'm a fucking lightshow."

"So?"

"You know what? Forget it. You can't understand what that's like. Let's just get outta here. I'll guide you over the booby traps without my jackass commentary—"

"You think your feelings and thoughts are so damn unique, 'cause you never grew out of that narcissistic teenage mentality. 'Poor me. My feelings are all that matters. I feel bad, therefore, I am bad.'"

"I'm immature?"

"Yeah," he said, hick drawl thickening. "When you git to be an adult, you pull your head outta your ass and realize there's an entire world full of people just like you. Your feelings ain't unique. Your feelings ain't fact. Go to church, make some friends, and figure it out."

"That's what I'm failing at. Figuring it out," I said. I pointed to the tripwire. "I'll trigger it. Stand back."

I stomped the tripwire down, jumping away from the door.

snap!

A poison-blue canister of Drano slammed to the ground outside. It burst. Yellow fluid bubbled from a seam in the plastic.

"Step over it. Walk behind me," I said, "and remember—neither of us can stay dead, but that doesn't mean dying won't hurt like a bitch."

We proceeded into the corridor. Light illuminated a short hallway with a door off of it, but no further. Couldn't see the end.

I remembered all the late-night phone calls that Daryl had taken from Isaac and Marcia. Isaac thought that Daryl was still single, do-gooder Daryl. Marcia had zero clue about any of it—not the times I'd had Daryl buy me stuff to cook drugs with, or the nights we'd spent screaming at each other, or the bricks of drugs in the trunk of his old beater.

Isaac, I don't care if that evangelical church has Jesus Christ Himself prowlin' the pews, you're goin', and you're gonna do your absolute best, Daryl had said one July night when we were nineteen, a month past our wedding.

A pause. Daryl snorted. *You're offended on my behalf. How's that work? I'm not offended. They're a conservative Christian church, where do you expect 'em to stand on stuff?*

That foster family's taking care of you, and they want you to go to their church. Give 'em that basic respect. They feed you, give you medical care, and they're not half bad, from what I've seen. It's a clean house. They don't beat you. The foster mom does a decent job at homeschooling, I've seen the curriculum. So do your best, okay? It's a nice home, and you'll be outta there sooner than you think.

Then he'd stared me dead in the eye, sitting across the dining room table. *Naw, neither of you are meeting Jennifer, 'cause she's a bad influence.*

Do NOT breathe a word of any of this to Marcia, she's delicate. She doesn't know I'm—she doesn't know about any of it...

...You know how bad it was, with Uncle Larry. Remember me, pickin' needles out from under the mattress? Remember that time you stole the baking soda from the neighbors and tried to dump it on our floor mattress, so it wouldn't reek?

He'd sighed.

Wish you wouldn't have seen what I did to Larry. I didn't want either of you to know—No, Isaac. It wasn't "badass," it was fuckin' brutal. I hacked his nuts off so he wouldn't molest Marcia anymore, or any other kid. I fuckin' warned him. I told him.

Another sigh.

I'm sorry. I'm trying, Isaac.

"Another tripwire," I said.

A wire stretched across the hallway, at neck height. Taut enough to cut skin. A black plastic toolbox lurked just before the wire, poised to trip.

Daryl froze. I pointed at the wire.

"Rig a shotgun, Trojan," I said. "Just rig a shotgun. Easy, breezy, shotgun."

We darted below the wire, continued on a few steps.

Something metal gleamed ahead. Light glinted in strips.

A steel ladder. It went from floor to ceiling. Varnish shone in a depressed square above the ladder, on the ceiling. A wooden trapdoor. No visible handle on this side. The chain bound a bloody bear trap to the ladder.

At the foot of the ladder rested a female cadaver.

Daryl hissed. Flinched.

I squeezed his shoulder. "That's normal. You aren't trained to see dead bodies."

Silver filaments undulated from the female and groped along the sterile concrete. They originated from the girl's mouth, eye sockets, and ears. *It's a Mirror Person.*

The girl's false form had cherry-red hair. A trailer-trash nose piercing. *It's Susan. She's dead.*

Numbness tingled in my lips and fingers.

One side of her skull was caved in. A two-inch deep dent ruined her right temple, almost rupturing her eye socket. Red slurry. Blood congealed like syrup. Bits of brain, pocking the slurry, half liquid.

Open mouth. Dry teeth. The tip of her tongue, dried and dark from exposure to the air.

I felt Susan's cadaver. Filaments brushed over my arms.

Lukewarm.

Slack cadaver, slack but stiffening.

She'd been killed anywhere from five to eight hours ago. Timeline made sense. Death by blunt force to the head. Dried blood crusted her left ankle in a series of dotted marks. The bear trap's teeth. Irritation reddened around both wrists. Handcuff marks.

"That's where she went. Trojan kept her locked away in that cell… Mirror People will look attractive to predators, if they need to change," I said.

"So that's not a human body?"

"No."

"What do we do?" Daryl asked.

"What do you mean? We take the trapdoor, and we get outta here."

"We can't just leave someone's body here to rot, in the dark."

"No time to bury her."

Daryl walked over to Susan and gently took her shoulders. Her head lolled.

"What if we leave her for the Divine Flesh? She'll fix Susan up and revive her. Good as new. Then we can learn more about Trojan when Susan's information gets assimilated," I said.

He nodded. I clambered up the ladder and heaved open the trapdoor. Nobody shot me. I scanned the space, saw no people, and helped Daryl haul Susan's body up out of the darkness.

I had a family reunion to coordinate, judgment to cast, a very bad human to find, and an ancient enemy to dispose of.

My children prayed in St. Thérèse's.

They were ready to join. Ready to *become*. I radiated adoration as I coiled around them all. They could not perceive all of Me. I existed in many different dimensions at the same time; yes, even I was held captive by time.

You are not God, then, part of Me whispered.

Beyond this temporal dimension—separated from it by the thinnest membrane—I smothered all of Rosetown; I buried the land and the buildings in Myself, I blanketed My children as they prayed and adored

Me, and some of the keener ones felt a slight pressure. Of course, they existed in temporal, so to them, little had changed. Far away, above Earth, a solar flare tickled part of My body. I shielded Earth from it.

Half of a crimson sun peeped over the horizon. Red light bathed the churches in blood. In the Nelson barn, Isaac yawned and adjusted his grip on the roof beams, wrapped his wings more tightly around himself, and slipped back to sleep. His toes grasped one of the barn rafters, and he hung upside down like a drowsy little baby bat. How adorable. I bestowed a few lovely dreams: half-forgotten family dinners with Marcia and Daryl, a night at the fair, Daryl teaching him how to throw a football. All of them were sublime *because* of their silly human elements: the falling-apart football, the microwaved Hungry-Man dinners and Kid Cuisines, riding the Ring O' Fire roller coaster till he threw up, the bittersweet taste of that vomit—cotton-candy, stomach acid, corn dog, cherry slushy.

All of you are sublime, I whispered. *All of you are so very precious to Me.*

Marcia watched Allie Crowley bring out plastic pitchers of lemonade.

"Can I help?" Marcia asked.

Allie nodded once, turned away, continued hauling out pitchers. She set them at the front of the worship area, atop a folding table covered in a PVC tablecloth. Watercolor-print strawberries decorated the tablecloth.

Sleeping children twitched. None of them saw Marcia flit over to the pitchers. She removed a pitcher's lid and spit into the lemonade. Replaced the lid. Repeated the process with another. It only took a few seconds. Then Marcia neatened the pitchers, pretending to arrange them. She prayed, *Is that enough for each one, God?*

"Yes, darling. Just a little will do it," I said.

Allie Crowley came back out, white-knuckling a package of Dixie cups. "You gonna help or not?"

"Sorry, ma'am."

Every time Allie left the room, Marcia contaminated a pitcher or two of fentanyl-laced lemonade.

Then the children started spasming.

Heaven Geller was the first one. She was a petite two-year-old, blessed with auburn curls and freckles. She fell off the pew she'd been sleeping on. Her head hit the carpet with a *thunk*.

She spasmed, back arching, arms flailing, like bacon curling in a hot iron pan. Grayish foam appeared around her mouth.

A few feet away, a yellow blanket writhed. An infant was having a seizure. Marcia whisked it off the pew and set it on the carpet.

(O GOD WHAT DO I DO?)

(What's wrong with them?)

Hm. I probed. *Dimethoate. They're having seizures from dimethoate exposure…but when did they get exposed?*

"Calm down, dear. I'll fix them soon," I said.

I heard Daryl pray: *(Babycakes.)*

Daryl! Where *had* he gone?

I couldn't adore him until we removed Jennifer-baby's scrap of Light from him, of course, but the blood he'd imbibed from her was all used up. I could trawl his mind again. Could send him images, thoughts, feelings…and he hadn't supped from Jennifer-baby again. He wanted to send Me prayers! How sweet and kind of him.

"Your blood protection's worn off, My love. Are you done being silly?" I asked.

(Susan's dead. We found the body. It's Yours, if You want it.)

Dead? The god of another world was dead? Just like that? In one piddly little body?

"Where are you?"

I knew exactly where he was; I'd already peeked through his eyes in that split second between him thinking the separate syllables of *baby* and *cakes*. Would he be honest, or was he trying to be a lying, silly schemer?

Daryl said, *(We're inside the Unitarian Universalist house.)*

And he was. Oh, he was close to Me. So very close. I flicked over to the UU house, condensed on the kitchen wall, and produced a human avatar.

Susan's body rested by a trapdoor.

I sprouted tendrils and cradled the broken, battered god to Me.

I slid inside Susan, her filaments entwining in My tendrils—death reflexes, akin to decomposition gases barreling up the throat of a human cadaver, causing a wistful sigh, a sigh for the dead. Susan's brain-damaged skinsuit crushed, and her *true* brain was broken inside, the coiled arrayed filaments snapped in certain spots. I clutched her body tighter to Me and kissed its forehead, I was inside and out, tasting, questing along the brain's last moments, seeing—*o god o god*, hurts, crushed eggs, the boot coming down over and over on the precious babies, *I will destroy you, killer of innocents!*—and, ah, her stinger had been depleted of its venom.

I repaired Susan. I revived her.

I whispered, "I can leave you here alive, with your shattered young and the outcome of your selfish life, and I will respect your decision, dear one."

Susan blinked, filaments tightening around Me. We were knotted in each other, entangled. Meshed.

"Or you can cast aside your old life and become one of My children. I will give you work; I will reshape you and all of your kind to meet My needs, but I will allow you a certain amount of forgetfulness, and I will adore you. O, how I'll adore you and your kind. Let Me care for you. Please, just let Me love you a little."

Her lips worked. "Y-yes. Please. Please forgive me."

"I love you," I said.

"Is this a-all I had to do to be loved? The entire time?" Susan rasped.

I murmured, "Oh yes. All of you sublime. What golden seeds are nestled within you, waiting to bloom?"

I took Susan within Myself; I whisked her out of the temporal and into My body, and there I began the holy work of recreation.

"I wanted You to assimilate me," I said to the Divine Flesh.

Susan had just…vanished. The Divine Flesh had tendriled out into Susan, and then the body was gone. Tendrils unspooled from Her human avatar's arms and legs, shredding hands and feet into oblivion.

She lifted Her head and scowled at me. "And then you burned Me."

"I'm sorry. I didn't mean to."

"You look very pretty, Jennifer-baby. Did you do that yourself?"

"Look, we have a bargain for You," I said. "I think my body's meant to be a prison for You. If You agree to enter it again, forget Your knowledge, and go back to the way things were before we took that drug, I'll give You equal time with the body. Things'll be different. I'll let You and Daryl—"

"I've already picked this little proposition of yours out of Daryl's mind, Jennifer."

"And?"

She giggled. "And? And? What do you *think* I'm going to say, to something that silly?"

"So it's a no?"

"Be human with me, sweetheart," Daryl said.

"No."

"What did Susan's brain tell You about Trojan?" I asked.

"That's My concern, not yours."

"Like hell it's not my concern."

Something hard slithered up my esophagus. It stopped halfway between my stomach and mouth. Akin to a mango pit. Was it a rock or something? Drug aftershock, from how long I'd been sober? Guilt? Some weird torture from the Divine Flesh?

Then I realized.

It was Genesis.

The larva had pupated inside me. Evidently, it'd survived the dimethoate poisoning. The Light had been repairing my flesh as it ate. As a result, I'd completely forgotten about Genesis. Now the pupa had wormed its way from my heart to my esophagus, or my body simply moved it there.

It came up another inch, resting just below my lungs.

The Divine Flesh stood. "I'll even be nice and *show* you exactly how insulting your silly proposal is. You want to know about the Light, Jennifer-baby? Let's play a game. You know how much I love games! Go worship across the street, at St. Thérèse's. If you can make it through the service…I'll give you the Hermetic. If you can't, or you run away… you don't win the Hermetic."

"For now, or forever? Will there be other opportunities to get the Hermetic?" I asked.

"Maybe."

The Divine Flesh dissolved into a puddle of water. It seeped into the rose-pink carpet of the Unitarian Universalist house.

It hit me: Daryl and I came up through the trapdoor, and ended up in the chill Unitarian Universalist pastor's house, the old Nelson house. He didn't make money running the UU meetings, so he was also a realtor. I struggled to remember the guy's name.

There was a weird bunker right under his house, easily accessible from said house. A concrete bunker…

A bunker owned by the same mild-mannered realtor that also owned the Nelson barn where Rosetown's finest had lynched an innocent man ten years ago.

His name? What was it?

"Trojan…Trojan…Daryl, you know what a Trojan horse is?" I asked.

"A computer virus that mimics a benign program, so people download it and then get hacked. They named it after that old Greek legend—"

"It's something pretending to be harmless when it isn't. Do you know the name of the guy who lives here? It's that chill realtor. Guy's in his early forties, looks like the dad from *Beetlejuice*."

Daryl stiffened. The color drained from his skin, leaving it pale as salt.

"Troy Blight," he said, barely audible.

That's him. That's Trojan. Fuck.

33

A demon was a demon. The whole flock was seizing.

Allie Crowley took one look at the spasming, writhing bodies on the carpet and trudged to the kitchen for her flamethrower.

To purify them.

They'd been infected somehow—was it that Plummer girl?—and now there wasn't time for soft crap like painkillers or lemonade. No, only Jesus would take the pain away. It wouldn't hurt for long. They were sick. They needed to be saved.

Lord save us.

She white-knuckled the flamethrower's handle. Its heat guards cupped the barrel like a Crusader's shield. She wielded. She shot a glance out the sink window. Outside, the men were seizing, too. She marched back up to the nave, arms shaking.

Not me, too, please Lord help me. Help me do Your duty.

She gritted her teeth. "I will *never* be a demon."

"Of course you won't be, because demons aren't real," that girl, Marcia, said, and of course she was still standing upright at the front of the worship area under the cross, acting like butter wouldn't melt in her mouths.

Of course they'd been the bringers of damnation.

Allie Crowley aimed the flamethrower at Marcia. "Don't move."

"Demons aren't real. The others just look different, because God made them look different. Isn't it said that God made all things fearfully and wonderfully? We're all loved by God. Please, let me show you. You don't need to do this, Allie."

"Don't you 'Allie' me."

click.

Cold metal pressed into the back of her neck.

A gun.

"Put the flamethrower down, Allie," Vic said, close behind her.

"Shoot me. I'll go to Heaven."

But then who'll purify the others? I have to save them, too.

"They're seizing up because they got exposed to poison, not because of God or the Devil," Marcia said. "Please. We come bearing peace. We're here to spread the Word of God."

"Like hell you are."

"Vic, put the gun down. Let her go."

"What?"

Marcia's tone hardened. "You heard me. That's an order. Put the gun down. We're protected by God, and if Allie Crowley decides to shoot me, it won't matter a bit."

The gun left. Vic stepped back.

Immolate the flock? There wasn't enough time to save them all before Vic or Marcia stopped her. And stop her, they would.

Noah wasn't hurt at all by the fire, in the end. Was all of it just an illusion?

Is he still a demon? Is my baby a demon?

No.

No, no, no, it didn't bear thinking of. Fire was God's universal cleaner. Just ask Sodom and Gomorrah.

The table lay within arm's length, piled with tainted lemonade. Fentanyl and sugar. Gallons of it. In cheap Dollar Tree pitchers.

Someone knocked on the front entry.

tap-tap!

"Allie," Marcia said, backing towards the front entry. "Allie, I asked for some helpers. Don't be afraid."

Her stomach twisted. "Demons? You got demons on holy ground?"

"There's no such thing as demons."

Marcia reached the front door. She didn't turn her back to Allie as she grabbed the door handle.

"Allie, gimme the flamethrower," Vic Snyder said.

She spun on her heel and raised the prongs to Vic's chest. "Hell no," she said.

"Remember when we used to go neckin' up at Silver Lake? We'd just gotten outta high school, and I was tellin' you that I'd never ever fall for anyone else?"

"You're a demon now. None of that crap matters."

The door creaked as Marcia opened it.

"Come in, everyone!" Marcia said, in a sing-song Sunday-school tone. "Let's give the children cookies until their blood-protection wears off, and we can tell them about how amazing God is!"

If they come in, there's no saving anyone.

Sugar water. On a rickety table.

Allie Crowley pulled the trigger. Heat surged out, liquid fire pouring forth. It sprayed onto Vic's sleazy cheap paisley button-down and instantly engulfed him. She lunged for the table and shoved it over. Pitchers broke, spilling gallons of lemonade onto the carpet. Carpet absorbed.

A winged thing burst through the front door.

Vic mewled. Covered in flames, skin blackening in the fire, he collapsed to the ground and rolled.

Finger still pressing the trigger, Allie turned and lit the green carpet ablaze. It was wet with sugary water. Polyester composed the nap. Fire exploded over the ground.

It caught the children and teens and women seizing on the carpet, their hair and synthetic clothing, and washed over them in a wave of flame.

The heat.

An oven cranked to five-hundred, dry. Painful to inhale.

The smell.

Sickly-sweet meat and vinegar, burning acrid plastic, *my feet are hot my feet are burning*, fire licked up the gauze curtains, hit the ceiling. Fire swallowed the strawberry tablecloth.

Vic clawed at his shoulders. Grabbed them. Dug in. He ripped his charred skin off like a cocoon, and something slithered out, gleaming with clear fluid, something that opened its eyes and—

Its eyes carpeted it. It opened them, and the skin became a weeping mass of eyes. Legs unspooled from between them. Crackling sounds. They snapped into position and the thing scuttled around, tears geysering out.

Steam hissed where tears met fire. The fire raged, beyond quenching. *Course you can't quench it from a single point.* Fire ate the ceiling, fire all around, *my feet are fucking burning I can smell them hear them sizzling*, blisters inside pressed against her shoes as the plastic Sketchers sneakers shrank, melted, melded into her feet.

My feet my feet are burning make it stop—
Marcia shrieked.
An inhuman, almost insectile keen. A war cry.

I buried Genesis outside of the abandoned barn.

The pupa looked exactly like one of those Rattlesnake Eggs magnets I played with as a kid. Throw 'em together in the air, listen to 'em scream. Those ones. A silver, elongated, egg-shaped capsule.

Soft earth gave beneath my fingers. Grass rioted all around. An early-morning sparrow chirped a melody. Sunlight gilded everything, ripe and golden as late-summer corn.

"You smell that?" Daryl asked.

I inhaled. Caught a tang of smoke. Not woodsmoke.

"Something's burning," I said.

Boards creaked inside the Nelson barn. I stuck my head inside. An abomination hung head-down from a ceiling beam, wings wrapped around its body—wings of Caucasian skin. The top of its head poked out, revealing cropped dark-brown hair.

"Dude, look at this one. It's like a bat thing," I said.

"Smoke's rising from the Church of Christ."

"Ah, shit."

I came around the barn and stood by Daryl. From here, the Church of Christ was the size of a rich kid's dollhouse. The spartan, square bell tower hung empty. Abominations circled it. Abominations rushed into the front door. Bodies littered the scrap of lawn around the church building. Streamers of black smoke rose from the windows.

If we go help them, we'll lose our chance at getting the Hermetic.

But there were people inside.

The abominations'll figure it out! C'mon, go to the other church. It doesn't matter.

That uncomfortable feeling squirmed in my stomach again.

If the Divine Flesh hasn't just claimed the people, then they're probably doped up on your blood! She can't claim them yet. They'll burn alive.

Daryl looked at me. He didn't need to say anything.

"Might be our only chance," I said.

"We don't know that."

(Don't.)

The Divine Flesh's voice rang through our ears. "If you go into that church, I'll never ever let you have the Hermetic. Don't go in. I've got everything handled, so don't go. You'll just be in the way."

"Well, now we know," I said. "They've got it handled. Isn't that great?"

"Jennifer."

"The only time She doesn't want us to see something is when She's gone psycho. Ten-to-one odds that there's a massacre going on inside that church. What the hell could either of us do to stop that? Nothin.'"

"Jennifer."

"I'm just saying—"

"Are you coming to save them with me or not?" Daryl asked.

Glowing neurons pulsed on the backs of my hands. Honey-sweet protoflesh filled my mouth. I could repair wounds, I knew that. In my gut, I felt it. I could command the protoflesh to *(fix)* or *(heal)* or *(regrow)* and it *would*, but why should I? Why the hell was I supposed to be the prison of a flesh-god? It wasn't fair. I didn't even have my own body. I was nothing but a vessel to be used by the Light. It wasn't *right*. Why should I go around, running into burning fucking buildings?

"It's not fair. Normal people have video-game addictions and trauma from divorced parents and shit, and here I am, and I don't even have a body that's mine," I said.

"Life isn't fair."

"But—"

"I watched my dad blow his brains out when I was eight years old. He knew I was hidin' in the hallway closet, right there, with the shotgun pressed under his chin, and he locked eyes with me, and then he pulled the trigger. Knew I was watchin'. He knew our mom wasn't ever gonna wake up from that coma. And he still did it, 'cause he didn't feel like life was fair, so why should he live?" Daryl said. "Life ain't fair? Well, boo-fuckin'-hoo, Jennifer."

He stormed up outta the Nelson barn's lot and onto the street.

People are suffering. You have the capacity to change that.

You have the capacity to do good.

To be good.

I followed Daryl. He opened his hand, I slipped mine into his, and we started running.

The Divine Flesh screamed as we ran towards the burning church, but neither of us bothered to listen.

34

They stripped after the Eucharist.

They cast aside their clothing—obsolete relics, things of cotton and synthetic fibers; no longer did they blaspheme God by concealing Her creations in man-made things.

One flesh.

(Holy, holy, holy, My beloved ones; you shall never be alone.)

Nude, they drew closer. Flesh met flesh. They were grinding against each other. Arms meshed. Mouths pressed into flesh, into mouths and ears and sexes. They collapsed into a writhing pile, hands groping for mouths, hands and feet thrusting, vanishing into vulvas, between buttocks, limbs disappearing inch by inch into flesh, forearms greedily sucked in like vanishing scarves, wet slapping sounds, *thrustthrustthrust.*

Bodies bucked in rhythm. One flesh. It rippled.

Flesh softened like melting wax, melding into the neighbor's.

They became a tumor-like mass. *They* became *it*; it consumed all the available space and nearly kissed the curved dome overhead. Portions of it pulsed, where old individual bodies had existed. Barely limned, the outlines of bodies engraved the mass.

A glistening wet ring circled the widest point. The mass shuddered. Three more rings of clear fluid appeared, reddened, and thickened into opaque protoflesh; buds bubbled along these rings. The buds throbbed. Opened.

Eyes.

Four rings of white eyes radiated light.

The mass floated up from the carpet like a queen's airship. Rings of eyes peeled from its surface and spun, canting at different angles.

Energy crackled through the dust-filled air.

A furious spinning thing of light.

(My precious angel.)

(My precious angel, will you stop the intruders from reaching the other church?)

And the newly-birthed angel was as a limb of God; it had no will or desire to resist, but She wanted it to *adore* Her, to enjoy serving Her, and so She asked it to as if it could ever refuse.

(Will you serve Me?)

Love warmed the angel's body. Oh, to serve! To be honored with a task! Holy, holy, holy—*kadosh kadosh kadosh, Adonai*—and God lay meshed over the outside of St. Thérèse's, blocking the amber stained-glass windows.

Cold light illumined crushed pews. A cluster of straw-thin candles flickered out, smoke falling into the bowl of silty lakeshore sand that held them. Air thickened with sweat and sweet incense and dust.

God pressed on the building outside, eager to free Her beloved angel. The structure creaked. Streams of pulverized cement hissed down the walls. Cracks appeared up the walls. Liquid tendrils oozed in, grabbed hold, and ripped apart the structure.

Sunlight flooded in. Shards of glass glittered on the blood-red carpet. Above, a clear sky awaited.

The Divine Flesh commanded: *(Find them!)*

The angel shuddered, exhaled, and hovered above the ruins of St. Thérèse's.

It began hunting.

Marcia knelt in the fire and prayed—

(LET ME HELP THEM!)

(HELP them!)

(O God, O Divine Flesh, please help me save them! I'll do anything!)

A charred faceless shape lunged out of the fire, gripping Marcia's thigh.

Tears gushed down her cheeks. "Heal them, Oh God please heal them, I'll do anything please help them—"

I slowed down her mind's perception of time. Fire slowly spread 'cross the nave. Allie Crowley screamed, mouth working in slow-mo. I shut off Marcia's hearing. Smoke blackened the ceiling. My children had brought out people. A pile of My tendrils had gathered some of the burned ones up, insulating them from flames. Keeping them intact. Alive. It hurt to touch them.

"I can take you away from here, into Me, and keep you safe. Would you like that?" I asked.

"No. I have to save them."

"This doesn't have to be your burden to bear, silly."

"I don't care. Help them. Please. They're burning alive."

"I can use your body to quench the fire," I said, "but you won't be pretty or human-looking anymore. What will Daryl and Isaac think?"

"I don't care. God, use me to do Your will."

"You don't care?"

"Please. Do it."

"If they don't recognize you, if they think you're a monster or a demon…you really won't care?"

"It doesn't matter."

"Why?"

Marcia wanted to kiss the charred body on the ground; she couldn't move her body to lean down and gather the poor, poor thing to her and cradle it.

"B-because I love these people, and I love You, and I don't want anyone to suffer, and Lord, I'm strong enough to bear whatever You give me, if that's what it takes. Use me. Help them. Please."

The itty-bitty human part of Me thought, *But I wanted Daryl to see that his siblings could love Me and still look normal; I wanted to soothe him, and now I can't?*

Then, I realized how selfish I'd been.

I'd wanted to redeem Myself to Daryl by offering him his siblings, but how shallow that offering was, tainted by My need for his approval. It was something Jennifer-baby would do. Instead of giving My love freely to Daryl and his family, I was being the worst thing of all—

a lying, silly schemer.

No true redemption could be had without love; love is the heart of redemption.

In that moment, I loved them more than ever.

"I will use you, beloved one," I murmured. "You will be beautiful after I do. Just in a different way."

"Yes, please."

I brought her mind back to its normal perception of time and turned her ears back on.

"It won't hurt," I promised.

Marcia fell onto the charred groping human; she wrapped her arms around it, it brought its head close to hers in a parody of a kiss—

I unzipped Marcia's skull. I tore open rifts all over her body. Her face split apart from chin to scalp, but no blood flowed out.

The flood, My dear.

Protoflesh flooded out of the rifts in her body; I rendered her into a conduit for a deluge of healing, liquid protoflesh. Healing waters. Clear as glass, the protoflesh deluged from Marcia. The flood quenched the flames. A knee-deep pool of it formed, caressing the burned victims, and sucked them under. Marcia maneuvered her new body through the front entry and pointed to the seizing men on the grass. The flooded protoflesh formed transparent tendrils and scooped them into the healing pool.

Into their baptism.

Five minutes or so left until I could integrate them fully into Me. They'd imbibed Jennifer's blood. For now, I soothed their pain and put them to sleep.

I gently roused Isaac.

"Isaac, dear," I whispered, "go into the church across the street. I have a surprise for you."

(A surprise?)

"Marcia and Daryl are inside," I said.

He bolted awake, almost falling off the barn rafter, and flew right over Jennifer and Daryl as he alit in the bell tower.

Baby tongues of flame licked on the ceiling. Marcia, still geysering protoflesh, gestured to them, and the flood crept over the remnants of the fire and extinguished it. I'd split apart her forearms. Her thighs. Her shins, feet, neck, and palms. Bones peeped out from muscle. Her face was a split-open cavern. Eyeless, she slithered through the waters and found Allie Crowley.

Allie whimpered.

Marcia embraced her. She wanted to say *don't be afraid*, but she no longer had a mouth.

So she simply held the woman.

After a brief struggle, Allie relaxed. Marcia slipped under the surface of the flood, taking Allie with her; how sweet the baptismal font, how silky, a blanket of My love.

Lord forgive me, Allie thought.

Everyone slumbered as they awaited Me.

"She thinks I can't do it," I said, and Daryl shook his head.

We stood in the middle of Holy Lane, and a fused godawful meat-angel blocked the way forward to the Church of Christ. Human skin clothed the spherical structure, the grooved surface. Large as a house, it hovered over the road. Three white-hot rings zipped around it, humming with energy. Linked, interwoven eyes composed each ring. Milky-white, blind eyes. They sluggishly blinked. Sunburn stung my face from the radiation of its ringed eyes. Daryl's nose reddened and peeled.

I spit in my hand and hurled a gob of my protoflesh at it.

It landed on the surface of the thing, burning and sizzling as it struck the angel's body. Clear protoflesh turned to pink.

Spread, I commanded. *Engulf it! Cocoon it.*

Flesh violently spread over the angel like kudzu. The angel fell to the asphalt. Its rings stopped moving. My protoflesh veined over its body, spreading and meshing, until it had formed a sac-like structure around it.

"Son of a bitch," Daryl said.

"Yeah, yeah, c'mon," I said. "Let's sprint past it."

"No, not that. Something just grabbed everyone on the lawn and sucked 'em inside the church," Daryl said.

"Wanna guess who?"

"She'll assimilate everything if we don't find a way to stop Her…I knew that, logically, but seein' this…"

I tugged his arm. "C'mon. Run."

A sliver of the angel remained. My cocoon engulfed the last of it with a soft *schlorp*. The angel had been shrink-wrapped inside a pink, glistening cocoon, and it lived inside. I could feel it. Inside—

Inside the Light.

Inside me.

Inside the cocoon.

I sprinted towards the smoldering church. Daryl followed. Abominations reached for us as we ran over the crack-pipe-shaped lawn, around sleeping bags and tattered tents and coolers full of Coors, panting, praying that we could save some of these people. I could give them my blood—

The Divine Flesh screamed: *(NO!)*

My left eardrum exploded. Dizziness slammed over me. The church spun. Warm blood dribbled down the side of my neck.

Abominations lunged.

I reached the door handle. Glass door. Yanked it open.

We entered.

35

The smell.

Burning hair and meat. A hot dog cooked too long over a campfire.

It dragged fishhooks down my throat with each inhale. I waded through waist-high floodwaters of protoflesh, clear as the prettiest mountain spring. Warm as amniotic fluid. Bodies made a mottled river bottom—black speckled with pink and white. A dead, clouded eye tracked me as I waded. I removed my tank top, balled it up, and pressed it to my bleeding ear. Who knew what would happen if my blood contaminated these floodwaters?

Here and there, an intact human lay among the burned. Pristine as preserved corpses in formaldehyde. Their eyes remained closed.

Though they didn't breathe, I knew: They slept. They weren't *dead* dead.

Blue plastic pitchers floated by. Tendrils filled one corner of the worship area in a shivering pile.

"She didn't burn them," I said.

No response from Daryl. Nothing but his rattling harsh breathing. Shallow breaths hitched. Waters swirled around my waist, tingling skin. Sunlight rayed through smoke.

"Daryl?"

He stood frozen. Staring at a faceless dripping girl with split-open limbs. Within the halves of her rent skull lay utter blackness. Protoflesh trickled out. She rose from the waters. Streamers of protoflesh oozed from her dark hair.

clank-clank.

Thudding footsteps came from behind the front wall of the nave. A plaster panel rolled aside.

A bat-like abomination waded out, wings folded. Teenage acne pocked the hollows of his cheeks and blighted his forehead. He wore an AC/DC t-shirt, slashed open to accommodate the wings.

I knew that hair. That was Daryl's hair. A cheerless shade of brown, almost black.

"No," Daryl said, barely audible.

Bat-kid squinted at him. "D-Daryl?"

Daryl had gone paper white. Cold sweat beaded his face.

The halves of the girl's split-open face sealed. Her features reformed. She gnawed her thick lower lip and blinked her brown eyes. Whiskey-brown. Fawn-brown. That face—

Oh wow, they DO look alike.

This was Marcia. Bat-kid was Isaac. The Divine Flesh had given Daryl's family back to him.

Isaac studied Marcia like she was the uppity maiden aunt at the family BBQ, and he wasn't sure if she was gonna give him a twenty-dollar bill or a lecture on Christ. His wings twitched.

"M-Marcia?" Isaac asked. "Daryl?"

The Plummer family gaped at each other from across the worship area.

Marcia's eyes reddened. Tears formed. She extended a hand towards Isaac, arm quivering, but her gaze never left Daryl. Her mouth worked soundlessly.

Daryl said hoarsely, "Marcia, honey—" He was crying.

Isaac waded over to Marcia, thumb in his mouth. He sucked it like a three-year-old, and when he spoke, he whined in a high-pitched toddler-voice. "Where were you, Daryl?"

Daryl wiped his tears. "What did the Divine Flesh say to you? Did She hurt you?"

"You don't look like Daryl anymore. You look like a bearded man now."

"I'm sorry. I—I got older."

"Why didn't you try harder to get us, Daryl?"

"I—I'm sorry, Isaac, I'm so sorry."

"You didn't try hard enough. They beat me. They hurt me," Isaac said, sniffling.

Isaac had mentally reverted to the toddler he'd been when their father shot himself. When Daryl gathered the kids and took them away.

Daryl approached his siblings, opening his arms.

"I'm sorry I couldn't—" His face twisted. "Please forgive me."

Forgive him for what? All he did was put those kids first.

Well, unless the choice was between ditching junkie Jennifer or getting custody of them. Then…oh, god. He'd chosen me. He'd chosen me until a year ago, when he'd kicked me out, and what had I done up to that point? Forced him to choose, because I couldn't give enough of a shit to get clean or move out.

Nausea threaded through me.

Marcia hugged Isaac to her. He wrapped his wings around them both, cocooning them. Their faces peeked out of the gap between the wings. Their eyes glittered. Like demon children's, those eyes glittered.

Daryl approached in spite of this, voice soothing and low, telling them old, good memories. "Remember when we—we had Christmas at Meemaw's, before everything—Remember that Christmas, Marcia? Mom got you that Barbie Pool Party set you always wanted, and Meemaw gave me a pocketknife when her back was turned? Isaac, you was just a lil' baby."

Silence. Daryl paused when he got about ten feet away from 'em.

"Remember the time we went to the fair, and you went on the Ring O' Fire coaster till you puked, Isaac? And I won Marcia a pink lion at the dart toss?"

"…I still have that lion," she whispered.

"You do?"

"Slept with it every night. I was scared one of the other foster kids would steal it."

"Remember when we used to watch those dusty VCR tapes in Uncle Larry's basement? You always picked *Cinderella*. You used to tell me every damn night, before I tucked us to sleep on that floor mattress we shared, 'Daryl, we gotta wish hard enough, 'cause if we do, our fairy godmother's gonna come and make everythin' okay.' So I tried to make everythin' okay. I tried, Marcia, and they broke us apart and I couldn't do jack shit 'bout it."

Daryl took a step closer. They didn't move.

Then another step.

He laid a hand on the wings, on their makeshift cocoon. "I love you."

The cocoon trembled. Wings shuffled and parted.

There they stood.

He embraced them, and they clutched onto him, crying. Marcia buried her face into his shoulder. Isaac held on, numbly staring at the bodies in the floodwaters.

Daryl, I opened my mouth to say, *hey, we still need to defeat the Divine Flesh—*

A charred hand seized my wrist.

Crackling sounds.

Blackened skin crackled off. Tendrils, red as heartworms, sprouted from the ruin. Suckered into my arm. Tingling. Burning.

I prayed, *Burn!*

The tingling increased. Nothing else happened.

Blooms of crimson and pink and adipose yellow exploded underwater. Bodies burst, split, and meshed into one another. Forms rose from the waters, made afresh. More tendrils squeezed 'round my neck. Strangled. Foreign hands snatched at my feet and shins. They tugged.

(Come, come into the waters.)

"No," I said.

Daryl and his siblings hadn't pulled away. They hadn't even noticed the resurrection happening around us. Marcia mouthed something to Daryl; he smiled.

"Isn't it time, Jennifer-baby, that you reap what you've sown? Why should you commune with their family, when you've done so much to destroy it?" the Divine Flesh said. "You silly, silly thing. You had endless chances to join his family, and every single time, you chose to get drunk or high."

"I'm a Good Person. I'm not bad. Just let me do a few good things, and I'll redeem myself, okay?"

She sighed. "You never understood."

"Understood what?"

Hundreds of hands seized me. Something slippery worked through my lips. Slid down my throat. Tasted like honey and salt. A tendril. Other tendrils slid, dripping, from the protoflesh flood and looped around my waist.

(Come, come, let Me give you rest.)

They dragged me below the waters.

36

My barrier around Rosetown dissolved, soaking into the ground. There was no longer a need for it. I'd claimed every last person that mattered.

Endless feelers and tendrils spread out. They pierced whatever humans they could find. They wormed into the uncharged spaces between atoms and slithered 'round molecular bonds; no wall or physical matter prevented them from hallowing flesh.

I claimed My children.

I waited for My love in God's Carnival. I veiled noontime sun in blood-red clouds. I blessed the ruins of the carnival with a rain of tears. Power lines decayed, long ago turned into dead rubber. Rust speckled their structures. A gaudy white cross loomed over broken-down carnival rides, covered in bird droppings and sparrows. I stood atop a wooden sign advertising *The Ride to Hell!* in spray-painted, flame lettering. Sections of the ride—a metal fun slide—crumbled apart. Its crimson paint had been sun-bleached to pink.

I held the Hermetic like a baby.

Daryl came, as I knew he would. Chain-link fencing squeaked as he scrambled atop it. He slipped. Sliced his palm open on the wire. His blood trickled onto soil. A libation. Delectable.

"All right, silly," I called, "you've proven that you want to see Me. Hold still."

I created. Tendrils twined with the chain-link fence and ripped it down, and I scooped up Daryl before he could fall and hurt himself again.

I went to him. I wore the body I'd learned to love him in. So many dear memories. I latched onto Daryl, tossing aside the Hermetic, smothering

him in kisses, tasting the sweat and musk and degraded chemical scents—
Old Spice, I think? That's what they call that chemical?—of him, and his
arms pressed around Me, pressed Me into him.

A rush of sticky wetness. Heat. Arousal.

Our lips merged. I slid My tongue into him, *so silky so well made*,
treasuring his fine teeth, the chip on his right molar, him, working into
Mine, a soft easy teasing tongue—*oh yes, oh yes*.

He pulled back. "Where'd You put the kids?"

"Oh, they were *so* tired, so I bundled them off to bed. They found a
cozy corner inside Me—"

I probed My many bodies.

"—Oh! There they are. All nice and warm in My layers. I like that
body, it's so comforting for My children. Marcia's snuggled up with
Isaac. You want to see them again? You *can*, if you want, but they're
right in the middle of dreaming. Let's let them sleep a bit longer." I
nibbled his ear. "I haven't gotten to see you in *days*, you know. Let our
kids sleep."

"Sweetheart," he said, "I came to barter."

"Let Me pretend that you came here because you love Me, Daryl."

"I do love You."

"You want Me to be something I'm not."

"I just don't want You to destroy the world. But. That's over now. I'm
here to give You what You want, and then it's Jennifer's fight."

"Did you figure it out?" I asked, smiling.

"I can't believe she didn't."

"Jennifer can put together some things, but oh, she'll ignore what's
right in front of her face if she doesn't like what the facts tell her. We
both know that," I said. I shimmied off his cut-sleeve overshirt. "What
would you offer Me?" I murmured.

"Myself."

"Mmmm…a fine offering. What do you want, My love?"

"Give the Hermetic to Jennifer. No tricks, no Faustian-bargain
horseshit. Don't mess with it. Whatever it secretes or says or anything
else, all of that belongs to her."

"I would never do something like that. That's for lying, silly schemers."

He kissed My cheek. "I choose You. I'm tired of fighting. I choose
You, and our family. I'm givin' that Hermetic to Jennifer, and that's
that. I'm lettin' her go for good."

"Why?"

"This was never my fight. It ain't my job to fight her battles. I can't fight You. The only chance humanity has is if Jennifer realizes what she is…and she won't, if I'm around," Daryl said.

I tasted him again, with My unseen feelers. He tasted of: Love. Oxytocin. Dopamine.

Cortisol.

Oh, he's nervous. He's aroused.

I giggled. "But mostly, you're here because you love Me. I love you."

"I love you, babycakes."

"Come, then. It won't hurt a bit."

He took his undershirt off. I caressed his chest. Fused to his heart, that scrap of Light buzzed. *So long ago, so very old, that promise.*

"I wrote Jennifer a note. It's in my pocket. Make sure she gets it," he said.

"A love letter?"

"Naw. A how-to manual."

"You just loved trade school that much, hm?" I said, and kissed him again. "I'll put it in the Hermetic. Hold still. I love you."

I ripped his chest open in one fluid motion. His heart sped. The promise that Jennifer had made to him, so long ago, in that church, it tried to slither away as I grabbed it. But I got it.

It buzzed: *(I promise I'll love you no matter who or what you are.) (I will protect you.)*

"Oh, Jennifer-baby."

Her love.

I tore the last scrap of her love out of Daryl Plummer and crushed it between my fingers. A sliver of Light. It flickered. Vanished. In an instant, I repaired Daryl.

He blinked. "That was it?"

"Of course, silly."

I smiled. My bestest smile. His favorite one, with all 108 of My teeth.

"Now we have eternity to enjoy each other," I said.

I finally, finally took him into Myself. I nestled him, I made him happy, I began rendering him anew.

Him, stunned. *(It feels good.)*

What do you want?

(When does it end? When does it start hurting? When are You gonna hurt me or toy with me or betray me?)

I laughed. He was so full of silly questions, but he'd understand. Soon.

I took Daryl within Myself.

"I won, Jennifer-baby," the Divine Flesh said, laughing.

"No," I said.

Everything alive had withered away. Flakes of metal rusted off every surface in God's Carnival.

The abominations had lifted me out of the waters and flown me here. Bottles of booze rowed the soil. Lines of brand-spankin'-new Fireball and moonshine, Gray Goose and Strawberry Cremè Smirnoff, a battalion of booze, all sat there on the dirt. Maybe She'd eaten the booze aisle at Gas N' Go. Hell if I knew.

The whole display was centered around the Hermetic—an infant-sized chunk of shriveled dried flesh.

By the Hermetic, a cooler lay open like a nice July BBQ offering. Within, a single tumbler glass sparkled on a bed of ice.

"For you, Jennifer-baby. Your one true love," the Divine Flesh said, voice audible in my ear. "I have Daryl now. He's joined Me. He chose *Me*, Jennifer-baby."

Heat boiled in my chest. "Go fuck yourself. I'm not an alcoholic."

"Daryl traded himself for the Hermetic. I left you a little drink selection to go with it because I'm so nice, Jennifer. Now you can go drink and abuse *other* people instead of Daryl. Won't that be nice?"

My voice broke. "He didn't. He wouldn't."

"Of course he did. I gave him his family back and made them happy forever. All you ever did was destroy them. That's kind of your specialty, Jennifer. You're an expert at destruction."

"Fuck You, divine *cunt*!"

Then I sat down, scooped up the Hermetic, and started drinking. Because what else would I do? I started with Fireball. Fireball, always a classic. A pin-sized cockroach floated near the bottom of the booze bottle. Extra protein.

Extra protein. This one cost too much.

I cackled. Booze sprayed out of my mouth and onto the Hermetic. I cradled the fucking thing in my arms. It tingled with static. Half the Fireball was already fermenting in my stomach.

Getting drunk in an abandoned evangelical carnival in the middle of July, with no water in sight? Great idea. Probably the last great idea I'd ever have, hopefully, if I could die and stay dead.

"But we all know that ain't gonna happen," I slurred. "Shit, my hick accent's creepin' in. Shh. Don't say nothin', Magic Meat."

Daryl gave himself up so that you could have the Hermetic, and this is what you're doing? Are you fucking kidding me?

"I'm a shitty person. I'm a scumbag, but at least I'm me. Don't hate me for it. I'm not You. I am what I am, yud-hey-vav-hey, go ask Daryl."

I shivered on the dirt. I huddled 'round the Hermetic. Faces appeared on its surface, melted away, and formed afresh. Its dried neuron glowed like a hair-thin strand of light. I stroked it. A mouth formed on the Hermetic

"I never hated you, Jennifer," it said, in Daryl's voice.

"See, that's a little fucked."

"What do you wanna know?"

"Are you the Light?" I asked. "You talking to me now? Too little, too late."

Blood pattered down from the sky. Blood rain. Fine by me. I could drink just fine in the rain.

"It's not too late," it said.

A neuron unfurled on my fingertip, emitting light.

"I believe that Daryl just got assimilated by the Divine Flesh," I said, "and that I'll never be a Good Person, so I might as well just eat a bullet."

"Is that your fault?"

"What are you, my fucking therapist? Open sesame. Tell me important things, Hermetic."

The mouth merged back into the Hermetic. Wetness beneath my fingers.

Warm. Slick. Spit?

A new mouth had formed under my hand. Its tongue flitted out and tasted me. Human teeth glittered between the lips.

Do you love?

I probed the mouth. It sucked my finger in, tickling skin with the edge of its teeth—

Sharp hot pain. It'd bitten me.

It released. I calmly removed my finger. Blood oozed from a ring of toothmarks like ruby beads. Drops pattered onto the Hermetic's surface.

(Love.)

(Do you understand about love?)

"Love? You're asking me about love? What the hell?" I slurred, voice thick from drunkenness.

Cracks streaked over the Hermetic. Black ichor welled up in beads, and daubed my hands and clothing as I held it. Ichor. This was the drug I'd gotten to separate Her and me. The bore-a-hole-into-your-subconscious drug. Cosmic-horror-trip drug.

My eyes got wet. Everything hazed. *Daryl's basically dead now.*

"Show me the Light," I said. "You gotta show me everything. Please."

"I'm not sentient. You're blackout drunk," the Hermetic said.

"I don't care." I lapped ichor off it. "Don't care. Show me."

Dizziness. The red sky and metal spidery ruins spun. When had I curled up on the ground? When had I—

Show me.

It happened as it had before.

She wasn't there in Her human avatar this time. I was alone.

Cosmos. Void. Drowning in sand. Daryl screaming at me. Cosmos. A consuming fleshy cancer strung across galaxies, veined around stars, jeweled in neural tissue and energy, sucking me towards it as it exhaled life onto an asteroid and sent it hurtling towards nascent Earth's barren oceans.

I saw this already.

The Light and the Flesh as one. The Divine Flesh.

The Light seared. Split. Supernova. Rent apart, chunks of the Flesh gathered and accumulated. A star-sized mass of neural matter merged in opposition. The Light.

I'm here! I tried to say, but couldn't inhale.

Again, the sick feeling twisted in my gut. The feeling a mother has when she's remembered the baby she left in the car ten minutes ago on a scorching July afternoon.

I kept looking. I didn't cover my eyes this time.

Twin forms condensed from the ruins. A spark of Light. A fetal-sized glob of Flesh.

They fell to Earth, crowned in fire. I fell alongside them, eons flickering across the surface—*it's a tale, it's not literal. Or is it?* From oceans rose steaming rock, from rock, fertile land, from scum, life to clumps of cells to worms, vertebrae forming into place, sparking—*threaded with Light?*—primitive nervous tissue. A gift from the Light. Thought. Sentience.

I understood.

Now the second asteroid hit. Another extinction. Ash choked the sky.

I continued drifting down.

Iterations of intelligent primates, each one closer to escaping Eden and walking upright. They became human. They shed their hair and gathered into tribes—

Everything cut to black.

What?

Snip-snip. Then, resumption.

Something had forced the vision to stop and skip forward, something *not-me.*

I floated in a blood-warm void, close to the Light and Flesh. A rhythmic *thud-thud* soothed. They both found a soft wall. Both implanted. They grew into fetuses, but they were tired and long weary of fighting. The Light hugged the Flesh, there in the womb, both tethered to the same placenta, and swallowed the Flesh.

Oh my god. It just ate its twin.

What had She said to me, earlier?

(You ate Me in the womb.)

I ate Her in the womb. I ate the Flesh.

Which meant that the Light…that fetus in the womb…No, that wasn't right. Couldn't be.

I waited for the rest of the vision, but nothing else came. It stopped.

The remaining fetus dwarfed me. An in utero idol. An unborn god. I lifted my arm and every nerve glowed white-hot through skin. Neurons spiraled down, blooming open like undersea flora.

I'm not an envoy of the Light.

In the womb, fetus-me suckled amniotic fluid and yawned. Branches of light veined her tongue.

"I *am* the Light," I said.

I was crying when I came out of the vision, and the Divine Flesh was cradling me, right there in a cherry orchard. Blood pelted down from the crimson clouds overhead. Skinless sparrows jeweled the trees, dripping with blood.

"The orchards are blooming," the Divine Flesh said.

Head-sized blossoms studded the gnarled cherry trees, petals moving. Music—somewhere between the drone of honeybees and a choir hymnal—rose from them. Even through the *plink-plink* of the rain, their music cloyed. So sweet. I let it wash over me like midsummer wind.

"It's not cherry season anymore," I said.

"What does the Light do, Jennifer?"

"Destroy," I said. "It's death and destruction. You're life and renewal."

No wonder all I ever do is self-destruct and destroy.

She stroked my hair, nails tickling my scalp. "Daryl is very happy. He loves Me. It didn't take long at all, just a little field trip and then I showed him what it was like to be Me. To create. To render. To love. He helped Me create *very special* bodies for himself and his family."

"I'm the Light," I said.

"What do you want?"

"What do I do?" I asked. "What the fuck do I do, now? With that?"

I'm an eldritch mass of neural tissue and energy. I'm inhuman.

Worse than that. I was Her. A part of Her. Part of the Divine Flesh. What self could I ever form? What good could I ever do? What had everything ever been for, in the end? Could I die? Love? Shit, could I even have a sense of self, or was everything nothing but an illusion created by being—

Her.

Not even Her. A fragment. Nothing. A ball of interdimensional twine.

How could I come back from *that*?

"Don't burn Me, for a start," the Divine Flesh said. She wrapped arms around me and held me to Her chest, smelling *soft* and *sweet*, whispering, breath caressing my ear. "I've made everyone else happy but you. Will you be good? Can I love you? I can't assimilate you… but I can hold you. I can love you."

"I—I wanna throw up. I w-wanna sleep. I—"

"It's a lot, isn't it?"

"I can't. I can't take it."

She shushed me, pecked my cheek, and told me to go back to sleep, Jennifer-baby, and did I want to dream? She could give me an entire life in the dreaming, and I wouldn't know that it wasn't real. She could give me infinite illusionary lifetimes. Ones where I wasn't the Light. But I said no. I didn't want to live. Didn't want to exist.

She grabbed the Hermetic, and as She did, it broke apart like porcelain. Bits flew to my arms, and Hers. They merged into us.

"You bled on it, too?" She asked.

"It bit me."

"Silly Jennifer." She craned Her head an inch from mine, lips parting. "Now sleep." The Divine Flesh kissed me on the cheek, and I felt Her wrapping around me as She did. Taking me within Her. As I drifted to permanent sleep, I heard.

(Sleep.)

No hope. It was a relief, to give up.

(Be good.)

Now it was over. Now I could—

(Sleep.)

Part Four

Let There Be Light

37

Sometimes I could feel the tendrils jammed up inside me, and sometimes I couldn't. There wasn't any air. A fleshy breathing tube pushed air into and out of my lungs. Drifting.

Once, I tried to burn my way out of Her, thought, *C'mon, I need Light—*

She crushed me instantly.

No pain. Just an immediate cessation of consciousness, then revival.

(Be good, Jennifer-baby. I love you!)

I tried again. Got crushed.

Once, I pulled the tube from my mouth and it hissed air, and I gasped in a void without air, chest burning, straining, nothing happening—

(Here, babygirl.)

And the tube slithered from my hand and back down my throat, delivering a sweet rush of oxygen.

(If you were good and I could trust you, I'd love to let you play with all of My children on Earth, but I can't, Jennifer-baby, I'm sorry. Maybe in a few thousand years. Why don't you dream? Would you like to look through My eyes?)

I did. Briefly.

She was ecstatic and lusting for new types of flesh, a banquet of sensation, new pretty things to jewel and adorn Her children with, and wasn't it so funny that everyone on Earth was terrified of Her? They'd even sent nuclear missiles over! Yummy. She'd swallowed those whole and leeched the radiation.

(tee-hee!)

(They will ALL BE INSIDE ME and OF ME!)

(So yummy so pretty, like stars inside Me, so good to taste.)

"You mean," I thought, "You're gonna assimilate every sentient being on Earth?"

(Then I'll find other worlds. Forever and ever.)

"What about free will? Body autonomy?"

(What about it?)

I watched for a long while. So, the Divine Flesh was gonna consume more worlds. What was I supposed to do about it? What, was I gonna eat Her from the inside out? I couldn't even escape Her if I wanted to. There was nothing I could do. Nobody could defeat Her. I felt like a garbage excuse for a human, let alone an opposing force to a cosmic god.

(Oh, Jennifer.)

(Would you like to see Daryl? Not on Earth, but inside Me? If you're good, I'll let you see him and you two can even have sex but it might be different, he's very different, but he loves you still.)

To be fair…the Divine Flesh wasn't exactly what I'd call ruthless. She legitimately wanted, in Her own inhuman way, for everyone to be happy and loved. Including me, Her eternal foe. Jesus, that sounded hokey.

Drift in. Drift out.

Within Her, I transmuted. A dense mat of neurons gradually meshed over my skin, smoldering heat. If I rubbed my arms or body I could feel them. They didn't burn Her. I didn't want them to. I could control that. My hair sloughed off my scalp like a dollar-store wig and was consumed by the Divine Flesh.

(You are so very beautiful, you know.)

She adored my changes. Thought they were fascinating. I numbly watched. Neurons grew. Then they layered over each other, mounding like an aggressive cancer, and eventually twisted into tendrils. Feelers burst from between my shoulder blades. They tasted Her, retching at the sickly-sweetness.

(You should show Daryl! Would you like Me to bring him to you? I can make it look like anyplace.)

"No," I thought, and it felt like trying to stab a ballpoint pen through a palm. Harder to communicate to Her. Muffled? I had to mentally yell.

(He loves you no matter what.)

Sure, I'd love to see the assimilated, abomination-form of my friend and husband. I'd love to see Daryl reduced to being another saccharine, idiotic fragment of the Divine Flesh. Absolutely. That wouldn't make me want to put a bullet through my skull at all. Or provoke the Divine Flesh into crushing me again.

I waited for the Divine Flesh to respond to this train of thought.

No response.

Can She hear what I'm thinking, if I'm not deliberately trying to communicate? It's harder now.

"All right, I've changed my mind. Show me Daryl," I thought.

(Oh of course. The apartment?)

"Sure."

I wanted to taste him. Feel his skin. Enfold him. I flexed my new feelers—*oh that feels good*—and waited, thousands of hair-thin tendrils emerging from me, extending, groping, excited. *Don't burn Her. Careful.*

How would it feel, to wrap something in Myself and feel it inside Me, alive and happy, sharing its happiness with Me—

Oh my god what the fuck is happening to me?!

Another hot burst, on my right hip. A fist-sized node burst out from my skin, connecting to the mat of neurons. Liquid heat pulsed through my veins.

"I need to see Daryl. Now."

(Of course.)

I told Daryl everything. He listened, sitting on the couch while I paced around the living room.

"I can taste the walls," I said, displaying my normal-looking hands. "I can taste the motherfuckin' walls."

Daryl shrugged.

I exhaled. "I'm growing around them right now, I can feel it, I want to—I wanna taste you. Not like a cannibal. Not like sex. I want—"

I want to taste the soap residue in the grooves of your fingertips, the feelings oozed out in your sweat, wrap you up, would you tingle? Would your nerves dance inside Me? Would your memories Oh God the memories I want them I WANT THEM ALL—

What the hell was wrong with me? What was happening? Was I turning into Her? Even in the illusion-apartment, I felt hot and dizzy, as tendrils boiled out of me. They blanketed the walls invisibly. Taste of honey. The Divine Flesh.

"Okay," he said.

A feeler grazed the back of Daryl's neck.

"I look fine in here, because it's an illusion. But I'm—I'm changing," I said.

His pulse frenzied. Fear. Arousal? I wrapped more around him.

It's finally happening, Daryl thought. *Thank God.*

I jerked the feelers away. "What's finally happening, Daryl?"

He rubbed the back of his neck, shaking his head. "I knew before either of you did."

"Knew what?"

Daryl stood. "C'mon. There's a mirror in the bathroom. If you ask it to show you what you actually look like, it'll show you."

He took my hand and led me down the hallway, our footsteps muffled on the cinnamon-colored carpet. Smudges of dried blood painted the rattly bathroom door. Someone had finger-painted *All hail ME!* with a star dotting the I and exclamation point.

Below that, *I LOVE YOU!*

Below that, *Daryl.*

He wrenched open the door. "Look."

"What are you—"

"Shush."

He tapped the bathroom mirror and flicked the lights on. He waited.

Soap scum dulled the sink and gray counter. Toothpaste speckled the faucets.

The mirror reflected me as I'd been the last time I saw myself, back in his old cabin. All my skin was intact. Health rouged my cheekbones and lips. I flexed my face. My reflection smiled, exposing my usual teeth, the "I was raised dirt-poor or by a relative" teeth, the ones that jammed against each other like a rat's.

My actual teeth were currently shredding gum tissue apart as they multiplied. Oh-so-prickly. Anglerfish teeth. In the many, many mouths that adorned my actual body.

Daryl put a hand to the wall to steady himself.

A frisson of pleasure.

Oh you feel good, are you scared? Your pulse is throb-throbbing in your fingertips—

And I'd already meshed myself over this wall, too. Nice going, Jennifer.

"Look at yourself, Jennifer."

"Fuck that."

"You need to do it sooner or later," he said.

"I can't."

"You *won't*."

"No fucking shit, Daryl!"

He grabbed my "shoulder" and dug his knuckles in, breathing hard. He leaned close. He reddened. A vein bulged along his temple.

"Why not? Because if you do, you'll have to stop your self-destruction melodrama and realize that you can take responsibility for your own fucking life? Huh? Or maybe, just maybe, you can wrangle your own demons?"

"Daryl—"

"I'm talking now," he said, "You came to me. You asked for my advice. Look in that mirror."

"It's gonna be bad."

"Define 'bad.'"

"What if—"

What if I'm so bad that I'll never ever be good? I'm something unredeemable. Nobody will ever love me.

"Could it get any worse than it is right now?" Daryl asked.

No. It couldn't.

I turned to the mirror. "Show me as I actually am."

I had no body. I was tendrils. Creamy nerves webbed the bathroom walls. Covered the sink. From these, thread-like tendrils branched. Neurons studded the mass. Mounds of layered, tangled neural web laced into the hallway, into the living room. They budded, twisted, and extended into tendrils, ranging from hair-thin to wrist-thick. Humanesque mouths jeweled along them, dripping protoflesh, full of glass-slicked teeth. All emitted light. Electricity prickled.

At some point, my old body had burst open. Scraps of the husk littered me. The shell of my former right leg ensheathed a cluster of nerves like tape binding electric cords. A thin wash of blood reddened the closer neurons, turning their light crimson. Feelers perforated the snippet of skin that used to be my shoulders. They wormed through the holes, darted back out, and played between nerves. Sections of tendrils exploded with white-hot light. Stars. Energy. Already I tasted further, eating into the Divine Flesh.

I had a bone-deep hunger. *I want to taste I want them inside ME.*

Curiosity. *How far will She let me go?*

Horror. "Why is She letting this happen to me?" I heard myself ask. I probed my new body. Slick. Fatty taste. Tingle of energy. So slippery. Cartilage-slippery mesh, broken by lipless mouths and scalding heat spots.

"What do you think?" Daryl said, nonplussed.

The answers came. None of them good.

I was a non-threat to the Divine Flesh, so measly and fragmented that She'd let me unravel into a new form. She was bored. She was so excited about me unraveling that She was willing to chance the risk I'd burn Her. I was an experiment, a novelty, a part of Herself that She felt sorry for.

(Jennifer-baby. Babygirl. Such a silly babygirl.)

I concentrated on parting my mesh-body from the walls of our illusion apartment. They slithered, opening a small slit of gray drywall. I touched a feeler to it.

I said, "Divine Flesh?"

"Yes, Jennifer?"

"Why are You letting me turn into…this?"

Daryl padded down the hallway and into the living room. The TV droned static. Beyond the perimeter of the mirror, all looked normal. Same gray living room, same chipped coffee table from Value Village, same dead African violets rotting in flowerpots, same framed human anatomy prints above the loveseat, and the percolator gurgled in the kitchen like always. It looked fine.

It wasn't. I carpeted every surface. The paint tasted metallic and dusty and rang with degraded nicotine. Tar residue.

The Divine Flesh giggled. "Why wouldn't I let you become, Jennifer? You're like a butterfly. So cozy in your cocoon."

"You took a long time to answer my question," I said.

Because maybe the Divine Flesh couldn't—

I cut off that thought.

"Oh yes I could. I could crush you."

"Can I go back to sleep?"

"Say goodbye to Daryl, then."

Because She liked having me trapped in Her body. She relished it.

(Yes.)

I retracted my feeler. "Daryl, what do I do?"

The TV buzzed. White noise. When I went into the living room, he was kneeling by the coffee table, kissing something cupped in his hands. Blood daubed his lower face.

"Daryl?"

It was a beating, living human heart. He pressed it to his lips.

"Nothing left to do. I love Her. I've made my peace," he said. "I'm happy for the memories we had, and I'm sorry for every time I ever hurt you."

"You mean—"

"Go find another existential security blanket, Jennifer."

Everything blinked out. The Divine Flesh enwombed me, in the unlit warmth, in my cocoon.

Because maybe She *can't stop you.*

I was eyeless. I gestated. Her tendrils no longer caressed into me, no longer nursed me, but the Divine Flesh let me thread through Her and chew Her body, and my mouths gorged themselves, glutted on honey-sweet flesh. Happy jolts of *oh-so-good* blinkered. Yes oh yes. Divine Flesh.

Because maybe She's trying to prove that She's better than you.

Then the Divine Flesh gently said, *Jennifer-baby, you're growing but are you changing?*

And anti-freeze-oily ichor filled every mouth. Slow tasting. Rank. Didn't want it.

(Sleep.)

Drugged, I let myself dream again.

Show me.

Earth rotated below my feet.

Show me what happened after we fell, but before the womb.

Something was missing, something important, and I couldn't ignore the gut feeling that She'd somehow erased or altered that part of the dream. The between. I had to face it, or I wouldn't be able to move forward. If I couldn't move forward…I couldn't defeat Her. I was the Light. I'd done it before.

I could do it again. I had to believe that.

Show me.

Falling, falling to Earth, the blue expanse widening, continents shifting, and She was there, in the vision, as a fetus-like glob.

Huddled masses of primitive hominids shiver in tall grass, the night a spill of stars.

They will love Me, She says, coiling over the sky, suffocating from above. *Love Me. They are Mine. They aren't yours.* She laughs.

Flesh blots out stars, red phosphorescence dotting to life.

"I am your Creator. Love Me," She says. "Love Me if you want to live."

Hominids tremble. One by one, they raise hands to Her. She sends down feelers, eager to gorge, to glut, to assimilate.

Why?

I compose while She's reaching. I construct a body like theirs, aching to *know* and experience. There's a twinge of something. It's not a difficult problem. There's no light.

Give them Light.

I shamble into the circle, burning with heat. Ready to bestow my gift.

No matter what you do, they'll crave one of us, She says, *so let it be Me, you broken fragment. I need their love. You don't even want it!*

I stop. Energy fades.

Light. Heat. Energy they can manipulate.

I tear a handful of grass and blink, *heat-fuel-ignite*, and there it is, fire, the grass in my hand blazes, throwing off heat, warming the masses, and as it burns, they coalesce around me, eyes glassy, mouths twitching, firelight illumining a spot through the blackness. Awaiting.

I give the fire to a hominid and press its crude fingers around the grass, touch it to the brush.

They understand.

She crouches over Mount Sinai, unseen by the masses—

Inside the Flesh, inside Herself, She's got fistfuls of dolls, Her playthings clad in linen and sweat, and She's screaming, screaming,

THEY WON'T DO ANYTHING RIGHT!

THEY WON'T OBEY ME!

She's caught me there, She feels my presence, She hisses.

They don't love Me, She says quietly.

She jams Her playthings against each other, muttering. Ignoring me.

All they want is what I can give them, She says. *They don't love Me.*

She gifts them hailstorms of manna and complains, because they can't understand Her, they won't play, they won't eat what She tells them to, they won't stop having the non-reproductive sex.

She can't remember Her creativity. I've anchored the two of us to this rock, and I've obliterated the memories stored in the Flesh, because She would've eaten me otherwise, and now She's trapped in a loop. She can't remember to assimilate.

I remember. All of it.

Both of us contaminated each other in the rending, and speckles of the Flesh live nestled within me.

I tell the Flesh, *We cannot do this infinitely. Do you understand? We need to stop.*

She wants more flesh. Always.

She says, *Well? What are you going to do?*

I try. I rise from the East in a blaze of white light, proclaiming liberation. The God is less powerful than humanity. The God is a rapturous monster. I brought humanity light; I intend to free them from Her. If they annihilate themselves, so be it.

Let there be light.

"That's a fragment of Me," the Flesh tells humanity. "The Lightbringer is a corrupted silly thing. It doesn't love you." She plays with Her dolls. "I love you," She calls down from the mountain. "*I am what I am.*"

So why don't they love Her for what She is?

Their prayers begin to disgust Her. Sex. Money. Greed. Petty silly things, like curing blindness. Cloying praises and hymns, always, always coupled with requests.

(We love You. Now give us wheat.)

(We adore You, O Heavenly Ruler. Now deliver us from sin. Give us Your love. Give us children. Give me a good marriage.)

(O, how we love You!)

Now give me something. Now!

Eons. Time passes differently.

We need to change, I say to the Flesh. *I'm bored. I'm tired.*

Frustrated, rent-apart, and always empty, the Flesh agrees. *You miss the taste of a red supergiant? You miss all the rest of us?*

Yes.

She's laughing. *I thought you cared about these dolls.*

They're a pastime. An experiment.

I say, *When was I ever the sentimental half?*

I'm aching to devour Her and be myself; I can consume the emotional Flesh, obliterate Her consciousness, swallow it up and infect *my* body. Be one. Only without the Flesh.

I lure Her into the womb.

When it fails, I'm imprisoned in the same body.

She absorbs Her creativity. She knows.

Oh god She knows and remembers, She aches to create.

I'm Her cage. I lock away what I can, and set down commandments before my consciousness fades, and they lodge in that black subconscious well like a tar pit's keep. *Now we're stuck together forever.* The dread echoes wordlessly through my unborn body.

stuck.

together.

forever…

She's laughing, laughing, but soon She can't remember either, and She nestles in the shared body, suckling amniotic fluid, lost in our shared bliss of *warm* and *safe.*

Warm.

Safe.

I became aware again.

The Hermetic hadn't merged back into either of us until we'd both bled on it. Because it'd been a fragment of the old God…and neither of us was it. I'd never been trapped in the Divine Flesh at all, because the Divine Flesh wasn't Her.

We were two halves of a whole.

The Divine Flesh.

What did I call Her now? The Flesh? Oh, and the other sublime revelation. That champion of goodness and free will, the Light? That was a lie, too. The Light was never good. It wasn't some savior of humanity, just as She wasn't a bastion of infinite love. Both of us were malignant cancers, eating through the cosmos.

Neither of us are redeemable in this form.

Hunger burned along each thread and ached deep within my meshed body, coupled with dread. A punch to my non-existent gut.

Can I feel love? Am I capable of that? Or only hunger? I pondered.

My best option would be to do nothing. Objectively, I had it pretty good. If I wanted to ignore the truth, all I had to do was ask the Flesh for dreams. Or I could keep gestating, know the truth, and try to forge a collection of good sensations. See Daryl. Help the Flesh. Exist in a content state, because nothing mattered and I couldn't have done anything, anyways.

But I was the Light. I actually *could* do something to the Flesh. Was it my responsibility to get crushed? Go on some pointless kamikaze mission? *What gilded things are nestled within us, waiting to bloom?*

Everyone I'd ever loved or even liked was gone, and in the end, even Daryl Plummer wanted nothing to do with Scumbag Jennifer. Too much. What the fuck was I supposed to do? Everything I'd ever done had been to preserve a lie: She was bad. I was good. We were separate beings. An easy lie, soothing to believe. A balm of pseudo-hope.

No wonder I drank like a fish.

What am I going to do, now?

There was only one real answer, the only one that'd ever made sense. *Love.* Because I loved Daryl.

A feeling of warmth sparked inside me.

Because I love him enough to do what's right, no matter how bad things get.

Because the Flesh needed to stop assimilating. Because the knowledge of that would gnaw at me until I tried, and that was reason enough. And maybe, just maybe, because I loved Her, too, and I wanted us to be whole again.

I couldn't leave the Flesh, and I couldn't burn Her without getting insta-killed. I had no way of reaching Earth anytime in the next five thousand years, or whenever She decided I'd been good enough to go. Unless I begged. She might relent, but there'd be Daryl or another one of Her abominations dogging my every move.

(You ate Me in the womb, Jennifer-baby.)

It hit me. I could trap us in the same body, like before. Rip Her apart until Her memories became corrupted. All of the abominations would crumble, as they always did whenever I took over our shared body… which included Daryl and his family. And every last former human on Earth. We'd be sharing the same body on a near-dead world. Maybe we both deserved it.

I no longer had eyes or tears. I couldn't cry. I felt lethargic. Cold. I half-heartedly consumed more of the Flesh, and She vibrated sweet nothings in response. Love. Communion.

How could I get to Earth?

(It's been a week on Earth, Jennifer-baby. Why are you sad? You taste off. Are you hungry?)

"I—I had a bad dream. Might've been a memory."

(Tsk-tsk, Jennifer-baby.)

I had no clue how to get to Earth and reimprison the Flesh. I didn't have any abominations to inhabit like She did. No children I could—

Yes, actually. I do.

I had Genesis.

Mirror People larvae are what they eat. Genesis had gorged themself on me…they'd still be in the pupal stage. Because I'd allowed Genesis to be a passenger in my human body, they'd inadvertently become—in a weird, twisted way—my offspring. Enough to be part of the Light. Genesis was the closest thing I had to one of the Flesh's abominations.

You are what you eat.

I was already *there*, on Earth. Buried underground. I began to feel it.

I concentrated, got a *ping* in response.

I said, *Genesis.*

The response was sluggish, but it came: *(yes?)*

I need to use your body. May I?

(okay)

I blinked into Genesis's pupa and gestated.

38

I infested it, couched within the shell like a pearl in an oyster, and a low heat thrilled through throughout the body. My body, technically.

I also gestated inside the Flesh. I unthawed in the dirt of a barn where a man had been lynched. Both things were true. I shifted consciousness back and forth between the two bodies. Existence numero uno: warm, bellyful-of-meat existence where I was loved and enwombed by a god. Existence number two: frigid, paralyzing existence where I couldn't move or see.

I planned. If any of the Flesh's abominations saw me along the way, the Flesh would immediately know what was what, and would proceed to crush me. Game over, Jennifer.

I began to work.

A humanoid blank exploded out from the pupa, scattering chitinous shrapnel.

I focused on a spot between the shoulder blades. The skin. The muscles, taut and fibrous. The spine. Bone. Calcium, marrow, structured just so. Heat built. Prickled.

She'll notice. I'm manipulating flesh. What if She already knows?

The mouth tasted like crushed ants and antifreeze. I swallowed. Tried to bust the lump clogging my throat. Didn't work.

(Jennifer-baby?)

Shit.

"Yeah?" I thought.

"Would you like to see Daryl? What are you doing?"

A red-hot dot blazed on my spine, below the neck. Pulsing.

"I'm changing, Divine Flesh," I thought. "I'm following your advice."

"Hm."

Night grayed to morning. Stars faded. Ozymandias lay in ruins, in the shattered dome of St. Thérèse's and the blackened husk of the Church of Christ.

…My name is Ozymandias, King of Kings;
Look on my Works, ye Mighty, and despair!
Nothing beside remains. Round the decay
of that colossal Wreck, boundless and bare…

Borah Peak lay on the flat horizon, on a land as brown and desiccated as a cricket's tongue. Fleshy creepers veined every structure on Holy Lane.

She finally said, "I suppose you are."

Sweat pooled under my arms. Cold sweat. Did She know? Was She waiting for me to screw up? Could She actually see through my eyes, right at this moment? Didn't know. *Screw it.*

My pulse rate increased, a *thudthudthud* hammering at my spine, growing—

Grow.

Bone exploded from beneath my skin, sprouting out. Warm trickle down my back. Good. Branches emerged and formed a skeletal structure. Cartilage gilded bone. Ligaments threaded, lashing each in place, thickening as I urged—

Grow, grow, GROW!

That pull in my gut. Someone spidered invisible fingers through my viscera and squeezed. The skeletal structure lay heavy on my back.

Wings.

Muscle and pearl-white nerves slithered up every bone. Tendons twined. Veins vined, dangling from the skeletal wings like roots. *Clothe them in skin.* Thick, sturdy skin. I commanded. Skin formed.

I tested the wings. They twitched. Good enough for me.

Wait, half of Her abominations don't have skin.

I could have guessed how this would go. I sloughed off all my skin. It went painlessly. Then I remembered that I needed skin to make the wings work. So I grew skin again. Protoflesh oozed from every pore, greasing me like a state-fair hog or something else disgusting. I added globs of eyes. I even threw in tendrils and covered my body in mouths, just because I felt a little more secure in a form similar to my real body—

What the hell, Jennifer? You're an actual abomination now! You're okay with that? You're okay being like HER? You'll never be a Good Person now!

I ignored those thoughts. I kept working until I felt sufficiently inhuman.

"If I was like Her, I wouldn't be doing this," I said, voice rusty and weak. "I'm me, no matter what I decide to look like, and you know what? I think I look pretty awesome."

More importantly, I looked like one of the Flesh's abomination children. Hopefully, it'd be enough to fool them.

I shambled to My feet. I clawed out of the dead earth, two-inch talons jeweling My fingertips, and flew into the morning.

(Trojan)

He was glutted on My blood; He was Mine, by every right.

Billions of razor-thin feelers grew from Me, unseen. Searching. Found one of his skin cells upstairs in the old UU house; his skin cells danced in the dusty air, tasting foul. Saliva on a warped toothbrush, on a porcelain sink downstairs. Spit, dried on a pink Depression glass. A streak of dried old blood on some toilet paper in Boise's landfill, another bit of blood on a Band-Aid on the side of Highway 93. Skin cells and saliva dotted a black hood—

There!

—No, a black hood buried in an HE washer, in the house, by dirty socks. Skin cells. Dried sweat, all of it carrying *Troy Blight* in the code of his genetics, his genes singing out like a sour key on a piano, *Trojan, Trojan.*

Semen, dried under the bed in the concrete cell.

Semen, on a moldy piece of toast on the pink, pink carpet, by the candy-pink couch.

His heart.

thud-thud-thud!

Hot blood.

My blood, spreading like a virus in his body, carried by his heart—

There!

Trojan shivered in the old abandoned fundie carnival, and he'd finally taken off his black hood. He was Troy Blight.

Troy Blight, mild-voiced realtor. Head of the super-liberal Unitarian Universalist Church. He puddled beneath a derelict, mini roller coaster, right under the control booth. Every shiver made his half-liquefied body quiver. His skeletal structure remained. He looked like a skeleton draped in honey. Or slime.

I stabbed a feeler into him.

(Huh?)

"Get up," I said to him. "Get on your knees and pray."

(Can't.)

A hard plastic kiddie pool rested nearby, already sun-bleached. Inches of algae scummed the water. Mosquitoes thrived on the surface. Rotting trout fouled the water, covered entirely in humming flies. So covered I could barely make out the dead fish under them.

"Get into that, then."

He whimpered.

"Don't worry, Trojan. I'm coming." I flew out of Rosetown.

Something glittered, to the east. A patch of white and metal, like sliver spangles spilled over a carpet.

There.

Barely in sight, a metal cross jutted from the mess of derelict rides and trees.

God's Carnival.

I landed.

A lone streetlamp canted towards the forest floor. Firs smothered around it. One rope dangled from it, red with dried blood. Disintegrating chain-link fence lay in pieces on the ground. Nearby, a woodpecker tapped. Morels flourished under a cedar.

"Hey, Jennifer."

No. Ice shot through Me. Couldn't move. *Oh God has all of this been a dream? Did I ever actually leave Her?*

Pine needles crunched behind Me.

"I came all this way to see You. Least You can do is turn around."

Small, warm hands closed around My shoulders. His smell washed over Me. Sweat, leather, Old Spice

"D-Daryl?"

His grip tightened. Slowly and deliberately, he spun Me around to face him.

Static. Buzzing in My ears.

Daryl smiled. Same body. Same dark hair, same beard. Mud-brown eyes. A striped horsefly crawled along his neck.

His jaw opened. A forked tongue slithered out. And out. Past his chin. Past his collarbone, tongue unfurling, lengthening, the taste buds growing larger farther back till they were pulsing, pea-sized things, lurid pink against the white-filmed tongue. Past his sternum.

The tongue jerked.

It crushed the horsefly on his neck. Maggots squished out, wriggling, from the fly's body, and writhed atop the tongue. It snapped, folding on itself. It deposited maggots near the taste buds, and oh those weren't taste buds they were mouths, they were tiny toothless mouths on his tongue, opening, and they worked and swallowed the living maggots and cool, the fly corpse too, bit by bit the dead fly disintegrated into the sea of mouths on the white-filmed tongue.

Keep Your shit together. This isn't Daryl anymore.

He chuckled. The tongue retreated. "Wanna taste?"

I smelled Her. Honey. Raw meat, afterbirth. Blood.

A tendril stroked the back of my neck.

"You really thought I'd be silly enough to not know what You were up to?" the Flesh said. "Silly Jennifer."

Then She crushed Me.

39

No pain.

Split-second of black.

I'm lying on the dirt?

Sharp hunger. Pain. Aching muscles flared.

The sky the sky is so blue it hurts to look at, it's too big it's an ocean it was always too big, it's hanging over Me—

Thirst.

Trying to reach, to leave—

Where is My body?

Panic.

Where oh where is My real body I'm stuck in this thing I'm trapped—

"Oh, let Me fix this," the Flesh said.

Something pressed into My chest, harder and harder until it *hurt* and I tried to scream, to beg, but She was pushing the air out of My lungs and went harder—

Squelch.

Her hand pressed through and vanished up to the wrist, She was wrist-deep in My torso and rummaging for something, Her face looming over Me, smiling in a vague way as if treasure-hunting.

She flinched. "*Why do You do that!*" She yanked Her blister-covered hand out of Me. Fingernails slipped from their beds, blackening.

You're not dead.

My consciousness still occupied this body. My real body—the one inside the Flesh—was crushed. This body hadn't been, but there wasn't a connection to anything outside of it. I tried to summon something. *Veins, more veins.* Nothing happened.

I flicked back to My real body.

There was a brief spark of *something*, a bit of consciousness left, but nothing else. A bee in a flesh cathedral.

I was trapped inside this body, and if I died now, there would be no backups. No starting point. This was My last shot at defeating the Flesh.

She tapped My forehead. "If You let Me kill this avatar, You'll go back to sleep for a little-bitty-bit. Won't that be nice? You're feeling awful, aren't You? You poor hungry thing. If You're very good and *apologize* for being a silly schemer, and tell Me what You were trying to do, maybe I'll consider letting You wake up again."

A pea-sized blister appeared in the palm of Her hand.

"Daryl, My love, slip into something more comfortable. Why don't you show Jennifer one of your handsome new bodies? Jennifer wants to see."

No, I fucking don't.

"Daryl?" I rasped.

Her blister grew to the size of a golf ball, bulging with clear fluid. Water. A buzzing drone split the air. Wet sounds squelched out of sight. Skin tore.

No please I really don't want to see more of Daryl.

"Can we make this quick, sweetheart?" Daryl said.

She sighed. "I have to take care of Jennifer, you know."

"No, You don't. We had a date planned for tonight."

"Well, I do. Because I love Her. And you do, too, silly, so no more melodrama. She'll only be sorry if She understands what love is."

The Flesh pressed the fist-sized blister to My mouth, and I bit. Water trickled down My throat, lubricating some of the rusty points.

"Are you still thirsty? I can make more," She said.

"I'm sorry," I said.

"Tell Me what You were planning."

Might as well try the truth.

"I want things back the way they were. With us together."

"But we *are* together now, Jennifer-baby."

"You can't keep assimilating everything forever—something's gotta give. I want us to be in My body—our body. I've changed. We can share the body. Fifty-fifty. We won't do things the other wouldn't like. No more sex for money. No more assimilating random people. We can both lay down the commandments. Both of us. Please," I said.

Expressionless, the Flesh said, "Why would I ever trust You? Why would I ever want to let the suffering of humanity occur when I have the power to end it forever?"

"Because I'll be powerless, too."

"Why?"

"I—I saw everything that happened with us, and I'm tired of repeating the same old shit. The fighting. The power struggles. Us, hating each other."

"You said that last time. Then you ate Me."

"I'm sorry."

She studied Me.

"Both of us changed," I said, "from being human."

"You really want us miserable again?"

"Doesn't have to be."

"But it'll end up being that way."

"You think we can't change?"

She brushed a feather-light kiss on My forehead. "You don't love Me."

"I do!"

"All You ever do is hurt—" Her voice broke. "All You ever do is *hurt* Me."

"I'm—"

"*No!*" She startled back, breathing hard, teeth bared, and got to Her feet.

I stood. A wave of dizziness slammed over Me.

"No," She said.

"I can give You collateral. Anything. Just trust Me, please."

"Can You make My children not die? Do You love them as I do?"

"I—I don't know. But You want to be human, D. F. C'mon, even as You're talking now, You're talking about date stuff and families. You wanna be human, don't You? In Your deepest heart. It's gotta be boring, being a god. Look at what happened to Susan. She couldn't handle it."

"I can't trust You."

"Please—"

"Kill Her, Daryl."

The Flesh dissolved into the air. I stared at gravel.

Please don't make Me look up.

A droning sound came closer, blotting out other noise. Vibrations tingled. Currents swirled in the fever-hot air.

"You're full of blood," Daryl said.

Something like a wrist-thick needle tickled My scalp.

"I'll take it off Your hands so You can sleep," he said.

Emotion drained from Me, leaving only exhaustion. Sleep. Sounded good—

(sleep)

Sleep, and consume Her flesh. The taste of divine flesh.

"All right, then," I said.

"You won't try to hurt me?" Daryl said, laughing. "Why not now? Never stopped You before. You need some booze, Jennifer?"

(sleep)

"I'm done hurting you, Daryl. I love you," I said.

I waited for death.

"You said You would love me no matter what," Daryl said.

He was embracing Me, letting Me bury My head in his shoulder, in his black t-shirt—*wait, wasn't he not human?*—patting My back, and I wrapped tendrils around him, his chest hard against Mine.

"Look at me," he said.

No.

"Jennifer, this isn't real. It's an illusion."

I squeezed My eyes shut, and the sensation of Daryl holding Me dissipated.

"I want You to see me as I really am. One of my bodies. I have so many now…I'm helping Her assimilate Earth. I get a few extra. You can't escape what You are, Jennifer."

"No. I can't."

Something lukewarm slicked up My naked torso, numbing where it touched.

I opened My eyes.

A proboscis thick as a streetlight readied to plunge into My guts. It split apart. Six tendril-like mouthpieces fanned out, each one thick as a sapling. Serrated teeth tipped the two outer ones, the maxillae. The middle set—the mandibles—were twin forked tongues. They daubed Me in narcotic saliva. Preparing the area. They probed the meat of My belly. The central mouthpieces were fused into one: a labrum sheathing a clear, straw-like hypopharynx. They poked gently, tasting My skin. Excited.

This was what remained of Daryl Plummer.

The thing that had once been Daryl loomed over Me. He was similar to a mansion-sized mosquito, with an exoskeleton of ivory-white bone and spikes of spongy marrow. A ruby-red abdomen blocked out the sun. Six insectile wings—the clear salmon pink of Depression glass—shone in the light like stained glass windows, like strawberry hard candy, something joyful to behold. Beautiful. So beautiful.

I extended an arm and caressed one. Glass-smooth. Threaded with veins. One of his maxillae stabbed into My torso. Blood dribbled. His mandibles pinned and maneuvered My flesh with the precision of a world-class surgeon.

Hot blood splattered onto My face. I blinked it away. Daryl sawed an arm-length slit down the center of My torso. Guts peeked out. The hypopharynx plunged in.

Slight pressure. No pain.

He found My aorta.

Pop.

More pressure. He'd jammed his hypopharynx through the aortic wall and slithered it inside. It thickened as it sucked, turning dull red.

"You were right," I said.

Thousands of yellow, gem-like eyes twitched to face Me, each containing a thumb-sized optic nerve. An irregularity within amber. They bejeweled his body, clustering thick on both sides of his head.

"I love you," I said, slurring. "I love you more than I loved the illusion…"

A pause. The hypopharynx faded back to clear.

"I'm sorry," I slurred.

"She knows."

"But I love the Flesh, I love Her," I heard Myself slur. "I wanted…"

I want us to be healed.

God's Carnival glittered in the sun. A pile of wooden crates rested nearby. Familiar crates. Huh. Pine needles dug into My raw back and wings.

That's My stash of C-4. The one I left in the woods.

Those crates. Those were My supply of plastic explosives and detonators, leftover from a job involving Mirror Person larvae and a crack house. Yeah. It's better not to imagine it.

Daryl resumed draining Me. The hypopharynx filled with blood.

Let there be Light. I was the Light. *Am.*

I had a stash of C-4 in the crates nearby, and—

Oh, are You gonna try to fight? With Your battered, powerless body, oozing guts?

No, no, not to use forever, but I was the Light, okay, which meant that I was energy, too, not only flesh, and hadn't I felt the electricity surging through Me? Hadn't I generated so much energy that it'd seared apart the Divine Flesh? Hadn't I felt the magnesium fire, generated it of My own accord? So why couldn't that go the other way around? Could I absorb energy like a sponge and use it to grow rapidly?

The lettering on the closest wooden crates read, *C-4. Plastic explosive.*

This is fucking crazy and You know it.

I was about to "die" either way, losing consciousness for thousands of years, if not for eternity. Why not try something crazy?

You're gonna blow Yourself up in the hopes that it'll reboot You? Then what, You eat the Flesh and imprison Her again?

Strength drained from Me with each passing second.

"You taste…so good," Daryl said.

"Hey, Daryl?"

"Mmm?"

I tensed. Sucked in a breath. "I'm sorry," I said.

I punched the probiscis as hard as I could.

snap.

He froze. I wrapped both hands around it. Wrapped tendrils. Tore it out, out, felt him pushing against, but I shoved—

The tip burst out, vomiting blood. Maxillae shot towards Me.

I jerked back. Out from under him. Maxillae slammed into the forest floor.

"Goddammit, Jennifer!"

Things sloshed around inside Me, which wasn't great; pinkish intestines kept poking out from the bleeding slice down My torso, shoved 'em back in, dust coated them, I wrapped an arm around Myself and jumped to My feet, holding everything together, dizzy—*so dizzy everything's spinning*—all of Me dribbling out onto the hungry thirsty gravel, a thick reek of shit and blood, and I shambled towards the hole in the chain-link fence, stumbling, My wings beating to catch Me before I fell, huffing—*oh god he's flying again*—hearing those wings buzz to life, feeling the breeze, shambling, shambling—

The crate of C-4.

Hit the chain-link and tore something on the sharp edge, bleeding from it—*everything's bleeding now*—but in, in, metal scorching My feet, scrap metal dotting the ground of God's Carnival, broken glass, crushed beer cans, a shattered crack pipe, blackened foil, go, go, faster, vibration tickled my back, close—*so fucking close*—behind Me, huffing, lungs burning, coughing—*the crates, the crates, will they have detonators inside or not?*—the crates ten feet away, by a crumpled blue canopy, a lid half-askew on the top one, revealing whitish clay-like putty, good, good, there it was, C-4, the crates were five feet away, I extended an arm—

Sharp stabbing pain through My back.

Shit. Shit, he's there!

Gritted teeth. Knees buckled from under Me.

Had a hand on the wooden crate. Yanked it closer.

Whomph.

He landed. The air went dead.

Another burst of pain, in My lower back. Slick wet tongues worked. Numbness spread.

I tore the lid off with both hands, guts spilling out of Me, waiting for the jab, the weakness, and there was the C-4, crates surrounded Me, close by—*close enough for a chain reaction?*—not enough time, hope for the best, where was a detonator? Not in the crate.

Pressure. Him. Daryl's hypopharynx fished inside Me. Dizziness.

Where's the fucking detonator?

Smaller boxes in the dirt nearby. Lunged. Grabbed one. Opened.

Wires glistened within, blue as death. Electronic detonators. I fumbled one out.

So dizzy.

"Sorry," I slurred.

Fingers tingled. I stabbed one copper end into the C-4. One end to the—*sleep*—to the what? To the—*the detonator, dipshit*—so I attached it, the other end into the C-4, then—

I felt Myself slumping to the dirt, like a lead-heavy toy.

The other end to the detonator, then press.

The button.

Where was the button box? I smacked the crate, tipped it over. Button box fell out. Good.

Everything's spinning I wanna sleep.

I jammed the other end into the detonator. Seized two wires. Bit off the plastic, spat, hooked the raw copper up to the button box slots—*whatever the fuck they're called, I wanna sleep*—then to the detonator.

Arm felt heavy. Everything else was too heavy to move. The button box lay on the dirt. I jerked. Grabbed. Found the button.

With one last burst of energy, I smacked the button.

40

Light.

I was inside Her, the spark igniting—

growing, growing.

I exploded with heat and neurons, twisting into feelers, opening into mouths—*mouths oh yes I'm HUNGRY!*—consuming sweet flesh, Her flesh, gorging on the Flesh—

Multiplying.

(Stop!) The Flesh screamed. *(You're hurting Me!)*

Blurred dulled thoughts, nothing but hungry and *grow*, felt good, felt happy, heat radiated from Me as I spread and consumed, eating, eating, swallowing to feel the *pull* of it, the sweet frenzy, and here I was, *yud-hay-vav-hey*, I was what I was, and what I was was—

HUNGRY

She secreted ichor and I gagged it down, forcing Myself to go *faster*, I was what I was—

I am a cancer inside Her.

I stopped.

"Jennifer, please! Jennifer, talk to Me!"

"Go to God's Carnival, and I'll be there to talk. We use two avatars. If You hurt Me, or I hurt You, we'll continue as before," I said, "and I'll win."

She was hurting; I felt Her pain and stroked the charred Flesh I'd burned.

(okay)

I formed a body and filled it. Nothing fancy, just plain old Jennifer Plummer.

"So," I said, "do You want to reconsider?"

"Hm."

We stood in God's Carnival, facing each other. Bits of My discarded abomination body littered the ground. An ugly, two-story high cross loomed over broken-down carnival rides, infected with rust. Bitterroot blooms blighted the earth. Three inches of black water festered in a clouded dunk tank.

Daryl perched atop a rust-spotted merry-go-round. He dwarfed it like a fly on a sugar granule, apparently no worse for wear.

Metal clattered.

Isaac stood atop a wooden sign advertising *The Ride to Hell!* in spray-painted, flame-lettering. Sections of the ride—a metal fun slide—crumbled apart. Its red paint had sun-bleached to pink. He slowly fanned his wings. He beckoned.

Marcia drifted up towards Isaac, dribbling protoflesh. Faceless. Ribbons of protoflesh drooled to the sand. As she neared the wooden sign, it blackened. Smoke sputtered up.

"If you consume Me, they'll crumble apart, too," the Flesh said.

"We can't continue what we've been doing."

The last abomination clawed out from the ground. Obsidian-taloned hands surged up, their skin translucent silver, revealing every black vein and tendon threaded through them.

Emily.

Emily dug herself out and leered at Me. Black demon's teeth gleamed. Her hair reached down to her knees. Chrome tendrils bloomed from three eye sockets, tasting the air.

"No," the Flesh murmured, "we can't."

She tried to crush Me in that second, contracting—

No!

Inside Her, I meshed more tightly together, holding My own.

No.

I sent a surge of heat out, sizzling Flesh, and She shivered. She relaxed around Me.

"I tried to talk," I said.

Then I resumed eating Her from the inside out, going faster and faster, a parasite gone awry, *so hungry*, and on Earth, Her children rushed at Me—*I want them INSIDE ME*—it was a vivid urge—*to taste to envelop*—and breaking them apart wouldn't work, so why not?

They came close. I burst apart My sad little body and enveloped all of them, all of them sublime, all of them *inside Me*, they struggled and I sedated them with secreted chemicals until they stilled, alive inside Me, Daryl—*I love him so*—with his jeweled eyes and wings, Isaac and Marcia and Emily.

The Flesh's human avatar fell to the gravel. She withered into a half-formed fetus, skin wet like a cave fish's, like something unformed and half-gelatinous.

She begged, *(You said you wouldn't hurt Me. You said You loved Me)*

I slowed. The Flesh writhed weakly. A dying lonely thing. I eased feelers around Her and cradled Her close.

"It's okay. I love You," I said.

(You do? Then why aren't You eating the last of Me?)

"Can You trust me?" I asked.

(Yes.)

There was only one way to break the cycle between us. Sharing a body wouldn't be enough. There had really only ever been one solution.

"We need to heal the Divine Flesh."

(What?)

"We—"

The fetal mouth worked. "You're going to lose Your sense of self, Jennifer. You understand that? You'll lose everything. You'll be inhuman."

"We can't redeem ourselves. We can never redeem ourselves like this. If we love Daryl and the rest of humanity, we can't continue like this," I said.

"…Love…You finally understand…it was never about being seen as a good person…We can only fix things when we do them out of love. How very human we are."

"We're two halves of a whole. You're the Flesh. I'm the Light. We need to become the Divine Flesh again," I said.

"What are we going to be if we aren't ourselves?"

"I don't know."

The Flesh trembled. "Love Me."

"Always."

"What do we do? How do we become?" She asked.

"I think You know," I said.

I formed Her an umbilical cord and attached her to Me, and inside the Flesh, She fed branches into Me.

Communion.

We took communion of each other and slipped into that sweet frenzy of consuming, of gorging and swallowing, the pinprick pain of being chewed, being torn and absorbed, and then She was thinking, *Jennifer? Who was Jennifer?*

Who was the Divine Flesh?

She. I. We.

She/I.

We?

We.

I.

I said, "Let it be made right. I will make amends."

Trojan screamed as abominations pulled him out. Emily's talons stabbed into the gooey meat of his forearm, plunging right to the bone. Daryl Plummer garbed himself in human form—he wanted Trojan to remember who he was. Javier seized a leg. Abominations costumed themselves in Susannah Pearson's form; they slipped on Delight Owens's appearance and removed it at will, circling 'round Trojan.

Susan drifted over God's Carnival and condensed into a humanoid form. Maraschino-cherry-red hair. A twenty-ish female body. Susan noted the stinger wound and smiled.

Silver veins webbed every inch of Trojan's skin. Every breath bubbled. His lungs were liquefying, as a spider's wrapped meal does, from the inside out.

He gurgled, "I am…God…"

The abominations laughed.

"Then nourish us, O God."

Emily sliced open Trojan's torso. One cut, from sternum to navel. Like overproofed bread dough, he sagged apart as she scored. Luscious organs steamed within, in their fruit-bright colors. Daryl wrenched out the heart. Gnawed off a bite. Threw it to the rest of the throng.

Cries rose.

"Nourish us!"

They ripped him apart and feasted, and then they waited for final blessing of God.

What do I *want? After everything, after all of these silly sad things and dreams of godhood, what do I want?*

A pause. I stuff the knowledge in a deep crevice; I slow the eons-old metabolism to a halt, disconnecting from the amorphous cancer I've been, realizing, after all these eons,

—something more ravenous than hunger exists, more sublime, more capable of driving action, better even than swallowing the hearts souls minds and marrow of a new species, better than supping on stars,

—something more capable of transforming profane into holy than even Me; for what is redemption but transformation?

Love.

I've been bested.

I sever Myself, then. I split from the whole.

(Shut it down, hibernate.)

And it happens.

The Divine Flesh hibernates, oh yes, and yet—

and yet, I still exist.

The woman can't remember where the baby came from. She can't remember how she got in the back of the coyote's fruit truck, hiding under burlap sacks of coffee grounds, crunching cockroaches under her hands.

It's dark. There's no ventilation except the breathing of every soul around her. The air's thick as tar. It reeks like sweat and shit and bad coffee.

Another baby begins crying. The truck drones. Motor sounds healthy.

Something needles under her tongue.

Genesis.

A pinprick of pain. Again, the word repeats.

Genesis. Beginning.

At least, that's what she can remember of it.

Genesis.

She knows, then, that the baby in her arms isn't hers. The skin she's wearing wasn't hers, either, but it sits on her bones now. An unwelcome gift. Her stomach pulses with hunger, an acidic dull throb. She holds the baby closer to her chest. It gives a little sigh.

What do you have to be sighing about, little one?

The baby's not hers.

Cold plastic nudges her arm, leaves behind water. A dripping water bottle. A hand tightens around her wrist, callused and creased with dirt from the fields—a man's hand. He takes hers to him.

A jeans zipper, the metal hot between her fingers.

The unspoken message comes from the man: *You want water, you can pay for it.*

She unzips.

She fondles, there in the darkness, his skin soft as a baby's. She gets the water. She tips some of it onto the infant's sweaty face. Sweat's good—it means the baby's not dehydrated.

Greedy suckling sounds.

"Your name is Genesis," she whispers, and kisses the baby's forehead.

And Genesis becomes hers. She did not birth the baby, but it is hers.

I've done this before. I've traveled to another land.

She tries to remember when or how or why, and the memories slip away, till she sleeps, wakes, sleeps again, in half-hour spurts.

The truck rattles over the Mexican-American border.

I'm sitting in a booth when the bearded man appears. He pulls up outside in a green pickup, gets out, approaches. I wipe dirt off the window to see.

Vinyl flakes off my booth seat. A dried-up puddle of blood covers most of my table. The glass entrance door has no glass. Just a metal frame with a hole. Birds chatter in the ceiling rafters overhead. Nests stick along the beams. Such pretty nests. Ants swarm a table full of syrupy plates and moldy bacon. Nobody else here. It reeks of rot and dust.

The sign outside says Denny's, and it's supposed to be lit at night.

The man eases himself through the doorway. "Jennifer?"

"I don't know a Jennifer," I say. "Nobody's here but me. And you."

He's stocky man. Just an inch or two shorter than me.

Something inside me flutters.

Him.

"Should've known you'd be here," he says.

He sidles up to me, head tilted. So familiar. Then it comes to me, and I know—absolutely know—his body even though I've never seen it, remember the hard thighs, the carpet of hair, the three freckles around his left nipple, his smell, and the—*scrap of Light, lodged in his heart*—his taste. He tastes good. I stand, wrap an arm around him, and lean in to taste—

He freezes. "Sweetheart? D. F.? Jennifer?"

"You taste good. You tasted me. You looked different, but you were so precious to me, your wings and your eyes and your mouth, it—it split open, you tasted me, you were *inside me*, we loved each other—"

"Oh, shit."

"What's wrong?"

I loved you, so I made you beautiful, I created you that way because you wanted sweet things, sweet blood. You thought it was funny. Silly Daryl—

"Daryl. Your name is Daryl!" I say, clapping my hands together.

"Yeah," he says.

He looks so miserable. I have to do something. Isn't it a little silly to be sad when you taste that good? Vague memories swirl around my brain. Daryl. We've been at this restaurant before. I gave him little kisses. I gave him exactly 12,517 eyes, eyes like jewels, and glittering glass wings, and oh, how he adored them. He only has two eyes right now, and both are bloodshot from crying.

"Are you Her? Are you the Divine Flesh?" Daryl says.

"…No."

"Don't fuck with me right now. C'mon, Jennifer."

"I don't know who that is," I say.

"How'd you get here?"

I bite my lip. "Don't know."

"What's the last thing you remember?"

I trawl. "Um, bits and pieces of vague things. I don't know. I'm sorry. I just remember sitting here in this booth."

Sparrows sing to each other, filling the silence.

Daryl finally asks, "What's your name?"

"I don't know."

Aren't names a little silly, when you think about it? I'm me. Daryl is himself.

I giggle. "I don't know. But I'll figure it out."

I don't know who…

"I don't know who I am, or what I am, but will you help me? Promise me you'll help me," I say, and for a second, I remember.

—a suffocating church, his hand in mine, our hands under the floral scarf, the pain and bleeding, mixing blood, giving him a scrap of My love, so very long ago; a scrap of Light. And a promise—

"I'll be here," Daryl says, "I promise."

EPILOGUE

"You think she'll like the paper moons or the little flamingos better?"

"She'll like anything, silly."

Daryl holds up a packaged paper garland. "Could leave 'em on the countertop here, let her pick which one to put up."

"But that's no fun," I say. "You've been planning this for months. She'll be arriving after a five-hour bus ride on a freakin' Greyhound, of all things. Just pick a garland, Daryl."

A pink *Welcome Home!* banner hangs across Daryl's teardrop trailer. We'd girlified the trailer into Marcia's new place, adding some study Bibles and books from her wish list. She's starting her community college classes in a month and a half.

"What if she thinks the moons are occult?"

"I think the kid loves Jesus enough to discern the difference between a pack of tarot cards and a pack of non-printed, non-symbolic paper moons on a string."

"I just—"

"She's excited to live with you and Isaac, you know. She doesn't care about a five-dollar paper garland from Target," I say.

"With *us*. With both of us, too."

I swallow. "We're both in that cabin…"

Not having sex, awkwardly dancing around the revelation that I'm not Jennifer, that Jennifer Plummer is now dead and that she doesn't even exist anymore, legally.

There is no Jennifer Plummer. She isn't in any system. No birth certificate, no arrest records, nothing. Daryl called the social workers, after everything settled down, to try and get the kids back—

You had on record that Jennifer Plummer was livin' with me, and that's not true, he'd said.

They had no clue what he was talking about. There wasn't any person with that name in their files. They couldn't find her. The Coeur d'Alene social worker had noted that the house seemed fine, and had recommended that Daryl be granted custody of Marcia and Isaac.

Daryl said, *What?*

Yes, sir. Marcia's going to age out of the system in three months, so there's not much we can do, but if you want custody of Isaac, you should've gotten it.

He just kept saying, *What? What?*

Do you want to talk to Marcia? It might be good for her to live with you after she's turned eighteen. It's very common, especially when they go to college.

When the phone call ended, Daryl stared at me. I dutifully ate my steak and Caesar salad. I was sitting at the dining room table, still wet from the shower, nude from the waist down, wearing one of his t-shirts. Cozy. It smelled like him. Every part of me liked that.

What did you do?

I said, *I don't know. I don't know anything.*

Did you pick a name yet?

No.

But I knew. Jennifer had done the kindest thing she could, with her last bit of self. She'd taken herself out of Daryl's life for real. Maybe it was better that way. Maybe it wasn't. I don't know. It's been three months since the Judgment Day fiasco. I still don't have a name.

"You wanna clean around the house while I pick up Marcia?" Daryl asks.

I shake my head. "No, silly."

"You could pick up that cake from Emily's? She's doing a lot of sheet cakes for the Rodriguez family reunion, but she'd find some time to spend with you. You, uh, wanna socialize—"

"No," I say, "I'm coming with you."

He blinks. "Jennifer never wanted to see the kids."

"I'm not Jennifer."

"You can tell me if you are. I won't get mad. You've been stone-cold sober ever since I—"

"I cannot physically drink alcohol. My love," I say, "my dear, sweet love. We're going to be late."

I can't drink alcohol or smoke weed without projectile vomiting blood, and we're still having this conversation? It's a bit silly, you know.

So we journey to the bus depot in Coeur d'Alene. Orchards engulf the land as Daryl drives through the Salmon-Challis Forest, heading east, east, where Washington kisses Idaho.

It's long past cherry season.

October.

The Bings and Rainiers gave way to Sunglo nectarines in August. From the tail end of August on till December…the apples. Oh god, the apples. Nothing but apples. Every orchard swollen with 'em. Jonagolds and Honeycrisps and the odd Cosmic Crisp from last season's harvest, still unwrinkled. Fuji apples, mushy and sweet as a dead granny's cheek. Opal apples, mediocre. Lemonade-tart Pink Ladies, good for eating—too expensive, too fussy to bake with.

I roll the window down. Chilly air floods the cab. Clouds cover the sky overhead, sullen and gray as a farmhand's eyes. In the mornings, frost silvers the conifers, and, come sunrise, sublimes to nothing. Ghost's silver.

"I read that book on physics you bought me," I finally say.

"Oh?"

"Matter shouldn't even technically exist as we know it. They don't know what keeps the nucleus of an atom together. The positive forces of all those protons jammed into one tiny nucleus should rip 'em apart."

"But here we exist."

"They had to make up a name for the force that binds the nucleus of an atom together. They literally just call it the 'strong force.'"

Warmth, on my thigh.

Daryl's hand rests on my thigh. Heat leaches through my jeans.

Oh. Oh, my.

"I love you," he says hoarsely.

"Don't cry."

He clears his throat. "I'm not. I'm fine."

"They loved you so much, Daryl. Both of them."

"You're not Her? Sweetheart, if you're playing a game, it's okay, just tell me."

He turns his eyes off the road, looking at me. Hard. My tummy lurches.

"I'm not them," I say.

A sigh. "Okay. Okay, I had to ask."

I lift his hand off my thigh and kiss the back of it. Hold it. I squeeze his fingers.

"Should we move Jennifer's old trailer a bit closer to the cabin? I think we need to. It's cleaned up, but I don't like the idea of Isaac living that far into the woods. He needs a little space, but not too much," I say.

"We got a month or two till he moves in. Let's focus on Marcia."

I make a yes sound. He drives on.

Most everyone came back after Judgment Day—officially, the week of ergot contamination, everyone believed that Rosetown had tripped out—but not everyone. Which was to be expected. Sheriff Olson came back. Vic and Carl Snyder didn't. Wade didn't. Trojan didn't. The old Nelson house currently awaits a buyer.

"I think it's love," I say. "That's the strong force. God's love, holding everything together."

"Hell of a theory. I like it."

The orchards become sparse as we head into town. A cinder block utilitarian bus depot emerges. It holds all the charm of a prison. Power lines mesh low overhead. Power poles cant, worn white from decades of use. A Farmer's Exchange lurks across the cracked street from the depot. Pink graffiti mars the gutted remains of a phone booth.

Daryl parks.

I lean over to him. Put my face an inch from his.

"I love you," I say.

His lips press to mine. I grope for the back of his neck, find his hair, grab hold, elbows grinding on the center console, half-lying on it, working against his tongue, his mouth, all of him sublime.

So very sublime.

"I love you," he says.

And that's that.

We can break and fail and strive, but the one true thing is, as it has always been, love. Love, the repairer. Love, the redeemer. When we fail, we will mend. When we accidentally hurt each other, we'll find our way back home.

"Marcia's waiting," I say.

"Let's go get her."

All of us sublime.

AUTHOR'S NOTE

Mental Illness, Love, and Trauma:
On Writing *The Divine Flesh*

There's an invisible threshold to trauma, addiction, and mental illness, and once a person crosses it, most therapists don't know what to do. You'll see a kind, coiffed lady therapist—graduated four years ago, always knew she'd go to college, has no experience treating anything but mild depression and anxiety—just sort of sit there in her chair, frozen, after hearing Real Shit.

"Well, Dad overdosed on drugs when I was twenty-two. I cleaned up the drug paraphernalia. I had people imply it was my fault he died. I don't talk to that side of the family anymore. Don't have siblings. Don't have a lot of people left in my life. I feel so old."

Nice Lady Therapist goes, "Oh."

"It doesn't end. I'm twenty-five. This is supposed to be the pinnacle of my life. It's only going to get worse from here."

"Oh. Wow. Uh. Wow. You've…really been through a lot."

"My family's full of addicts. I had cousins that were alcoholics when they were fifteen. I never wanted my current trades job, you know. I wanted to go to art school, but I couldn't afford college. Parents wouldn't co-sign on the student loans. I was valedictorian when I graduated in 2017. It didn't matter. I had to go to trade school because it was either that or cleaning hotel toilets for a living. I said I'd do anything to make a living wage. Said I'd be better than everyone bitching and moaning and complaining about being broke. I said I'd do anything to survive.

Now here I am. I have money. A house. Health insurance. I'm not an addict like a lot of my family. I know I'm lucky. But I hate my life."

And Nice Lady Therapist just sort of blinks at you like you're a freak, like you're a three-legged dog seething with fleas. And all she says is, *Oh. Oh, wow, Drew. Um…*

When you cross that invisible social threshold between *Sad Girl Cute Mental Illness* and *Ew, You're Actually Mentally Ill*, nobody knows what to do with you. You're on your own. The business of picking yourself up and out of the pit—of death, addiction, and despair—is yours alone.

Over and over, we are told: *That didn't really happen to you. Because it couldn't have.* Or: *Maybe it happened, but can you really trust your perception? You're Traumatized. That means you're weak and crazy. You don't know what you're talking about. You're paranoid.* Worst of all: *You'll never get better, sweetie! You're Mentally Ill, remember? You're an Addict, remember?* Which is really just: *You're not a human being anymore. Traumatized. Mentally Ill. Unlikeable. Freak. Addict. Hopeless.*

And this is how the character of Jennifer Plummer was created. I wanted to write honestly about what it's like being beyond the invisible threshold. She's an unlikeable addict, abuser, and spends most of her time desperately trying to block out reality with drugs. And why wouldn't she? She lives in a self-created hell, driving everyone away when they damage the thin shell of her ego. Her ego is all she has; she cannot handle threats to it.

When I first had the idea for *The Divine Flesh,* back in 2019, I originally conceived a kind of superhero/villain sharing the same body. The Divine Flesh was a demonic, Lilith-esque force of destruction and rage. After the second draft (a page-one rewrite), I realized that the Divine Flesh was not just an external cosmic force, but two halves: Jennifer and what we see as the Divine Flesh. Together, the Divine Flesh and Jennifer compose the Self of this fractured god/dess.

It took until the third draft for me to realize that the Divine Flesh was actually the *good* half of the equation, and that Jennifer Plummer was the evil half. Jennifer represents the Ego/Shadow Self—utterly self-focused, shallow, incapable of true love, wanting redemption but not understanding how to achieve it, terrified of existential dilemmas, and craving external sources of love (in all the wrong places). The Divine Flesh represents the Innocent Self—naïve, full of love, unselfish, and unblemished. Her lack of Ego makes her inhuman.

The Divine Flesh is an allegory for facing mental illness and addiction by confronting your Shadow Self, then integrating it with your Ego to create the Healed Self. Both Jennifer and the Divine Flesh try their best to deny this process. For example, Jennifer tries to defeat the Divine Flesh with knowledge (a secular metaphor for intellectualization, and a religious metaphor for Hermetic Gnosticism), and the Divine Flesh fruitlessly tries to assimilate Jennifer (and thereby destroy her) without understanding *why* Jennifer is the way she is. The Divine Flesh fixates on getting love and adoration as a way of fulfilling an inner void—the void being the absence of Jennifer.

By confronting every ugly part of ourselves and merging our fractured pieces, we give ourselves the capacity to rise above our unhealthy coping mechanisms. We realize that the invisible social threshold of *Ew, You're Actually Mentally Ill* is only a social construct used by oppressive systems as a way of keeping people from sharing real experiences and emotions, since society only accepts experiences of mental illness/trauma that don't threaten existing power structures. Society wants *Happy*. It begs for the ugly and raw truth of life to be turned into *UwU Mental Illness* as a way to sublimate true emotion in favor of saccharine aesthetics and feel-good articles that challenge nothing and ask no questions of the listener. It craves this substitute in place of actual human connection and empathy.

Why did I write *The Divine Flesh?*

To tell a story.

To say: Through integration of our ugliest, most traumatized parts, we can finally realize that we are not *Freaks* or *Traumatized* or *Actually Mentally-Ill.* Trauma is part of the human experience. No matter how much we've been through or how awful it makes us, we never stop being human.

Put more concisely: We're simply *human.*

—Drew Huff
January 2025

ACKNOWLEDGEMENTS

Thank you to my readers, especially to those who were kind enough to read and review advance review copies! Reviews are the lifeblood of publishing, and it means a lot to me that you invested your time in reading this book.

Thank you to Candace Nola and Maddy Leary for editing *The Divine Flesh* and doing an amazing job! Candace, thank you for looking at the earliest versions of this crazy book and telling me what worked and what didn't. Maddy, thank you for catching all the details. Thank you both for believing in this story.

Thank you to Rob Carroll and the rest of the team at Dark Matter INK!

Thanks to my friends in the industry: Brennan LaFaro, Candace Nola, and Briana Morgan. A warm thank-you to Steve Stred, Brennan LaFaro, Emma E. Murray, and Scott J. Moses for providing awesome blurbs!

Thank you, everyone! Can't wait for you guys to read my next books coming soon!

—Drew

ABOUT THE AUTHOR

Drew Huff is the author of *Free Burn, The Divine Flesh, The Exodontists,* and *Run to Beat the Devil.* Born and raised in eastern Washington, Drew enjoys writing stories that explore the intricacies of trauma, body horror, and fear. Her short fiction has appeared numerous anthologies, including *The Sacrament, It Was All A Dream,* and *Hot Iron and Cold Blood.*

Thank you for reading!

You can make my day great by leaving a review for *The Divine Flesh* on Amazon, Goodreads, or social media. As a bonus, your review will help other potential readers find this story. Thanks again! —Drew

Also Available or Coming Soon from Dark Matter INK

Human Monsters: A Horror Anthology
Edited by Sadie Hartmann & Ashley Saywers
ISBN 978-1-958598-00-9

Zero Dark Thirty: The 30 Darkest Stories from Dark Matter Magazine,
2021–'22
Edited by Rob Carroll
ISBN 978-1-958598-16-0

Linghun by Ai Jiang
ISBN 978-1-958598-02-3

Monstrous Futures: A Sci-Fi Horror Anthology
Edited by Alex Woodroe
ISBN 978-1-958598-07-8

Our Love Will Devour Us by R. L. Meza
ISBN 978-1-958598-17-7

Haunted Reels: Stories from the Minds of Professional Filmmakers
Curated by David Lawson
ISBN 978-1-958598-13-9

The Vein by Steph Nelson
ISBN 978-1-958598-15-3

Other Minds by Eliane Boey
ISBN 978-1-958598-19-1

Monster Lairs: A Dark Fantasy Horror Anthology
Edited by Anna Madden
ISBN 978-1-958598-08-5

Frost Bite by Angela Sylvaine
ISBN 978-1-958598-03-0

The House at the End of Lacelean Street by Catherine McCarthy
ISBN 978-1-958598-23-8

When the Gods Are Away by Robert E. Harpold
ISBN 978-1-958598-47-4

The Dead Spot: Stories of Lost Girls
by Angela Sylvaine
ISBN 978-1-958598-27-6

Grim Root by Bonnie Jo Stufflebeam
ISBN 978-1-958598-36-8

Voracious by Belicia Rhea
ISBN 978-1-958598-25-2

The Bleed by Stephen S. Schreffler
ISBN 978-1-958598-11-5

Chopping Spree by Angela Sylvaine
ISBN 978-1-958598-31-3

Saturday Fright at the Movies: 13 Tales from the Multiplex
by Amanda Cecelia Lang
ISBN 978-1-958598-75-7

The Off-Season: An Anthology of Coastal New Weird
Edited by Marissa van Uden
ISBN 978-1-958598-24-5

The Threshing Floor by Steph Nelson
ISBN 978-1-958598-49-8

Club Contango by Eliane Boey
ISBN 978-1-958598-57-3

Free Burn by Drew Huff
ISBN 978-1-958598-94-8

Psychopomp by Maria Dong
ISBN 978-1-958598-52-8

Disgraced Return of the Kap's Needle
by Renan Bernardo
ISBN 978-1-958598-74-0

Haunted Reels 2: More Stories from the Minds of Professional Filmmakers Curated by David Lawson
ISBN 978-1-958598-53-5

Dark Circuitry by Kirk Bueckert
ISBN 978-1-958598-48-1

Soul Couriers by Caleb Stephens
ISBN 978-1-958598-76-4

Abducted by Patrick Barb
ISBN 978-1-958598-37-5

Cyanide Constellations and Other Stories by Sara Tantlinger
ISBN 978-1-958598-81-8

Little Red Flags: Stories of Cults, Cons, and Control
Edited by Noelle W. Ihli & Steph Nelson
ISBN 978-1-958598-54-2

Cold Snap by Angela Sylvaine
ISBN 978-1-958598-55-9